TRUE IDENTITY

Deirdre Jonker

Publisher: Inspiring Publishers,
P.O. Box 159, Calwell, ACT Australia 2905
Email: publishaspg@gmail.com
http://www.inspiringpublishers.com

A catalogue record for this book is available from the National Library of Australia

National Library of Australia The Prepublication Data Service

Author: Deirdre Jonker
Title: True Identity
Genre: Fiction

Paperback ISBN: 978-1-922920-51-5
eBook ISBN: 978-1-922920-52-2

Prologue

When a father loves his daughters very much, he's willing to do anything for them. In the emergency room, Arabella was in pain and the look she gave me after Amy was born hurt me. Her heart was getting slower, and she started breathing faster. The doctors told Arabella that she was not going to make it. Her last words were, "Save the children, Gabriel Ambrose. I will always love you, no matter what." After she died, Gabriel screamed and ran out of the clinic room in pain, trying to save himself from attacking my children.

Arabella, with her long dark brown wavy hair and brown eyes, was pushing out the two girls. "Oh goodness, this hurts." Arabella screamed as she was holding Gabriel's hand. Gabriel, with his silk shoulder-length black hair and red eyes, felt this anger and fear building inside of him.

His brothers couldn't stop him from destroying chandeliers, candelabras, and other stuff. That was probably the worst moment of his life. His wife was dead, leaving him with two girls. I need to kill those girls. Suddenly, his other three brothers surrounded him.

"Don't do it, Gabriel. They are your children," said Lucien, one of Gabriel's brothers.

"Yes Gabriel, you must check yourself and go upstairs where the nurse is weighing the children and putting them in glass boxes. Oh, here comes Amelia," Daniel.

"Gabriel, I know a way for you to keep Arabella with you forever. Here is the spell to put her in limbo. Keep it safe and here is a locket with both you and Arabella's pictures in it, she said.

"My family, how can I raise two children of my own?" Gabriel snapped.

"Put them up for adoption, Gabriel, till you are ready to finally confront them about who they really are. They are probably bound to find out, anyway, with their powers," Lucien said.

"I know a couple in Oregon named the Martins who are having trouble having children of their own," Gabriel said before he took off for his office.

"Get a hold of those people and off they go. But when Amy turns eighteen and Ginger turns eighteen, they come back here, right, Alistair?" said Gabriel once Alistair and Darcia came running into the room. Alistair with his black neck-length hair and blue eyes, wearing a casual outfit of jeans and a checkered blouse. Darcia, with her shoulder-length brown hair and green eyes, wearing a tight short-sleeved white blouse and skinny jeans with brown boots, was watching Gabriel planning the next eighteen years.

"Right Gabriel," Alistair while swallowing his saliva.

"You are correct, Alistair. Oh, by the way, before I forget, Alistair, when the time is right, could you and your group go over to Oregon after Amy turns eighteen? Ginger will be eighteen as well, so that is probably the right time to tell them who they are. I want to protect my babies from my horrible mistakes," Gabriel said with a smile, while clasping his hands together.

"Of course, Gabriel, we don't want our species to go extinct just because of you," Alistair said in a reassuring tone. Gabriel scoffed at the comment and walked off, leaving Alistair, Darcia, Amelia and his other three brothers standing there in an awkward way. "I guess we should bury the body and put her soul in limbo." Darcia sighed.

"Alistair, let me ask you something," asked Darcia. "Why didn't Gabriel turn Arabella into an immortal like us?"

"Because Amy and Ginger were still inside of her and if he puts his blood in her, it could have killed Amy," Alistair said with sadness in his eyes.

"Amy and Ginger are already an immortal by blood. How can that kill something like that?" Darcia asked.

"I don't know," snapped Alistair. "Stop asking me questions and let's get some stuff done." After Arabella was buried in the backyard, the rest of the group came into the parlor and they put a spell on Arabella to put her in limbo.

"Did it work?" Gabriel asked.

"Let's try this. Arabella, if you hear me," said Lucien. "Please turn the lights off and on real fast."

At first, nothing happened. "Sounds like she's gone forever," said Gabriel in a sad way. "Wait a minute, did you guys see that? Arabella, is that you?" Darcia asked.

The lights went off and on in a few seconds. "Congratulations boys and girls, she's not gone forever." Gabriel went crazy and grabbed himself a glass of blood from the table and gulped it down. "Now I will call up the Martins and tell them my children are for rent for eighteen years till they will come back to me."

It was ten in the evening in Oregon, and Athan suddenly got a phone call from an anonymous dialer. "This is Athan Martin. How may I help you?"

"Ah Athan," said Gabriel. "You won't believe this, but I have two girls I want to put up for rent adoption."

"Oh my goodness, are you serious? That's great. When will they come?" Athan asked excitedly.

"A group of my friends will drop them off at your door," Gabriel said.

"May I ask you for your name?" asked Athan.

"Of course, it's Gabriel Ambrose and I tend to travel around and remain at a residence wherever I feel welcome."

"Oh my goodness sir, it's a real honor for you to call us." Gabriel felt relieved but also sad inside for leaving his daughters in the hands of humans. "There is one more thing you must know, Athan," Gabriel said. He waited a minute or so to continue. "My daughters came from my wife, who had just passed away. I am an immortal and my blood runs in the family."

"Oh dear," said Athan. "Does that mean they are immortals as well?"

"Yes they are," said Gabriel. "So what you must do is don't tell them anything except that they are adopted if they ask, but I highly doubt that."

"Of course, I would never say anything about that. Anything else I must know?" Athan asked.

"A week after my daughters' eighteenth birthday, I would like to claim them back."

"What?" chuckled Athan? "Why would you want them back? You are giving them to both my wife and I."

"I will lend them out to both you and Emma and, at the age of eighteen, the same group who will drop them off will take them back home to me, whether you like it or not." Athan sighed as she leaned against the back of his bed with confusion.

"I guess we can live with that. Just take them over and, at the age of eighteen, both your daughters will be returned. Anything else I must know?"

"No, that's all I have to call you about. Sweet dreams and do not do any weird things while my children are there. They are my precious little treasures and if anything were to happen to them, you would have me to deal with, understand?"

"Yeah, of course, well, let me say goodbye now."

"Good evening Athan," Gabriel said. After he finished talking, he walked back to the parlor where his family was sitting.

"Well, what's going to happen now, Gabriel?" asked Daniel with his arms crossed.

"The Martins will accept my children and, at the age of eighteen, they will be returned safely back home, where the rest can happen. Now Alistair and Darcia, you know what to do, right?" Gabriel asked, with his eyes focused on Darcia's.

"Our boys will also be traveling with us," said Darcia. "They were very excited to hear that you have two daughters. Who knows, maybe there might be a little romance between them."

(18 years later)

Chapter 1

Weird Week

One Saturday afternoon, Amy drove into her driveway from the grocery store and walked into her house, having her two golden retrievers jump on her. Athan and Emma helped her put the stuff away. Amy was living in Oregon in this suburban house with a garden in the back with a driveway for the cars.

"Hey sweetheart, at five o'clock, the Thompsons asked us to ask you to babysit their two children, James and Lucy," Emma said while drying her hands with a towel.

"Okay," Amy said. "I'm going to call Steven to see if he would like to babysit with me. They would let me bring a maximum of two people to babysit." Steven was the guy Amy met when they both took English together. Steven tutored Amy in some of the homework and literature and their relationship built from their connections and thoughts. Amy admired Steven's brown neck-length hair and brown eyes. He was mostly clean-shaven but had stubble. He mostly wore jeans and a long dark blue sweater and walked with a swagger.

"See you later, honey. Oh yeah, bring Sammy and Lilah with you to your room and don't forget to feed them," Emma said. Amy walked into her room and put the TV. A few hours later, she heard her mother call her.

"Amy, could you come down for a second? We have to have a talk with you."

Amy got off her bed and ran downstairs. "What's up, mom?"

"Here is twenty-five bucks to buy yourself some dinner wherever you want to go. You better go now, so you'll have enough time to get there. I charged your phone for you, so if there are any problems, call your father or me. Have fun."

Amy, with her dark shoulder-length brown hair and blue eyes, got in the car, put her purse into the seat next to her and drove off to this cheap diner, and went and bought a chicken dish and a medium cup of soda and sat down next to a window.

"Hey. My name's Larry Harrison, and you dropped your keys," said a man with blonde wavy hair and blue eyes, wearing jeans and a light brown jacket.

"Oh, thank you," Amy said with a smile.

"You're welcome, he said with a smile on his face. After she finished eating, she walked over to her car and drove off to the Thompson family. Once she arrived, she rang the doorbell.

"Can I help you, darling?" asked an elderly woman in the doorway.

"Is this Thompson's residence?" asked Amy in a confused way.

"Amy," said Mrs. Thompson. "Welcome. Come in and we'll be on our way," said a middle-aged woman with light brown hair and green eyes, wearing a black dress and shoes.

"Hey Amy," said Mr. Thompson with his black hair and dark brown eyes. "Here's a list of what the children need to do. They have homework they need to do, so please help them if they need it. All our information is on the refrigerator door, and good luck," said Mr. Thompson as they walked out of the house.

"Hey you guys, are you ready to have a fun evening?" Amy asked when she saw the children in front of the television.

"Yep. One of our favorite TV shows is on and we promise to do our work and stuff afterwards," said Lucy with her light brown hair and green eyes, wearing a floral onesy.

"Okay. I'll just sit over there reading my math book. How long will it take?"

"Another fifteen minutes," Stanley said while his eyes were glued on the TV. He took after his father with his black hair and brown eyes.

"Okay." Amy, she sat down with her math book and started reading about the history of algebra.

Out of boredom, Amy decided to rest her eyes a bit. Ten minutes later, she opened up her eyes, and the children were gone. "Lucy, Stanley, you guys upstairs doing your homework?" There was no response. Amy walked upstairs and saw lights on in their bedrooms. Amy opened the door and found them doing their homework together. "Do you guys need any help with your homework?"

"No, we're fine," Stanley, said.

"Okay," said Amy. "If you guys need anything, just call me and I'll be up here in a few. I'll be reading a book I brought. Before I forget, have you two already eaten dinner?"

"Our mother has already ordered us a pizza and it should be here in about fifteen minutes. Just go downstairs and relax and if we need you, we'll holler," said Lucy.

"Okay." Amy walked downstairs, minding the door for the pizza person to come. After the pizza delivery arrived, the children and Amy sat down at the dining table.

"So," Amy said. "What kind of homework do you children have to do?" Amy asked with a smile, looking at Lucy and Stanley. Stanley wiped his mouth with his napkin before he answered.

"I have to fill in the correct word types of nouns and proverbs for school tomorrow." Amy smiled and looked over at Lucy, who had tomato sauce all over her face, causing Amy to chuckle.

"My teacher has me do add and subtractions for math. It's pretty easy." Amy nodded and watched them eat.

When the evening arrived and the children had brushed their teeth, Amy watched the children tuck themselves into bed. Even though Lucy and Stanley's parents were rich enough for the children to have their own bedrooms, Lucy and Stanley shared a room together in separate beds. "Do you kids have a night routine? Story time?" Amy asked as she watched the children snuggle under their covers.

"No, our parents just turn off the lights for us. They stopped reading to us since we were young," said Lucy. Amy nodded and smiled.

"Okay. If you need anything, I'll be downstairs waiting for your parents to arrive." Amy smiled before she turned off the lights and closed the door. Amy walked down to the living room and decided to continue reading her algebra book to avoid making any loud noises.

About twenty minutes later, Amy heard one of the kids shriek. She ran upstairs and saw Stanley spasming in his bed. Lucy was next to him, holding his hand and whimpering. "Amy! I think we need to call our parents!" Lucy said with tears in her eyes.

"Mommy!" Stanley cried as he gripped his sheets. "I need my mommy!" Amy quickly called their mother, and it went to voicemail.

"I'm calling the paramedics. Hold on a moment," Amy said before she dialed the alarm number. Moments later, the paramedics came and placed Stanley on a gurney and took him to the emergency room. Amy and Lucy sat on the front seat.

The doctors placed Stanley in one of the beds and grabbed an IV drip. "What seems to be the problem, ma'am?" asked a female doctor with dark brown hair and caramel skin with black eyes. Amy exhaled and tried to remain calm.

"I don't know. I am just the babysitter and the parents never mentioned any problems I should be aware of." Amy sighed as she kept her focus on Stanley, who started to relax. Lucy was breathing fast. Amy held her close and tried to help her remain calm.

"Has this happened before?" Amy asked Lucy as she crouched before her. Lucy shook her head. Just then, Amy's phone rang. Their mother was on the phone.

"Amy, is everything all right?" asked the mother with concern.

"I'm at the hospital. Stanley appeared to have had a spasm of some kind." The mother shrieked.

"I should have mentioned this. We are on our way. Which hospital are you at? He has these episodes. Did Stanley take his medication?" Amy's brow furrowed.

"Medication? Not that I can remember." Amy sighed. Amy mentioned the name of the hospital and the parents both arrived within an hour. Both parents came running toward the waiting room where Amy and Lucy were sitting.

"Oh, thank goodness Amy. Where is he?" the mother asked, panting.

"The doctor said he is going to be fine. He is just resting in that room." Amy pointed to the room Stanley was in. Both his parents and Lucy walked over to him with relief.

Suddenly, Amy heard a male voice she recognized from a distance. She looked over and saw Steven waving at her. "Amy?" Steven asked. "What happened?" Amy smiled and shrugged.

"Nothing much. The parents are here to take over. I'll wait and see how this will end. Could you sit with me for a moment?" Amy asked, watching Steven sit down next to her, holding her hand.

An hour later, the doctor returned, and the family went to go home. Amy got to her feet and looked over at them. The mother walked over to Amy and hugged her. "Thank you so much for being there for him, Amy." Amy hugged her and then released her. The mother handed Amy her money. "Do you need a ride back to our place for your car?"

"I'll have my boyfriend drop me off to pick up my car, but thanks for the offer." The father patted Amy on the shoulder. "Thank you, Amy. That was very brave." Amy chuckled and shrugged. "That's what I do, sir," Amy said with a smile.

After the family left, Steven and Amy got into his car and dropped Amy off at Thompson's house so Amy could pick up her car. "It's a shame we both have separate cars, Amy. I would like to spend some more time with you." Amy smiled and hugged him. "Perhaps somewhere next weekend? I'm feeling quite exhausted from this evening." Steven smiled before he kissed her. "Well, sweet dreams, Amy." Steven got in his car and drove off, leaving Amy to get into her car. When Amy had returned home, her parents were in the living room watching TV.

"Hey Amy," Emma said with a smile. "How was your evening shift?" she said with humor in her voice. Amy rolled her eyes and shook her head.

"Those two are bad parents. They never told me that their kid gets these weird episodes and that he needs medication." Amy chuckled. Her parents looked up at her with concern. "Their son had spasms, and I had to take him to the hospital to get it all sorted out," Amy said.

"Oh dear," said Emma. "Well, are you okay? Do you need anything? A cup of tea?" Amy smiled and shook her head.

"No thanks. I'll just go up to my room and get ready for bed. I feel quite exhausted from it all." She bid her parents good night and walked up to her room.

When she entered her room, she saw a letter on her bed with no return address on it.

Dear Amy,

I saw you today at the hospital and realized you were very good at taking care of those kids and you kept your cool and you weren't scared of whether the kid was going to die or survive. I'm just very proud of you and wished to meet you in person.

Cordially,
L. Harrison

P.S. Meet me at St. Benedict Monastery at 12:00 sharp. We'll have lunch together somewhere.

After Amy read the note, she went to the bathroom and brushed her teeth and hair; put her pajamas on and went straight to bed. The next morning she went downstairs and ate a bowl of cereal, got dressed, and drove off St. Benedict Monastery and parked about fifteen minutes away so she could walk there to see why this person chose this place to meet her. At noon, she looked around but couldn't see her mysterious date.

"Good afternoon Amy," said a male voice behind her. Amy turned around, holding her pepper spray, and saw a guy wearing a parka, a hat, and sunglasses leaning against the corner looking at her.

"Who are you?" Amy snapped as she looked around, trying to find another person.

"Harrison. Larry Harrison."

"How do you know my name and what is about this meeting?" Amy asked as she was fumbling in her pocket for her phone.

Larry took off his sunglasses and hat. He has brown eyes with blonde ear-length hair. "No, I'm not looking for a relationship, but I need one more person in my group and then we're complete and we can do our rituals, have fun, etc. You seemed like a caring person who would also love to join a group. I saw your expressions filled with worry, nerves, happiness, and feeling excluded."

"What?" Amy asked in a confused tone. "What is this, anyway? Some form of cult recruitment?" Amy snapped. Larry smiled and walked towards her. "Please stop," Amy said with fear in her voice. "How do you know me?" Amy asked, starting to feel this panic inside of her. Larry kept his distance and focused on Amy. "You truly have no idea who I am?"

Amy shook her head and started to feel paralyzed. "You are your father's daughter, do you know that?" Larry asked with a smile. "You have his eyes." Amy started to walk towards her car and felt her hands shake. "Gabriel is looking forward to your return. Both you and your sister's return," Larry said with a smile. Amy got into her car and drove off to her house. When she returned home, her mother was in the kitchen, preparing herself some lunch.

"Amy?" Emma asked with surprise. "Where have you been?" Amy tried to keep as calm as possible and walked over to the living room, seeing her father reading the newspaper and the dogs in their beds. "Oh, nowhere. Just thought I would fill the car with some gas." Amy smiled and sat down, trying to keep as neutral as possible.

"Oh, that's so nice of you," Emma said as she smiled. She brought her plate to the table. The dogs immediately got up and hovered around Emma. "No, this is my lunch. You two already got your kibble." Emma chuckled. Amy felt this weird feeling inside of her. What did Larry mean by the name Gabriel? Amy tried to distract herself from that moment. That evening, Amy walked up to her bedroom and saw another note. Again, with no return address.

"Now what?" Amy snapped. When she opened the letter, she saw it was from the same guy, again.

Dear Amy,

Forgive me for not properly introducing myself. I did not want to come across as a scary and untrustworthy person. Could we meet each other again? Or would it be better for me to meet you in a more open environment? Please meet me at this one restaurant. The address is below the letter.

Cordially,
L Harrison.

Amy got this weird feeling inside of her and hid the letter in her drawer. Who is this guy, anyway? Amy sighed and shook her head in disbelief. This is not happening. Amy decided to see who this Larry Harrison was, even though she felt it was not going to end well. Amy mustered up the strength and decided to go against her instincts and find out more.

The next morning, Amy told her parents she was going to hang out with her best friend Jenna. Her parents gave her some money to spend on some shopping. Instead, Amy drove over to the restaurant and saw Larry sitting at a table with two menus. "Amy," Larry said cheerfully as he waved her to him. Amy looked around and saw other people eating and talking. "I'm so glad you made it, Amy." Amy looked at him and stood by the table.

"Who are you and what is this name, Gabriel?" Amy snapped. "I have been having dreams about a man named Gabriel, so please tell me before I leave." Larry smiled and gestured for Amy to sit. "Please." He whispered. Amy reluctantly sat down in her chair while keeping her purse close to her. "Well, my name is Larry Harrison. I live with my family in Florence in a mansion of fifteen people. Some of us are adopted. Would you like to meet them tomorrow night for a few hours and then we can hang out and go to dinner tomorrow night at a different restaurant?" Amy felt puzzled. "You don't have to say yes or anything about this offer."

"No offense, Larry, but I already have a boyfriend and he's not going to be happy about me dating another guy, so excuse me. Tell me more about you before I leave."

"Well, I grew up in Florence with my brothers and sisters. I went to college to study medicine. I don't have a girlfriend… yet." Amy nodded, wanting him to continue. My birthday is February ten nineteen ninety-nine, and I moved to Oregon to meet other people. Now it's your turn." Amy wasn't sure if she wanted to lie or tell the truth.

Chapter 2

The Introduction

"If I tell you a bit about myself, will you tell me more about what this man named Gabriel is about?" Larry smiled and nodded. Amy rolled her eyes, realizing she was doing the dumbest thing.

"I am a babysitter and I work at this grocery store a ten-minute drive from my house. I live with my parents and sister and two golden retrievers, a brother and sister. Um, I'm a junior in high school and have a boyfriend who also goes to that school. We give each other drives to school sometimes if our car is in the shop or we feel like sitting with each other and talking about our days or weekends you know. Excuse me for a moment; I need to visit the bathroom. I'll be right back" Amy walked to the bathroom and did some breathing exercises and closed her eyes for a minute and returned to the table.

Larry was gone, but he left his parka and sunglasses. He returned with his cell phone in his hand.

"Sorry, I had a phone call from my mother. She finds it wonderful to have you come over, but I told her to wait to see if your parents, I mean family, are all right with it." Amy barely knew the guy and wondered why he had such a sudden interest in her. Amy started to forget about what she was going to ask him.

"Let me just ask my parents about this. They don't let me go out with strangers. After lunch, Amy dropped Larry off at the gate of his mansion. They waved goodbye to each other. Later that evening, Amy went over to her parents' to ask them if she could go on a date with this guy she had just met.

"What? Absolutely not. Plus, we don't even know who Larry Harrison is and you have to babysit tonight. You are babysitting Morgan family. Two girls and if we find out you brought that guy over, you'll be grounded for a month and we'll teach you about the facts of life every day till you come to your senses. Got that?" yelled her parents.

"Yes, mom and dad, I'll go and call him up and cancel our date. Hello, this is Amy. I've come to tell you that I can't come to your house tomorrow night."

"Oh, that is too bad. I wanted you to meet my brothers and sisters and family. We could've done a lot of fun stuff this evening," Larry said over the phone.

"I have to hang up and get ready for a presentation about a historical figure tomorrow."

"See you around," said Larry. She hung up. Amy felt weird after Larry called her babe. The next day, Amy went to school and had calculus during first period.

"Good morning class, we're going to talk about lesson twenty-five. Open your books to page one-fifty-six and do the exercises on that page." The teacher smiled and nodded, watching the students grab their books. After that class, Amy went to her history class and she was the first person to give her presentation. After school ended, Amy drove back home to get ready for dinner and to babysit.

"Hey Sweetie, how did your presentation go?" asked Emma as she was setting the table.

"It went well." Amy walked up to her room and put her bag aside and went over to the bed. There's a note from Larry on the bed.

Dear Amy,

I'm sorry to hear that you can't see me that much anymore. However, there is a way that your parents don't have to know. Meet me during school times in the woods at lunchtime and we can hang out for forty-five minutes and we can do *this every day till you're off parental week. If not, then we'll have to find another way. Or maybe I can stop by the house you're babysitting.*

L. Harrison.

After, Amy put the letter down, and went downstairs to grab the house phone. "Excuse me Amy, could you clean up the kitchen and do the laundry because I'm having some people over tonight? I will be on call if you need anything. Who are you calling, if I may ask?" Emma asked.

"I'm calling a classmate to ask what our math homework is." Amy responded in desperation.

Emma sighed, "All right. I don't quite believe you, but go ahead." Amy walked up to her room and called Larry up.

It was ringing, but no one answered the phone. "Hey Larry, I would love to meet you tomorrow during lunch time and hang out together from twelve till quarter till twelve forty, then I have five minutes to get to class. Give me a call sometime, either now or tonight at twelve. Tonight I will be babysitting these two girls named Charlotte and Caroline. I could give you a call and give you the address and thirty minutes before they come back from their night out, you can leave and I can make sure everything is all right. Anyway, give me a call and I'll see you later! Bye."

After dinner, Amy drove over to the Morgan family to babysit two girls.

"Okay, now over here you'll find the emergency phone numbers, our cell phone, the phone we're staying at. We let the kids stay up till nine-thirty and then they have to go to bed because tomorrow's a school day. Thank you for coming. See you between eleven and midnight. Hope your parents don't mind."

"No problem. They're okay with it," Amy said with a smile.

After they left, Amy went over to see the girls watching a movie.

"Hey girls, my name is Amy, as you already know, and if you need anything, I'm here for you," Amy said with a smile.

"Cool," said Caroline. Amy heard her phone ringing. It was Larry calling her up. Amy ran quickly into the bathroom and answered.

"Hey Larry, I'm glad you got my message."

"Yeah, so where's the place you're babysitting those kids?" Larry asked. Amy gave him the address. "Jump into your car after I put the kids to bed. I still have some questions that need to be addressed," Amy said.

"Okay, just call me. See you later." Amy walked over to the TV room and told them they still had thirty more minutes to have their nightwear on and brush their teeth. They both walked upstairs and Amy followed them and stood with them while they brushed their teeth.

"Amy, our mommy always reads us a bedtime story before we fall asleep. Here, could you read us this book?"

"Sure, of course." Amy grabbed the book and waited for the girls to fall asleep. Thirty minutes after Amy left their room and walked downstairs to pretend to read her math book, she called her friend Larry instead and he jumped into his car.

"Mommy, please don't leave me, mommy!" screamed Caroline. Amy ran up as fast as she could turn the lights on and saw Caroline having a panic attack. Amy ran over and grabbed her arm and stroked it, trying to wake her up and shook her.

"Caroline, listen to me. What's going on? Tell me now!" Caroline was in shock and she was staring at the ceiling of their bedroom.

"Amy, I'm scared." Charlotte screamed. "We should call an ambulance, or even better, I'll get her medication in the bathroom." Charlotte ran over to the bathroom with the house phone, just in case they weren't in there. Larry rang the doorbell.

"Did the ambulance come here so soon?" Amy ran quickly and fell down the stairs, and twisted her ankle. She got up from her pain and hopped over to the door.

"Oh my goodness, Amy, what happened to you?"

"Need help. Caroline. Panic attack, call an ambulance." Amy panted.

Larry grabbed his cell phone and dialed for the ambulance service and he ran upstairs to their room, seeing Charlotte holding Caroline's hand and talking to her in a calm voice, telling her that she was going to survive as usual. Ten minutes later, the ambulance arrived and the three of them grabbed Caroline and jumped into the ambulance. After they got to the emergency room, Larry, Amy, and Charlotte waited in the waiting room.

"It's okay, Charlotte, your sister is in good hands and if she's been through this a couple of times, your sister will live. Okay?" Amy said, trying to keep her calm.

"Okay." Caroline sobbed.

"So Larry, you have already graduated from high school, right?"

"I think I already told you, but just in case, I'm a junior in college," Larry said.

"There goes our night tonight. On Monday during my second break, I will have an hour's break so we can hang out somewhere, get a cup of coffee and a donut or muffin at coffee shop which is like ten minutes from campus." Amy sighed. "I want to hear more about this Gabriel's name," Amy said, keeping her focus on Larry's eyes.

"I'm already there waiting for you." Amy couldn't help but chuckle and the three of them waited together for the doctor to come. After an hour later, a male nurse told Amy that she was just having a panic attack and nothing to worry about. Both Amy and Larry walked Caroline to see her sister.

Later that evening, Larry took Amy and the two girls back to the house and Amy waited till the parents arrived. "Amy, could you stay with us till we fall asleep? I'm sort of scared that it might happen again," Caroline said.

"Sure. I would love to sit here and wait for you to fall asleep and for your parents to arrive." Ninety minutes of snoozing with the kids, the parents walked upstairs and handed Amy her forty dollars and Amy told them that she had gone to the hospital due to Caroline's panic attack.

"Oh, my goodness, is she all right?" asked Mrs. Morgan, with her short black hair and brown eyes. "And who are you?" the mother asked as she pointed at Larry. "I never remembered mentioning additional visitors, Amy." Amy sighed.

"This is Larry. He is a friend, I guess," Amy said with a chuckle. The mother grabbed her wallet and handed Amy the money.

"Is everything else okay, Amy?"

"Both girls are fast asleep and everything's good," said Amy while she put her jacket on.

"Well, thanks again and thank you, Larry," said the mother. "Have a safe drive home and goodnight."

"Goodnight." Amy and Larry walked outside and got into her car and locked the door. It was pitch dark outside.

"Well, that was an exciting evening?" Larry said with a chuckle as he walked Amy to her car. "I guess we will be seeing each other again soon?" he asked. Amy looked at him with irritation. "What?"

"I don't even know what to say, Larry, if that is even your name?" Amy responded. "How did you find me?" Amy whispered. "How do I remind you of this Gabriel fellow?" she asked, keeping her hands on the door of her car. Larry didn't respond. "How am I supposed to feel comfortable with this sort of behavior? I get random notes from you on my bed and you want to keep having dates with me? I'll see how I feel before I make any commitments. You were brave and kind to help me out this evening, but I don't even know you so well," Amy said.

Larry shrugged and walked over to his car. Amy waited for him to leave before he got into his car. She turned on her headlights and drove off slowly so she wouldn't make any mistakes. As Amy was driving home, she noticed a dark figure standing on the side of the road. Amy's instincts were kicking in slowly as the figure started to walk towards her. Her hands started to shake, as the figure was about ten feet away from her. Suddenly, the figure appeared running towards her, causing Amy to stop abruptly. The figure stood on top of the car and crouched down. Amy was frozen with fear but quickly managed to push down on the gas pedal, hoping that the dark, manlike creature would fall off. Out of panic, she covered her eyes and crashed into a trash barrel. When Amy uncovered her eyes, the creature was gone. Amy quickly got out, but there was only a scratch on the car. Amy quickly got back into the car and drove back home.

As soon as she got to her house, she walked upstairs to go to bed, but her parents and sister were still up sitting around the dining room table.

"Hey, is everything all right?" asked Amy while yawning.

"Oh Amy, thank goodness you're home. We were so worried that you got kidnapped or something," Emma said with desperation. "We tried calling your phone, and it just kept going to voicemail."

Amy sighed. "After I was done babysitting at eleven thirty, I got into a car accident, but no damage that much to the car and I am fine," Amy said with fear in her voice.

"Why couldn't you call us?" asked Athan, trying to avoid getting angry with Amy.

"How was I supposed to know that a girl snuck up on me and asked me for a ride?" retorted Amy.

"It is time to go to bed, all of us, so we can get up in the morning and go for our morning jog." After everyone walked to their rooms and closed their doors, Amy jumped into bed and fell asleep without putting on her nightwear and brushing her teeth. She was very tired after her long day. The next morning, Amy woke at ten o'clock with a high fever and a clammy body. Her mother came into the room with a cup of tea and a sandwich.

"When I went into your room to wake you up, you looked pale and hot and you were breathing irregularly so I let you stay home. I know about this fellow Larry Harrison. I just talked to him on the phone and he seemed like a really nice guy with manners. I invited him to come over so we could meet him," Emma said.

"Oh," Amy whispered.

"Can I get you something from the grocery store?" asked Emma.

"Yeah, could you get me some frozen fruit bars and some chicken soup?" Amy asked with glassy eyes.

"All right, you just rest in bed. Last night I went to the bathroom, and I saw a light coming from you room. You were sprawled across your bed with your coat still on and your light shining in your direction. Your father and I dressed you in a nightgown and then we went back to bed. You may feel a bit drowsy, so when you walk down the stairs, be extra careful," Emma said before she kissed Amy on her head and left her room.

"Hey Athan, do you need anything from the store?" Emma asked.

"A six-pack of beer and a few bags of pretzels," said Aaron. "I'm going over to watch a game with some friends this evening."

"This evening? Why isn't it on the refrigerator, like we discussed years ago?" asked Emma.

"Are you going to help me or do I have to get in the car and drive off to the same store to buy some stuff tonight?" Athan snapped.

"No. Now I'm going to get Amy and me dinner and some stuff tonight and you can have a gay night with your friends," Emma said, feeling herself getting upset.

"Whatever." sighed Athan.

"That's it! Go to your party with your drinks and snacks." Emma yelled before she got into the garage. Emma stormed out of the garage and grabbed her keys before leaving the house.

"Amy, come here and take a look at this person on TV."

Amy moaned and mustered the strength to respond. "Dad, I'm not feeling so well. Could you bring me some fluids, like a glass or bottle of water?" Athan got out of his chair and walked over to the kitchen. He grabbed a sports bottle filled with ice cubes and took it up to Amy.

"So Amy, how are you feeling?" asked Athan in his fatherly voice. He looked down at Amy with concern.

"A bit woozy and sick to my stomach and I have a headache." Amy sighed.

"Let me get you an aspirin and a stomach reliever."

After he walked off, Amy felt something coming back up and ran to the bathroom and threw up. "Amy! Oh my goodness, are you all right?"

"No, I..." and she threw up again in the toilet and washed her mouth. A few seconds later, she threw up again and again for a whole hour, and then she walked back to bed and fell asleep. At quarter past one in the morning, Amy woke up in a panic and screamed for a few seconds and her parents ran in and grabbed her face and cupped it and quieted her down.

"Amy, Amy, wake up. Amy!" shouted Emma.

"It's okay sweetie, daddy's here," said Athan. Amy woke up and sat up and breathed for a bit, and then she told her parents that it was just a nightmare and they left after twenty minutes. The next day at eight o'clock, Amy drove to school feeling a bit tired and walked to her biology class, where she was paired up with a female classmate named Martha.

That girl loves to talk about one thing. Pony's and dude ranches. After that, she had calculus. She wasn't that good at calculus and after school on Thursdays she had to go to a tutor's class for two hours. Then she had her first twenty-minute break, where she just walked alone through the hallways and library and opened a required book for English. After that, she had gym class. What Amy realized was that she had become an outcast at school.

Nobody wanted her in their team, but they were forced. At noon, she walked outside to meet Larry to drink coffee and eat a chocolate doughnut.

"So Amy, how's school so far?" asked Larry, while stirring his coffee with a wooden spoon. Amy looked at him, irritated.

"Not fun. I'm an outcast. I have to meet up with the school councilor because of my bad grades. I've had a horrible flu." Amy sighed while resting her head on her hand.

"I've heard from your mother. She told me that you were asleep during the whole day and that you were indisposed," Larry said. "I did show up at your parent's house and they seemed very nice and loving to me. I even bought a bouquet, as per tradition, when you go to someone's home," Larry said with a smile.

"Oh my goodness, I wanted to talk to you and ask if you'd keep me company because I was bored out of my mind. I read all the books in my room before. TV was boring, my music was boring, I wanted to go outside, but every time I started walking again, I would throw up," Amy said with sadness.

"What a drag. So, what do you have after your lunch break?" snickered Larry.

"History, Art, psychology, physics, and then I'm done for the day."

"Will I see you tonight at another babysitting gig or something?" asked Larry.

"No, I'll try to call you when I get back home and talk to my parents about my panic attack I had."

"What happened?" asked Larry in a shocked way.

"No, it's nothing. I woke up screaming." Amy chuckled out of embarrassment.

"Okay, thanks for telling me this, but don't you have somewhere to go, like school?" Larry asked, placing the empty coffee cup on the table.

"Oh my goodness, I have history class in about fifteen minutes. We have to make it or else I get detention today," Amy said, trying to control her panic.

"Well then, we better get going." When Larry walked Amy back to campus, they talked about school, friends, and college. As soon as she waved goodbye to him, she ran up to the classroom and ran to the nearest seat she could find.

The teacher stood in front of the classroom, with her arms folded across her chest. "Please open your textbooks for the next chapter. We will be discussing some more historical figures. At the end of the semester, we are going to be performing a play on one of the topics of your choosing. For homework, do the required pages and answer the questions on pages hundred and thirty to one hundred and forty and answer the questions in long sentences. Some of you will be reading their answers in front of the entire class and remember." The teacher smiled and sat down to let the students do their work.

The next class Amy had was art. Amy walked quickly over to the art room and sat down at the table nearest to the door. It took the rest three minutes to gather their bags and books and stuff. The teacher grabbed out the paint and brushes and bowls of water per table and smiled at her a couple of times. "Hey Amy, how are you?" asked this male teacher with dark brown hair and glasses. He was one of those teachers that enjoyed flirting with girls.

"Fine thanks, need any help?" asked Amy.

"No, I've sort of got everything under control. But thanks for the offering. All right, you guys settle down. Take a seat anywhere because we're going to continue painting our self-portraits and being extra careful with the paint. We don't want to send someone to the nurse's office or send anyone home with a stain."

Amy grabbed her picture from the pile. Two of Amy's enemies by the name of Heather and Sharon put some red paint on her stool. Amy didn't immediately see it and sat on something that felt wet. She turned around and saw some red paint on her pants and tried to wipe it off. Amy heard Heater and Sharon snicker behind her and glared at them. "Mr. Marsh," Amy asked. "I need to see the school nurse." Marsh looked at her with panic.

"Here's a form hallway pass. Go down the hallway and turn right and then left."

"But sir, I don't feel weird," Amy responded.

"I know you don't, but just go." While Amy walked down the corridors, a group of seniors laughed behind her back. Amy looked back; feeling confused, but continued walking. As soon as she got to the nurse's office, she told Amy it was paint. "Some kids are trying to pull your leg. The nurse washed her pants in the basin and tried to dab at it.

"We might have a lost a found of old gym shorts, if you want to wear something dry?" said the nurse. Amy shook her head. "It should be dry within the hour, Amy. Try to watch where you sit the next time."

"Thank you ma'am, I'll just be going to class now and I'll see you sometime in the hallway. Bye." Amy closed the door behind her and walked back to class wearing her soggy jeans. She walked over to her psychology class because she spent the entire art lesson in the nurse's office.

When she got to psychology, she saw Heather sitting by the window. The teacher looked confused at Amy. "Ms. Martin, you are late." Amy sighed.

"I had to go to the nurse's station, ma'am." Amy responded before she sat down. "Are you all right?" asked the female teacher with grey hair and blue eyes.

"I'm fine. Just had a little accident," Amy said as she looked over at Heather, who had a smile on her face with her blonde wavy hair in a ponytail and her blue eyes filled with malice.

"Okay. Where did I leave off? Oh right. Last week we were focusing on mental health awareness." The teacher kept talking, while Amy started to lose her focus and started thinking about whom Gabriel could be.

"Who's next? Let me see, Amy, what would you ask a patient if you were a psychologist?" Amy snapped out of her daydream and looked at the teacher. "Amy? Please answer," said the teacher. Amy had to think about how she would respond to such a question. Heather looked over at her and rolled her eyes.

"Could you ever forgive someone who physically abused you?" asked Amy.

"Interesting, but I think we know what to answer to that one?" said Heather, snickering.

"But it depends on why, how, and where this person physically abused you," Amy said.

"Interesting girls, how would you like to go through debate teams? We'll be having them next Wednesday afternoon."

"I would be glad to run for anything, ma'am," Amy said with confidence.

"You know I'll be there too, ma'am, and I would love to debate Amy," Heather mocked.

"To be continued. What other questions could you ask a patient? Yes, you." The teacher pointed to another student. The lesson went on for another twenty minutes. "For your homework for this

Wednesday, write down what we just discussed and we will be having a little psychology simulation. Write down at least ten questions about psychology and write a four-page essay on psychology and have the following questions in your essay. Who, what, where, how, when. Okay? Good. See you next time."

It was break time that lasted only fifteen minutes and Amy walked over to the physics lab and grabbed her cell phone while no one was watching and called Larry.

"Hey Amy, how's school? Are you out?"

"Attention students, the physics teacher is sick today, so whoever has physics in a few minutes can go home right now or if you have a class after that, you're free to eat lunch or study or whatever except phones. Any phone which is on will be confiscated till Friday," said the principal over the intercom.

"Well Larry, I just got out, but I have to go before something bad happens to me."

"Later, Amy," said Larry. After she hung up, Amy grabbed her stuff and walked out of the building fast and jumped into her car and drove off to a quiet place and put on some classic tunes and closed her eyes. She then drove home. When she got near her house, she drove slowly because there was a group of people walking into her house. She turned her lights on and drove on slowly. She grabbed her stuff, got out of the car, and locked the car to go inside the house.

"Hey baby girl, how was school? Why are you out so soon?" asked Emma.

"Physics teacher is sick and I'm out." Amy responded.

"Well, anyway, meet this group of six who will be joining us this evening."

"Hey." Waved Amy and then she walked up to her bedroom, closed the door, took her shoes off and lied down on her bed. "Amy, could you take the dogs out or else no TV or computer tonight?" Emma screamed from the stairwell.

"I'm coming," Amy replied. Amy put her sweats on, tied her hair in a ponytail and walked downstairs with their leashes, then called them to the door.

"Hey Sammy and Lilah, come here so we can go for a nice jog in the park." The two dogs ran to her and jumped on her, knocking her down while licking her face and hands. "Whoa here, let me put your leashes on." She walked off with her dogs. Later that evening, Amy got back; the eight of them were sitting in the living room talking about their lives and other stuff.

"So Amy how was your walk? Did you come across anything exciting?" asked Athan.

"Nope, so when is dinner ready? I'm starving." Amy moaned.

"In a few minutes, could you set the table and feed the dogs for me unless you're too busy with something?" Emma asked.

"Sure." Amy was setting the table and feeding the dogs. After that she jogged up to her room to lie down on her bed to turn the TV on.

"Ah, I finally get to relax." A few moments later, there was a knock on her door.

"Hey Amy, I'm Bryan. Do you have a minute before dinner starts?"

"Okay?" Amy said, feeling uncertain about who this guy was. She did have to admit that this Bryan guy was quite handsome with his light brown neck-length hair and blue eyes. He was wearing black pants and a black jacket that looked very expensive.

Bryan composed himself before he started talking. "Amy, what I'm going to tell you may sound very weird, stupid and it may not make any sense, but someone very important wants to meet you." Amy chucked weirdly and fell back against her wall and cupped her face and laughed. Bryan chuckled along with her, not knowing how to properly handle this situation. "Perhaps it might be better if we talked about this after dinner. My family will be explaining it all to you." Bryan smiled and left the room.

"Amy, it's dinner time. Come down." Emma yelled. Amy walked downstairs and sat next to her father. The other people also joined the dinner table and served themselves a modest portion.

"So anyway, why don't you tell us about what you're learning in school this year?" Athan asked.

"Well, father, I'm doing physics, calculus, World History, art, music, and other classes. In a month, our mentor is going to take us to an art workshop. It costs fifty bucks a person for the bus, art, and gift shop."

"We'll talk about that later. So what are you learning with calculus?" asked Emma.

"All sorts of mathematics stuff mixed and this Friday at three o'clock, I'll be having a placement test." Amy responded.

"I knew my little girl had it in her." Athan punched Amy out of comradely.

"Athan, could you help me in the kitchen by bringing some stuff out?" asked Emma.

"Coming, dear," said Athan before he got out of his chair.

"Anyway Amy, did Bryan go up to talk to you about the big news?" Alistair asked.

Amy started to feel the same fear she had when she met Larry. "What's going on?" Amy asked in a suspicious manner.

"You may think that you're safe, but we have to get you to Australia where he can't find you fast. Joshua has already packed your bags and we're ready to go. Your parents also know about this. We're going to stay here for another week and the eight of us will board the plane to Australia. If, by any chance, you feel uneasy or if you receive any weird messages, let us know and we can deal with it," Alistair said in a soothing voice.

Amy got out of her chair and walked over to the kitchen when Athan and Emma stopped talking. "Mom, dad? What's going on? Who are these people and what do they want?" Amy asked, feeling this fear inside of her. Athan and Emma smiled and walked towards Amy. "What?" Amy asked with fear in her eyes. Athan and Emma just smiled.

"Why don't we join our guests at the dining table?" Athan responded. The three of them walked back to the table.

"Excuse me for a moment." Amy walked to the balcony and looked at the dark sky and leaned over the fence and sighed.

"It's beautiful, isn't it?" said Bryan, making Amy feel more at ease with this situation.

"Yeah, I've always loved the night when I was a little girl. It seemed peaceful and quiet."

"You still have three more hours before bedtime. What are you going to be doing? Oh, by the way, your parents don't have enough room for all of us, so we'll be staying at the nearest hotel about an hour away."

"Good," Amy said, forcing herself to smile.

"You're not so happy about this, are you?" asked Bryan.

"No, do I look happy about leaving my home and traveling to Australia because I'm being chased after by some weird person who's trying to kill me?"

"Now come on, it's not so bad. Just think, this as a vacation and all of us are backpacking and touring. Well, I have to go. Catch you tomorrow. We'll be going over the guidelines and trying to make the best of our adventure." Bryan smiled before he walked back inside.

The next morning, Amy walked downstairs, still not sure what she was going to be facing. Athan smiled at Amy. "Good morning, sweetheart, how did you sleep?" Amy looked at him and shrugged.

"Fine," Amy said in a morose voice. "What do I need to know about this situation? Is it still happening, where there is an unknown variable chasing me?" Amy asked as she grabbed a red apple. Athan looked at Amy, but didn't answer. "Of course," Amy whispered.

"When you go to school today, just remember to stick to the lie about having to leave for a family gathering. Alistair told me he would help you out with the story," Athan said with a smile before he placed a plate of scrambled eggs and bacon in front of Amy. Amy looked at it as if it were poison, but decided to eat her breakfast. Alistair and Darcia put on their thick coats and hoods and got into the car with Amy.

Alistair and Darcia sat in the back of the car. "So Amy," Alistair said. "We will pretend to be your family and help you with the story of your dying grandmother and how important it is for you to be present." Amy listened to the story, but kept her eyes on the road. "Try to park as close to the school as you can," he said. Amy nodded.

It was an overcast and rainy day, but Alistair and Darcia were still quite sensitive to that type of weather. When Amy parked as close to the building as possible, the three of them got out of the car and hurried into the building. Some students looked over at Amy with confusion, but Amy ignored their judgmental looks. When they got into the principal's office, Amy led the way.

"Good morning, principal Jefferson. May I introduce you to my extended family?" Amy gestured, but forgot their names. The principal smiled and extended her hand.

"Good morning," the principal said. "How can I help you today?" she asked with her short blonde hair, blue eyes, thick dark blue eyeliner, and dark pink lipstick. Alistair smiled and shook hands with her, and then Darcia.

"We are Amy's aunt and uncle. We have traveled from overseas and we were hoping to allow Amy to leave school for about a year or so? Our matriarch… her grandmother, has passed away, and it's important that she is present for this occasion. There was no other time or place to have her funeral," Alistair said as he looked at Amy. Amy rolled her eyes, which the principal responded with confusion to.

"Is this true, Amy?" the principal asked. Amy nodded. "For how long did you ask?" the principal asked.

"About a year?" Alistair said. "This is not just a one-day or week occurrence. Our family has big traditions. We have families all over the world that are coming to see her in the weeks to come," Alistair said, before he grabbed Darcia's hand. The principal squinted her eyes in confusion.

"Well, I suppose that is okay. Will Amy be continuing her school online or would she continue that during her summer break?" the principal asked. Darcia exhaled at her questions. "It's quite unusual for a student to be gone that long, hence the question," said the principal. Darcia nodded.

"I suppose she will be finishing her work off online. Other than that, she has a week to pack and we have a week to organize our travels, as well. Other than that, we have no further questions or requests," Darcia said with a smile.

The principal nodded. "Very well," the principal said. "I'll notify Amy's teachers and get this whole thing sorted out. Unusual, but you two are here in person. Thank you for coming in. Will Amy be staying for her classes today?" Alistair nodded.

"Yes, for the coming week, she'll be here," Alistair, said with his charming smile. The principal nodded.

"Okay. Pleasure to meet you," the principal said. "Amy, you should be getting to your psychology class right now." Amy nodded and left the room without greeting Alistair and Darcia.

Alistair and Darcia walked back to Amy's car and got into the back seat. "That went way better than I had expected," Alistair said, as Darcia got herself as comfortable as possible. "I'll have Bryan pick us up in a bit," she said as she dialed for Bryan on her phone.

When Amy entered the psychology class, she walked over to her friend Jenna and sat next to her. "Good morning to you. You look different today?" Jenna said teasingly. "Lack of sleep?" Amy chuckled.

"Yeah. There has been some family drama taking place. Plus, I got told by an aunt and uncle who are visiting us that I will be gone next week to attend my grandma's funeral somewhere." Jenna looked confused. "I'll tell you about it over lunch," Amy whispered.

This brown-haired, slender female teacher came into the room with a floral dress and short-heeled shoes, carrying her bag. "Good morning students," the teacher said. The students responded with a good morning in return. "Today I was thinking about doing a mock simulation of what it means to be a good psychologist for a patient. I know you all have friends in this class that you want to pair up with, but today, I feel that I'll pair you up with people you normally do not communicate with. As part of the social aspect," said the teacher.

"Amy, I will have you paired up with Heather. Jenna, I will have you paired up with Martha," the teacher went on, while naming some of the other students. "Remember your homework of asking questions psychologists would ask their patients? Why don't we try out some of your questions?" The psychology teacher had each pair present their mock psychology simulation. The students appeared to be having fun, which gave the teacher a positive feeling of the activity. When the bell rang, the students grabbed their bags and walked over to their next class.

The teacher cleared her throat. "Amy, can I have a word?" the teacher asked. Amy nodded. "I got a memo from the principal that you will be out for a while? Is there a reason for this? She mentioned a funeral or some family gathering?" Amy nodded.

"Yes. My grandmother had arranged this big formal gathering that would be taking place in the coming weeks. It's important for me to be present. The principal proposed that I finish my work off online."

The teacher looked confused. "If there is anything you want to talk with me about, Amy. You know you can trust me, right?" Amy rolled her eyes, feeling antsy.

"Look ma'am… Umm. What I'm about to go through with all due respect is none of your business or anyone else's."

"Amy, I may be a teacher, but I might know what's going through you."

"You do?" asked Amy in a surprised way. She had a feeling as if the teacher was spying on her, but didn't want to draw attention to her facial expression.

"No. But you know you can trust me if you ever need someone to talk to." Amy smiled and nodded. "I will not force you to tell me anything, but if you ever need someone to chat with, please come to me. You may go before you get into trouble with your next class." Amy smiled and walked off.

After health class, Amy had to go back to get instructions from her teacher. "Amy, is there a problem in your family?"

"No, what are you talking about?" sighed Amy in annoyance.

"You're leaving this Saturday for six months or more. Is there a problem going on?" asked the teacher with a smile on his face.

"No, it's just that my grandma is dying and I have to be there to be there for her. She loves me more than her own daughter."

"I understand, but in my eyes, I think you're exaggerating. I don't think you should be gone that long," said the health class teacher.

"Plus, there will be an end of the year party and a family reunion there. Very special." Amy responded with anxiety in her voice, trying to get a chance to walk away.

"Stay here for a moment. I need to get something. Don't go anywhere." Amy ignored the teacher and jogged out of the building and ran as fast as she could home. When she got home, the phone rang, and she answered it before her parents got to it.

"Hello Amy, I'm glad we have got to talk. Didn't I tell you to wait in the classroom till we were finished talking? I was going to give you instructions on how to avoid having relations because of depression, but now I can't do it for you till you get back here. I was also going to give you a bag of health class materials."

"Who is that, Amy?" whispered Emma.

"Amy, you cannot just leave school during the day."

"Not now. I really can't come over." Amy hung up.

"Amy, who was that?" asked Alistair, worried.

"My health class teacher, who's annoying. It seems like all of my teachers are not letting go of the fact that I am leaving for this grandma reason."

"Good job," said Alistair.

Later that evening, Amy lied on her bed and tucked her hand under her pillow. She felt a note under it. It was a kitty cat-waving farewell.

Dear Amy,

I heard you have to leave town because of someone's harassing you. I'm going to miss you a lot and I will never forget you whatever happens. I would really love to spend some time with you in a quiet place eating junk food and ice cream and laughing about stuff. I want to give you something special before you leave. Maybe we can eat some lunch or dinner somewhere. I really need to see you before anything bad happens.

My phone number is on the bottom of the end of this letter.

Love,
Larry.

"Amy, it is dinner time. Are you coming?" Emma said. Amy walked downstairs together and sat down across from her parents, eating their dinners in silence.

"So Amy, I heard you got a phone call from your health teacher? What did he want from you?" asked Athan, curious, wondering if Amy told anyone about her situation.

"Oh, nothing much except for talking to me about this personal situation, and I refused."

"That's good. Keep telling all those people for another two days and then you're home free," Alistair said with a reassuring smile.

"Okay, but let me finish my dinner and I'll be up in my room relaxing and bracing myself for this adventure," Amy said before she placed her fork on the side of the plate.

"Sounds good. Anyway, what have you kids been doing back in the hotel room?

Anything you'd like to share with us? Darcia, Felix, Silas, Joshua, or Xander? What have you guys been discussing?" asked Alistair, giving them a stern look.

"Well, Alistair, it's nice you ask that. We've been discussing this situation and we know that Amy is going through a rough time and we'd like to do something very special. We know that she likes this Larry guy and maybe she could spend the last two days with Larry at his house where she can hang out with him and go shopping for anything as long as it's below five hundred bucks. She will be treated like a queen till everything settles. What do you think about that, Amy? Sounds good?" Asked Darcia.

"Okay. Sounds lovely. Oh yes, mommy and daddy. Larry would like to see me. Is that okay with you guys?" squeaked Amy out of happiness.

"Sure, as long as you five will be watching over her, hanging around his house and guarding her and watching her from the rooftops, talking quietly. Okay?" said Emma.

"Sure thing," said Joshua. "We would be honored to watch over your daughter."

"So when does he want to see you, Amy?" asked Bryan.

"Tonight from eight in the evening till tomorrow morning, and perhaps afternoon?" said Amy.

"Oh no sweetie, it's lovely that he wants to spend time with you, but you're too young to be sleeping over at another man's house. Out of the question," Athan said.

"Athan, could I have an audience with you in the kitchen?" asked Emma.

"Sure honey," said Athan. He and Emma walked over to the kitchen and closed the door. Five minutes later, they both walked out the door.

"Amy, your father and I just discussed that you are allowed to see Larry, since you're going through a rough time and you're being a good sport about this."

"Oh thank you, you guys," said Amy before she hugged and kissed them.

After dinner, Amy ran upstairs and put some makeup on, styled her, grabbed some of her clothes and pajamas. "Sweetie, you're going like that? asked Emma.

"Bryan, are you and the other four ready to guard our baby?" asked Athan.

"Sure thing, Mr. Martin. "She's under the best care," said Bryan with a smile.

"A father loves to hear those kinds of things. I really appreciate that," said Athan before he waved goodbye to Amy.

"So Amy, where does this Larry guy live?" asked Joshua when he got in front of the wheel. Amy gave him the address where Larry lived. "It's like about twenty minutes from my house." Amy responded as she put her seatbelt on.

"Okay," said Joshua after he buckled his seatbelt. "Everyone put your belts on. This isn't the first and last time I will mention this." About a half hour later, they got to the mansion. Amy was the only one who entered the gates while the others hung out in the car waiting for anything to happen.

"Oh my goodness, Larry, is this the girl you've been talking about?" screeched Buffy.

"Yes she is, mother," said Larry when he put his arm around Amy's shoulders.

"Hi Amy, my name is Buffy Harrison, and this is my husband, Nathan."

"It's a pleasure to have you here at our mansion, Ms."

"Martin. Amy," Amy stuttered out of nerves.

"Oh course it is." And both Buffy and Nathan giggled.

"Now Amy, let me give you a tour around our home. Will you be staying here with us?" she asked.

"Larry invited me over tonight and tomorrow morning and perhaps afternoon. We are still discussing that part. I brought my own gear with me," Amy said with a smile.

"Splendid. I will show you where the guest room is unless you and Larry have already made plans together," Buffy said with a raised voice.

"Um, I'm not sure. It's all up to Larry, I guess," said Amy, when she looked up at his face.

"You see those five women over there playing cards? They are the maids on this floor. They make fifty bucks an hour, so they don't seem like servants to us. And in the west wing I have my room and in the east wing is William's territory, in the north is Bianca's territory and south is Ethan's territory, but the other kids have to share their spaces with them. There is a lot of room for everyone. All the kids are in their rooms doing their work. In the basement we have a workout center. Over there, in back of you we have an inside and outside swimming pool. Next to it we have a sauna and steam room. Next to that, we have a Jacuzzi. We have a library with a piano in it. The pianist usually plays classical music for us. We do not really believe in rock, tangy noise. It's just not music in my eyes. We have bathrooms on each floor. In total, we have six floors. We have stairs and an elevator. We also have a small museum and an art gallery where some of us like to paint. During the weeks, all our kids have their own teacher for each subject. Down the three halls we have our kitchen. It's gigantic," Buffy said as she walked Amy up to Larry's room.

"Oh, my goodness Larry! This is your room?" Amy's mouth dropped.

"You like it?" asked Larry with a tiny smile. "Please don't get too overwhelmed."

"I'm speechless. It's just like a fairytale. Oh my." Amy fainted and woke up on Larry's bed with him next to her reading Michelangelo's work.

"Larry, what happened?" asked Amy drowsily.

"You got overexcited like any other person who enters this house and you passed out," Larry said, trying to avoid a chuckle.

"Oh Man, how embarrassing. Why am I in these purple silk pajamas that say Buffy on them?"

"My mother was nice to offer you a pair of pajamas and the maids dressed you in them and put you in my bed so you wouldn't panic," said Larry while his eyes were still on the book.

"Oh, my goodness, the last month has been weird for me. I just can't believe it," Amy whispered.

"Do tell me. I'm very curious to hear from you since we haven't spoken in a long time," said Larry in an excited way.

"A while ago, I came back from school and I saw this group of seven people sitting with my parents together and talking. My mother told me that they were staying and I was all right till one of their sons, Bryan, comes up to my room and tells me that someone's after me. I laugh and he walks downstairs and later, while we're having dinner, his father talks to me about someone chasing me. I start to get scared and then I find out I have to leave this Saturday to Australia so that he or she can't find me. All of us besides my parents, sister, and dogs can't come with me. I am so scared and tense, it is not even funny."

"It's good that you got that out. But before you continue, I already know that you're going away. Heard it from your parents. They trusted me to keep this a secret and I promise I won't tell anyone else," Larry said as he placed the book down next to him.

"Thanks Larry, I really appreciate. I would like to stay tonight and tomorrow night with you, but I will have to ask the whole group about this. But I promise to keep in touch with you while I'm gone," Amy said.

"Can you also promise me one more thing?" asked Larry with a questioned look.

"Yes," Amy said in a curious tone. "I can promise you a lot of things."

"Could you try to stay away from the surfer boys? It may sound harsh, but I think our relationship is going very well and I don't want to break it."

"I understand, but I'll see what I can do, because it is pretty tempting," Amy said.

"Why don't you try to get some sleep so we can hang out more tomorrow morning? We can go jogging and I want to show you this beautiful place, this beautiful lake," Larry said as he smiled before he left the room to make sure Amy was comfortable.

"I'd love to. Let me grab my cell phone and call my parents up and talk to them about this," Amy said as she looked around to see where her bag was.

"Your stuff is downstairs in the living room. There's a map at each corner if you get lost."

"Thanks," Amy said before walked downstairs. As she walked down the corridors, she saw the names of the kids that live there. Suddenly, she saw a shadow facing her.

"Hello? Is someone there?" asked Amy with fear in her voice. There was no response. The shadow was walking towards Amy. Amy ran down the other way and the shadow ganged up on her. Amy turned left and opened the nearest door. She ended up in the cleaning closet and turned the light on. She tried to keep her breathing even, but she was very scared. She was looking for something she could find to defend herself with. There was a window cleaner, a broom, and other chemicals. She grabbed a cleaning spray and snuck out quietly and ran quietly down the hallway and ended up in the bathroom. Down the hallway, she saw a light shining brightly and ran towards it. It was these two boys' room they stayed in.

Amy knocked on the door. "Is there someone in here?" asked Amy in a quivering tone.

William, with his short brown hair and blue eyes, opened the door. "Yes, can I help you?"

"Yeah, which way is the way to the living room? I need my purse."

"I'll show you the way down so you won't get lost anymore," said William, and they both walked over to the living room.

"So Amy, what do you think of our house? Larry told us that you fainted out of excitement, just like my ex-girlfriend last year."

"Oh," Amy giggled out of nerves. "I guess this is a good place for girls to practice fainting." William chuckled.

Moments later, they got to the living room. Amy grabbed her bag and both of them walked back to Larry's door and they waved goodnight. As soon as Amy got back to bed, Larry was already asleep. She walked over to his bathroom and called her parents up.

"Hey mom?" whispered Amy.

"Amy, what are you still doing up? Are you okay?" Emma asked.

"Yeah, long story. Is it possible if I stayed at Larry's house tomorrow night as well, or the entire day? Just as a going away hangout?"

"Can we talk about this tomorrow morning? I need to sleep." Emma whispered.

"Okay." And they both hung up. The next morning, Amy woke up at ten thirty alone.

"Larry? Are you in here?" whispered Amy, but there was no response from him. Amy walked downstairs to the dining room and found everyone sitting around the breakfast table eating eggs, bacon, sausages, potatoes, tomatoes, salmon and a lot of other breakfast foods.

"Morning Amy," said Buffy. "Did you sleep okay?"

"Yeah," Amy yawned while stretching her body and walking towards an empty chair.

"Here, we saved you a spot right next to Bianca. The maids will get you whatever you want," said Buffy.

"So Amy, are you going to stay here with us today or do you want to go back home?" asked Nathan.

"I was going to call them up and ask if I can stay one more night here before I have to get back. I'll call them after breakfast," Suddenly, Amy's phone starts ringing.

"Hello? Oh, hey mom," said Amy.

"Yeah, you have to be back before dinnertime. You're staying at home tonight cause you're leaving tomorrow morning at seven in the morning."

"Okay, I understand mom. Okay, I'll tell them," said Amy before she hung up.

"Bye."

"So what's the upshot, Amy?" asked Larry while drinking some coffee.

"I have to be back around fiveish," said Amy while pouring herself a cup of coffee for herself.

"Larry can bring you back home, but before you go, we can hang out together," said Nathan in a cheerful tone.

After breakfast, Larry and his family took Amy down to the porch to show Amy the sights that were seen at the house. Then he grabbed several glasses of pink lemonade and they toasted to Amy's last moment together. "Amy, I really want to prove how much I love you." Amy was about to speak until Larry put his finger in front of her mouth. "Like so." Larry cupped Amy's face and planted a delicious sweet kiss on her lips. "I love you, Amy, and will always love you," Larry said before he handed her a bracelet with the family crest. "Now we will perform the ceremony," Nathan said before he gave Amy a glass of water and chanted some Latin words. "Now you will forever be protected by the Harrisons."

Larry then took Amy's hand and walked her to his car, and they drove back to her house. On the porch, they kissed each other goodbye and hugged each other tightly and went their own ways.

"Hey Amy, how was your evening at Larry?" asked Emma while drying her hands.

"It was pretty good. Today they gave me a family crest," Amy said before she pulled it out of her backpack. It was a silver pendant with a picture of Larry on it. It had sapphire stones and red-pink stones on it.

"Amy, you have a lucky boyfriend," said Emma.

Later that evening, Allistair's five sons had entered the house and went into the living room, where Alistair and Darcia were talking to each other about their plans for tomorrow.

"Hey Dad," said Bryan when he saw Alistair sitting at the dining table.

"What is it, son?" asked Alistair with a concerned look.

"I kind of have a nice warm fuzzy feeling when I'm around Amy. She just makes my heart beat fast," Bryan said with love in his eyes.

"Our baby boy is growing up to be a nice young, handsome man," Darcia teased.

"Darcia, cut it out. We will be taking the bus over to the airport and the eight of us will go into the bathrooms and change our appearance while Amy sits at the gate with her stuff and reading a book. She won't even know who, what, and where we are. We might even take different flights out, but what Amy has to do is look calm and relaxed. Furthermore when we board our plane, we will be sitting down. If Amy wants pretzels or water, the seven of us will switch off and get whatever she needs. When we land after in Singapore to catch our next flight out to Australia, we'll be looking the same and we'll have a three-hour layover and we'll sit kind of far away from her so no one will get suspicious of us. After we arrive in Australia, we will get our luggage, catch the shuttle bus out to where we're staying and we'll get whatever Amy wants or needs. We're also going to visit the beach and Amy can go swimming and meet other people," Alistair said before he grabbed a glass of water and gulped it down. "Okay?"

"Sounds good. So Amy, are you scared?" asked Emma while massaging her shoulders. Amy never liked those kinds of questions.

"I feel worried and queasy," Amy said. "Is this normal?"

"It sounds like you're coming down with the flu. Just take this day off. Maybe you can go to bed earlier," said Athan. Amy walked up to the bathroom, brushed her teeth and hair, put her pajamas on, turned her TV on, and closed her curtains. Later that night, Bryan snuck up to her room and went right next to her and helped her sleep by singing a lullaby.

"That's soothing Bryan, keep going," Amy whispered.

"You're not asleep yet?" Asked Bryan in a confused way. "I thought this lullaby put one to sleep."

"No, I can't sleep after this weird news about leaving my family and friends. I just can't keep my mind out of it."

"They were doing this ceremony, and they wanted me to be a part of a farewell ceremony this morning and I drank some water." Bryan sighed for a moment and right after Amy was asleep, he jumped into his car and drove off over to The Harrisons' residence and rang their doorbell.

"Excuse me sir, but can't you see that it's in the middle of the night and you're disturbing our rest?" said Nathan, wearing his pajamas.

"Oh, I'm deeply sorry. Are you the father?" asked Bryan.

"Yes, I'm the head of this household and you'd better get out of here or else I release the wolves," Nathan said with anger in his eyes.

"And again, I'm so sorry, but do you by any chance know Amy Martin?"

"No, haven't heard or seen that person. Now leave." And he was about to close the door.

"Amy's not feeling well and she's getting weaker by the second and she told me that you were doing a ceremony with her. Is that correct or am I lying?"

"Why don't you come in and drink a nice warm glass of milk with me?" Nathan said.

"No thanks, I'm not thirsty." Bryan snapped as he felt his canines growing inside his closed mouth.

"Anyway, what you're saying is true. Larry was so upset about hearing that Amy was leaving in a few hours and he wanted us to give something to her that would make Amy be his forever."

"Well, could I talk to Larry or somebody and have you guys undo this spell because she's in no condition to follow our plan tomorrow to protect her from a group of people who are chasing after her."

"Why on Earth do they want her?" asked Nathan in a sarcastic tone. "Fine, I will go over to Amy and give her something that will soothe the sick feeling." As soon as they arrived back home to the Martin residence, Bryan and Nathan walked over to Amy's bed.

Nathan was the one who loved having peace between two opposing forces and poured some liquid stuff into a glass and gave it to Amy and she fell asleep.

"So Nathan, what did you do and how long will she be asleep and will she be okay to travel tomorrow on a twenty-eight hour flight? It's pretty laborious."

"I understand. Well, I gave her an antiserum to stop her from fainting feeling uneasy. I mixed it with some water and added an Advil to stop any kind of pain that may occur."

"Will she be all right tomorrow?" asked Bryan in an annoyed tone.

"She will be fine. She won't remember anything from today or anything. It'll just be a nightmare for her. Don't say anything, just play along or else she might get a concussion and end up somewhere terrible."

"Like where?" asked Bryan in a worried tone. "Amy should never have gone over to your place."

"In limbo or purgatory," said Nathan.

"My goodness," said Bryan. "Well, anyway, thank you for saving my sweetheart and we might or might not see each other again. Who knows?"

"Goodnight. Maybe I can get some sleep tonight. Have a safe trip." And Nathan drove Bryan back to his car so that he could drive home and everyone could forget this ever happened.

"So Bryan, how did you get that guy to come over here and nurse Amy back to health?" asked Darcia.

"I just had a long conflict with him and he almost sent the dogs after me, but he looked deep down in his heart and found a soft spot."

"It is one in the morning and we should sleep for another five hours, so we have ninety more minutes till we have to wake Amy up and get her going.

"I'm going to stay awake the whole time," said Alistair. "I need to do something. I will get us ready for the trip tomorrow. I'm already bringing the suitcases down and getting our tickets so we won't waste any time at the airport because we're on a tight schedule and we need to move, move, move," Alistair said before he jumped into the car and drove off to the hotel.

"Well, Darcia, now that your hubby isn't here, do you already miss him?" Bryan asked teasingly.

"Very funny. I am going upstairs to Amy's room and watch over her," said Darcia in a snide way.

"I'll join you," said Bryan. "Um, excuse me, boys, but where do you think you are going?"

"We're going to walk around picking up some girls," said Xander.

"Make sure to be back around sixish," shouted Darcia. Joshua and the other guys walked out of the front door.

"Will do," said Joshua. The five of them walked out the door and down the streets.

"So Bryan, why are you interested in this girl? What happened to Giselle?" asked Darcia.

"Oh Giselle, I remember her blonde curly hair, she always wore blue ruffled dresses and a bow in her hair. She and I went steady for a few years till I found her kissing another man at our hangout spot. I was crushed, and I ran back home. It felt like she drew through my heart. I was upset for six months and later I continued with family businesses and now I'm here."

"Nice story," said Darcia, out of boredom. Later, at four in the morning, everyone started to assemble to get ready for the trip. Amy woke up and went to the bathroom and went back to bed.

"So we should let her sleep till quarter till six and you, Darcia, at six, start dressing Amy slowly so she won't wake up and when it's time, she'll already be dressed and ready to go," Alistair whispered.

"Got it," said Darcia. Then she went to the kitchen and poured herself a glass of water and leaned against the sink and closed her eyes and breathed in and out.

"What are you thinking about, Darcia?" asked Bryan.

"I'm afraid of what might happen to Amy. She is in a bad condition, and a group of immortals are chasing her and all this. It's too much for me. I can't handle it. Too much pressure."

"Yeah, I feel the same way. But what doesn't kill us makes us stronger, right?" Bryan asked.

"Yeah, but not with everything," Darcia retorted.

"True that," said Bryan while staring out into space.

"Anyway, today Amy will be all right. Another part of the plan is if anyone tries to bother with Amy, we'll have to go in all together," said Bryan.

"What time is it, by the way?" asked Darcia.

Bryan checked his Rolex watch. "It's six o'clock."

"So another ninety minutes," said Darcia, while sipping from the glass.

"Yes," Bryan said.

"So what are you going to do when this weird thing is over?" asked Darcia.

"I don't really know yet. Maybe if I get closer to Amy, we might hit it off or something. She's a very special girl." Darcia smiled and nodded before putting the glass on the counter

"I'm going upstairs to check on Amy, see how she's holding up." And she walked off.

At quarter to seven, Darcia got a pair of sweats from the washroom and pushed the covers to one side and took her pajamas off and put her sweats on slowly. At ten till seven, Bryan walked upstairs to wake Amy up.

"Hey, Amy. Wake up. We have to go to the airport to fly off to Australia. Wake up." Amy opened her eyes a bit and mumbled something he couldn't understand. Bryan turned her big light on, pulled the covers off the bed and cradled her in his arms, and carried her downstairs to the living room.

"Where am I? How did I get here and what?" whimpered Amy.

"You're at home in the living room and we're about to take off to the airport," whispered Bryan.

"Where's everyone?" asked Amy in horror.

"Alistair is at the airport with the other five guys waiting for us, so we'll have to catch that train and bus to get there. So are you ready?"

"Where's my backpack?" shrieked Amy.

"Alistair's got it. He put some books and your music and some snacks and other stuff in it plus your diary so you can write down any thoughts that are bothering you. Your parents are over there taking their car back, so let's make a move on." Once they got to the airport by transportation, they met everyone. Amy hugged her parents tight, and they kissed each other and cried a bit. After that, the eight of them walked through passport control and walked over to their gate.

"All right Amy, just walk over to gate. We're going to change into our new selves," said Xander.

Amy did as she was asked to do and went over to her gate and opened up her backpack to see what Alistair packed her. Amy still felt a bit dizzy. It was hard for her to keep her head up, but she had to fight that and be strong. She saw some candy, peanuts, fiction books, and her music with earphones, some other stuff and a letter from an anonymous person. She opened the card and saw the kitty cat-waving goodbye.

Dear Amy,

I am so sorry I didn't listen to you or anything about the situation at my house. I didn't want you to leave Boston. I am very sorry that you had to drink that garbage and I swear to my blood that I'll never do that again.

Love Larry Harrison.

Amy felt weird, sick, and sad and needed a shoulder to cry on, but unfortunately, there was nobody there for her. She felt so vulnerable.

For a second her eyes began to water, so she ran into the nearest bathroom and locked herself in the bathroom and sobbed.

"Excuse me, ma'am, but are you okay in there?" asked a young woman standing in front of her cubical.

"Oh, I'm all right, it's my first time I'm traveling alone and I'm homesick already."

"Yeah, the first flight as a teenager can be very exciting. I remember my first day."

"What happened?" asked Amy.

"I was crying in the bathrooms and I bit the bullet and got on the plane and I read my favorite book."

"Well, I'm not really on vacation," said Amy, as she was drying her eyes with a tissue.

"Business or family stuff?"

"Exactly," Amy said with a feeling of relief instead of having to lie and get caught lying about something. A few moments later, Amy went back to her gate and a few minutes later, she boarded her plane and ended up sitting next to a cute Australian guy from Sydney.

"My name's Amy," said Amy with a smile on her face and a feeling of comfort next to him.

"The name's Avery and I'm going to be visiting my family from college."

"So you go to college in Oregon?" asked Amy.

"Yes, and I really love it. It's better than school. I just hate being pushed around and making me feel inferior and stupid." Avery said as he was getting himself comfortable.

"Yes, I'm still at school, my last year, and then I'm off to college. What are you?"

"I'm a sophomore and quarterback and I get tons of girls. It's all fake in my eyes." Amy nodded.

Several minutes after the plane took off, Avery went to the bathroom and Amy grabbed his backpack quickly and snooped around to see if Avery was the one.

She saw that he had the same candy as her. She put his backpack back before he came back and grabbed her book, pretending to read. She also grabbed herself some red licorice candy.

"Hey Avery, want one?" Amy offered while holding some candy in her hands.

"No thanks. Hey, I also have the same candies and the same bag. Don't you just love candy shops?" he asked with a smile on his face.

"Yes, I do," said Amy. Once the airplane started reaching its destination Amy continued reading one of the books Alistair had packed for her. She was very distressed and cried a little, but quietly so no one would hear her.

"Well, Avery, I guess we'll be seeing each other in this airport," said Amy.

"Guess so." And he put his stuff in the backpack and waited. An hour later Amy went to the train and got on and went over to another concourse. Then she searched for her luggage but she didn't see anything. She already saw Avery go past passport control again, and she was getting desperate that her luggage didn't come through.

"Excuse me miss, but we have your luggage, right through that door," said Darcia in her disguise wearing a scarf. "Now follow the crowd to recheck your luggage and go on to your next gate."

"Thank you very much." And she rechecked her luggage and ran to her gate, even though she was on time. She sat near the entrance and grabbed her book to keep her mind occupied.

"Hey Amy, isn't it just fate that we're sitting together again?" asked Avery.

"Funny," Amy said. And he sat down next to her and grabbed a book about prehistoric times.

Once Amy got on the plane, she made herself comfortable and continued reading her book in peace.

"Oh, my goodness, Amy? We're sitting together again. Isn't that weird?"

"Uhuh," and she continued reading. Later, she fell asleep and got woken up by Avery, who was getting his backpack.

"Well Amy, it was nice meeting you and maybe we'll see each other on the shores of Sydney. Take care and he walked off to the luggage belt.

Chapter 3

Australia

Amy went over to the luggage belt, grabbed her stuff, and walked over to the exit.

"Amy! Amy!" yelled a group of people. She walked over to them and they grabbed her and shoved her in a rental car.

"Finally, we can get out of these horrible clothes," Bryan said, while taking off the wig and mustache.

"Come on, you guys. Couldn't you guys get my attention another way? I was sort of scared for a moment," Amy said as she put her seatbelt on.

"You're safe and fine. We'll be staying in this cottage for seven people and we'll protect you as promised," Alistair said in an assuring way. Once they arrived with their luggage and stuff at the cottage, the woods surrounded it. From the outside, it looked like a piece of trash.

"I wonder what it's going to look like on the inside," said Amy.

"Darcia and I will have to go to the reception desk and get the keys to this place. We'll be staying here for two weeks and find another place to stay," said Alistair.

"So Amy, did you enjoy sitting next to Avery? He seems like a nice guy," asked Silas with his dark brown short hair and black eyes, wearing the same outfit as his brothers.

"Oh yes, he's deep, interesting and handsome," Bryan said. The boys laughed loudly.

Amy turned the other way and ignored them and waited for the other two to come back from getting the key.

"So Amy, did you dream about anything special?" asked Bryan.

"She probably dreamed about Avery," Joshua said. The boys laughed out loud again. Amy was getting annoyed and upset about being away from her family and being laughed at. Alistair sighed in annoyance, causing Darcia to glare at her sons.

"Can't you guys see that I am in no state of being teased or being made fun of? I am away from my family. I had to travel alone, plus you guys promised to treat me like a princess. What happened?" Amy snapped.

Once the taxi arrived at their destination, Alistair and Darcia walked into the reception house and sat there waiting for them. Amy felt like they had punched her in the stomach really badly and wanted to cry, but she held it in. She was scared of what might happen to her. About twenty minutes later, Alistair and Darcia walked out of the reception house and guided everyone over to the front door of the cottage and opened it. As soon as Alistair turned the lights on, it looked really cozy, warm, and welcoming.

"Amy, you could be the first to pick out your bedroom. It'll have to be sort of in the middle," Alistair said, while he was brushing his hair with his fingers. Amy walked up and checked every room. She noticed that there were two beds per room. She chose a room with beautiful wall decorations. She put her two big suitcases next to her bed and walked downstairs to see what everyone was doing.

"So Amy, did you see a room you liked?" asked Darcia, while she was brushing her hair.

"Yes. I noticed that there are two beds in a room. I don't really understand."

"You didn't think we were going to leave you alone at night, did you?" asked Alistair.

"Well, I don't know. I was hoping to have a room alone since I am the only teenage girl in this group," Amy said.

"Tonight will be weird for you, but I can assure you that in a few days you'll be the same Amy as you were at home," Darcia said while she was hugging Amy.

Amy nodded and sat down at the table, putting her hands under her chin while looking around the table.

"Amy, you'll be bunking with Bryan," said Darcia. "The rest of the guys will choose their own partners, but one of you guys will be sleeping alone. Is everyone okay with that?"

"Sure," everyone said in a tired way while yawning and stretching their arms and legs.

"What we're going to do right now is rest, freshen up and chill and tomorrow we'll explore Australia," Alistair said. "I'm going to get settled into our room. How does that sound?"

"Good," the group said in a chorus. Amy walked up to her room and went to lie down. Bryan came up and joined her. Four hours later, Bryan got out of bed and woke her up.

"Where am I and what time is it?" asked Amy while squinting at Bryan.

"You're in Australia in this cottage and everyone besides me and you are going to the grocery store for food tonight. Alistair asked me to wake you up, so you will sleep better this evening."

"Okay, I'll get up." Amy yawned. Both Amy and Bryan walked downstairs and saw that everyone was gone.

"So, Bryan, I feel woozy. Did you bring any kind of medication?"

"What do you need, some painkillers?" asked Bryan.

"When did they say they'd be back from the grocery store?" asked Amy.

"In a couple of hours, they will be back." Bryan responded.

"What are we going to do in the meantime?" asked Amy.

"Alistair asked me to tell you that we'll be dining in formal and that I'm supposed to give you this purple velvet gown tonight. The males wear tuxes and the women wear gowns. Plus, you guys will have to wear makeup. It's our tradition."

"I'm not so sure if I'm okay with this. Could I just be exempted?"

"No, since you're part of this club, you'll have to join us or get lost, so you'll end up somewhere horrible," Bryan said before he walked away.

After everyone came back, Amy walked over to Darcia to talk to her. "Hey Darcia, is it mandatory to have to wear a gown for dinner?"

"Oh, Bryan wasn't supposed to tell you we were and yes. You have to wear a gown. I'll help you with your makeup and hair. You'll also have to wear black heels, which Alistair picked out for you," Darcia said with a smile.

"Now let the ceremony begin," Alistair said after he chimed his glass with a knife.

"What ceremony?" asked Amy in a confused way.

"The ceremony of welcoming our new guest, who is you, to our circle of grace. What we're going to do now is hold each other's hand and whisper something nice in their ear and talk for five minutes about this situation," Alistair said. Alistair, Xander, Joshua, Bryan, Amy, Darcia, Raymond, and Silas held each other and did their ritual.

"So, when will we be eating?" whispered Amy to Bryan.

"Now, everyone go ahead and fight each other for the best seat in the dining room," Alistair said, trying to be funny. Nobody laughed and walked over.

"Hey Amy, I was wondering if you wanted to walk outside after dinner, maybe get some ice cream," Bryan asked.

"Sure. I'd love to get some ice cream after dinner and hang out," Amy said with a smile.

"Well, Bryan, you might want to use the car and hang out in case something bad is going to happen," Alistair said.

"So, Amy, tomorrow we're going to be hunting gorgeous Australian guys," Darcia said as she winked, causing Amy to chuckle.

"That sounds like fun. When you mean hunting, you mean hitting on them, right?"

"Of course, we are no hunters. Go ahead for ice cream," said Darcia with a smile.

"Wow, Alistair, this is really nice spaghetti. You got the texture right." Xander said as he was waiting for Amy to leave.

"I try my boy," Alistair said while he leaned against the chair. After dinner, Amy and Bryan freshened up and got into Alistair's rental car.

"So Bryan, why did you want to get some ice cream with me and not with your brothers?"

"I'll answer that in a bit. I want to go to a parlor and get an ice cream coup you and I could share," Bryan said.

"Sounds cool, but I didn't bring my wallet," said Amy in a depressed way.

"Don't worry. You're here on vacation and you need to relax," Bryan said when he put his arm around Amy's shoulders.

"Wow thanks Bryan, I really appreciate that," said Amy. A few minutes later, they arrived at this fruity ice cream parlor.

"Good evening, a table for two?" asked a male waiter with black hair, wearing an ice cream parlor uniform holding two menus.

"Yes. Is it possible for us to sit at that booth over there in the right side corner?" asked Bryan.

"Sure. Follow me, please. Here are your menus and enjoy yourselves." He then walked over to one of the waitresses standing behind the counter.

"So, Amy, choose something. It can be anything you want."

"Okay. Oh look. This coup has strawberries with vanilla ice cream, chocolate ice cream and other fruits, chocolate sauce, and whipped cream," Amy said, sounding excitedly.

"Sounds delicious. We'll go with that. Excuse me Garcon. We're ready to order," Bryan said. "We would like number fifty."

"Anything to drink with that?" asked the waiter.

"We would like to have a bottle of sparkling water to go with our ice cream," Bryan said.

"Okay. It'll take twenty minutes for the ice cream to be made," said the waiter and walked off.

"So Bryan, why did you take me here?" asked Amy with a serious look.

"Perhaps this is too soon, but I have fallen for you," Bryan said as he played with the tablecloth.

"Whoa Bryan," Chuckled Amy. "I'm already seeing someone who will probably dump me before I get back from Australia. It's a bit too fast for me, but I don't want you to leave my life. Ask me in a week. I have changed my mind."

"I'll wait for a week…" but before he finished, Amy leaned across the table and kissed him.

"That's my sign to you, Bryan, to heck with everyone. My answer is yes. I'll be your female companion. I bet Larry is already scouting for other girls. Plus, I feel this sort of connection with you that I did not feel with Larry," Amy said with a smile.

"The feeling is mutual," said Bryan.

"Hey, what is this? Get out of my parlor and never come back," the manager screamed with a phone in his hand. Amy and Bryan ran out of the parlor and drove back to their cottage.

"So Bryan, how was the parlor?" asked Alistair, looking at both Amy and Bryan.

"It was okay. The parlor was closed, but Amy and I are boyfriend and girlfriend."

Alistair and Darcia chuckled. "That was fast," said Alistair, and they both gave a high five. "So where's the girl?"

"Amy is upstairs getting ready for bed," Bryan said as he was heading for the stairs.

"So, what are your plans for tonight?" asked Alistair, with humor in his voice.

"Dad, you sick little man. I'm not talking about girls with you for a long time."

"Fine by me. Just have a pack of safety stuff with you at all times," Alistair said. Bryan walked up in disgust. Bryan then walked over to the room where the rest of the boys hung out.

"Hey Bryan, how was your date with Amy?" asked Joshua.

"Okay. So what were you guys doing?" asked Bryan.

"We went for your evening walk and we're surfing the television," said Xander.

"Tomorrow we're going to look for Australian girls. You're welcome to come along unless you have to guard Amy, chaperon, or be there in the distance," said Silas.

"I would love to check out some girls at parties. So Josh, do you have a girlfriend? If yes, who and what is she like?" asked Bryan.

"I do. Her name is Jessica. She has brown hair and brown eyes. She loves wearing black clothes. She and I are going steady. When I get back, I'm going to propose to her," he said in an exciting way.

"That's wonderful." And the five guys fist bumped each other and continued talking about guy stuff. Later in the evening, Bryan walked back to his room and saw that Amy was fast asleep. The sound of her breathing made Bryan feel happy and fuzzy inside.

"Good night Amy," Bryan whispered close to Amy's ear.

"Night," replied Amy softly, and he fell asleep in his bed. The next morning, Bryan got up, took a shower, and went downstairs for some breakfast. On his way down, he smelled waffles being made by his father.

"Good morning parents," said Bryan. "I hope everyone slept okay."

"Morning son, how'd you sleep? Where's Amy?" asked Darcia, while sipping from her coffee.

"I slept like a baby and Amy is still asleep. We should let her sleep. She is going through a rough time, and I heard her cry in her sleep. I didn't bother to wake her up," Bryan said as he sat down next to Darcia.

"Poor kid. Here are your waffles and enjoy yourself," Darcia said while yawning.

Josh, Raymond, Xander, and Silas walked downstairs in their clothes and took a seat at the table.

"Where's Amy?" Raymond yawned while pouring himself a cup of coffee.

"Asleep," Bryan said.

"Here you go boys, enjoy your waffles," Darcia said when she brought over a big plate of waffles.

"Thanks mom," the four boys said in a chorus. At ten thirty, Amy walked down in her pajamas and saw that Alistair and Darcia were at the table. The five boys were taking showers, getting ready to check girls out at the beach.

"Morning, Amy. We saved you a batch of waffles. Here's the syrup and butter." Bryan went down and kissed Amy on her head and took a seat next to her.

"Hey Amy, I heard you cry in your sleep last night. Did you have a bad dream?" Bryan asked as he watched Amy cut a piece of waffle from her plate.

"Actually, I don't remember what my dream was about," Amy said.

"The guys and I are going to the beach in twenty minutes. You are welcome to come and join us," said Bryan.

"That sounds like fun, Bryan. You should take Amy with you guys and have a good time. I promise that you and I will go shopping sometime this week or next week. You don't have to hang out with the five guys all the time," Darcia said, as she smiled at Amy.

"Thanks, that sounds like fun. I am up for a nice shopping spree with another female," said Amy.

"I'll wait for you to be done with your waffles," Bryan said as he sat there patiently in the chair next to Amy. After Amy finished breakfast and got herself read, the six of them jumped on the trams and went over to the beach. It was an overcast but also warm day for people to be at the beach.

"We should go where there are not that many crowds screaming, dogs barking, and kids screaming," Bryan said, holding Amy close to him.

"Okay," Amy said. They laid out their towels and formed a circle around their backpacks and snacks and began talking about girls and guy talk. Amy got bored and got up.

"Where do you think you're going?" asked Bryan, challenging.

"Swimming," Amy said with a smile on her face.

"Wait while we come along with you," Bryan said. The six of them ran over to the water and stood there.

"Hey you guys, we should have a race to see who the fastest swimmer is," Joshua said.

"Get on your marks, get set and go." And they ran as fast as they could and started swimming like a wild animal that wanted to kill them was chasing them. Several minutes later, Amy got a cramp in her side and screamed for help. Bryan heard her and called everyone and went down to save Amy. After that, he carried her to the towels and gave her mouth-to-mouth.

"Amy, come on Amy, it is not your time to leave us." He did that for several minutes until Amy regained consciousness.

"Bryan, I was so scared," Amy whimpered. "This has never happened to me before," Amy whimpered as she was rubbing her eyes.

"It is okay. You and I are going back home," Bryan, said. He cradled her in his arms and carried her over to the nearest public transportation.

"Excuse me sir, but is that girl okay?" asked an elderly man while holding a shopping bag.

"Yeah, she's just a bit tired," said Bryan, as he held Amy close to him.

"Okay," he said and continued standing next to Bryan. As soon as Bryan opened the door to the cottage, he placed Amy on the couch and went to get her a glass of water. He heard a weird banging coming from Alistair and Darcia's room.

"Oh, goodness," Bryan gasped. He grabbed Amy by her arm and swung her over his shoulder and ran out as fast as possible.

"Bryan, could you slow down? The bouncing up and down is making me want to throw up," Amy moaned.

"Just a minute Amy, we need to go to a better place," Bryan said as he ran for another two minutes till he was as far away from the cottage as possible.

"Please tell me that was not real, Amy," Panted Bryan out of anxiety.

"Oh it was Bryan, it was," Amy chuckled. "It most definitely was real."

"There are way too many pictures going through my head right now," Amy said.

"Please stop, it's not that funny." Bryan snapped. Amy sighed, steadying herself against Bryan's body.

"I know, but those are just nerves. I probably know how it feels if I heard my parents," Amy said with a chuckle.

Once things started to settle down, Amy and Bryan walked hand in hand through the restaurant lane to see if there was anything they could eat.

"Hey, aren't those guys my brothers standing over there in front of that restaurant?" asked Bryan while pointing his brothers.

"Yeah, let us go and hang out with them. Maybe you can tell them what happened," Amy said with a chuckle. Amy and Bryan walked over and walked into a fish restaurant and sat down at a six-table booth at the end of the restaurant. A pretty red-haired woman wearing a diner uniform with heels came over with her pad and menus and handed them to Amy and the other boys.

"What would you like to drink?" asked the waitress.

"We'll have six waters," Raymond said.

"Okay, coming up," said the waitress before she walked to the bar and filled all of six of their glasses with ice and a slice of lemon.

"So Amy, how are you feeling?" asked Raymond.

"Average I guess." And she turned to Bryan to see his terrified expression.

"Bryan, you look stressed out. Why?" asked Raymond.

"Can you guys not tell mom or dad or anyone or even laugh out loud?"

"Sure. What's the news?" asked Silas.

"When I carried Amy into the house, I heard mom and dad very loud."

"Oh dear, Bryan, gosh darn. Are you all right? Do you need to talk to mom and dad?" the other boys, including Amy chuckled.

"So Amy, after lunch, you want to ditch these guys and get some ice cream, again?" asked Bryan with humor in his eyes.

"Sure, but this time let's keep in neutral and no more making out, or we'll have to leave the parlor again," Amy said with a chuckle.

"Got it," said Bryan with a smile on his face.

After lunch, Amy and Bryan went to get some ice cream at this stand and walked over to this park ten minutes away and sat down in front of this lake and sat there relaxing.

"So Amy, do you miss your family back home?" asked Bryan.

"Yeah, I really do, and I can't stand the thought of someone chasing me for a sick reason. I really want to be back in my room watching movies with my dog, eating dinner with my parents and sister. For the last month, my sister and I've not been going well but when I was babysitting and rushing to the hospital, my sister was in the background in case I needed a ride or an extra person. I really appreciate everything she's done for me."

"Do you ever tell her that?" asked Bryan when he moved away to face Amy.

"No, not really, but I do show her by my facial expression that I appreciate that."

"That's good enough, I guess. Do you miss your friends or school?"

"Um, school… no. Friends, yes. I remember my friend Jenna. She was a really good friend. We would always have our Friday after school shopping days. We would watch a movie every three weeks with other friends. I do miss those times."

"I totally understand your dilemma. Being away from your friends and sister seems very hard," Bryan said as he smiled.

"You know what I'm feeling right now?" asked Amy.

"What?" asked Bryan.

"It feels like I'm in a movie right now and you and I are the main characters and the rest of your family is like the backup characters or something like that."

"That sounds nice," Bryan said.

"Say, what time is it?" asked Amy while looking at Bryan's left arm.

"It's about a quarter to five and we should probably leave after our ice creams."

"So you want to walk around the park to see what there is to see?" asked Amy.

"Sure." The two of them walked around for thirty minutes and walked back to their cottage to eat dinner.

"Hey Bryan, did you and Amy have a nice time today?" asked Alistair, as he held Darcia in his arms on the couch.

"Sure, except for some moaning I heard up in your bedroom today?"

"What were you doing outside our bedroom?" snapped Darcia.

"Amy got cramps from swimming in the ocean, so we came back for a bit. I got a bit uncomfortable and ran out with Amy on my back."

"Son, can I have a word with you upstairs? I think we need to have a talk about this. I am not mad at you, but since you heard us, you probably want to get away from us, but since the killer is on the loose, we need to stick together as a support system and protect Amy," Alistair said.

"Can we talk after dinner? What is Darcia making?"

"I don't know. I'll be upstairs in a sec and we can talk about this before it gets out of hand."

"But dad…" moaned Bryan.

"Move it," Alistair snapped as he led Bryan towards the stairs. Bryan slumped upstairs to his room and sat on his bed, listening to his father's speech about the facts of life.

"Hey Darcia, what are Alistair and Bryan going to talk about?" asked Amy.

"Amy, could you come upstairs as well?" asked Alistair in a demanding way.

"Sure," said Amy. She walked upstairs and saw Bryan sitting all uncomfortably on the bed.

"Bryan and Amy, I know what you may've heard may have made you two feel uncomfortable, but as you know, we didn't know you guys were coming up the stairs. That's what we do when we're alone sometimes. If we don't do whatever you heard us do, we are either doing what we do best or walking around the area for some fresh air," said Alistair.

"Ahem father, may I talk to you in the other room across from ours?" asked Bryan.

"Sure," said Alistair. Both Bryan and Alistair walked over to the other boy's room and locked the door.

"Father, please don't speak about this dying thing to another person. Just talk about it in front of Darcia or my other four brothers, but not people like Am," Bryan whispered.

"Bryan, she probably doesn't even understand or know what I'm talking about," said Alistair.

"Father, please don't mention this again. Could you at least promise me that?"

"Bryan," sighed Alsitair. "I think it's time for her to know who we are in person and stop running from it, because if the day comes that she finds out who we are, you can really damage her brain big time," Alistair said.

"She's going through an okay time that I see by her expression," said Bryan in a low voice.

"But don't you think she's trying to hide her depressed, sad, look and think more positive?" asked Alistair.

"Maybe? I don't know. What do you mean, it could damage her big time?"

"She could faint or go into a coma, so tonight after dinner, while we're having a moist chocolate cake with a strawberry on top, the seven of us will tell her."

"Fine, but it might not go well as planned," Bryan said.

"We'll see. Now go to your room and keep Amy there till dinner time and I'll tell the rest of the group." After Alistair and Bryan finished talking, Bryan walked over to Amy.

"Amy, my dad wants you and me to stay up here. They're planning to get you a surprise so you can't go down till it is dinner."

"What should we do in the meantime?" asked Amy, hoping the surprise was not scary or dangerous.

"We can play truth or dare or maybe something like that." He leaned over to Amy's face to kiss her, but she pulled away. "Is there something wrong, Amy?"

"Oh, nothing's wrong. I just don't feel like kissing right now." She went over to her bed and laid down on her right side while staring at the wall.

"Amy, are you sad about leaving your family?" asked Bryan.

"No," said Amy. She turned to her left shoulder and tucked her pillow under her neck and started doing breathing exercises.

"While you're up here, I'm going to check up on everybody," Bryan whispered.

"See you later Bryan," Amy whispered to Bryan. After Bryan closed the door quietly, he walked downstairs.

"Bryan, what are you doing down here? You're supposed to be upstairs stalling Amy," Snapped Darcia.

"I am. She's upstairs lying on her bed taking a snooze," said Bryan.

"Okay. Now can I have everyone's attention? This evening we're going to let Amy know our family secret, since she's going to be with us for a very long time," Alistair whispered.

"Um Alistair, I don't think it's a good idea to do this," Darcia said.

"Yeah, Alistair, don't you think she's gone through a very tough time?" asked Raymond.

"Maybe we can postpone it for another time when she's really in jeopardy and then out pops our other side," Alistair said in a sarcastic tone.

"Dad, I just don't think it's a good idea for her to know two days after leaving her family. Maybe the attacker won't come for another two-three year," Bryan said.

"Okay. I guess we can wait for a month or so," Alsitair said. He then walked off to the kitchen to pour himself a glass of wine and gulped it down in one go.

"Hey Alistair, I know we may've shot down your plan, but give it some time. You'll know when the time is right. Have patience," Darcia said, while her arms were around Alistair's body.

"Okay, Darcia," Alistair said. He leaned over Daria and kissed her tenderly on her lips and they hugged each other. Later that evening, Bryan called Amy down to dinner and everyone ate quietly.

"So Bryan told me you guys are planning, me some kind of surprise?" asked Amy.

"Yeah, we'll be taking you somewhere for dessert at a pastry shop and eat it by this beautiful place. You'll see," Alistair said with a smile. After dinner, Amy walked up to her room and opened her laptop to check her email. She saw that Larry, Ginger, Jenna, and her parents wrote her emails.

She clicked on Larry.

Dear Amy,

I am so worried about your wellbeing in Australia. I can't really sleep that well thinking you are dead or something. I really miss you, so is there any way that you and I could have a phone conversation so I know you're alive? Just kidding.

I do hope you haven't met any cute surfer or anybody and forgot about me. Anyway, email me whenever you want to talk.

Larry

Amy closed her email and began to cry a bit. She missed everyone and felt horrible about leaving him or her. "Hey Amy, we are about to go outside for a drive. Come and join us?" Bryan asked as he stood in the doorframe.

"Um, give me a second. I am just reading my emails and looking over my work. See you downstairs soon," Amy said before she clicked on Ginger's email to see what her sister had to say.

Dear Amy,

Mom and Dad are so worried about you. I know you're doing okay. Lilah and Sammy miss you so much, but I give them lots of treats and love, so when you come back, don't be surprised to see that they love me more than you.

I got a couple of A's and B's at college. Your friends have sort of forgotten about you. From mom and dad, they tell me that your teachers keep asking me about you and I tell them it's none of their business, short and snappy.

Anyway, call mom and dad ASAP. Mom keeps crying, either in her room or in the bathroom. It's getting on my nerves.

Ginger.

"Amy, come downstairs and ride with us. You can sit in the front seat with me," Bryan said. Amy walked downstairs. "You weren't crying up there, were you?"

"Um, no I wasn't. I just got some dust in my eyes."

"Okay. Let's go," Bryan said as he opened the door for Amy to get in.

"Where are we going?"

"The seven of us were thinking about taking you somewhere special and quiet. But first we're going to get some dessert," Bryan said in a soothing tone.

They went to a drive-through and ordered Amy a sundae. "Amy, when we get to this special place we're going to do a little introduction and you'll be meeting some of our friends and eat your sundae there," said Alistair as he kept his eyes focused on the road.

"Okay." And she looked outside where it was dark and the area was creepy with all the trees and weird-looking shadows.

"Alistair, take a left over there and we're here," Darcia said while reading a map. The six of them got out of the van and followed Alistair and Darcia into the woods, where there was a fire and five other people standing there with no shoes on.

"Alistair, Darica. Welcome back. You can put your coat and shoes over there and come and join us," Audrey said with her light brown short wavy hair, blue sparkling eyes, and slender figure wearing a tight autumn coat. Amy took her shoes and coat and placed them on top of Bryan's.

"So, this is the girl?" asked Logan with his short black hair and blue eyes, wearing a black sweatshirt and jeans.

"This is Amy. We need to protect her," Alistair said, holding Amy close to him.

"Hi, my name is Logan and these are Audrey, Mackenzie, and Caleb."

"Nice to meet you," said Amy while crossing her arms. Bryan saw her shivering and grabbed his coat for Amy.

"Amy, let me tell you about these people. They are the brother and sister of Alistair and Darcia. They're immortals just like us and others around here," Alistair said. Amy had her eyes on Cameron's blonde-length hair and dark brown eyes and cheekbones. He smiled at her and it made her to smile. Audrey and Mackenzie stared at Amy with an unwelcome look and scowled.

"Hey Amy, here's your caramel sundae and a spoon," Bryan said. It had already melted, but Amy didn't care.

"So what kind of ceremony will we be having this evening?" asked Amy while eating her ice cream.

"Logan will explain," said Alistair. Logan, with his dark brown hair, brown eyes and pretty red lips, started explaining. Amy just stared at his lips and felt dazed.

"Amy. It's time to perform. Relax and enjoy," Bryan whispered.

The eleven of them showed their fangs, black eyes, and long nails. Amy stood there frozen and dropped her ice cream and fainted. The next thing she remembered was that she was in the car on her way back to the cottage. The next morning, she woke up and walked downstairs, seeing that everything was average. Everyone was eating eggs and bacon. "Wow, I had a weird dream that we went to this field and you guys turned into creatures," Amy said in a quivering tone.

"That was no dream, Amy. That was real and so now you know who and what we are. We are immortals and we have come to protect you and introduce you to the others in this world. Care for some breakfast?" asked Alistair with a smile.

Amy grabbed a cup of coffee and sat down next to Raymond. "Amy, you don't look so good. Maybe you should rest and relax today, maybe do some schoolwork before it is the end of the year and you fail this year. That would be a shame," Bryan added.

"Here, have some bacon and eggs," Darcia said, while placing a plate in front of Amy.

"Thank you." And she took a bite from her eggs and leaned on her elbow. After breakfast, Amy walked up to her room with a cup of coffee to her laptop and went over to her emails and continued to read them and reply to them.

She went over to Jenna.

Dear Amy,

I am so sorry that you're having family issues and you had to move back to Australia. I miss you so much.

Guess what, you'll laugh your head off. Heather went to prom last week, and she took this guy, Damien, to prom. She was wearing those cleats she had bought and as she walked over to Damien. She tripped and fell onto this vanilla sheet cake. The whole school burst out laughing and she ran out of the building in tears and ran home. It was hilarious. Anyway, tonight I'll be babysitting The Thompson's. Take care and I hope to see you again.

Jenna.

After Amy read that, she immediately replied.

Dear Jenna,

Can you keep a huge secret? I'm not in Australia because some family problems. I'm away from home because some killer who wants me is hunting me down. That's funny about Heather. Those Thompson kids are so adorable. If you need to go to the hospital, tell them you know Amy, they'll laugh their butts off.

Anyway, I'm still alive, scared, and sad and I miss you, too.

Love,
Amy.

After that, she went over to her parents' email and began reading.

Dear Amy,

Mommy and daddy miss you a lot and want you to be back in our arms and between us. Last night, the three of us watched old footage of us in Paris, Italy, and Germany.

I hope those seven people will catch that guy soon so that you can be back at our house and we will be reunited. You will also be very famous; you will be on the TV and in the newspapers.

We'll be sending you your birthday stuff, plus Jenna and Ginger and other presents, to your new address in six months.

Love you lots,
Mom and Dad

"Oh my goodness, what's happening to me?" Amy cried. Darcia heard Amy in her room and walked in.

"Amy, are you okay?" Darcia asked from outside the bedroom.

"No. I miss my friends and family, and I want to go home," Amy sobbed. Bryan entered to get his cell phone. "Amy, my goodness, what happened Darcia?"

"She's homesick and tired. Maybe we should get her some painkillers or sleeping pills, or something," said Darcia. "I will tell Alistair." Darcia walked downstairs.

"Amy, I know it's tough for you, and I understand. You want to talk about it?" Bryan asked while hugging her.

"Yeah. I just read some emails from my friend Jenna and she hopes to see me again and my parents want me to reunite with them. It's so sad."

"It must be very hard to read these heart-wrenching emails," Bryan said before Alistair and Darcia came into the room.

"Hey Amy, are you okay?" asked Alistair as he stroked Amy's back.

"I'm just homesick," Amy said while her lip quivered.

"Alistair, can I talk to you in the other room for a sec?" asked Darcia in a demanding way. They walked over to the other room and closed the door so Amy couldn't hear them. "Alistair, is there any way for Amy to contact her friends and family? I mean, look at her. She is stressed out. She probably can't see them again."

"I understand Darcia, but if we call up her house, the murderer could do something bad," Alistair whispered.

"She doesn't have to call them but email them and ask them to go to a hotel phone or airport phone or even a hospital phone outside their house."

"I don't know, Darcia," Alistair said while rubbing his eyes.

"Look inside of yourself and find your warm, loving side and ask yourself there." Darcia walked out of the room, down to the living room, and dropped down on the couch between Joshua and Silas.

"Hey Darcia, what's going on upstairs?" asked Joshua. "Why is Amy crying?"

"Amy's homesick and is crying upstairs right now." Darcia sighed, while biting her thumb nail.

"It must be hard for her not to comprehend why this is happening to her and who she actually is," Joshua said.

"So what do you guys think we should do to cheer Amy up?" asked Darcia.

"Maybe we should buy her some jewelry or a nice chocolate cake," said Xander.

"Xander!" said the five of them in a chorus. "Why should we buy her a chocolate cake?" they said.

"Most girls like chocolate cake and I can go for some right now," Xander said.

"Jewelry sounds nice, maybe a locket with her family in it," Darcia said with a smile.

"And Bryan," added Raymond.

"But where do we find a picture of her family?" asked Darcia, while she covered her mouth as she yawned. Just then, Alistair and Bryan walked downstairs.

"Hey Alistair, how's it going up there? Amy still crying her eyes out?" Joshua asked.

"Not really. We were thinking about visiting some family members around the world. Maybe they could help us. Like the Italian, Greek, Croatian, and the Romanian group," he whispered. While they were talking downstairs, Amy emailed her family and friends.

Dear Mom and Dad,

I miss you so much and I can barely handle being here while he or she or they are out there.

I'm still alive, but I feel dead inside. I have been having weird dreams about people killing me or holding me hostage and people killing you guys.

There is no way I can probably see you guys soon. I'm just emailing you guys to know that I am still alive and I miss you so badly. Give my regards to everyone; Sammy and Lilah, Ginger, Jenna, and Larry.

Your loving daughter Amy

Amy snuck downstairs to get herself a glass of water and overheard them talking about planning a surprise for Amy. "Hey Amy, how are you feeling?" Darcia asked. "We know you feel bad, depressed, confused and homesick, so we were planning on visiting some family members across the world. We will be happy to pay for your plane trip and make sure you and Bryan stick together for a long time." Amy felt speechless. She wanted to say thank you and that sounded lovely, but nothing came out of her mouth.

"You don't have to say anything at this moment," Darcia said with a chuckle. "Before I forget to ask, but do you have a picture of you and your family together?"

"Yes, in my suitcase," Amy said as she headed for her bag.

"Maybe we will see them for a second? Or Bryan, you should go up with Amy."

"Sure," said Bryan. Both Amy and Bryan walked upstairs and ten minutes later, they came down with a beautiful picture of Amy and her whole family standing in a meadow with a blue sky and some shrubs in the background.

"Who took this picture, if I may ask Amy?" asked Alistair, walking over to Amy.

"A close friend of the family. She and my mom were very close and people always asked whether they were sisters," said Amy, trying to stop herself from crying.

"That's nice," Alistair said with a smile. Amy walked upstairs to go over to her box of pictures. There was a picture of Amy and her two dogs; Amy and Ginger as babies; Amy and her parents at Disneyland; other pictures of her family. What caught her attention was a picture of Amy and Larry eating ice cream in front of the ice cream parlor. She never even got her picture taken with Larry. Amy looked at it real close and scanned every part of the picture, but couldn't make heads or tails out of it. Then she saw an old letter that Larry had written to her about meeting each other for the first time.

She heard her email making a message tune. She opened it up and saw that Larry had written her an email.

Dear Amy,

I'm glad to hear that you are okay. I heard it from your parents over the phone and they screamed with joy. What I wanted to ask you is: do you see that picture of you and me in front of that ice cream parlor we used to go to and the note that is in your box? I wanted to have a memorable picture of us together. However, whatever you do, if you see any dubious signs or people acting weird or even wild animals acting weird, do not listen or look or even follow them. Some family members and I will meet you in Italy next week and we will start clarifying things, because whatever is going on is messed up and I want to reunite with you again.

Please keep in contact for any kind of news and report it to me ASAP! Got it!

Larry.

Amy deleted that email and closed her laptop and walked downstairs again.

"You guys, I would love to meet your family around the world," Amy said, keeping herself as normal as she could.

"We're going to visit some Italian friends. They know about your situation and they're going to help you and make sure nothing bad will happen to you, plus the seven of us will support you in any way possible," Alistair said.

"Thanks guys, really much. I really appreciate everything what you guys have done for me."

"Amy, you don't have to say that every day. That's sort of our job protecting people who we care about," said Darcia.

"Even though you're having mood swings and crying, we'd still treat you like one of us," Bryan said in a playful manner.

Amy smiled and hugged Bryan really tight. He carried her to the couch and put her between Joshua and Raymond. "So Amy, would you like to have a nice omelet with scrumptious fillings made by Alistair?" asked Darcia.

"Well, I am also sort of hungry," Bryan, said as he interrupted Amy in a winey tone.

"Well, your omelet is on its way, so you just sit back relaxed and we'll make these couple of toppings extra special for you, and would you like some hot coco with lots of marshmallows in it?" asked Alistair.

"I would love a nice cup of hot chocolate with marshmallows," Amy said.

Alistair and Darcia walked into the kitchen and started preparing Amy's lunch.

"So, Alistair, when are we going to leave for Rome?" whispered Darcia.

"Next week Monday. So we have like about five days till we have to leave. I got everyone Italian dictionaries and Italian learning tapes for Amy so she can communicate a little with Dante. He's the leader of his Italian group." Alistair whispered while tossing the omelet.

"Does he also speak English?" asked Darcia, with concern in her voice and eyes.

"Yes, but he prefers to speak Italian with his brothers," Alistair said.

"Oh?" Was the only thing that came out of Darcia's mouth. Amy walked upstairs to pack some of her clothes and her shower stuff. "Amy, your lunch is ready," Darcia said while carrying the hot chocolate to the table and putting some mini marshmallows in it.

Amy walked down and sat at the table. The omelet looked like an artwork by one of those famous painters. Her hot chocolate looked really lovely. She wanted to take a picture, but that would make her look weird. She grabbed her knife and fork and cut a piece. It tasted like heaven. There was also a straw cookie in her hot chocolate. "Thank You," said Amy with a smile.

"You're very welcome, Amy," Darcia came by and kissed Amy lightly on the top of her head.

"You guys come and join Amy," Darcia snapped, watching the four boys walk over to the table.

"Hey dad, could you make me an omelet?" asked Bryan.

"Sure, would you also like a foot massage, a nice glass of water with some ice and a slice of lemon, and would you like to be addressed as Lord Bryan?"

"I have my own nutrients. Come and join me upstairs, brothers," whispered Bryan.

"I need to call Dante to make some arrangements with him and other stuff. I'll also call the other world members and tell them about Amy's dilemma." Alistair walked over to his room and closed the door.

"Hey Dante, it's me, Alistair," Alistair whispered in a hushed voice. "She's with us."

"Buona serata, Alistair. How are you doing, brother? How are the rest of the family members?" Dante said in a velvety voice.

"They're fine. You know about Amy Ambrose, right?"

"Yes. Everyone in my family knows about Amy. When you arrive, we'll give her something so she'll be able to fight like an immortal princess. Amy will be staying in the West wing with Adrianna, Francesca, and Alessandra. They will look over her while she slumbers at night. You have to come and see everyone again."

"Don't worry. We'll be there next Monday," Alistair said in a whisper.

"Splendida. Now Alistair. Do we have to prepare any meal or drinks for Amy?" Dante asked with curiosity in his voice.

"Darcia and I will take her out to eat every night," said Alistair.

"Does she know that we're immortals? I mean, does she know of Gabriel?"

"Yes, and No. The seven of us, and the Australian crowd, showed her. She fainted after we turned around. It was hard for some of us to look at Amy. She won't find out about Gabriel till we arrive in Romania," Alistair said, as he started to feel uncomfortable about the whole lying to Amy.

"I just talked to Gabriel a few minutes ago, and he's waiting for her to finally meet her. And don't worry, when Amy arrives, she'll be in good hands. Ciao," Dante said before he hung up.

Alistair walked back to everyone and told everyone the news. Later that afternoon, the eight of them went out to dinner at this steakhouse. After they finished, they drove back to the cottage. Alistair and Darcia went to their room to get ready for bed. Bryan and Amy walked upstairs, got on Amy's bed, snuggling. The other days they were hanging out by the beach doing their regular stuff, getting ready for their trip to Rome.

Chapter 4

Italy

When Amy woke up, she gathered all of her belongings and put them in a duffle bag and backpack and walked out with the whole group to one of the taxis. Alistair and Darcia walked into the reception to return the key. As soon as they got to the airport, everyone was around Amy protecting her from any harm. They checked in their luggage and walked over to their gate and got out their reading books.

Amy got out her diary.

Dear Diary, 10/03/07

Well, there's been a lot happening to me. A month or so ago, I came back from school and these people told me I was in grave danger. At first I didn't believe them, but later they were really going a bit too far about this thing, so I gave in and we went to Australia so he wouldn't bother me. Now we're on our way to Italy to meet these weird people. The reason I say weird is that these people are not ordinary people. They are immortal. I saw a couple of them transform into these monsters. I fainted, and that was the great excitement of this trip. We'll be staying in this manor with some Italian people. I miss Larry and my family. I wonder who this murderer is, maybe a hot, dark, mysterious, super handsome guy or maybe a creepy monster. Anyway, the time is ten thirty in the evening and I'm still alive, thank goodness. Amy

The ground flight attendant made an announcement. "Could a Ms. Amy Martin come to the information desk?" Alistair and Amy walked over to the desk at the gate. "Ms. Martin, you have been promoted to first class," said the attendant. Alistair smiled and used his powers on her.

"Berdine," said Alistair while reading her nametag. "My female companion needs to have one of her male companions next to her."

"I'm sorry, sir, but she was the only one promoted unless you want to change her ticket to sit next to her male companion?"

"Yes, I would," said Alistair.

The attendant clicked on the keyboard. "Ms. Martin, I've changed your seat to a window seat," the attendant said before handing Amy her new boarding pass.

"Splendid madam," Alistair said sarcastically while guiding Amy towards the waiting area.

"Bryan, you'll be sitting with Amy," said Alistair.

"That won't be a problem for me," said Bryan, with a smile. Then he winked at Amy, causing her to blush.

The eight of them got up, showed their tickets, and boarded the plane. As soon as Amy and Bryan got to her seat, they started kissing each other until Alistair came by and swatted him on the back of his head. "Stop that," he snapped. Once every passenger got seated, the flight attendants demonstrated the safety instructions. After they departed, the captain turned off the seatbelt sign. Amy and Bryan snuggled together. "So Amy, I saw that you were writing in your diary. Does that help you calm down or center your thoughts?" whispered Bryan.

"Yes, it does. I do it whenever I'm depressed or nervous or even when I'm happy about something," Amy said while Bryan was kissing her hands.

"So, what are you going to order for a drink?" asked Amy.

"I would love some water with ice cubes and a slice of lemon," said Bryan.

He then opened up the airplane magazine to glimpse through the pages. Amy pulled up her backpack to see if there was a book in it that she could read. She got hold of one of her books. Alistair must have put it inside when they left Oregon.

"How's the book, Bryan?" asked Amy.

"It's pretty good. What are you reading?" asked Bryan.

"I'll be reading the airplane magazine," said Bryan as he reached for the front compartment. Just then, the flight attendant came to their row.

"Would you like anything to drink?" the flight attendant asked.

"Yes. One water with ice cubes and slices of lemon."

"Anything for you sir," the flight attendant asked. Bryan shook his head. She opened up a small bottle of water and grabbed a cup of ice cubes and a lemon slice. Bryan handed Amy her cup and kissed her hand real soft and smooth. It made Amy get goose bumps.

"Are you okay Amy?" asked Bryan with a smile on his face.

"Yeah, never better," Amy, whispered. "Never better."

"Hey Amy, wouldn't it be funny if the murderer was on this airplane sitting either in front of us or somewhere next to us?"

"Yes, Bryan, that would be so funny. I would pee my pants and have a mighty fine time," Amy said sarcastically before she took a sip of water. The coolness of the water felt so delicious in her throat.

"See? You're seeing the bright side of this journey," Bryan said. Amy didn't respond to him and opened the book to page one. "Hey Amy, want to know what happens in the book?"

"Why, you didn't read it, did you?" Amy asked.

"No, but Darcia did, and she told me and ruined it for me. Now I can't read it anymore," Bryan said with a chuckle.

"No," said Amy, while going back to her book. Several hours later, Amy got up and went to the bathroom. Bryan followed her.

"Hey Amy, do you really have to go to the bathroom?"

"Yes," Amy snapped.

"Which number do you have to go?" said Bryan, with a smile on his face.

"That's none of your beeswax, mister," Amy snapped before she locked the door.

Bryan chuckled before he turned around and saw Allistair scowl at him, mouthing for Bryan to return to his seat.

"Bryan, what are you guys doing? One more time if you put the moves on her she and I are switching places and you'll be sitting back there with Raymond and a stranger," Alistair snapped before he pointed to Bryan's seat.

"Sorry," Bryan whispered. He walked back to his chair and continued reading the airplane magazine. Amy walked back and grabbed her pillow and leaned against the window and slumbered off. Later on, the flight attendants came by with some lunch. Amy woke up and dug into her cheese sandwich. "Wow Amy, you eat like someone who's been locked up in a closed for a week without food," Bryan whispered. That sort of made Amy mad, but she was very hungry and wolfed down her food in five minutes and went back to sleep.

"Wow," Bryan whispered. Several hours later, the flight attendants came by with the garbage trolley and some beverages. "Hey Amy, would you like to have a drink?"

"Sure, please get me some water," Amy said. There was some turbulence going on.

"Bryan, I'm scared." She grabbed his arm, and he placed his arms around her. Moments later, the flight attendants came by with forms and prepared for their landing in Rome.

"When we arrive at our family's manor, we'll take a nice long walk around the area for some fresh air and to stretch our legs," Bryan said.

"I'm up for some fresh air," said Amy, while stretching her arms and legs.

Amy listened to half the flight attendants, pulled her chair up, and put her stuff back into her backpack and got ready to meet them. When they got out, they walked at a fast pace to the luggage belt and waited. They waited and waited and waited for fifty minutes, collected their luggage. "Will we meet your family here?"

"No, they sent a limo and their butler," Alistair. When they went outside, they saw a long hummer limo with a guy in front of it.

The eight of them got into the limo. "Good Afternoon lords and ladies, off to a nice month with Dante and his family. It's about a two-hour drive. Hope you don't mind." the driver, an elderly man, said in his uniform.

"Yes, we have our special girl with us," Alistair said. What seemed like many hours later, Amy saw the side of the manor. She saw a gigantic lawn and two huge fountains and ten statues of lions going into the manor.

"Oh my goodness, you guys," whispered Amy while she was staring at the manor. Amy had always seen pictures of manors, but she had never seen one close by.

"Yeah!" whispered Bryan. "I am getting pretty excited."

"All right, you guys. Here we go and you guys are expected at Dante's manor," the driver said before he stopped the limousine.

"Thanks, driver," Alistair and Darcia said. The driver walked to the door and opened it for everyone to walk in with the luggage. First nothing happened until this beautiful girl came running down to meet them.

"Oh, my goodness, is that Alistair?" asked Francesca. Francesca was wearing this red-colored gown with a bow that went across her chest.

"Oh, my goodness," yelled other girls running down the stairs to hug the other five guys.

"Oh my goodness, Alistair, this must be the girl who we need to protect, um excuse me, I need to check something. Catch you later," She said as she smiled at everyone except Amy.

"Amy is sort of in a situation and we need to protect her," Alistair responded.

"Buongiorno," said a deep male voice. Dante came walking down the stairs wearing black pants and a black shirt, and a house jacket. He has black shoulder-length hair and purplish eyes. They hugged each other like they had not seen each other in like forever. "And you must be Amy." Dante kissed her on her hand.

"Hey boys, long time no see and you Darcia, welcome to our manor in Rome. Adrianna wants to see you so badly. Go upstairs and surprise her," Dante said. Darcia wanted to please her, so she walked upstairs to Adrianna's room.

"Welcome. Alfred, could you take their luggage in the elevator? I am going to show them around and could you call the other three brothers of mine to meet Amy so they know who they're dealing with?" Dante said as he led Alistair's group around.

"Certainly, sir," said Alfred as he grabbed the luggage trolley and walked towards the elevator.

"How was your flight?" asked Dante with a smile on his face.

"Pretty long and boring. We need to walk off this airplane feeling," Alistair said.

"At level four, we have a spa center for the women and a sport center for the guys and a steam room. We have an inside and outside swimming pool and an outside pool. We have signs at every corner of the house, so if you get lost you'll know where you are. So Amy, you know about our huge secret that we only tell very close friends," Dante said.

"Yes, it's pretty exciting news," Amy said out of nerves.

"Don't worry. We'll protect you like you're a chamber with gold in it," said Dante, which caused Amy, laughed nervously.

"You will be on the same level with Francesca, Brianna, Adrianna, and Darcia, which is the West wing," Dante said, gesturing to the different areas of the mansion.

"Awesome." whispered Amy sarcastically, and loud enough for Dante to hear.

"In case you are thirsty or hungry, Alfred will fetch you a snack from the bar on your level. We have a small movie theatre on level five, which shows the newest films. We have everything you need, my dear," Dante said.

"Okay," Amy said with a smile on her face.

"Well, I will let you freshen up in your wing. I will have Regina send you up some shampoo and conditioner. Just relax and take it easy. The elevator is down the hall to the left, but I will walk with you because I have to go up to my wing," Dante said. Amy and Dante walked in and stopped at Amy's floor, and he went up.

"Wow," Amy whispered. "I never thought I would ever be in a manor."

"It is quite magnificent," a female voice said. Amy turned around and saw another woman her age wearing the same dress as Francesca. "Hi, I didn't mean to sneak up on you. My name is Adrianna and you must be Amy. I've heard about you."

"Yeah, I can barely sleep that well," Amy said in a morose tone.

"No worries. We're going to have a blast with you around, and we'll keep an eye out for any suspicion. Come along. I will show you your room and your very own bathroom with bath and shower. Have you ever been in a manor before?"

"No, but I went in my ex-boyfriend's home before I left on this crazy adventure slash nightmare," Amy said as Adrianna was leading her.

"Well, you are in for a very special treat. I'll give you your handbook with rules and regulations and other stuff."

"You have rules?" Amy asked.

"Dante is very strict about these rules, but he will make an exception for you since you are 'special'," Adrianna said as she led Amy through these corridors filled with paintings and art.

"Is that a camera in the corner over there?" Amy pointed.

"Yes. Dante is also strict about that too, just to make sure nothing bad will happen to us," Adrianna said. "All right, this is the room you'll be sleeping in. It is nothing special."

"Nothing special, oh my goodness," said Amy as her mouth fell open.

"Over there to the right is your huge bathroom, to the right is your king-size bed, there in front of you is your closet with gowns and dresses and, of course, shoes that is also part of the rules we dine in formal, we eat lunch in less formal and breakfast we eat with our Pajamas and robes," Adrianna said, pointing at everything.

"Oh my goodness," whispered Amy.

"You got that right sister, now let's continue your tour around your bedroom. Over there is a huge window looking over the courtyard. Regina and this other guy are our servants."

"Great, so where can I take a shower?" asked Amy.

"The washroom is there. Regina will fetch your shower gels, your robe, a towel, and some slippers. I will be waiting downstairs, so if you need me, just holler into this call box and say, Adrianna, I need you and I will be up in no time."

"Wow, thanks Adrianna," Amy said.

"No problem Amy, just pretend you own this place," Adrianna said. She left and Regina, with her dark brown hair and brown eyes, wearing a maid's uniform, came into the room with some shower supplies and set them on her bed.

"Thanks Regina," Amy said with a smile on her face.

"You are very welcome, Amy." Regina left. Amy walked into the bathroom with a surprised look. This bathroom looked like half the size of her bedroom in Oregon. Amy got into the shower and relaxed. When Amy was done, she got out, finding a blue formal gown on her bed with some accessories and a pair of shiny blue heels.

"Hey Amy, are you ready to go downstairs for dinner? It is midnight and you'll be meeting the rest of the family. I'll help you with your look," Adrianna said. She dried Amy's hair and made it all nice and shiny and put her hair up with a clip and put a shiny clip across her head, after that she helped Amy into that dress and put her pumps on. "Now it's time for some makeup. You look like a pink and peach." After Adrianna helped Amy, they were ready to dine with the family. "Now we will be escorted by some guys with a flower so, be prepared." Some guys who were going to escort Amy and Adrianna knocked on the door. "That must be the two guys who will escort us knocking on the door," Adrianna said before she opened up and Amy's mouth went open. There was a handsome guy with brown, neck-length curly hair with brown eyes and a tuxedo with a red rose in his hand.

"Hi, I am here to escort Amy Ambrose. My name is Romeo." He kissed Amy's hand really softly and grabbed her arm and pulled her softly out the door. Amy didn't realize Romeo had used a different surname.

"So, Amy, I will be your escort for this evening. I'm one of Dante's brothers."

Amy was speechless and let herself get lost in the moment.

"We will be downstairs in no time, so just relax and breathe normally." When they got to the dining room, everyone was standing behind their seats, waiting for everyone to arrive. Behind Amy were Adrianna and another gorgeous guy with blonde curly hair and a smile that would make her go crazy.

"Ladies and Gentlemen, I would like to invite this lovely young woman named Amy Ambrose who we will be protecting. Everyone, this is Amy in the beautiful royal blue gown," Dante said. Amy felt embarrassed and giggled nervously.

"Thank you," Amy whispered before she bowed and walked back to Romeo.

"Now please, sit." The men took the women's seats and pulled their chairs and pushed them, and then they sat down themselves. Regina and Alfred took out a big bottle of champagne and some water.

"I would like to propose a toast to Amy, who has been a brave and strong girl for surviving this horrific nightmare. To Amy," said Bryan.

"To Amy," the others said. Amy was blushing and felt so embarrassed having fourteen faces smile at her. Francesca didn't bother. Regina brought out a huge bowl of what looked like raspberry juice, except it didn't smell like that.

"Enjoy," Dante said, gesturing for everyone to drink.

Amy looked confused at what the butlers put in front of her, causing her to gag a bit. Dante looked surprised at Amy. She looked at Bryan, who was slurping the red substance from his spoon, and looked at the others.

"Oh dear, I forgot that you are used to human foods," said Dante. "Forgive my manners."

"That's all right," sighed Amy. "I think I still have a candy bar in my backpack upstairs."

After everyone finished their meal, Adrianna took Amy up to her room and picked out these beautiful black silk pajamas with the word Ambrose on them.

"How did you know I was coming?"

"Like Dante said this evening, we are immortals, and we all have the same power. It gets annoying after a while. When we're mad at each other, it turns into a huge fight and sometimes we end up near death."

"Sounds exciting," said Amy in a sarcastic tone. "One of your sisters doesn't seem to like me."

"Who doesn't like you, Amy?" asked Adrianna in a shocked way.

"The person who greeted us first I guess," Amy said.

"Oh, Francesca. She is always like that with new people. Later, she will come closer to you. Just have patience. Anyway, I will leave you for you to get ready for bed. If you are not tired, you can always walk down to the library and pick a book out. I put your manual on your desk over there. Furthermore goodnight."

"Goodnight," said Amy.

Amy walked into her huge bathroom and turned the faucet on. She looked so beautiful in her royal blue dress. She brushed her teeth and then walked back to put her pajamas on. She went over to the library to pick a book out. When she got there, she saw Romeo reading a book with a gold rim around it.

"Oh hey," Amy said. "I mean to disturb you," said Amy, surprised.

"No worries. Come in and pick out any book from the library," Romeo said.

"So what book would you recommend?" asked Amy.

"All of them I guess," Romeo said. "We have romance novels, fiction books, comedy books. Just to get a conversation going, how are you doing?"

"I don't know exactly. I feel depressed, guilty, and confused. It feels like this is a nightmare," Amy said as she sat down on one of the velvet purple chairs in the library. Romeo sighed.

"You can grab any book you want," Romeo said with a smile before he continued reading. Amy decided she would prefer to sleep. "Sweet dreams." The other days Amy spent in Rome, they went everywhere with the crowd and saw almost everything, like some cathedrals and a couple of churches and domes, and they saw different historical museums and a lot more. Two weeks went by in a snap.

"So, Dante, in a few months we'll be having our annual family gathering in Romania. You guys have to come," Alistair said, trying to make it sound like there was a party going on. Everyone we know around the world. Bring any friends and family members to this gathering."

"I forgot to give Amy a protection serum that will last in her body for a very long time. You wouldn't mind, will you?" asked Dante.

"Not at all, but is that really necessary?" asked Alistair, with a confused look.

"We did promise Gabriel," Dante said.

"Anyway, this evening at dinner, we will give her a special drink. We will tell her it is medicine, well actually it is a kind of medicine." When they got back to the manor, they all went their separate ways till dinnertime.

"I would like to do a tiny ceremony for Amy and give her this special drink," Dante said.

"The last time I was in the middle of a ceremony, I ended up somewhere messed up," Amy said.

"Well, in this case, you will feel powerful and high for a day, then it wears off, but you will have the power inside of your body to fight anything."

Dante handed Amy a goblet with something that looked like water. He tilted her head back and let the stuff go down her throat. When she was finished, he handed Regina the goblet and looked into her eyes to make sure nothing would damage her body. "So Amy, how do you feel?"

"Average, I guess," she whispered.

"Good," he smiled and walked back to his seat. "Now you may continue eating this deer. My brothers and I hunted for you Buon appetito. After dinner, we have a special treat for everyone. We are going to be having a masquerade ball for all the people in Rome at this palace this Friday."

"Wow." Amy whispered when she was drinking her water. After dinner, everyone went his or her own way.

"Dante," said Alistair, making a beckoning gesture. "Can I have a word?"

"Certainly, Alistair," Dante said.

"Dante, you have to come. Amy is glowing." Adrianna shrieked in terror. Alistair and Dante ran up to Amy's room, seeing her glowing. Amy was breathing really fast. Alistair and Darcia ran to her side and grabbed her hand.

"Amy, can you hear me, Amy," Alistair repeated that till she looked at him and spoke really softly.

"Oh, goodness, Alistair, I am really sorry for doing that to Amy. I didn't know she would react this way to the serum. Most people react normally," Dante, said, with fear in his voice.

"Well, Amy is not dead, thank goodness. We should bring her a nice cup of cold water for her to drink," Alistair said reassuringly.

"Where is Bryan?" Amy whispered.

"Bryan, I'll get him for you," Dante said. He walked off to the East wing to bring Bryan to Amy.

"Bryan, Amy needs you quick before she might pass out," Dante panted. The two of them raced really hard for Amy. "Amy, Amy, Amy. Can you hear me?"

"Yes," she whispered.

"Bryan, you need to kiss her on her mouth quickly," Alistair snapped.

Bryan cupped Amy's head gently and pushed his head slightly so their lips would meet. Suddenly, the windows flew open.

"What happened?" The other four brothers said when they ran into Amy's room.

"Amy's body could not handle the powerful medicine I gave her and again, Alistair, I am so sorry about this," Dante whispered.

"It's okay Dante. We just need to let her rest until tomorrow morning." The next day, Regina went into Amy's room with a glass of water and a painkiller before she woke Amy up.

"Good morning Amy, how are you feeling?"

"Good, but I feel weird after what happened yesterday. My body feels like it was on fire."

"Take a drink of this cold water." There was a knock on the door.

"Come in," said Amy groggily.

Dante and his three girls walked into Amy's room. "Amy, what I gave you yesterday was something that would protect your body from any harm and you'll heal faster."

"Is the burning part, part of this whole protection?"

"Yes. Some people don't even feel anything, but your body is probably sensitive to that," Dante said as he sat on the edge of Amy's bed.

"What's going to happen to me?" asked Amy, feeling uncertain and scared.

"So long as the murderer is not near us, we still need to keep an eye out for any suspicion. You might want to rest this entire day. Regina will take care of you."

The four of them walked out of the room to talk to the rest of the people.

Darcia entered the room with Bryan to check up on Amy to make sure she was okay.

"Hey Amy, how are you feeling, sweetheart?" asked Darcia, looking concerned.

"Fine, so what's the upshot about this whole adventure thing?"

"You're going to meet everyone around the world so they can protect you from any harm. Just relax and snooze if you want," whispered Darcia.

"Bryan, why do these kinds of things happen to me, like seizures or heart attacks?"

"Maybe your body isn't used to being away from your home so long and the traveling may have something to do with it or the tension you're feeling about being chased," Bryan responded as he reached for Amy's hand.

"Could you keep me some company while I lay here? Maybe read me a book or sing?" Asked Amy as she was squeezing Bryan's hand.

"I will sing you one of my favorite old songs I heard once upon a time before you were born," Bryan said as he held Amy's hand.

"Your voice sounds very beautiful. Please do not stop." After Amy fell asleep, Bryan walked downstairs to checkup on everyone and left outside for a nice walk with someone.

"Hey you guys, what is up?" asked Bryan.

"How is, Amy? Is she all right? Do we need to take her to a doctor?" Darcia asked.

"No, she is asleep," said Bryan as he let himself drop into a chair.

"What are you doing downstairs? Go up and watch over her," said Alistair.

"Or else what, you'll spank me, send me to my room, take away my privileges?"

Alistair looked over at Darcia in an irritated way. Bryan ran up as fast as possible and sat in the chair next to the bed. He saw some fiction books and decided he would open one of the books and read it. Two hours later, Bryan went down to eat some lunch. When he waited for the elevator, two guys walked up to Bryan.

"Hey Bryan, how is the girl? Are you planning on getting married to Amy?" asked Angelo with his black hair and dark eyes.

"I'm not quite sure. We're taking it easy since this whole charade is going on," Bryan said. "So, are you two with Adrianna or Francesca?"

"Romeo is with Francesca and Angelo is with Adrianna. It's nice having girlfriends." Said José the other guy that also had black hair and dark eyes.

"Yeah. So you guys are married, right?" asked Bryan.

"No, but I'm planning our wedding next year in January," Angelo said. When the elevator came, the three of them walked in and went downstairs to the kitchen to eat something they could find.

"Here is that leftover deer," Bryan said, all excited.

"All right, here are three plates," Bryan said before he sliced a piece for Angelo and then José.

"Would any of you guys like some wine or champagne? I'm going down to the cellar to get a bottle of something," said José.

"Why don't you bring up the Roman wine and let's toast to our beautiful women?" Angelo said. After Bryan served himself some deer and poured everyone a glass of champagne, they waited and sat around the table. "To women," they cheered and took a sip from their glass and put it down.

"So Bryan, how old is Amy, anyway?" asked José.

"She is eighteen, going on nineteen in three months. She's a junior in school." Would she not have graduated two years ago with her brains? So, her birthday is when?" Angelo asked after he wiped his mouth with his napkin.

"Her birthday is May tenth nineteen ninety-one. When she was in ninth grade, she dropped out of high school due to peer pressure," Bryan said.

"What day is it today? We do not want to miss the ball this Friday," said Bryan sarcastically.

"It is Tuesday. I bet Adrianna is going to plan a birthday for her since they're close." Moments later, Alistair and Dante entered the house in their jogging suits and went into the kitchen. "Wow, Alistair, you're a fast runner."

"So are you Dante, but do not act surprised at our condition," Alistair panted.

"So Bryan, how is Amy? Is she still sleeping upstairs?" Alistair asked.

"Yes, I left out of boredom, and I was hungry. Is Darcia mad at me about Amy?" Bryan asked before he took his last sip of wine.

"No, she's just overprotective of her. Do not be so hard on her, son. Relax," Alistair said.

"Hey Dad, what is for dinner?" Bryan asked, before he looked at Dante.

"We're having what we usually have. It's in the garage, so the manor will not get dirty. We will be eating at one in the morning. Is Amy up for a nice dinner again?" Alistair asked, before he poured himself a glass of wine.

"Sure, let me go upstairs and wake her up," Bryan said.

"Poor girl, but at least she is protected a bit from any harm," said Dante. "Are you still going to introduce her to Gabriel?"

"Soon," Alistair whispered. Amy came downstairs holding Bryan's hand. "Look who finally came out of bed."

"Hey Amy, how are you feeling?" asked Dante.

"A bit tired, but all I need is some fresh air." Amy said as she felt pain throughout her body.

"Bryan, you can take Amy out on our personal hike following the path that starts at the beginning of the mansion," said Alistair.

"Are you up for a hike Amy?" asked Bryan, holding Amy in his arms.

"I will give myself a couple of minutes. If I really cannot continue, I'll go back. If I'm up for a longer walk, we will continue," Amy said.

"Would any of the other boys like to go with us, Alistair? Maybe Raymond, Joshua, Xander, and Silas?" Bryan asked?

"If you want to invite them, use the call box," Dante said.

"Hey you guys, do you want to go on a walk with Amy and me?" asked Bryan.

"Sounds like fun. When are we going?" asked Raymond.

"We will be leaving in five minutes," Bryan said.

After Amy and the five boys left the manor, the boys went jogging ahead, leaving Amy and Bryan together. "Amy, in a few weeks you're going to meet another group. Some of those people are rude, but pay no attention to their behavior. If by any chance something bad happens, you and I will run back to your house and family and I will protect you no matter how long or hard it will take," said Bryan.

"Really?" asked Amy in a concerned way.

"I want to give you this necklace of a unicorn. The reason I chose this is because it reminded me of you and it is very special."

"Oh my goodness," Amy whispered.

"May I?" asked Bryan while holding the necklace.

"Yeah, of course," Amy said. When he put it on her, she turned around. "Bryan, I will take very good care of this necklace, I promise."

"That necklace is my promise to you that I will die for you anytime and anywhere."

Amy leaned into Bryan's chest and cuddled with him. "So you want to continue this walk or go back to the manor?" Bryan asked.

"Continue walking. I need the exercise so badly my body is screaming at me." Moments later, they caught up with the other four guys pushing each other into the bushes and laughing.

"What took you guys so long? We thought you were eaten my cougars or mountain lions," Joshua said teasingly.

"There are no mountains or lions here, only snakes and spiders. I hate those critters. Both of them are mean and vicious and dangerous and aggressive," Bryan said.

"I have heard about this story where this little girl walked into a spider web and thousands of tiny spiders jumped on her and started eating her alive," said Silas.

"Yeah right," Xander said.

"It is true. I saw it in a magazine. There was also a picture of a spider there."

"Besides our spider conversation," said Bryan. "Do any of you guys, including Amy, want to run for a bit?"

"I'm not really up for it; I'll just walk for a bit longer and return to the manor for dinner. You guys run without me," Amy said before she crossed her arms.

"I will stay with you, Amy. It is a bit too dangerous to be walking all by yourself in your condition," Bryan said.

"Thanks Bryan, but if you really want to run, go right ahead."

"No, I will stay behind and walk like a wimp."

"You're so not a wimp, Bryan. I bet if I weren't fatigued, you'd probably be out running. I have a question for you. Will I become one of you guys, meaning immortal?" Bryan knew he was not allowed to tell Amy anything about whom she was or any information and tried to think of a good answer.

"There is a cottage in the distance. Want to check it out and go in to see if there is anything special in it?" Bryan asked, trying to change the topic.

"We can walk over, but not inside. I am not walking into someone else's property."

They walked over to the cottage and knocked on the door. Nobody answered.

"Come, shall we go to dinner?" asked Amy. "What I don't understand is why Dante serves your liquid meal around midnight?" asked Amy while they walked towards the manor.

"Ahem Amy, but what were you and Bryan doing outside? You were supposed to be ready for the three guys to pick us up," Francesca snapped. "Now go in to your room and put your gown on." She walked off with a heavy sigh.

"Amy, don't mind Francesca, she is just a bit cranky, because she's not the center of attention but you. Come in and I'll make you pretty like those other days," Adrianna said as she walked with Amy and Bryan back to the manor.

"May I escort Amy to dinner?" asked a blonde guy with curls. "My name is José". This time, he came with a white rose and kissed Amy's hand. When they arrived, everyone was standing neatly in front of their chairs. The men pulled the chairs from the women and pushed them forward as usual.

"Now, ladies and gentlemen, it is Thursday and that means tomorrow we will be going to this palace in Rome. We will also be eating and drinking there. At midnight we will drive back here and relax, so special people like Amy can sleep," said Dante. Amy felt her stomach cringe at all these parties and ceremonies. It made Amy want to throw up and let this nightmare end. "Enjoy your meal," he said.

After dinner, José took Amy up to her room and walked back to his wing.

"So Amy, what did you think of José? Quite the charmer?" asked Adrianna.

"He was the one who found me when I was being attacked by a group of guys. He fought them off for me and took me to his apartment before he became one of them. He placed a lukewarm towel over my forehead and put some classical music on so I wouldn't get too overwhelmed. After that, he took me home. Dante was in my apartment sitting in one of my dining room chairs. The last thing I knew was he gave me a drink from this goblet with some of his blood. The same night I was sleeping in the bed you're sleeping in," Adrianna said as she was brushing her own hair.

"Wow, what an interesting story. I'm confused about one thing. The stuff he gave me that one night before I went crazy. Did he put his blood in it or was it just something strong?" asked Amy.

"It was not his blood for sure, because if someone had another choice, he would leave them alone and look for other victims. If he saw someone he did not like, he would wait for the opportune moment and kill him or her. Not because he is mean, but he would do it to protect other people or teach whoever needed a lesson, and teach them a lesson they will never forget their whole lives. Oh my goodness, listen to me; I'm just keeping you up. Goodnight and remember, you are safe no matter where you are," Adrianna said before she left Amy alone in her room.

"Thanks, Adrianna. I really appreciate that and I am very grateful for everything."

Amy walked into her room and turned on the plasma screen TV. The news was on about someone who escaped jail and was looking for somebody. "He has black hair; he has thick muscles with two dragon tattoos on both arms. The police are driving around checking everywhere if they can find this man. Anyone who finds him should report him immediately, as he is no ordinary man. He seems to have psychic abilities and is very powerful. In other news," the reporter continued.

Amy walked over to the window to look over the courtyard; in her corner of her eye she saw a shadow. "Keep it together Amy, there is nobody looking for you anywhere," She murmured to herself. Suddenly, there was a knock on the door.

Amy gasped for a moment. "Come in." Alistair and Bryan went into her room. "What Dante gave you was some kind of potion that protects you from any danger. If you get cut, slashed, beaten, or something, you will heal fast. In a week, we will be going to visit some other family members. Anyway, we found a way for you to have contact with your friends and family. Downstairs is a phone you can use. First, you'll have to dial this number, and then call this airport payphone. Remember, you can only call them for twenty minutes," Alistair said before he rolled his eyes out of despair.

Amy looked confused at Alistair. "Thanks Alistair." Alistair and Bryan left after a few minutes to get the phone ready for Amy to use.

"Oh, my goodness sweetie, I cannot believe it is you. How are you feeling, Amy?" Emma asked over the phone.

"Oh Mom, I miss you guys so much and I want to be back home! The dogs miss you. Your father misses you, and your friends. Oh my goodness. In a couple of months, it will be your birthday. Sorry we cannot be there for you," Emma said causing Amy to laugh and cry at the same time, "Here is your father wants to talk to you."

"Hey Amy," Aaron said.

"I miss you so much. It is really killing me to be separated from you guys like this," Amy said.

"Sweetie, it is just as hard for you as for me. Dinners are really quiet. We are going to miss your birthday. Here Jenna wants to talk to you."

"Hey Jenna, my goodness, it bites here without you. I mean, I am sort of the only girl in my group and I need to talk to somebody," said Amy.

"Amy, school bites without you; they just made Heather student body president. What's going on over there?" Jenna asked, feeling uneasy about the email she read from Amy a few days ago.

"Nothing much. I get to travel to Italy and other exotic places."

"Man, I wish I had been there with you. We would keep each other company and whatnot. Anyway, if I was there, what would you ask me because I only have ninety more seconds with you."

"At this moment, I cannot think of anything. Larry wants to have his turn to talk."

"Hey Amy, how is your little adventure?" Larry asked teasingly.

"Not good. My body hurts."

"Just remember to breathe, drink plenty of water, get fresh air and exercise, eat healthy and, plenty, and remember I will always have a space for you in my heart, Amy no matter where you are, how, what, and when I will always love you. Well, goodbye and we'll talk or email some more in the future. Goodbye and good luck." And they both hung up.

"Amy, are you okay? You sounded really despaired," asked Alistair.

"No, it is nothing. I want to be upstairs alone in my room, trying to catch some sleep," Amy said before she walked up to her room, got into her pajamas, and turned the lights off. The next day, Amy walked down in her pajamas and robe to eat some breakfast that was prepared for everyone.

"Good Morning Amy, did Alistair give you the number to contact your parents?" asked Darcia while pouring herself and Amy some coffee.

"Yes," Amy said.

"Regina made some special pancakes for you," said Darcia before she winked.

"Special pancakes? What does that mean? You did not put any weed or drugs in it?" Amy snapped while analyzing the pancakes.

"No," Darcia said. "Special meaning they were made especially for you with all the love surrounded in this manor." Just then, Dante entered the room.

"This evening, we will be having a masquerade ball. Regina will dress you up nicely. The limousine outside will drop us off. There are some others out there that don't know about Amy, so we will keep her sort of in the middle of our group. Silvio will also be there. He's sort of the organizer of this ball. Other than that, we are going to have a good time. Today, you guys can do whatever you have planned and addio to you," Dante said.

"Hey Amy, want to go shopping for clothes with me and the other girls? I will buy you a maximum of five outfits, maybe six. We can also eat some lunch somewhere and have some girl time together since you're the only teenage girl in this pack," Adrianna said cheerfully.

"That sounds like fun," said Amy in an excited way.

"We will leave outside in thirty minutes, so don't rush with anything. Remember, you are on a little vacation. Raymond and Silas will help you with your homework and everything, so just relax. The only thing you need to watch out for is any mischief," Darcia said reassuringly, waiting for Amy to finish her breakfast.

"Okay," said Amy. She took a sip of her coffee and a bit from her pancakes. She could barely swallow with all this emotion going through her body like crazy.

"You do need some girl time; you do not want to be spending the whole time with guys," Darcia said, trying to sound funny.

When Amy and Darcia got into this car that fit nine people, Adrianna drove over to this shopping street. "So Amy, what is your size in clothes so we can help you pick some stuff out?"

"I am an American size ten. I do not know what that is in Italy," Amy said. Darcia, Amy, and Adrianna walked in the front while Brianna and Francesca walked in the back. "Hey Fran," said Brianna, "Cheer up, do not hate Amy cause we are focused on her right now. I will also go shopping for you."

"I am not at all angry about what you said. I just do not like her attitude or appearance. I'm glad she will go in a few days."

"Francesca, maybe you should give her a chance; get to know her a bit, maybe talk about something," Brianna said teasingly.

"No, and you guys cannot make me. Plus, she has an eye for Romeo. He and I are getting engaged soon and if they hang out more, she'll steal him from me."

"Amy and Bryan are together. When she leaves, you and Romeo can be together forever, I guess, until you get bored with him," Brianna said as she linked her arm with Francesca's.

"I just want to get these few hours over with," Francesca whispered.

"Don't think about Amy right now. You and I can look at ball dresses or bridal gowns if you want, while the three girls can spend time with Amy and talk about stuff. I do want to spend some time with Amy before she leaves," Brianna said. Francesca sighed and nodded her head.

"Amy would like to go into this shop," Adrianna suggested. All of them walked into a teenage clothes store. Amy tried on a couple of shirts and jeans and modeled them in front of everyone. "You should get that blue shirt with those giraffes kissing each other with those dark blue jeans." An hour later, they walked into a couple more shops and came out with shopping bags.

"We should sort of get back to the manor and have some lunch and get ready for the party tonight," Darcia said. "I do not really care. We could eat some Chinese if you up for it?"

Francesca was getting annoyed with Amy having the urge to push her into the sewer, but she held it in, enduring Amy putting on a fake smile whenever they made eye contact. Slowly, they turned around and headed back to the car to get back to the mansion. When they got back, Regina and the other maids were in the kitchen preparing some kind of wok dish.

"Hey girls, did you guys enjoy shopping today?" asked Alistair, as he was drinking down a glass of wine.

"Yeah, we got Amy a couple of new outfits, a sort of gift from the gals," Darcia said. Francesca ran upstairs to get away from Amy.

"In a few hours, we will be going to the party, but before that would Amy like to have some food we prepared for her?" Alistair asked.

"Sure. I am kind of hungry from all that shopping," Amy said.

"Good," Alistair said. Regina poured the noodles on this plate and set it in front of Amy with some water with ice cubes and a slice of lemon. "Enjoy."

"Thank You Regina," Amy said. Darcia sat across from Amy, keeping her company. Dante came down in his usual casual suit, sitting next to Darcia. After Amy ate her noodles, she walked up to her room, seeing Adrianna sitting on the edge of her bed waiting for Amy.

"Here are a few choices of hairdos you can pick from. You can have it down or you can have it prom style and I'll search thru your closet to find a nice formal gown for you. But first you should take a shower, so you are nice and clean. Here is your towel and robe. I'll be in my room," Adrianna said cheerfully.

"Thanks Adrianna."

Amy went in and took her shower. When she came out, she saw Francesca sitting in one of the chairs, looking at Amy.

"Hey Amy, Dante told me to come up and do your hair and help you in your gown while he had to discuss something with Adrianna," Francesca said with a smile.

"Thank you Francesca, but if you really do not want to, you do not have to."

"Sit here in the chair and I will get some supplies for your hair. Amy sat there quietly in front of the makeup mirror. An hour later, Francesca helped Amy get into this thick purple velvet dress.

"You might want to run a brush through your teeth. They look a bit, never mind." She walked out of her room and went over to her own room to get ready. Amy felt a weird vibe from Francesca and checked her teeth to see nothing out of the ordinary. Once Amy was ready, she walked down to the Limousine and got in with the rest of the group.

"So, Amy, whatever happens, do not run. Just stand where you are and we'll come and back you up. Remember to wear your masks at this party. Amy, you are going to be the belle of the ball, Bryan said.

"I am sort of nervous about this whole ball," Amy whispered.

"Do not be nervous. I will be your dance partner this evening and if you need to use the bathroom, Adrianna will escort you, so nothing bad happens," Bryan whispered.

When they got to the ball, there were like about a hundred other immortals and humans waltzing together. "Hey Dante, remember me, Silvio? Meet my lovely bride Katherine. We met six months ago at this opera. Hey Darcia, you're still looking beautiful, as ever," Silvio said with a smile before he kissed Darcia's hand.

"Hey Silvio, remember Alistair and our sons?" Darcia asked, gesturing to them.

"I remember Bryan when he was a newborn. Darcia, may I have this dance?" asked Silvio.

"I would be honored," Darcia said as Silvio led her on the dance floor.

"Well Amy, are you ready to go into the crowd and dance like crazy?" Bryan asked. Amy and Bryan walked onto the dance floor. Everyone formed a circle, staring at Amy. "Bryan, they are staring at me. I do not feel comfortable," Amy whispered. Bryan looked at Alistair and he came very fast through the crowd to get to them.

"Oh, my goodness, that's Gabriel's daughter. I feel like taking a small nip from her," said a woman in a black dress with ruffles. The music stopped, and they all stared at Amy. Adrianna, Adrianna, Dante, and Francesca came in front of Amy. "Dante, what is this? Why did you bring her here? You know these people cannot hold in their urge. I want to ask you to leave and come back when you think you're ready," Silvio asked.

"That was pretty tense; those people were looking at me very hungry. We should get home very fast before they all come out and chase us. Amy, you're safe and you can't be touched, I promise," Bryan said while squeezing her hand.

"Next Monday you guys will be safe on your airplane off to our sisters. Relax, you are not going to be harmed," Adrianna said in a calm, soothing voice.

As soon as they got back to the manor, Bryan took Amy up to her room and did a room check to make sure nobody was in there disrupting anything. "Bryan, can you stay here with me and sleep next to me so I will not die?"

"I will not sleep with you, but I will watch over you while sitting in this rocking chair and listen to you breathing silently."

"Oh Bryan," Amy leaped in and kissed her as soft as a feather and made out with her for five minutes straight. Then she went to bed with a smile on her face. When she was fast asleep, Bryan snuck out of her bedroom and went downstairs.

"Hey Bryan, I am happy I'm not the only one who is still awake," Darcia whispered.

"Oh well, thank goodness, right?"

Chapter 5

Greece

That morning, Amy woke up and packed her stuff in her duffle bag, packed her backpack, and got dressed, getting ready for her nightmare on a plane again.

"Hey Amy, are you ready to meet some Greek people?" asked Alistair. "They will give you a little vaccination somehow, so don't be afraid of anything."

"Sure, when do I get to speak with my friends and family again?" Amy asked, feeling tired and worn out from this trip.

"Soon Amy. On this airplane you get to sit next to Raymond getting to know him. Then you can get closer to the other guys," Alistair said.

"Okay," said Amy. The eight of them got into the Limousine. Alfred took them to the airport.

"Okay, we have to go to check in our luggage and go to departures. If anyone gets hungry, there is probably a food court," Alistair said.

"Oh, my goodness, is this line going to Athens?" asked Xander, looking down the line with disgust.

"It sure looks like it. It is good we left the manor early so we'll be at our gate on time," Darcia said teasingly.

About thirty minutes later, the next check-in desk opened. "Good morning. Will all of you be flying to Athens?" asked the flight attendant.

"Yes, it sure does look like it," said Darcia in a sarcastic way.

"Oh," the flight attendant said in an annoyed way. "Well, here are your boarding passes and passports. Your gate is on the boarding passes and your departure time is twelve thirty. Have a great flight. Next please."

"Anyway, now that the first pressure is dealt with, let us head out to our gate and relax. If anyone is hungry, you can go and eat something. If Amy gets hungry, someone will have to walk with her," said Alistair before he sat down and placed his backpack in front of him.

"How long of a flight is it from Rome to Athens?" asked Bryan.

"The flight will take about an hour and nineteen minutes," Darcia said, before she sat next to Alistair.

"Thank goodness it is not as bad as going from Australia to Rome, which was a very long flight. So when are we bringing Amy back to Oregon?"

"When things start to mellow down for the others, understand?" Alistair snapped before he opened up his phone to check for messages.

"Yes, father, I understand," Bryan said. Amy walked over to the row of chairs and sat down next to Bryan digging though her bag to find anything to read.

"Hey Bryan, want to switch books cause I do not have anything to read?" asked Amy.

"Sure." They switched books and started reading at the same time.

Several minutes passed and the group of eight boarded the plane and went to sit where they were assigned. "Hey Amy, we will be sitting together, how lovely," Raymond said. Amy giggled nervously, smiling up at Raymond while he put his backpack in the overhead cabin. "You want me to put your backpack up in the compartment?"

"No thanks, I will just keep it here under my seat," Amy said. Raymond went to sit down and grabbed an airplane magazine and sighed while flipping through the pages.

Amy got out her diary, writing about her feelings.

Dear diary, (sniff sniff)   *10/10/07*

I'm starting to get a bit teary-eyed. I really miss my family, especially Ginger. She has always been there for me from kindergarten to high school. I really want to take everything back I've ever said to her when we were fighting.

"Amy, are you crying? Do you need Bryan to come and switch seats with me?" Raymond asked with concern in his eyes.

"No, I'm fine," Amy, said.

Anyway, in forty-five minutes, I'm going to meet more immortals. I cannot handle this much pressure anymore!

"Hello, do you want to drink something?" asked a flight attendant.

"Yeah, I would like some water with ice cubes and a lemon," Amy said.

"What about you?" the flight attendant asked Raymond with a smile.

"I'm fine, madam," said Raymond with a charming smile.

"Here you go; hello, would you like to drink something?" the flight attendant asked Alistair who was sitting behind her.

"So Raymond, what is the next immortal group like?" Amy asked out of curiosity. Raymond sighed at how he was going to formulate his answer. "The family consists of several girls and their parents. Some of them are very quiet and relaxed and the others are a bit loud and exciting, as I would formulate it," Raymond said.

"What will happen to me when we get there? Your parents said they were going to give me a serum like the Italians. Is that true?"

"Yes, that is true. There is going to be a 'party' in your honor where there is frozen blood, what humans would think is ice cream, but it is not, and then you drink from a goblet or a glass. It is better than an injection," Raymond said.

"What are you thinking about? Your expression seemed really uptight and stressed out about something," Amy said while she kept herself from panicking.

"Oh, it is nothing, but Vanessa, the mother, will read your future and tell you something."

"What?" Amy asked with a concerned expression.

"Oh, nothing, but are you ready to be responsible for three other people? In two months and we will be celebrating your birthday in Romania. We will be staying at this castle owned by Gabriel, the headmaster. Every woman or girl who looks at him immediately falls for him. His is thirty years old, but in his new life he is about a thousand years old. He also has three other brothers. The four of them have four wives. Anyway, back to the Greek family members, Thalia and Vitani are the ones who are the quiet ones. They both work at a dress shop. The other two girls, Margaret and Allysa, work as waitresses at this restaurant twenty minutes from their house. Alarick is the husband of Vanessa. Vanessa is the house mom and Alarick works at the newspaper company. Any other questions?"

"So far, I am fine with asking questions. I'm going to continue writing in my diary."

To be continued with this diary session, after listening to Raymond about his family. I really want to be in Larry's arms right now. Anyway, back to my sister. If anything bad happened to her, I would always be in the background for her. If she were in my situation, I would congratulate her for being so strong. Well, wait till we get to Athens to hear more.

Amy.

"Attention passengers, we are approaching our destination. The weather is thirty-two degrees Celsius. If, by any chance, you miss your flight, the airport is provided with a place for you to slumber till the next morning at six in the morning. We hope you had a wonderful flight and we hope you'll fly with us next time. Thank you," said the flight attendant over the intercom.

Oh my goodness, what if those people don't like me? Amy thought as started to feel anxious. After the plane landed, the group of eight walked to the luggage belt. Amy felt her stomach cringe again. She felt like crying, but she didn't want to look bad in front of the whole family. "Hey dad, is that Vitani and Thalia over there?" Bryan asked as he pointed at two beautiful brown-haired women in gowns with Greek designs on them.

"Yes, they are, my son. Amy, you see those two girls in their blue matching dresses?" Alistair said.

"Those two girls with dresses standing in front of the crowd," asked Amy. "Are they not dresses over-rated in this century?"

Alistair chuckled. "Yes, they are our cousins and nieces. They are old-fashioned, you know."

"Yay," whispered Amy, trying to act excited. "This is going to be exciting."

After everyone got his or her luggage, Bryan took Amy's hand. "Hey Amy, no matter what happens? Just stay close to me. If you walk with Vanessa, she will talk your ears off. The father will tell you about the origins of words and the four girls will either be mean, envious, or nice to you. I do not want anything bad to happen to you. I'll make sure you and I share a bedroom together," Bryan said.

"Thanks Bryan, I am so nervous," Amy whispered while breathing heavily out of her mouth.

"O theé mou," said a female voice with a Greek accent. "It's Alistair, Darcia, and the boys!" A woman came running towards them wearing caprice and a shirt that says I heart Athens.

"Wow Vanessa, you look so beautiful and colorful," Darcia said teasingly. She looked at Amy with a smile saying a middle-aged woman wearing caprice.

"Is that Bryan?" Yelled the two girls in blue, hugging him and the other males. The Greek group surrounded Alistair's group. "This must be the one," Vanessa said before she kissed her cheek.

"Yes. This is Amy Ambrose," Alistair said while he had his arm around her. Amy furrowed her brow with confusion. *Ambrose? Why did he call me that?* Alistair winked, and they continued walking.

Vanessa walked over to Amy and hugged her tightly. "No worries, child, you are safe with us."

"Thank you," said Amy. Just then, a guy with black hair came up to Amy and hugged her.

"I am Alarick, and we're going to give you a gift next week to make you strong and powerful. Well, come on, we need to get to our house so Amy can freshen up and we can show her Athens and other islands." Everyone got into this car that would fit nine people. Darcia sat on Alistair's lap in the front with Vanessa and Alarick. Amy sat on Bryan's lap next to Xander and Raymond; Joshua and Silas. The four girls sat in the trunk area.

"So Amy, how did you get this guy or woman after you? What made you the person everyone likes?" asked Alarick, wondering if Amy knew the actual truth.

"Let me answer this one for her, Alarick. She herself does not know why," Alistair said.

Amy was looking outside, ignoring half of what they were talking about. She did not feel comfortable being alone on this mission; she preferred to do one hundred math questions than to be in her situation. She felt insecure, unsure, confused, depressed, and vulnerable. She would also have to pick between Bryan and Larry.

"Here we are, our beautiful Greek house," Vanessa said as she gestured to the house.

It looked like any ordinary suburban house she'd been in. She didn't want to get out of the car, but she had to. "We already have the sleeping arrangements. The four girls sleep in their own rooms, Darcia and Alistair in one room, the four guys sleep on mattresses downstairs by the TV, Bryan and Amy sleep together in one room. We'll show Amy where she can drop her stuff off at the house," Vanessa said before they got out of the car. Vanessa led the way for Amy to her room. It was a small, cozy room with hearts all over. There were two single beds with pink sheets on them.

"The bathroom is next door. We have extra toothpaste just in case, anything you need, we will get it for you. For dinner, you do not have to do anything special like what the Italians or the Romanians had you do. Dinner will be served in about five hours. After dinner, we will have a special Greek dessert for you. This month will be very special for you. We can go shopping and meet some Greek friends who know about our secret, and in two weeks I'll give you a little potion for your situation. We have movies here if you want. Sometimes the girls would want to do makeovers and paint their nails while the guys walk around the hardware stores and camping stores," Alarick said with a chuckle. "Look at me, I am just talking for so long. I will be going downstairs. If you need anything, just let one of us know."

"Thank you," said Amy. "I really appreciate everything you have done for preparations." Amy walked over to her bed and put her suitcase on her bed and grabbed her shampoo and conditioner. Bryan came upstairs with a relieved look.

"Those Greek girls are a bit too much for me. Thank goodness we get to sleep together in one room instead of you with one of those girls."

"Yeah. Anyway, I was thinking that you and I could take a walk down to a shopping mall to hang out," Bryan said as he sat down on his bed.

"Sure. I just have to take a shower before we leave. I smell so bad from all that traveling and the tense feeling," said Amy as she opened up her suitcases.

"You and me both, Amy," chuckled Bryan.

Vitani and Thalia came skipping up the stairs. "Hey Bryan, we were wondering if you would like to walk to the store with us and our dad. Giselle is outside. Want to talk to her?" asked Vitani.

"Who's Giselle?" asked Amy with a concerned look on her face.

"She is Bryan's girlfriend, but then she dumped him and later she got a concussion and now she and Bryan are together. She and her mom had already made marriage plans, so he is taken. She also wants you to see her in her bridal gown and go over a few things. Who are you again?" asked Vitani.

"She is probably the maid or the suitcase carrier or some low-class person," said Thalia before they both giggled.

"Excuse me?" Amy was ready to get off her bed and punch Thalia in the face.

"Now Ladies let's not fight right now. We should be happy and excited about the twenty-nine days we'll be staying here."

"Maybe the maid can set the table for mommy, since mommy does her best to take care of us," said Vitani. Amy wanted to bite their heads off but held herself in and placed her pajamas on the bed. The two girls left the room with a grin on their faces.

"Bryan, can we not stay at a low-cost motel or something away from those girls?"

"No, but what we can do is to avoid them at all times except for meals and the ceremony for you. With me, here they cannot do anything."

"Bryan, who is Giselle, and what is this about you and her still dating and getting married? I thought we were boyfriend and girlfriend."

"Amy, I haven't spoken to Giselle for over seven months. Back then, she never returned any emails or phone calls. We sort of grew apart from each other. You and I are boyfriend and girlfriend, except if you still have feelings towards Larry. I am not going to stop you, so you cannot stop me with Giselle and me. Look, Giselle and I are not going to get married. It's a bit too soon for me to say I do at this moment."

Amy walked over to the window and saw this blonde girl wearing a pink dress carrying a basket. "Is that blonde girl standing out there, Giselle?"

"Yes, but I am not going outside to meet her. I do not feel like dealing with a screaming girl giving me kisses and hugs," Bryan said as he walked away from the window.

"Do you not ever tell her to stop doing that, or does she own you?"

"Nobody owns me," snapped Bryan. "I'm going to take a shower unless you want to, but I think I should go first because I'm done in like five minutes," said Bryan.

The other girls came upstairs to the room Amy was in. "Hi, I am Margaret and this is Stella. Our sisters can act a bit on the rude side so do not mind them. We know about your situation and we're going to protect you from any harm. You know about the ceremony. You do not have to drink. You can also get a shot if that will make you feel any better," said Margaret before she hugged Amy.

"Yeah right, I'm going to gulp that gunk down and it's over with," Amy said with a chuckle.

"There is also going to be cake and Greek ice cream and some drinks. You do not drink any alcohol, do you, Amy?" asked Stella.

"I am eighteen years old, but I do not really feel like drinking alcohol in this condition of mine. No offence girls," Amy responded, trying to keep as relaxed as possible.

"You should try this Greek liquor. It tastes like mint," Margaret said.

"I would rather not, anyway, Bryan and I are going to take a walk down the streets and hang out with each other," Amy said as she looked in the direction of the shower.

"Tomorrow all of us are going to be cruising around Athens taking pictures and getting so souvenirs and we'll be eating Greek food for lunch and have a blast," Bryan said, with a twinkle in the eye.

After the two girls left the room, Amy looked over at Bryan and their eyes met. They were moving closer and closer and closer till…

"Hi you guys," screamed Vanessa. "I want you to meet Ruffles. She's our cute little doggie! Oh, I hope I'm not disturbing anything."

"No, we were just relaxing and nothing. We were thinking about going outside and walk around," said Amy.

"That sounds like fun. I will get everyone to go, so nobody gets cabin fever," Vanessa said as he was leaving.

"Vanessa," Bryan asked, but she was already downstairs screaming at her family to get them outside.

"Darn it. There goes our day together down the toilet," Amy said in desperation.

"We will have other times together for you and me. Do you want ruffles to join us as well?" Bryan said with a chuckle.

"No, thanks Bryan." Amy sighed. "Oh goodness, someone else is coming up the stairs."

"Hey, can I come in?" asked Darcia.

"Sure, come on in and join the crowd of just me and Amy." Darcia walked in, looking surprised and relieved about being away from Vanessa.

"Bryan, we made a huge mistake coming here with Amy and ourselves. Vanessa can't stop talking about money and her clothes and her shoes and the way guys look at her. She also has this loud laugh that can break someone's eardrums."

Bryan chuckled. "Vanessa is also being wild with us, too. We were just having a moment here together and suddenly she came in here with her dog. We want to have some alone time, but she is assembling the whole family," Bryan said in annoyance.

"Just endure with it today and tomorrow the eight of us can walk around. The family downstairs is just going to be looking out like spies," Darcia said.

Amy lied down on her bed. "Ouch, this bed is so uncomfortable. It is like lying on a board with nails sticking out."

"Here, let me try. You are right here and try this other bed," Bryan said as he moved aside for Amy to get comfortable.

Amy went over to the other bed to try it. "This bed isn't as bad as the other one, but still bad. How does one sleep on this thing?"

"Let's get out of here before the ceiling comes crashing down on us," Bryan said.

Amy, Darcia, and Bryan left the room to see what everyone was doing downstairs. "Look who is here? Amy, you can sit between Maggie and Stella. Alarick is telling us about his days in the marines," said Vanessa with a smile on her face.

"Amy and I were about to leave and hang out with each other before anything bad happens to Amy. We want to be with each other as long as we're both alive," Bryan said.

"That's sweet. Enjoy your lovebird moment while Alarick and I are guarding the house," Vanessa said.

"But mom, were we not going to go outside with all of us and go sightseeing?" asked Vitani.

"Maybe we should let Amy and Bryan be with each other while they still can," Vanessa said before she winked at Amy.

"Hey you guys, do you want to hang out with Amy and Bryan?" asked Alistair to his sons.

"We were thinking about hanging out with the four daughters. Maybe see a movie or walk around shopping streets," said Raymond.

"Okay, well, see you guys till dinner," Bryan said to Vanessa and Alarick.

Amy sighed in relief. "Thank goodness we are finally alone," Amy said to Bryan while holding hands together. They walked onto this shopping street filled with crowds of people and kids that could run over your toes or bump into your ankles. "Want to go somewhere quiet, like a park looking over a lake or a street that is quieter than here?" asked Amy.

"Sure," Bryan said. "The two of them walked over to this park where people were jogging and walking their dogs. Two women jogged past them, looking at Bryan in a flirty way. Bryan winked at both of them.

"Bryan, are you trying to ruin our relationship, or are you ready to move on?"

"Those are just two girls. Amy, I can tell that you still have feelings for Larry. I see you talking to him through email most of the time when you're on the computer." There was silence between the two of them. Amy felt so sick and depressed that her eyes began to water.

"Amy, are you crying?" Amy didn't respond since she was pushing down her emotions. Her stomach hurt and she wanted to run back home, but she could not. "Oh goodness, Amy I am sorry about what I said to you about Larry and my ex friends. You are in a messed up situation and I can understand you want to talk to your friends, and maybe I should relax a bit more. Say there is an ice cream parlor down the street. Want to go in and get some?" Bryan asked, before he kissed Amy's hand.

"Actually, I'm not that hungry. I do not want to go back to your Greek family. I do not feel like walking. I just want to go back home to Oregon and see everyone again," Amy said, trying to control her breathing.

"I understand and I will back you up as much as possible. It is just I can't be babysitting you twenty-four hours a day. There is a reason why I have four other brothers, and I also need some Bryan time where I listen to my music or read a book or relax somewhere," Bryan said.

"You want to go back to the house and relax till dinner time? Maybe you and the two girls can play mommy and daddy," Amy said teasingly.

"You can be the baby, Amy since you're acting like one right now," Bryan said sarcastically causing Amy to glare at him.

"Whatever Bryan, let us go home and go our own ways till we go someplace else."

"Fine," Bryan snapped. They walked home, went their own ways and relaxed till dinnertime.

"Diner! Everyone, come to dinner!" Vanessa screamed. Amy walked down very depressed and stressed out about her life, her relationship with Bryan, getting murdered by someone, being held hostage. "So Amy, did you have a nice walk?" asked Vanessa, trying to make conversation and bond with Amy.

"Descent," Amy said. Vanessa handed out big cups that were sealed shut and you could not see what was inside it.

"Enjoy your meal for this evening. Alistair, can I talk to you for a second?" Vanessa asked. Alistair got out of his chair and walked outside with Vanessa. "What is going on with Amy? Does she know her true identity yet?"

"No, she does not, because Gabriel wanted to surprise her. She will understand it soon, but at the moment. She cannot drink what immortals drink, so it is best that Darcia and I take her out to a restaurant or grocery store this evening."

"Okay, I understand. I will keep my mouth shut and nobody needs to know anything till the right moment," Vanessa whispered. Alistair and Vanessa walked back to the table, seeing everyone drinking, except for Amy.

"Amy, smile a bit and relax. You are safe," Alarick said while putting away his newspaper. Amy put on a fake smile and put her face in her hands. She wanted to run out of the door to a motel or hotel and stay there a few nights, but her legs were being stubborn.

"What should we talk about for dinner conversation? I know. How about we talk about how Alarick and I got married twenty years ago?" said Vanessa, overly excited.

"I remember I was wearing this light blue dress with a bow. I had my hair in two ponytails and a pair of blue heels. Your father was wearing a tuxedo. He and I stared at each other for a long till he comes and sits across from me at my table. We were talking about Greek food and that restaurant. Here I'll show you a picture," Vanessa said before she came back with a photo book.

"Oh, is it not beautiful how mom and dad met," Margaret said to Vitani.

"I would rather leave the table to go upstairs and do my homework for tomorrow. Oh, that is right, Amy. Do you have to go to school at all?" Vitani asked.

"At this moment I am doing schooling online, so I will not fail this year and pass."

"What grade are you in?" Vitani asked.

"I am a junior and will become a senior in a few months. I also get help from Darcia, Alistair, and the other five guys," Amy responded as she avoided eye contact.

"Fascinating, so you're not doing your work? You are not going to get any smarter if you let someone else do your work," Vitani said provocatively.

"Amy, we have a huge surprise for you before you leave to your next destination," Vanessa said. "Tomorrow we are all going to be watching every corner, every suspicion and everything. Amy can go shopping or hang around with everyone." After everyone finished, Amy walked up to her room and opened her diary.

Dear Diary,   *10/15/07*

Today I'm not that happy. Bryan and I are now wobbly, and I'm afraid he might dump me for Giselle. What I can do tomorrow is get some information. I am hoping to book myself a ticket back home and forget about these immortals who want to mess with me! Anyway, I still need to endure for another twenty-nine days and see what happens next.

"Hey Amy, I want to apologize for what happened while we were talking about. I know you are in a bad state and I know how girls get when they see their boyfriend's exes," Bryan said, trying to sound sympathetic toward Amy.

"Thanks Bryan, I was a bit jealous of Giselle and your Greek cousins."

"So we forgive each other?" Bryan asked.

"We forgive each other," Amy said. He grabbed her face and pinned her to the bed, and kissed. His skin was so soft and smooth it gave Amy goose flesh.

"Wow Bryan, that was beautiful. How about some more?" whispered Amy.

"Okay." He grabbed her face and continued with kissing her.

Then they moved on to Amy's bed and made out for fifteen minutes straight. Suddenly, there was a knock on the door.

"Excuse me, it is me, Raymond. Can I come in for a few?"

"Sure, come on in and join the party," Bryan said with a chuckle until Amy punched Bryan lightly.

"How are you two managing with this family? I can barely handle their conversations and their laughter," Raymond sighed as he sat down on the edge of Amy's bed.

Amy and Bryan burst out laughing so hard they fell back and could barely breathe. "Stop it, they might hear you and ask you to two come and join us."

"Okay, Okay we're stopping." But they couldn't.

"Amy, do you want to go outside for a nice walk and enjoy one of us instead of Bryan, so you'll get a chance with all of us? It is time for us to go hunting as a group again. Bryan, if you are not down within five minutes you will put our family to shame. Amy you are welcome to join us, but Bryan you really need to come with us," Darcia hollered.

"Fine, I'll go with you guys on your hunting trip. Hey Amy, would you like to see how we hunt our prey? Unless you want to be stuck here with girls who taunt you. No, you have to. Darcia and Alistair put you under my care. Here are your shoes and you better put away your diary and precious belongings," Bryan said before he put his shoes on.

"Okay," Amy said before she got her shoes on. The eight of them got into Alarick's car and drove off to this party center to get them alone so they can feast on human flesh. Amy didn't feel good about this and told them she'd be waiting in the car for them. An hour later, the five guys came out with five girls and got into the van.

"Hi Amy, meet Alyssa, Brittney, Brianna, Beverly, and Carey." Amy felt so bad about what was going to happen to them. She wanted to tell them, but she would probably look like an idiot or the group might get mad at Amy and kill her or something, so she decided to keep her mouth shut.

"Smart choice," Bryan whispered to Amy. Amy giggled out of nerves and was embarrassed. She pretended like that never happened.

"So, Bryan, where are you guys going to take us?" asked Brianna.

"You will see Brianna, you'll see," Bryan whispered.

"Here we are in the parking lot. Now we need to walk up that hill," Alistair said. The thirteen of them got out of the van and walked up to the hill. Amy did not feel good about what was going to happen next. She wanted to run back to the van and lock the doors, but her legs kept on walking. While they were walking, Darcia grabbed Amy's arm.

"Hey Amy, I know you feel uncomfortable about this little get-together. If it gets too much, close your eyes and cover your ears. We will be done in about a few minutes."

A few minutes is pretty short Amy thought. Darcia walked over to Alistair and wrapped her arms around him while they walked. Amy didn't have anyone to hold on to except herself. After ten minutes of walking up the hill, Bryan stopped walking.

"So, Silas, what's going to happen next?" Alyssa asked.

"We are going to play a game of tag, us five against you five girls. Trust me, you will like it. Amy, you might want to be closer to Alistair and Darcia," Bryan said.

"We will give you girls a sixty-second head start," Joshua said. The boys started counting.

Amy ran back down the hill to the van, hearing growling and howling. She heard the girls scream and ran to the car. It was dark outside. Suddenly, she heard a growl coming from this dark spot in the woods. She was frozen, could not move a single finger. She leaned against the car so tightly she could barely breathe. It started coming towards her and towards her and towards her until it jumped out at her. Amy got down and started running up the hill as fast as she could. "Help," Amy screamed, but she couldn't see anybody except the trees. She heard this creature in back of her. Suddenly, she tripped over a twig and twisted her ankle. The creature walked over to her. It turned out to be a black wolf with silver eyes staring at her. The wolf nudged her body around. Amy started crying loud that even the people at the other side could hear her. The wolf ran back into the forest when it saw another creature run over to her. It turned out to be Bryan.

"Oh Bryan, I am so scared. I want to go home so bad and I twisted my ankle," whimpered Amy in pain.

"It is okay, Amy. You are safe with me. I will carry you on my back down the hill to the car." As soon as they got to the car, everyone was inside, waiting for them.

"Hey Amy, what happened?" asked Darcia.

"There… was… A… wolf… chasing…. me," Amy panted.

"What did he or she look like, Amy?" Alistair asked with a worried look.

"It… was… black… with… silver… eyes."

"Oh no, don't tell me it's one of the court members in Romania spying on us?" Darcia asked.

"It might've been Adrian coming to check on whether we are breaking any rules or not." Alistair sighed with irritation.

"When we get back to the house, I am going to call up the court members to see who was behind this," Alistair said before he started the engine of the van. When they got back to the house, Bryan carried Amy up to their room and placed her on her bed.

"Are you hurt Amy? He did not bite you or scratch or anything, did he?"

"No, I just sprained my ankle when I was running," Amy said. Bryan could hear everyone arguing downstairs. Bryan stayed up with Amy, helping her relax.

"Here, take some vitamins that I brought with me for you. I knew something like this would happen one of these adventurous days," Bryan said as he opened up a bottle with no label on it. He dropped a couple of tiny white pills in his hand before he handed them to Amy. Then he grabbed her a glass of water.

"Here, take these with some water and in a few hours you'll feel so relieved and happy, like this was all a bad dream," Bryan said as he smiled.

Raymond went upstairs to checkup on Amy. "Hi Amy, how are you doing?"

"She twisted her ankle so she couldn't walk that much. I will have to have her on my back for a while; we can't leave her alone in this house," Bryan said.

"Tomorrow we are going to walk around Athens and hang out with the whole family. If you guys want to stay in this house, just go for it. I hope your foot will feel better soon, Amy," Raymond said with a smile.

"Thanks Raymond, I hope so too," Amy whispered.

"Well, goodnight and hope you won't get any nightmares about weird things," Raymond said before left. Bryan went over to Amy's bed to give her a light foot massage. "Ouch, that hurts."

"You want me to get Alistair and Darcia up here so they can see whether you need a doctor or some rest?" asked Bryan, with a twinkle in his eye.

"Sure, get them for me, Bryan," Amy said. A few moments later Alistair and Darcia came walking up the stairs.

"Hey Amy, let us check out that foot of yours," Alistair said while he sat down on Bryan's bed.

"It does not look that bad, except you probably need an ice pack or something cold to wrap around it to make the swelling go down. Let me ask Vanessa."

Darcia walked downstairs to get an ice pack for Amy's swollen ankle. Vanessa and Alarick and the four girls came running upstairs to Amy.

"Oh, my sweet child, how did this happen?" asked Vanessa.

"I sprained my ankle while I was running from this wolf in the forest while the other eight were hunting," Amy said, trying to control her breathing.

"Why did you let Amy out of your sight? You know she's in a vulnerable state," Alistair snapped.

"Look, we had five girls with us," Bryan said defensively.

"That is no excuse. You let Amy out of your sight and she got chased and hurt. "Gabriel is not going to be happy," Alistair snapped. Vanessa put the ice pack on her swollen ankle.

"Ouch!" Amy screamed.

"Sorry about that. I see that Bryan handed you some painkillers," Vanessa said. After everyone except for Amy and Bryan, left the room. Amy began to cry a bit, but she did not want anybody to see her, so she was shoving down her emotions, but her emotions started taking over her body. Amy put a pillow against her face and cried.

"Amy, I'm so sorry for everything," said Bryan, crawling onto the bed. He leaned over Amy and pressed his lips against hers.

"Bryan, Bryan, Bryan, you don't have to apologize for anything. If I never have run down that hill, I never have seen that wolf and run," Amy whimpered.

"No Amy, you did not do anything wrong. Besides, if you hadn't noticed that wolf, we wouldn't have noticed anything and we would probably get surprise attacks from Gabriel," Bryan whispered. Just then, Bryan's phone rang. "Hello, oh hey Mrs. Martin, how did you get this phone number?" Bryan asked Emma over the phone.

"I got it from Gabriel from Romania, the supposed leader of your group?" Emma said over the phone.

"Well, Amy is right next to me," Bryan said as he handed Amy the phone.

"Oh, my goodness, I want to be in your arms right now. I'm messed up right now! I think I'm cursed because you will never guess what happened to me this evening. While the eight of them were hunting, I freaked out and ran down this hill and this black wolf chased me, and then I tripped and sprained my ankle badly. I am so scared and I'm homesick," Amy whimpered over the phone.

"Oh, baby, I do not know what to say. I am speechless and I might faint a bit. Your father and sister and I really love you and hope you get back to us soon," Emma said in her motherly tone.

After the phone call, Bryan quickly hugged her, and she cried on her shoulder. "Bryan, I cannot take this anymore," sobbed Amy.

"It is okay, Amy. You are safe, and I promise not to ever leave you again. I'm going to stay here and watch over you while you sleep to make sure nothing bad will happen to you," Bryan whispered before he kissed her on top of her head.

"No Bryan, it is not your fault, I ran down and tripped, it is not your fault and…"

Bryan shushed Amy. "Amy, it was my fault and I will not leave you!" Moments later, Amy fell asleep. Darcia came upstairs to checkup on Amy.

"Hey Bryan, how is Amy doing?"

"She is asleep, and I'm guarding her with my life," Bryan said, placing his arms around Amy.

"Do not let anyone get to you, but next time, keep an eye out for Amy."

"Thanks mom, I really appreciate you talking to me. I have to breakup with Giselle and get it over with."

"That sounds like a good plan Bryan, you are really maturing and everything," Darcia said as she smiled before she left him and Amy.

"Thanks mom I'm going to call Giselle and tell her the big news about us," Bryan said before he grabbed his cell phone to call up Giselle.

"Hey, this is Giselle."

"Hey, this is Bryan and we need to talk about something."

"Oh, no, you're dumping me for that Amy who is not even in love with you?"

"She is not happy since she's running from a group of mean people who want to kill her," Bryan responded.

"Okay, but can I come over for a few minutes and we can talk this out?"

"I am sorry Giselle, but my heart is for Amy! Farewell," Bryan said and hung up. After he put the phone away, he walked back to Amy from the bathroom and made sure she did not wake up because of hitting her foot. All Bryan saw was a beautiful girl slumbering innocently. The next morning, Bryan carried Amy downstairs for some breakfast. Alarick was serving some scrambled eggs and some bacon for Amy. Amy felt like something ripped her heart out and stomped on it.

"Good morning Amy, are you feeling any better than yesterday?" Alarick asked.

"I feel okay, but I am not really in the mood for breakfast," Amy responded.

"Did you guys plan to do something? Alarick and I are going to keep our eyes and senses sharp? Our children will be indisposed for a few hours. If you and Amy would like to stay here and relax a bit, maybe watch some movies together. We have some fiction and nonfiction movies. Oh yeah, I almost forgot. Please take a drink this potion and your foot will be better this evening. You will be a bit stronger than usual, so do not get scared about that," Alarick said with a smile before he handed Amy the drink.

"It tastes like liquid candy, but a little chunky. Should I be worried about what will happen to me right now?" Amy asked, feeling worried.

"You should not worry about anything, just drink it and you'll feel great! Say, Bryan, if you want to take the car, you are allowed to. Whatever you do, do not lose the keys," Alarick said. After everyone left the house, Bryan and Amy were left on their own. "What should we do today? Do you want to watch a movie or go outside? Your wish is my demand," Bryan said, while kissing Amy's hand.

"I would like to get some fresh air. If I stay in the house the entire day, I will go crazy," Amy said.

"We will take Alarick and Vanessa's car and drive around till the car has no more gas," Bryan said with a chuckle.

"Sounds like fun." The two of them got into the car and drove around for a minute to see what there was to see in the car.

"Hey, there is a zoo. Do you want to look at the monkeys and laugh at them? See the lions or tigers?" Bryan asked.

"No, thanks, I feel sad for those animals that are tortured like that. What if you changed into a lion and you were taken to a zoo where little kids would scream and throw stuff at you?" Amy asked.

"I would hate it. So you want to see some of the sights and tour around Athens before we go on with our adventure around the world?" Bryan asked while he looked over at Amy.

"Sure, that sounds like fun. Could you slow down a bit? We are going to crash into another car and get hurt if you speed up like that?" Amy said before she chuckled.

"Chill out, Amy, we are not going to die. We are not going to get a ticket either unless you want to spend some time in the slammer?" Bryan asked teasingly.

"No, thanks, I am too pretty to be in jail. I mean, look at me with my brown hair and green eyes. I could be a supermodel," Amy chuckled.

"Where are we going? Cause if we're going to sit in this car the entire day, I will go crazy too." Bryan stopped at this outside mall to look around and buy some souvenirs and laugh at street acts and have a good time with Amy. Suddenly, there was a guy wearing a parka, sunglasses, and a hat stalking them.

"Hey Bryan, there is a guy in back of us staring at us. It might be a killer, right?"

"Amy, go ahead, walk into this store and I will wait outside for him to come by and slam him against the wall." Amy walked inside and the strange guy walked in another direction when he saw Bryan.

Moments later, Bryan entered the store. "Amy, the coast is clear and come out so we can continue our day together. Remember, I need to watch you at all times or else something bad will happen to you," Bryan whispered. Amy walked out looking worried and a bit uncomfortable. "Hey, it is okay. When I'm around, nothing can happen to you. I'm stronger than most of my other brothers and parents. I can fight off four or five people at a time."

"Bryan, do you think you're winning my affection by telling me how strong you are?" Amy said before she chuckled.

"You want to see my six-pack? Giselle told me that I was bestowed this gift cause I'm special." Bryan smiled.

"Well, Larry told me I am an angel because of my beauty."

"Okay, let us drop this conversation. Want to get some lunch somewhere or chocolates?" They walked into this Greek restaurant with this Greek waiter guy who had a thick accent. He grabbed two menus and escorted them to a booth.

"Well, what a surprise Bryan, Giselle was talking about how you dumped her with that other girl you're sitting with," Giselle's mother said in a snide tone.

"Hi Kate, this is my new girlfriend, Amy. She is from Oregon," Bryan said as he placed his right arm around Amy, holding her close.

"How nice, well, continue with your meal and enjoy your stay here in Athens, Amy," Kate smiled sarcastically.

"Thank you madam," Amy said. "This is a beautiful place to visit."

"Oh my goodness, Amy, I feel so stupid and awkward right now. We should be grateful she did not call you names or smacked you, but of course I would have protected you from her," Bryan said before he chuckled.

"Thanks Bryan, so what looks good on this menu? I know you do not eat human food and since I have not been eating that much, I will go for a two person meal," Amy whispered as she analyzed the menu.

"Up to you Amy, but I do need to check my wallet for some money for us to spend on ourselves. Oh look, a couple hundred-euro bills. We are fine. So Amy, we have been sending in some of your work and you are getting good grades. You will be finished with school and will pass soon. No worries. Your teachers are pleased with your essays and explanations," Bryan said with a smile.

"Do you think the teachers actually believe I am doing the work?" Amy asked teasingly.

"Of course, we can read your mind and see how you formulate things in your head," Amy said before she chuckled at Bryan's response.

"Darn it, why do you read my mind? It is like my diary. Those are personal thoughts," Amy snapped.

"We got our powers from the court members in Romania," Bryan said.

"Here you go, a nice big platter of our famous Greek meat that we scraped off," the waiter said.

"Do you think the chef spit on it to give it extra flavoring?" Amy asked.

"Amy, do not gross yourself out. It is not worth spending money on food you might not eat because you have to say something gross." After finishing her meal, she and Bryan went walking the streets in Greece till they drove back to the house to watch a movie together and cuddle up. To their great dismay, they saw Vitani and Thalia watching TV in the living quarter.

"Let us go upstairs to our room before they torture us by playing with them and doing their work for them," Bryan said before he carried Amy to their room. Bryan placed Amy gently on her bed and took his shirt off, to reveal his porcelain-sculpted upper body. He hovered over Amy.

Bryan went with his lips over to her neck real smooth. It felt like a silk blanket going over her body. Then he went back to her lips and kissed her so softly she barely felt it. "Oh goodness," Vitani whispered. "What are you guys doing on this bed, making out like idiots?" she screamed. "Bryan, where is Giselle?"

"Today during lunch break she came up to us and told us that you dumped her.

Vitani, no offence, but get out of this room for a minute so Amy and I can have a private moment to ourselves," Bryan chuckled.

Vitani stomped out of the room and ran downstairs to Thalia. Hours later, Vanessa and Alarick came back from their hunting trip. Vanessa had some blood on her teeth.

"Hey you guys, did you have a nice time roaming around Athens? Did you get anything like souvenirs?" asked Alarick before he dried his hands on the kitchen towel.

"No, not really. What we were planning on for the next few weeks is to roam some more around Athens and visit one of those Greek islands," Bryan said softly.

"Sounds like fun," said Alarick. "This evening Alistair and Darcia told me you're going hunting again and this time, keep Amy close to you," Alarick said. At six o'clock in the evening, the eight of them got into the van and drove off to the same place, get some girls and enjoy a nice cat-and-mouse game. This time, Alistair and Darcia let Amy run with them and follow them. After they got back, they went to sleep. As the days were going by, Alistair took the seven of them to visit other little islands.

It was the last day before they were going to leave Greece and move onto another group. "Amy, this evening we'll be doing a special ceremony for you. Margaret and Stella baked the cake, and the other two got the ice cream and chocolate sauce and whipped cream. I will now be making the potion, so you just relax upstairs in your bedroom with Bryan and relax till dinnertime. After the evening, all of us will celebrate you being here by going hunting for humans at parties. The girls and Alarick have been very good at staying away from human blood, so that they deserve a treat," Vanessa said, before they all clapped for each other.

"Cool," Amy whispered. "Bryan, you want to go upstairs with me and relax like what Vanessa said?" Amy asked.

"Sure, let us go up and relax till dinner and the big ceremony for you especially." Vanessa called everyone downstairs after an hour passed.

"Wow Vanessa, the cake looks so delicious. Since we are immortals, we will let Amy eat this cake and ice cream," Amy said with a smile. After dinner, they walked into the living room where there was a chair in the middle and ten chairs were around it. When Vanessa walked into the kitchen, they were chanting some weird Greek song. "Now it is time to chant the potion song and Amy drinks this stuff in this goblet. After you drink it, feel free to have some champagne afterwards. Here you go Amy," said Vanessa.

Amy felt weird about sitting in the middle while everyone watched her drink that stuff. After Amy drank the potion, she felt sick to her stomach and ran to the bathroom trying to throw up.

"Bryan, stop her before the potion doesn't go through her body," Vanessa screamed. Bryan grabbed Amy and put his hand in front of her mouth, tilting her head.

Chapter 6

Croatia

The next morning, Vanessa and Alarick dropped the group of eight off at the airport. "So, where are you guys taking me next?" Amy asked.

"You are going to meet our Croatian family, who are also immortals who disguise themselves as regular people. After that, we will celebrate your nineteenth birthday in Romania, where you will meet the head person, Gabriel. You will so like him, he is a lot of things," said Alistair as he helped with bags.

"Well, aren't I in for a nice treat to meet immortals and drink potions? So let me ask you guys something. Who is actually chasing me and why and where are they now?" Amy snapped, feeling herself getting angry.

"Calm down," Alistair said, trying to control himself. "There is a group who wants you because you are a very special girl who is going to find out soon who she is. You, Amy, are a unique person. You have a special gift that we cannot tell you about. You only have to find out yourself. If you were not that special, you would be a hybrid and become a queen." Amy did not say anything and felt this heavy pressure on her shoulders and back.

"Gabriel sent out some scouts a while back to capture you and take you to him alive. He knows about you, Amy. He can read people's minds across the world and know where they are," Alistair said.

"So why does he not come and capture me? Would that not make more sense?" asked Amy, trying to act sassy.

"We should be quiet now, Amy, since we're amongst other humans. We do not want to cause any problems," Alistair said, while grabbing everyone's passports and boarding passes.

"Bryan, what is your Croatian family like? Is there anything I need to know about them so I am prepared for anything?" Amy asked, rolling her eyes.

"They are calm, nice people that will wait on hand and foot for their guests. Their three sons and only daughter are very nice; we keep in touch a lot. The leader of that group is Kristjan, and he is the younger brother of Gabriel, so they have the same qualities and appearances, only a bit different. They love to eat humans, so we'll be eating out most of the time, so us five boys will look over you while you sleep, go to the bathroom and shower, and everywhere. They know about you, Amy, so they can keep themselves detained. The wife, Helen, is also a flesh eater and will do everything to get what she wants. She will use her psychic powers, so you and I will be together for a long time till we get to Romania. Our Romanian family is so nice, but they are also human eaters. We will form a circle around you whenever you walk, so there is no way for them to harm you," said Bryan as he grabbed the airplane magazine. The flight attendant made the announcement about the flight to Croatia.

"Bryan, I do not feel comfortable about meeting your human eating family. What if they bite me or kill me?" asked Amy, terrified, knowing she was going to die somehow.

"You are a very special girl whom everyone knows about, especially Gabriel, so you are mostly under protection and if they were to harm you, they would get killed by Gabriel," Bryan said as he held Amy close to him.

"Who is this Gabriel and how does he know a lot about me and what is his interest in me?" Amy snapped, causing Bryan to ignore her. He closed his eyes and pretended to fall asleep. And again, Amy could not stand being in an airplane and meeting new people. After an hour, Bryan opened his eyes before landing.

After they landed, the group of eight walked over to the luggage belt to pick up their luggage and see the family. "Hey is that Alistair and Darcia," asked a woman with blonde hair and a short dress. "Hi, I remember you boys when you were new to this whole immortal life and this must be Amy. It is an honor to have you here in Croatia. You know what we will do to you right for a tradition?" the woman asked.

"Yes, I do like any other family from Rome and Athens," Amy said before she giggled out of nerves and playing with her hair.

"Good, I'm here alone because the other guys and girl could not make it. Come along." She seemed nice, but a bit overexcited to see Amy. Amy was so scared her hands were shaking, her heart felt like it was going to rip out of her skin and she felt like throwing up. They got to this beautiful new black van that could fit nine people. As soon as they got out of the car, the five boys surrounded Amy and Alistair and Darcia, who walked beside Bryan and Joshua. Bryan held Amy's hand really tight so she wouldn't faint.

"Kristjan, come and meet our guest friend Amy Ambrose," the woman said in a raised voice. Amy looked confused again by the surname.

"Welcome Amy to our home, sweet home. It is an honor to have you staying with us," said Kristjan with a fake smile across his face and gulping at Amy. Amy looked up at his shoulder-length blonde waves and blue eyes and marble complexion. "I believe you may have met my wife, Helen?" He gestured toward the woman with the loud voice with her wavy brown hair and brown eyes wearing tight hipster clothing.

"Thanks. It's an honor having you let me stay here," Amy said in a nervous way.

"Come in. Helen will put your duffle bag in your room. May I get you something to drink? We have water?"

"I would like to have some water," Amy responded nervously. A woman with short brown hair tied up with a hair tie, their housekeeper, entered the living room.

"Libby, could you get Amy a glass of water?" Kristjan asked. Amy felt uncomfortable sitting on the couch, having five faces staring at her like they were going to kill her.

"So, Alistair, does your little companion know about our secret?" asked Kristjan.

"Yes, she does, so whatever should happen, try not to do anything to Amy."

"Excuse me," said Libby in a harsh manner. "What are you talking about?"

"Libby, do not start anything now. Get Amy her glass of water." Dmitri snapped.

"Yes, sir, would anyone like anything to drink?" Libby asked.

"No thanks. Just water for Amy," Alistair said. "Anyway, this evening we were thinking about hunting with Amy," Alistair said as he winked at Amy.

"That is wonderful," Kristjan said. "We were also thinking about hunting ourselves since we are not humans. Excuse us," said the three boys. "We need some fresh air." As soon as they walked off, Amy's heart was beating faster.

"So Amy, Alistair and Darcia have told a lot about you, so how is it living in Oregon?" asked Kristjan while he kept his gaze on Amy.

"It is pretty nice with suburban houses and our neighbors," Amy said in a hoarse voice, trying to sound normal when talking to people who want to have her as the first course.

"Do you go to school?" Kristjan asked while keeping his eyes on Amy's.

"Yes, well, I used to, but now, since I'm in this dilemma, I'm doing an online schooling system," Amy said.

"Interesting. Our kids are doing their education here at home, so nothing bad will happen. You know we're immortals, right? We give ourselves these shots, so during the day we are normal and then the serum wears off at night and we go hunting. We usually have to watch out for police and guards, so we will not have a repeat like last time," Kristjan said as he watched Helen enter the living quarter.

Amy was speechless and smiled and nodded at everything they said. She felt very uncomfortable with the way Katherine was looking at Amy with her blue eyes and long brown hair and pearl complexion every time she took a sip from her water. "Do you have any questions you would like to have answered if no, we should go off to do our own stuff? Oh yeah, this evening either Helen or I will give you this drink after dinner. You probably already know what will happen. We are not going to do anything special, so no worries," Kristjan said. Amy nodded in agreement and grabbed Bryan's hand. Then they walked over to their room to see what their room looked like even though Bryan hardly slept.

"Amy, while you are sleeping, my family and I will hunt humans, so if you wake up and we're not here, do not panic and always stay calm. The way you can contact me is by talking and I'll hear you in my head. Tonight I will lock the door so nobody can harm you. If they were to attack you, you would have to scream my name and I will be by your side in less than a minute," Bryan said as he was walking back and forth, trying to remember everything he was ordered to tell Amy while he was gone.

"You must be very fast and a showoff," Amy said teasingly.

"Whatever Amy. I am strong and fast and you will never be able to catch me, since you are slower and clumsier than me," Bryan retorted. Amy scoffed. Later, Amy and Bryan walked over to the nearest fast food for takeout. Amy ordered two hamburgers, fries, and a diet soda. They walked over to the park that looked over this lake where Amy got to eat in peace.

"Say, Amy, since you are eighteen and almost finished high school. Have you ever thought about college?" asked Bryan.

"You know, I have not thought about that. I'm worried that we can never see each other again after this whole joke is over," Amy said before she finished her last bite.

"Sorry I ever brought that up. We still have nine more months until they will leave you alone and by then you will have had enough of being around me."

"Never, Bryan. You and I were meant to be together and I will never leave your side," Amy said before she snuggled close to Bryan.

Bryan used his sleeping powers on Amy, and she passed out on his lap. He carried her back to her room and placed her on the bed gently. "Hey Bryan, are you ready to hunt with your brothers and family? We promised we would not hurt Amy whatsoever," Kristjan said. "Since she is Gabriel's offspring."

"If Amy dies, I will kill you and your whole family and I will do more horrible stuff to you," Bryan snapped.

"Bryan, you are not as strong as me or the court members. I know how important Amy is and I am able to keep my cool around Amy, but not other humans. Anyway, is my Croatian family ready to hunt?" asked Kristjan.

"Yes Kristjan," Helen said.

"Hey Alistair, are you ready to hunt humans we find on our path? When we get back, Bryan and Raymond will watch over Amy while she sleeps. The other ones will enjoy a nice evening, either walking around or whatever. Let's go before we get crazy and the young, pretty people return to their homes. Let's go to a party and feast," Kristjan said to everyone while he was busy unlocking the front door. When they got outside, they started running till they found any kind of person.

"I call the first woman I see!" Bryan yelled to Alistair.

"Bryan let us go to this dance down the street and do the cool move so the girls will look at us with interest and then we will go inside to see what there is to see," Alistair said.

"Whatever, dad, I will just go with the flow no matter how ridiculous I look while strutting with my father."

"That is the spirit, my son! Now let us walk smooth and cool," Alistair said before he demonstrated the walk and the boys sort of blended in while Darcia walked, fast into the disco as normal as possible. When they got through, they looked around to see whom they could pick and feed on.

"I claim little miss blonde who's wearing that leather outfit looking at me," Bryan said. The other four guys went in separate directions to see whom else they could find. "Hey, I'm Bryan, and I noticed you looking at me. Would you like to step out with me for a bit and walk around in the dark with a strong person next to you?"

"I am sorry, but I already have a boyfriend and he is walking towards us with two beers," said the girl.

"Okay, nice to meet you and enjoy your beer with your boyfriend," Bryan said. Alistair saw Bryan and walked over to him.

"Real smooth son, do you not remember how to get the girls and boys? You have done a good job in Athens. Why mess it up right now? Darcia and I will get three people and your brothers are waiting outside with some male friends and girlfriends. Just wait outside for us and we will be out very shortly," Alistair said in a reassuring tone.

Bryan was disappointed at not getting that girl he wanted, but in his head he found out a way to get her without her boyfriend. He would smell her trails and go to her place and kill her. A few minutes later, Alistair and Darcia came out with two college girls and one male adult. "Sarah, meet my son Bryan. Bryan, meet this lovely woman named Sarah. Start talking, Bryan," Alistair said. Sarah was a Caucasian woman who had black hair and was wearing this beautiful pink gown with a pair of black heels. *Maybe I should clean this dress and shoes and give them to Amy as a gift.* Bryan thought.

"Come along Bryan, so we can show these people our wonderful surprise," Alistair said.

Bryan jogged after them and got into the front seat of the car next to Alistair. "Hey Bryan, it is not that bad that you didn't get that beautiful girl who has a boyfriend. Whatever you are thinking, do not even think about it or else you and I are flying back home and we will hang out at home. I will take away your powers and privileges. Think about if you were a girl and there was a guy that wanted to kill you. Would you like to die at the age of twenty-five?" asked Alistair.

"I guess not, but are we not created to hunt for people when we're hungry and for the fun of it?" asked Bryan while staring at the darkness outside the car.

"Never mind now. Let us get out and enjoy our meal, unless you want to wait in the van and let your brothers and mother and I enjoy it."

"I will go and hunt with you, because it is part of our family rulebook and tradition, and plus, I'm hungry," said Bryan.

"Attaboy Bryan, you see? Whenever we have the serious talk, you're always smart enough to do the right thing," Alistair said with a smile on his face.

They got out and did their usual routine with their victims and walked back down the hill to the car. To their greatest surprise, they saw a strong-sized male figure with short silver hair and black eyes leaning against their van.

"Good evening Brother, remember one of your court masters, Adrian? Gabriel is waiting in Romania and Alistair, you're under death row for letting getting Amy hurt. Remember that evening in Athens when you were hunting and you let your precious Amy out of sight before I saw her? You had better go back to Kristjan and Helen's house before something bad happens to her." Suddenly Adrian's cell phone rang.

"Hello Gabriel, Alistair is right next to me." Adrian handed Alistair the phone.

"Hello Gabriel, please call back your spy and tell him to leave us alone."

"Alistair, you messed up big time. Come back to Romania and give me five good reasons why I shouldn't hunt you down and end you myself."

"Look Gabriel, why are you suddenly annoyed at us for going back to Oregon to pick Amy up? I mean, those were your orders," Alistair said. There was an awkward silence on the phone. "Hello, are you still there?"

"Alistair, Amy is not old and strong enough to possess some powerful gifts and, as her and Ginger's father, I would like to keep them with me till she's ready."

"What do you want me to do, bring her to you so you can deal with her?" asked Alistair, annoyed.

"Yes. I want you to take her to me alive so I can run some tests with her and see what I have to do. You have three weeks till we see each other and I want you, Ginger, and Amy to come to our place," Gabriel snapped.

"Yes Gabriel, I will make sure she is there within three weeks alone or else I am dead," Alistair said in a sarcastic manner.

"Correct. Bye Bye." They both hung up.

"Well, I have to get back to Gabriel and get a golden metal for seeing you guys, so I bid you adieu," said Adrian. He disappeared into the forest.

"Dad, you are not taking Amy to the Romanian coven, right?" Bryan asked.

"Bryan, you are still too young to make decisions. I do not want Amy to die so soon, but since both Amy and Ginger are Gabriel's daughters, they have the power to overrule someone like us. Come on, so we can make sure the Croatian family members are not eating Amy." As soon as they got back to the house, they heard Amy moan like crazy. "Oh dear, Amy is in trouble. Let us go," Alistair gasped. Then the seven of them ran up to Amy's room, seeing Amy hyperventilating like crazy.

"Amy breathe, relax. Bryan is here. Amy, wake up and snap out of this! "Kristjan, what the heck happened to Amy? Why is she like this?" Alistair yelled.

"Helen gave Amy her potion and now it's taking over her body like what happened in Athens." Bryan clapped his hands real hard close to her face till Amy woke up.

"Bryan, Bryan, Bryan…," Amy said in shock. Bryan picked Amy up and carried her downstairs and gave her a glass of water. "Do you remember what happened?" Bryan asked.

"Well, I remember I was dreaming about seeing five male people who were telling me I possessed a valuable gift and I had to die, then I got woken up by Helen and they gave me this gross red stuff and then it felt like my body was on fire." The next day Amy woke up with Bryan sitting on her bed looking at Amy and holding her hands and kissing them very smooth.

"Good morning, Amy. How are you feeling?" Bryan asked with a tiny smile.

"Fine, I guess. Why do you ask?" Amy asked, feeling uncomfortable.

"Yesterday you were hyperventilating, and you felt like you were on fire. You were having a nightmare about five people that wanted to kill you. Amy, we need to have a talk about what might happen to you in Romania," Bryan said, while remaining calm.

"What is going to happen to me when we get to Romania? I am not going to die, am I, or end up being held hostage?" Amy asked, feeling herself panic.

"Not exactly, but the Romanian leader wants to meet you and run some tests with you to see what they can do to protect you," Bryan said, realizing he did not handle the situation that well.

"What kinds of tests will they do? Shots, do I have to take my clothes off and do something embarrassing?"

"No, it's nothing like that. Are you ready to hear the truth and burst into tears, or should I wait another time?"

"What is the truth that'll make me cry like crazy?" Amy shrieked, feeling tears in her eyes.

"I should let Alistair or Darcia, or someone else tell you this, because it might ruin our relationship. I will get someone up here to tell you the big news."

"Wait, Bryan. I trust you, and I know you'll have a shoulder for me to cry on."

"Let me make sure it is okay with my family," Bryan said. He ran downstairs and heard Darcia talking to him. Twenty minutes later, Bryan came upstairs and locked the door behind him.

"Bryan, are your parents okay with you telling me the truth?" Amy asked.

"They do not want me to tell you, but darn, I am going to tell you."

"Okay, okay Bryan. Maybe you should not tell me about this important news."

"Bryan, you will open this door now or you will be so sorry! Bryan!" Alistair yelled. Bryan opened the door and walked out of the room so they would not embarrass him in front of Amy.

"Amy, did Bryan tell you what you were not supposed to hear or see yet?" Alistair snapped.

"No, he didn't. Now, could one of you guys tell me what this is all about before I go insane?" Amy asked, feeling desperate as she was looking at Alistair's concerned expression.

"Do you know your ancestors in the past, Amy?" Alistair asked.

"I never knew I had ancestors in the past. They must be very interesting? Wait a minute, how do you know them?" Amy asked.

"It was around the time when Gabriel had turned me. I was in jail for being framed. I was sitting there with my prison buddy for stealing jewelry. Then I saw him wearing this leather jacket and sunglasses and he said my name and paid for my bail. The next thing I knew, I was at his castle lying in this bed. When I got up, I felt weak and horrible. I saw him standing on the patio, looking outside. I drank from this goblet and I felt the same as what you felt last night. Next, I was hunting with him and three other guys and four women for humans. Since I still had my human instincts, I felt so bad for killing innocent people and they knew what I was going through, but didn't do anything. They did not want to cause any problems. A hundred years later, I met Darcia at the nightclub where she and I met; later our relationship grew and grew. Gabriel found out about my human friend and threatened to kill her unless I changed her. I felt culpable for my situation."

"What happened, but when will I hear about my family?" Amy asked.

"Just listen. So, two hundred years later, we went over to Romania to see what my penalty was going to be. It turned out that Maggie Stevenson was James's niece who is the great-great-great-great-great grandmother of you and she is the sister of Darcia. She was going to give herself up to me, so Darcia and I could get married under one circumstance. I had to change Darcia into what I am. I told Darcia the news, and she ran back to Romania to complain to Gabriel, but he was not there. He left Darcia there to die. I was waiting for her at the entrance of the building till she came out crying. I walked over to her and hugged her and told her I was going to change her. That evening, I used my powers on her. A few moments later, I was teaching her how to hunt. I was so proud of her being a quick learner. Later on, Gabriel saw what happened to Darcia and told me he was very proud of Darcia and me. Maggie had this gift that, would give some of the females in your family tree a gift that if you wanted to kill someone, you could just, by the snap of your fingers, but you'd have to be careful with this gift. It's not for any weak individual, only the responsible people, apparently you too," Alistair said before he took a break.

"Oh my goodness, um, I'm pretty confused," said Amy, surprised.

"I understand, so that is why the court members want to meet you so they can see who you are and what gift you own. I will bring Bryan back in so he can soothe your emotions. Bryan, get your butt in here and take care of Amy!" Bryan jogged into the room and waited until Alistair left.

"Bryan, I am so mystified and I feel like crying, but it just will not come out."

"I understand, but that's the truth and you still have three weeks to hang out with Helen, Catherine, and Darcia and have a girl's day before you're stuck with us guys again," Bryan said.

"Bryan, protect Amy! Gregory has lost it and he wants to kill Amy!" yelled Helen.

"Amy, I promise I will not hurt you. I just need to eat something!" Bryan whispered.

"Gregory, get out before something bad happens to one of us." Kristjan and Roy grabbed him by his arms. Then, Zachary jumped ahead, calming Gregory down. "Gregory. Cool it. You are not really hungry. Come. There is a cute redhead out there," Kristjan said while subduing Gregory.

"I need to have Amy's power so badly let me go you jerks!" Gregory snapped. Kristjan jumped on Gregory and bit him so hard he nearly died from losing too much blood. "Dad, what the heck was that!" shouted Gregory so loud the neighbors ran out their houses. Gregory screamed.

"I am sorry, son, but you were out of control and you just had to calm down." The four of them walked down to the basement to talk to each other.

"Amy, I'm sorry about what happened. Let us go outside and explore Croatia, just you and I and we can eat some lunch and eat some dessert afterwards."

"Bryan, I feel upset and I want to die instead of being hunted by five people who want my gifts. In a month, I will be nineteen years old and then I will go to college and get a job and eventually move onto the great beyond," Amy said.

"You are lucky Amy. I am stuck in this life forever till I have to wait for someone to kill me painfully. When you get old, you can die in your sleep," Bryan said before he chuckled and he hugged Amy. Later that day, Bryan and Amy went outside to explore Croatia.

"Hey Bryan, want to go over to the beach and swim together? It is overcast," Amy asked.

"That sounds wonderful. Let us get out of here before someone tries to hurt you again." They got their swimming suits on and jumped in the car. All of a sudden, Joshua and Xander ran as fast as the car and jumped in.

"What are you guys doing here? Amy and I were planning on going to the beach together," Bryan snapped.

"We are also Amy's chaperons and we are not leaving her side. Besides, if Katrina sends out some of her spies you couldn't take four of them on. She also has another ten helpers in Romania," Joshua said.

"Silas, Katrina would never send her collaborators out into the human world so everyone would know what we are," Bryan said with a chuckle.

"Who is Katrina?" asked Amy in a worried way.

"She is the queen of Gabriel. When they are together, they could wipe out thousands of people in one go and both of them have a good appetite when it comes to killing people, whether they're humans, wolves, vampires, witches, you name it. When they're apart, they're still powerful, but not as powerful when they're together," Bryan said as he held Amy close to him.

"I will have to meet her in Romania, right? And have her eat me for dinner?" Amy asked with fear inside her body.

"You are not going to die when I am around. Remember that necklace I gave you? That is my promise to you that I will never, ever let you go. Anyway, we are not going to be at the beach with you guys. We're just going to keep a weathering eye out for anything distrustful." When they arrived at the beach, Amy and Bryan walked down to the beach. They walked a bit further away from the crowds so they could have some privacy.

"Hey Arthur, aren't Amy and Bryan a lovely couple? I mean, look at them. They look so happy and they're going to splash each other and chase each other, and eventually they'll kiss each other. I bet Darcia is already making wedding plans for the two lovebirds," Raymond said.

"Whatever. What actually happened to Kyra? Aren't you still boyfriend and girlfriend?" Xander asked.

"No, she dumped me for some beach boy down in Arizona about a few years ago," said Raymond, feeling sadness inside of him.

"Yeah, I remember that now. That you got home and your face was blank and you couldn't talk. Anyway, I know you have a crush on Amy. I mean, look at her in that light blue swimsuit," Xander said with a chuckle.

Raymond didn't respond to that, since deep down inside, he thought Amy was good looking. Joshua and Silas walked down the beach and looked around to see if there was anything interesting going on. "Say, Raymond, you want to get hooked up with those two girls sipping their soda pop? Maybe that will take your mind off of Amy and Bryan," asked Joshua.

"No, thanks. I would rather walk along this shopping street and relax till we have to defend Amy for some kind of reason," Raymond murmured.

"Goodness, you are not fun. If I were you, I would walk over to one of those girls and see if they are something. Wait a minute. Those two girls are Katrina's human representatives and I know they want to hook up with us and take us to Romania so we can either get killed, tortured, or join them," Joshua whispered.

"How do you know those are not regular college girls who are on vacation enjoying a nice day?" Silas asked.

"That's what they want us to think, but I am way smarter to believe that. Let us go over to Bryan and warn him," Joshua said.

"Xander, I am sorry to say, but ever since mom brought you home from the hospital, she accidently dropped you on your head, making you stupid. Later on our nineteenth till twenty-third birthday, dad's gift was changing us into these monsters," Silas murmured. While they were talking, the two girls came over to them and accidently bumped into Raymond.

"Oops," said girl number one. "I'm sorry about that."

"That's okay. It happens to us all on a beautiful day like this." The two girls giggled and started having a conversation about the water. They both kept glancing over at Amy. "Anyway, see you girls around and maybe we can hang out again sometime," Raymond said while Joshua and Xander were smiling at them.

"How about tomorrow? We would like to go to this Croatian dance with you guys. You can take some friends with you if you want. Here's a flyer with the date, what will happen, where, etc.," said one of the girls with her silk brown hair and green eyes.

"Cool, we might see each other there! Bye," Raymond said with a smile.

"Way to go Raymond! You see, if you wait a little longer, you will get a girl. Let's go and pick out two tuxedos, high hats, and two canes to make it special. We can practice dancing together, you and me, and we can laugh our heads off."

"Goodness Xander, are you not over prepared? I am not even sure if I want to go and dance. Maybe I just want to hunt for humans and relax for a bit," Raymond said as he walked with the flyer in his hands.

"Xander, a party means people, which means we can escort them outside and kill them. Look, it says on the flyer from eight till two in the morning and we do not go to bed, remember?" Raymond responded with a grin.

"Let's go back to Bryan and tell them about those girls' names I forgot."

"Bryan! Bryan!" yelled Xander.

"Hang on a minute Amy," Bryan said. "My idiotic brothers want something. Let's hope it is important or else there will be problems."

"Bryan, Bryan…," panted Xander. "There are two of Katrina's servants back where we were and I think they saw you guys and are going to report it to Katrina, so they might kill you and Amy."

"Seriously? We should get back to Alistair and Darcia and get the heck out of Croatia, and go to Romania to clear some stuff up before things get out of hand," Bryan said sarcastically.

"Or we could relax out on the beach and go swimming out there and enjoy ourselves," Xander retorted.

"No. Let's get out of Croatia and go to Gabriel and Katrina," Raymond said. The six of them went back to the house to talk to Alistair and Darcia. "Alistair, Darcia, we have something very important to tell you guys," To their surprise, they saw Alistair and Darcia sitting together on the couch with the two girls from the beach.

"Well, well, well, what do we have here? A lost puppy that needs a home to go to?" said the other girl with silk blonde hair wearing a white floral beach dress.

"Remember us Bryan?" said the brunette girl.

"Yes, I remember you, Rochelle and Cassie. I remember you killed your own boyfriend to get your hands on me, but I'm sorry to say, but Amy and I are already together so, hah," Bryan snapped.

"I do not want you, pup. Gabriel wants to have a word with Alistair, so let's go and see them," said the blonde girl who Bryan recalled was Rochelle.

"I am sorry, but you can't take us like this. We are meant to protect Amy," Alistair said, as he grabbed Darcia's hand.

"Gabriel sent Rochelle and I to bring you guys over to them. He said that three weeks were too long," Cassie said in an irritated tone.

"Dad, say something. You can't let them take us like this because that snot of a Katrina wants to kill one of us," Bryan snapped.

"I'm not going to die like this," Alistair snapped.

"Unbelievable, father, how could you let them do this to you?" Alistair looked and Darcia and kissed her hand.

"Hey what did I just say?" snapped Rochelle. "Vamoose pronto. Let's go to the airport and fly to Gabriel."

"Bryan, what is going on?" Amy stomped out of the house and started running down the streets. Bryan caught up with her and pinned her to the nearest wall.

"Calm down Amy, nobody is going to die this time or any other time. We're just going to have a nice talk with these people and an hour later we'll leave for Oregon and you will never ever have to deal with me again."

"Let me go, so I can fly back to Oregon alone and reunite alone without you guys!" Amy screamed.

What the heck is this about? Amy said to herself. *I wonder if there's an Internet café around so I can book myself a one-way ticket back home.*

"There is an Internet café about a hundred blocks down. You might need a car with your flip-flops and heavy legs," Bryan said.

"What the heck is your problem? Can't you see that I'm not in that mood right now to argue? I am probably going to die sooner than I thought. I might not see my family again," Amy snapped feeling herself panicking.

"Just get in the van Amy, and let us try to think positive and happy thoughts and sooner or later this discussion about you being a human will end," Bryan said in a calm voice. Amy got in the van annoyed and having the urge to strangle Bryan for this insensitive behavior. "It will be all right. Just have some patience and relax. I swear on my life that you will not die whatsoever. If someone has to die, it will be me or one of my brothers," Bryan said as he reached for Amy's hand.

"It's just not fair and if you die, I will die with a broken heart. You and I have been through a lot and if you leave me, I mean I love you so much. Even though you and I fight, I will always love you and appreciate your protection, but I still want an apology for calling my legs heavy," Amy said, feeling tears falling down her cheeks.

"I apologize for calling you all those names, but I am also sort of nervous about seeing those two again," Bryan said before he kissed Amy's hand.

"Did you have some kind of relationship with Katrina and she wanted to kill you?" Amy asked.

"Okay, we're at the airport. Everyone out pronto!" Cassie yelled.

"Are you making a mockery of us, because if you are, I might as well end you myself," Bryan retorted. As soon as the ten of them got out of the car, they ran through customs, passport control, and got to their gate.

"Does the Croatian family know about what happened to us?" whispered Amy.

"Probably, but they have their own problems to deal with that we don't know about," Bryan whispered back.

"Like, what kind of problems? You can read their minds or know something right, because you are family?" Bryan used his sleeping powers on Amy and she fell asleep till Bryan snapped his fingers.

"Wow Bryan, you still have your sleeping power. That's what I've always loved about you and your pretty gorgeous eyes and voice," Rochelle said.

"Enough Rochelle. I am with Amy, but she keeps asking me questions about the family secret and sometimes she needs a timeout from all of this."

"I know what you mean. My ex-boyfriend would always ask me questions, and sometimes he just asked too much, and I'd have to put him to sleep," Rochelle said before she chuckled.

"Does Gabriel know that we're going over to Romania to see him?" Alistair asked.

"Of course. He can actually see you and hear you. Whatever you say, do not say anything negative or else you will be put in a torture jail for a week and later get tortured while you'll be hearing crazy wild music."

Bryan smiled at Rochelle and grabbed one of Amy's packed books and started reading it.

"I remember I read that book. It warmed my body up, and it made me happy inside even though I'm a toxic cold pit." Bryan was getting annoyed but he didn't want anyone to know what was wrong with him.

"I'm going to leave you alone till we get to Romania, because I have this awkward feeling that you want to strangle me," Rochelle whispered. Bryan smiled and nodded. A few moments later, the flight attendants were going to make a speech about the flight. Later, the second-class passengers were boarding very slowly. "Why does boarding always take so long?" Bryan laughed for a sec till he saw Alistair's expression and his face went back to pain. "Let me see seat thirty six," Bryan murmured.

Amy started to wake up from the forced sleep Bryan put her in. "My goodness," whispered Amy, so only she and Bryan could only hear.

"I know what you mean." Moments later, four people got aboard the aircraft and ten minutes later, they departed Croatia to go to Romania.

Dear Diary,   10/17/07

Well, the Croatian trip turned out to be a bust. My stomach is turning because I am about to meet the court members who will decide my fate and either kill me or let me go under conditions. I am so scared I feel like crying, but I do not want to embarrass myself in an airplane filled with people. I miss my family so much I would give anything up just to see them one last time. The flight attendant will come by shortly with beverages and I am afraid I might throw up from all the anxiety that's going on in my head right now. I can barely sleep or eat. I cannot laugh anymore. I'm so upset right now and I want to scream so loudly. When we arrive, I might be dinner for someone because when I am in this situation I cannot defend myself, because I am weak and scared. I wish I had gone to a taekwondo class with my friends so I could show off my moves. I am alone in *my world and I'm not sure if I can continue on with living a fearful life. Maybe I should let them kill me so I can get this horrific nightmare over with. Anyway, that is my problem for the day. Amy*

Bryan looked at Amy and held her hand as tight as possible. "I will always be there for you, even though you and I argue about something stupid. I will never ever leave your side whatsoever," Bryan whispered.

"Oh Bryan, you make me want to cry out of happiness and hug you so tight."

"We'll get through this. You are not alone facing those people. You still have me and my brothers and parents, and other family members don't worry too much," Bryan said while he held her hand in his. "Remember those potions you had to drink in Rome, Athens, Croatia? That potion will protect you forty percent from harm, and that is enough for someone like you. You will not be the main meal or anything, mom's the word."

Amy started getting tears in her eyes but she dried them off quickly before Bryan even saw her. "Amy, try to relax." They hugged each other so tight.

"Excuse me, madam and sir, would you like something to drink?"

"I would like water with some ice cubes and a slice of lemon for my special girl." He smiled at Amy with his smile that can make a woman faint.

"I'm going to continue writing in my diary. There is something fun to do on an airplane?"

Dear Diary,   *10/18/07*

When I was in Croatia, I found out that I am very special and that Gabriel (head of court) wants to meet me. I feel discombobulated and scared about what they will do to me. Maybe they'll suck me dry or torture me slowly or something. Oh goodness, I think I'm going to throw up.

Amy jumped over Bryan and ran to the lavatory. "Amy, are you okay? You're not throwing up, are you?"

"Yes… I… Am… Oh my…" Amy was throwing up everything and Bryan waited till Amy was finished and escorted her back to her seat. An hour later, Amy dozed off in her seat and leaned against the window. Bryan felt Amy's forehead and looked at her complexion to see if he could find anything. It felt warm and clammy. Bryan took his jacket off and put it on Amy so she wouldn't get cold fast.

"Hey Bryan, is Amy okay?" asked Darcia, and sat next to Bryan in the empty seat.

"We should let Amy sleep and see if there's a hotel room available somewhere, so no one would bother Amy in her condition," Bryan whispered to Darcia.

"We are going to be staying at our family's home down in Bucharest and the next day, we will visit the court members," Darcia whispered.

"That sounds like fun. What we need to do is keep an eye on Amy, so nothing bad or stupid will happen," Bryan whispered before he smiled.

"I can't argue with that, but I think they won't attack Amy, but just in case, keep Amy with you. Are we clear on that because if she dies we're all dead?" Darcia asked. "Anyway, I hope Amy will feel better when we get off this airplane because it will make things a lot easier for me to deal with," Darcia said before she walked back to Alistair and discussed some plans with him. "Hey Alistair, we need to talk about what will happen to us when we arrive in Romania? What will happen after we've collected our luggage and leave the airport?"

"Gabriel sent two human servants to come and pick us up with two hummers, enough for the ten of us."

"Amy is not feeling well and Bryan was thinking about booking a room for him and Amy to stay. Would that be a wise move?" Darcia asked.

"No, Darcia. We are not going to be spending on hotel rooms when Gabriel and Katrina have rooms for their human friends who take care of business while they slumber down in their basement. Besides, they will not harm Amy whatsoever or else the deal between me and Gabriel is off and I have to kill him in front of his queen," Alistair whispered.

"What about Katrina? She is pretty mean when it comes to something like that. She is also pretty strong mentally," Darcia said with a sigh.

"First, we will meet our family and settle into their mansion and freshen up a bit. Does Amy know that we need to wear business suits when we face them? If not, you have to take Amy out after putting our suitcases away and measure her and see what color suits her."

"I do feel so sorry about letting this happen to Amy. I mean does Gabriel or Katrina know how strong Amy is?" Darcia asked.

"They want to talk to her and get her to return to her original self, again. I do wonder why Ginger isn't here with us," Alistair whispered. An hour away from their destination, Amy woke up with Bryan watching a movie. He did not seem to be bothered by all the action. If Amy saw something like that in her state, she would faint, throw up, or cover her eyes and ears.

"Hey, you're awake. How are you feeling? Maybe you should snooze for another forty-five minutes. Would you like some water or a cup of coffee?"

"I would like to have a nice cup of dark coffee so I can stay awake and focus more on what will happen," Amy said as she sighed.

"Oh yeah, do you by any chance have a business suit, because if you don't, you and Darcia will have to run down to a shop and buy a suit for you. It's one of the customs in their handbook," Bryan said before he sighed.

"No, I do not. I do not feel like going shopping right now. I want to take a nice warm shower or bath and sleep for a very long time."

"Do you take milk or sugar with your coffee?" Bryan asked.

"I just want to have a black coffee with two cubes of sugar," Amy said before she closed her eyes.

"Amy, are you sure about the sugar? If you are eating sugar, your blood will be sweeter."

"Right now, I don't care whether we die on this airplane or if I turn into someone like you."

"I'm going to continue watching this weird movie," Bryan murmured. Minutes later, the captain turned off the movies to make a speech.

"The fun is about to begin when we collect our luggage and go into the hummers. Oh boy, am I excited," Amy said hysterically.

"Think positive and happy thoughts, as least you have us backing you up? You get to sleep in a nice castle tonight with me or whoever in this family; you're getting good grades from your teachers and more."

"Whatever," Amy sighed. After they got off the airplane, they walked slowly towards to luggage belt and collected their stuff.

"Hey Raymond, would you mind watching Amy for me for a while? I need to talk to dad about our plans and what will happen next. Do not do anything while I am gone," Bryan snapped.

"Chill out bro, I am not going to hurt the little lady." When they got to the luggage belt, the other passengers were getting their trolleys.

"So why do you guys not ever lose control and accidently kill one of these innocent humans?" Amy asked Raymond.

"It is not easy. If that is what you are thinking, Alistair taught us how to control ourselves when someone walks by us. You know what happens if they know whom and what we are? They will try to kill us and do horrible stuff to us. I do not feel like going into detail right now."

"Okay, I understand." Amy walked over to Bryan's side and they hugged each other. "So you have got enough of Raymond? Or are you infatuated with him, but you want to hide your face? I have noticed that you have stopped thinking about Larry Harrison. Do you not have any feelings for him anymore?"

"Well, with all this drama going on and court people wanting my possessions, I do not really think about home that often, although I still miss them terribly."

"Attention ladies and gentlemen coming from Croatia, your luggage will come soon, in twenty minutes later than we'd expected, so sorry for this issue. Thank you for your cooperation and for the people who will miss their flights will get a free flight the next day at seven," a female voice said over the intercom.

"Aw Man I'm going to miss the darn flight." A couple of people said next to Amy and Bryan.

"It's too bad for people who will miss their flights and have to leave the next morning. I remember when I was thirteen years of age I was visiting my cousins in Louisiana and I was on my way back to Oregon and I had to stop at Dallas to make a long story short. I had to spend the night there and the next morning at noon I was back at home with my family. They were pretty mad about what happened," Amy said.

"I bet they were. So, are you getting bored with me yet?" Bryan asked.

"No, not really. I mean, I would prefer to be with my own family right now and walk my dogs and have catfights with my sister and stuff."

"You'll see them soon, don't worry," Bryan said as he held Amy close to him. Later on, everyone got their luggage and headed out towards the exit of the airport to meet their human helpers.

Chapter 7

Fleeing

As soon as Alistair and his group of others left the luggage belt, they went to the bathroom, covering every part of their body. They did not want anyone to know their secret, putting on chic long jackets and hats. "Master Gabriel and Mistress Katrina are expecting you. They are very happy to see that Amy is still alive and seeing you guys after all those centuries," the drivers said.

"Hey Bryan, are that man and woman human?" Amy asked as she stood behind Bryan.

"Yes, they wanted to live a luxurious life and sleep in fancy beds, eat gourmet food, get paid fifty dollars an hour while taking care of their home etc.," Bryan whispered. Amy felt anxious. As soon as Alistair, Darcia, Amy, and Bryan got into the first hummer, they drove off with the other three guys in the car in back of them.

"Hey Amy, don't worry about the king and queen, they're still asleep till eight o'clock and then you will meet," Alistair said, as he grabbed Amy's hand in a comforting, fatherly manner.

"So there is no killer chasing me? Only a couple of immortals that want my gift? Why did you take me to all those places?" Amy asked feeling herself getting frustrated.

"So they can give you potions to protect your body just in case they might try to do stuff to you," Alistair said with a smile.

"What do you mean by doing stuff? I'm not going to die, am I?" Amy snapped, releasing her hand from his.

"Not as long as we are there. If we are dead, you are probably not going to survive that long unless they invite you to join them. Once we have arrived and your suitcase is in your room, you and Darcia will go shopping for business suits, so you will not stand out that much. Plus, they love wearing suits," Alistair whispered. Amy felt uncomfortable. She could not think straight anymore. She wanted to escape.

"That might not be a good idea to do, Amy. Remember that we're not humans," Bryan said with a smirk, pointing at his head.

"Why do you guys always have to read my mind? It's like reading someone's diary and that can ruin that person's life," Amy snapped.

"It is not like that. After we have had a nice talk with those people, we can get lost in Bucharest and see what there is to see," Bryan said with a smile while holding Amy's hand.

What Amy would have preferred was to lock herself in her room watching movies and going on the computer, surfing the internet and chatting with her friends and relaxing till it was dinner time at her house. While Amy was looking outside, Bryan put his arm around her shoulders. "Well, look at where we are going to be staying? Is she not a beauty?" the male driver asked. Amy smiled and nodded, even though she wasn't too thrilled about meeting people who wanted to kill her.

As soon as the hummers arrived at the gate, the male and female driver pressed a green button and the gate opened. When everyone got out, Bryan grabbed both Amy's and his luggage and rushed her inside. There was a door that probably led down to the basement where the family slumbered.

"How many people live in this castle, besides Gabriel and Katrina?" Amy asked as she was looking around the entrance of the castle.

"I have not been here in a while, but wolves guard the castle and there are about a couple of them who live here and they tend to gather more and more each year to create an army," Bryan said as he walked ahead of Amy.

"Like those teenage movies?" Amy asked. Bryan chuckled and stopped talking about the topic. "Anyway, what are they going to give me this time? I need to know why I am such an interest to Gabriel? How are we related?" Amy asked, causing everyone to gasp. "What?" Amy asked in a confused way.

"Never mind that, Amy," Alistair said. "Now how about we go and take your suitcase up to your room and Darcia will walk with you over to get you fitted properly?" Alistair asked trying to remain calm.

"Come on, Amy, let's go and shop. Do you have a special color that fits your hair color? You should wear a black suit with black heels," Darcia said, as she grabbed Amy's arm.

"I'm such a lucky girl who gets to wear a black dress suit with black heels?" Amy said in a sarcastic way.

"Wait here for a moment and let me see if one of the drivers will drive us to the nearest shop," Darcia murmured. The male driver got into the car and drove Amy and Darcia over to the mall.

As soon as they got to the mall, it looked quite empty, as if it was abandoned. Most of the shops looked closed and dead inside. Darcia grabbed Amy's wrist and pulled her into the women's section and pulled out a size thirty-eight suit dress, and pushed Amy into the dressing rooms. "Come out when you have it on. If it does not fit, just come out with the suit and we'll get a different size." Amy felt a bit happy being in a shopping mall, but she preferred to go with Jenna because at least they could laugh about the clothes and laugh when they did not look good. As she was standing in front of the mirror, she did not like wearing it, but if it got her out of the court meeting, she would wear it even though she looked like her mom.

"So how is it coming, Amy? You know we only have three more hours, so if you are ready, come on out and then I will buy you something delicious to eat," Darcia said as she sat on one of the chairs outside of the changing rooms.

"Sure, that sounds like fun, I guess," Amy sighed.

"Say Amy, what is up with you? You seem so serious and depressed. Is this about the court? Or do you not you like wearing it?" Darcia asked, as they were looking for an open restaurant for Amy to eat.

"I guess all the above. I'm afraid this is the last time I'll set foot in a shopping mall or meet a handsome husband and have babies with someone, or ever do anything. I do not want to deal with any pain or torture. I cannot handle this anymore," Amy said as she felt her eyes water.

"There there Amy," Darcia said, trying to keep Amy as calm as possible. "I swear on our blood that nothing bad will happen. Alistair would never let them harm you, nor my four boys or the other family members. Now let's get something to eat and drink for you!" She grabbed Amy's wrist again and pulled her into the food court and stood in line at this pastry restaurant. "Two chocolate smoothies please and one chocolate muffin, one large chocolate creampuff, and two chocolate doughnuts." When Darcia got her change back, they sat over at this table and enjoyed their food. "Oh, man, some guys just winked at me. I do not feel comfortable when they are making kissing faces at me," Amy whispered.

"You are a beautiful young woman, so do not ask me to go over there and smack their faces. They are not worth my time," Darcia said, as she watched Amy eat. Bryan and the other boys walked into the mall. Josh spotted them.

"Guys, isn't that Amy and Darcia over there?" Josh asked while pointing at them.

"Hey Amy, let us see your dress. Darcia, could you stop feeding her sugar? The sweeter she gets, the more they cannot stop the urge to attack her," Bryan said while looking at the food with disgust.

"You guys, nothing is going to happen to Amy unless you want her to die?" Darcia sighed while rubbing her forehead.

"What!" shrieked Amy?

"Just kidding, you are not going to get hurt. Let's finish so you can model for Alistair and the other guys," Darcia said as she winked at her.

"Whatever," Bryan said. "We were on our way to the game store and sports shop. We ran here from the castle and in an hour we'll be ready! See you later," Bryan said before he gave Amy a pat on her shoulder.

"So, Amy, are you ready to go home? The driver has been in the car waiting for us and you need to wash your hair and put on some makeup," Darcia said. Amy shook her head. When they got inside the castle, it was very quiet everywhere. Amy looked around and there was nobody except Darcia and the driver walking upstairs. "Amy, you still have one hour to get ready here. Take this purple fuzzy robe. I will be here when you come out of the shower," said Darcia as she walked next to Amy.

"Hello, is Amy in this castle?" asked Alistair over the intercom.

"Yes, she is up in her room. Send the maid up to get her ready because I've been dealing with Amy's needs that I forgot about mine," said Darcia. The maid came upstairs with a towel and got Amy's makeup and suit ready. "Here you go Miss Ambrose. Please sit here and relax while I take care of your makeup." Moments later, Bryan brought Amy down wearing his suit. Gabriel stood at the bottom of the stairs with his black silk hair down his back, his red eyes, marble complexion, strong built body, and pink lips that he kept closed till he would officially meet Amy.

"My name is Gabriel, and this is my queen Katrina. We just got up an hour ago. The fifteen of us will go and talk about this situation when we get to our meeting area. We will see you all in an hour while we prepare ourselves. Ta ta." Katrina scowled at Amy and grabbed Gabriel's arms. The other members of the castle walked over to their limousine and drove off.

Amy turned around with this blushing feeling and felt like fainting. Hours later, the five of them walked over to the main room and saw them sitting on two thrones with the other three on both sides.

"Welcome, my loving family, to our second home. Amy, I want to apologize for not meeting you that well. My name is Gabriel, and this is my wife, Katrina. The other five members are our close brothers and sisters," said Gabriel. He grabbed her hand and shook it softly before he kissed it. "It is a pleasure to meet you."

He grabbed her body before she fainted. "Alistair, want to take her before things get out of control?" Gabriel asked, while holding Amy in his arms.

Alistair raced over and snapped his fingers, and she woke up. Gabriel walked back to his throne and grabbed Katrina's hand and held it tight. "Alistair, why have you not told her? I almost bit her when she almost fainted. I know she has the potions in her that would save her from any problems," Gabriel snapped before he looked at Amy with this hungry look. He squeezed Katrina's hand really hard again.

"Gabriel, if you want her, bite her," Katrina whispered. Gabriel looked at her with a painful look.

Amy managed to steady herself against Alistair. "Amy, how would you like to join our group of immortals?" Gabriel asked with raised eyebrows. "Unless you already know the truth behind that question?"

"Well, I don't know?" Amy shrugged. "You are the Gabriel I've been hearing about? I heard that name, even when I was in Oregon," Amy said, as she looked over at Alistair with confusion.

"Amy, whatever you do, do not give them your powers, do not give them!" Darcia shrieked.

"Vladimir shut Darcia up. So Amy, what is your answer? I can see that you are uncertain. Alistair scheduled our meeting this evening. Amelia, could you help me out here? Amy refuses to respond?" Gabriel asked with tenseness in his voice.

"Raymond, Bryan, stop her!" yelled Darcia at the top of her lungs. Daniel and Lucien ran over to the two guys and held them in the headlock position.

"Amelia, do your work." Gabriel said in a controlled, low voice.

"Yes, master." Vladimir grabbed Amy's neck and Amelia walked over to Amy and placed her hand over her head and used her mind game on her. Gabriel could feel Amy's mind weakening.

"Gabriel, stop Amelia, please!" screamed Darcia.

"Amelia, do not kill her, just weaken her." The other twenty wolf guards were standing in the background, watching all the action going on. Amelia stepped away from Amy and scowled at Alistair before she walked back to where she stood before.

"Amy, I must apologize for this, but I need to know if you want to join my group and be fierce and powerful or be a weak human who can't use her gifts," Gabriel said with a hint of desperation in his voice. Amy thought about it again for a moment and looked at Alistair. "I am very sorry, but… I prefer to stay human and go back to Oregon and live a human life," Amy said in a flat, monotone voice.

"Is that your final decision?" asked Gabriel, knowing the answer.

"Yes, it is now. May I please leave and go back home where I belong and finish my high school so I can continue on to college?" Amy said, feeling herself going numb.

"Nobody is stopping you, Amy? It is just, why do you not want to stay young, beautiful, run fast, be strong and powerful and take revenge on the people who you used to hate?" Amy did not respond to Gabriel's question and walked toward Alistair and stood by his side. Gabriel smiled and nodded to his guards to escort Alistair's group outside without Amy. Gabriel and Katrina got off their thrones to shake hands and wave goodbye to them. "Gabriel, you cannot have Amy, so she will be coming with us back to Oregon and she can decide to either be Bryan's mate or to wait longer," Alistair said in a stern tone.

"It's just weird that one prefers to stay human. I mean, when I gave these people a choice, they were all thrilled to become immortal," Gabriel said before he used his magic to put her memory of her being a baby in her mother's arms inside her mind, causing Amy to freeze.

"Daddy?" Amy asked with fear. Alistair grabbed Amy fast and placed his arms around her.

"Amy, snap out of it and you're coming back with us," Alistair snapped.

"Huh? What just happened?" Amy asked, looking confused.

"Nothing. Just run along with us and get the next airplane back to Oregon." As they were running, Gabriel locked all the doors with his mind.

"Please, Amy, reconsider staying with us for one week and then you can make up your mind and I will let you go," Gabriel begged. Amy was scared and confused. She kept looking at Alistair to read his mind.

"Amy, do not even think about it!" Seconds later, Gabriel undid the locks and let them go.

"Gabriel, what about the girl?" asked Katrina. "We cannot just let her go right now?"

"Wait for the opportune moment, Katrina. Soon I will leave this area and do checkups on Amy without her knowing it. I will save her when she needs to be saved," Gabriel whispered.

"What about Bryan? He stays with her at all times," Katrina said in a panicked tone.

"I will need to take Claudia, Audrey, and Vladimir so they can distract them, and I will bring Amy back here," Gabriel said.

"You and I will always stay together, right?" Katrina asked with uncertainty in her voice. Gabriel didn't respond to that and walked back to the lounge down in the basement area.

"Hey Amy, are you okay? Did he hurt you at all?" asked Alistair, worried, as he checked her upper body, neck, and eyes.

"I don't think so. I have a splitting headache. I need to rest for a moment. So was that the meeting of your group?" Amy asked, feeling foggy headed.

"Yes, but they will be checking up on you, Amy. Whatever you do under any circumstances, do not do anything you could regret later. Now your birthday is in a couple of weeks. Have you thought about that?" asked Silas, as he walked to the other side of Amy.

"Silas, she just got through a weird meeting, so let's just take her back to the airport. Hey Amy, you still have six months to do whatever you want before your year is over," Darcia said. Just then, Gabriel and his three brothers walked through the door to them.

"Alistair, you cannot leave yet. We still have to give Amy our special drink. Please bring her back in," Gabriel said with a charming warm smile.

"Gabriel, she is not in the right state to go through more problems. She is tired, and things could go wrong," Alistair said with desperation in his voice.

"Alistair, can I talk to you for a moment in private? Please follow me down to our resting area." Alistair thought about it and sighed before he walked with Gabriel down to the basement area. As soon as they got to the resting place, Gabriel smacked Alistair across the face. "Are you mental or what? Why would you not tell Amy the truth? You did not even know about Amy or Ginger's existence till we told you guys two years ago. Amy does not even know who she is. Why would she want to live a pathetic human life?" Gabriel asked.

"We are not going to give Amy over to you right now," Alistair retorted.

"You already know that it's time to give her over and return her back home," Gabriel said, leaning against the wall, blocking Alistair from leaving the area.

"Gabriel, we need to have a vote with all covens to see what we should do."

"Assemble all the family members," snapped Gabriel while glaring at Alistair.

"Why? You are in no state right now to be receiving your daughter back home, Gabriel. The whole plan of having you place immortal children up for adoption so they could become human? It broke everyone's heart when Arabella had died in your arms that night, Gabriel. Darcia and I talk about it occasionally with each other. The hungry feeling you have toward Amy needs to simmer first before you can get used to her again. Do not forget poor Ginger, who is still in Oregon," Alistair said, feeling his energy slowly drain.

Alistair walked back upstairs to get out of that place to take Amy back to Oregon. "You know Alistair, if you take her back home, you guys will not be around her that often. I can put on my cloak and travel back to Oregon and take her and run back there fast and, of course, I'd use my powers on her," Gabriel said with a smirk.

"You know how wrong that sounds? We are not going to leave immediately from Oregon. We might stay in a motel and change our appearance so she wouldn't recognize us," Alistair snapped before he walked up to Darcia.

"Darcia, let's get the heck out of here now!" Alistair snapped, before Darcia, Amy, and the four boys walked out. Bryan flung Amy on his back and ran with the other six. When they got to the car, they helped Amy put her clothes and stuff in her duffle bag and grabbed her backpack. Then they got to the airport and there was a two-hour line waiting to check in their luggage. "Oh heavens, how should we get through this?" Bryan moaned while his arms were around Amy.

"We could say that our airplane is boarding right now and we really need to get on," Darcia murmured while she was watching how fast the women were working. "Or we could just endure this line and wait till it's our turn while Gabriel and his tribe are after us," Alistair said before he used his powers of persuasion. "Excuse me, excuse me, this is an emergency. Please get out of the way."

"Pardon me folks, but you cannot cut in line like that. Please step out of the line and go to the back," said a security guard. Alistair looked into the security guard's eyes, hypnotizing him.

"We need to get on this plane as fast as possible." The security guard nodded.

"Next please," the attendant said. The seven of them walked to the desk so they could check in. When they were finished, they walked over to their gate.

"Say Amy, we will travel back home and you can celebrate your birthday with your family. Gabriel's group will not bother you anymore. We will be leaving and going back home from where we came," Bryan said with relief.

"So, the journey is over? No more having to deal with any problems of me having this amazing possession?" Amy asked.

"Correct. We will bring you home safely. You and Bryan can exchange information if you want and wish each other the best," Alistair said with a smile. Amy was happy hearing that her journey was over, but she also felt a bit depressed inside because of all the excitement that happened to her. She actually loved being around new people.

"Should I warn my family members before they throw away my stuff out of grief?" asked Amy.

"Whatever you want to do, you can call them on those payphones at the airport in Oregon and tell them you're back," Alistair said. Amy felt like crying out of happiness, but she shoved down her emotions and leaned against the chair and relaxed till they had to board the airplane. Just now, a flight attendant made her announcement during the boarding process.

"So Amy, how does it feel to go back home? Awkward? Whatever you do, do not tell our secret. Just tell them about your dead grandma and that it was so sad and there was a cake with her picture on it. Just lie, but do not say anything really happened, Bryan whispered. A young guy with brown hair came running with his briefcase onto the plane. Amy walked in with Bryan and they went over to their seats.

"Hey Amy," Alistair asked. "You don't look so happy about returning to your home. You are not going to run into any problems anymore."

"It's not about Gabriel and Katrina. It's just that this whole journey took a lot of energy out of me and I'm sad that we will never ever see each other anymore. You guys reminded me of my family, and now it is time to say goodbye," Amy said, feeling sadness built inside of her.

"Don't worry Amy. You will get used to your own routine again and go back to babysitting and getting good grades, and walk your two dogs again. We still have another ten or twenty-four hours of flying and when we drop you off, we will still be around for a few days and tell your parents about your trip," Bryan said with a smile before he kissed Amy's hand.

"But Bryan, I do not want you to leave me anymore. You could live with me,"

Bryan smirked and opened up the magazine in front of him and read a bit till the captain got on the speakerphone.

Five minutes later, the aircraft took off from the runway and went into the air. "Amy, I know you are crying and, instead of making things worse, I am going to switch places with Raymond so he can keep make you more comfortable."

"No, Bryan, don't leave me on this flight. I really want to spend my last moments with you," Amy said in a hushed voice.

"I was not going anyway, and you fell for it. I just have to use the lavatory." Amy put on one of the movies on the airplane and continued watching it even though it wasn't that funny for the first few minutes. After that, she turned to an action movie. "Amy, can I talk to you for a moment?" asked Raymond.

"Sure, I could use some company," Amy said.

"I need to tell you something before we arrive in Oregon," Raymond said.

"Yes?" Amy said, even though she already knew what he was going to ask.

"I will miss you a lot once we leave back home," Raymond said. "These weeks, as horrific as they were, were one of the best moments of my life."

When Bryan came out of the lavatory, he walked down with a swagger, which caused some of the women to gawk. Raymond got out of the seat and put his earphones back on.

"I saw Raymond talking to you. I know we all will miss you, Amy," said Bryan. "If you do want me to live with you, I can suggest that plan to both Alistair and Darcia." Bryan said as he looked behind him at Alistair.

Amy smiled at Bryan before she wrapped her arms around his arm. "It looks like they're coming down with beverages," Amy said. "I will have sparkling water with ice cubes and a slice of lemon."

"Amy, you look tired. Try to get some rest and I'll wake you up when we get off the plane and get on the shorter flight. I will get you some sparkling water, because I love you with all my heart," Bryan said.

"Oh Bryan," Amy whispered before she wiped her eyes. "Thank you."

"Amy, come here." They switched sides so Amy's face faced the window. He hugged her tight and let her cry on his shoulder.

"Excuse me," asked the flight attendant. "Would you like something to drink?"

"Yes, we would like two sparkling waters and with ice blocks and lemon slices." Bryan let Amy go so he could grab the drink and put it on his table. Amy breathed a couple of times to get her mind focused again. "Excuse me, ma'am, but do you need anything?" the second flight attendant asked.

"No, I'm fine. I just need a drink and relax for a while," Amy said.

"All right, but if you need anything, press this orange button and I will be over in less than five seconds." Amy nodded and smiled at the stewardess and continued cuddling with Bryan.

"Excuse me Amy, my parents would like to talk to me. I will be back as soon as possible, so just relax and breathe in and out. We are still stuck on this airplane for at least another six hours," Bryan whispered.

"Hey parents, you summoned me? Anything you guys want to talk to your son about?" Bryan said in a sassy tone.

"Bryan, I heard and saw Amy cry. What did you do to her? You did not tell her that we were going to leave her? News flash we are not. We're just going to stay at a motel or hotel nearest to Amy's house. We'll have a disguise on. As you probably heard in your mind that Gabriel wouldn't stop hunting Amy, so we are going to protect her without her knowing it. They might use the same tactic as us," Alistair whispered.

"Should I tell Amy or keep it a secret?" Bryan asked. "I hate seeing that girl like that. Wait a minute, Alistair. Was it not our deal to bring Amy over to Gabriel like you were assigned to do eighteen years ago?" Bryan asked.

"Yes, we were, but plans have changed and we're going to wait until Amy settles down for a while, instead of getting dropped off at the castle, causing her to freak out and escape and run back to Oregon. Give both Amy and Gabriel some time. Our task will be completed soon. For now, forget that we even had this conversation. Go back to your seat and comfort Amy," Alistair snapped.

Bryan walked back to Amy so she wouldn't get worried or sad again. "So Bryan, what were you guys discussing, if I may ask?"

"We were discussing what Gabriel told Alistair when they walked down to the basement," Bryan said, trying to cover up his lie to Amy.

"Do I need to know?" Amy whispered.

"Not really. It isn't a really a nice story you would want to hear. It is scary." After a while, Bryan and Amy dozed off, leaning on each other, holding each other's hand. Time went by till they had two hours to go sitting on that airplane. "Hey Amy, want to drive my dad crazy and make out?" Bryan asked with a smile on his face.

"Not really," Amy responded with a chuckle. Just then, the airplane was experiencing turbulence.

"I have always loved turbulence, ever since I was on an airplane with my whole family. Guess what, we missed dinner now. We are probably going to have lunch.

You can have mine. I am back on my special diet living off human flesh. Are you scared?" Bryan said.

"Not really. After that time in Athens, I am not really scared of your kind anymore, and with Gabriel and Katrina. They won't be hunting me anymore, right?" Amy asked, making sure nobody was listening to their conversation.

Bryan put his earphones on and watched any movie that he pressed so he wouldn't have to deal with Amy and her questions. Amy waited till they had landed so she and Bryan could talk.

"Pardon me, would you like chicken or pasta?" The steward asked.

"I will have the pasta and my boyfriend will have the chicken." After the steward went over to Raymond and Arthur, Bryan got up and walked towards the bathroom with a brown bag he had in his hands. Alistair watched Bryan to make sure he was not doing anything that could cause a riot. Darcia walked over to Amy to keep her company.

"Hey Amy, you do know why Bryan left to go to the bathroom?" Darcia asked.

"Not really, but I might have a hunch. He is on this special diet, am I right?" Amy asked.

"Did Bryan tell you this? If only he could have waited for us, we would have said it in a nicer way. I guess the way Bryan said it does not sound that bad," Darcia said with a smile.

"He told me you guys live off of human flesh and that made me feel uncomfortable," Amy whispered while cracking her knuckles out of nerves.

"You want me to talk to Bryan and make you feel comfortable again?"

"No, that is fine. I am kind of glad to be back with my family, but I do not want to see you guys leave." Darcia looked at Alistair to see if it was okay to tell Amy the truth. He shook his head and went back to watching his movie. "There comes a time for seeing each other and saying goodbye," Darcia whispered.

"That's true," Amy said while holding back her tears.

"If you feel lonely, here is my email address and I will respond to you within a few minutes at night. During the day, I would like to avoid crowds and the sunlight." Just then, Bryan returned, looking normal as usual. He popped a special breath mint in his mouth and sat down next to Darcia.

"Hey mom, what brings you to our row on the airplane? Not telling Amy anything that you should not tell her?" Bryan asked.

"Of course not, Bryan. I will leave you two kids alone to chat for another two hours. When we arrive at the airport, we will mosey on to shops and hang out for an hour and go through security and board that plane back to your place." As Amy and Bryan were relaxing in each other's arms, two hours had passed in a snap and they were in the airport. They had to change planes, letting all the passengers pass so they could walk very slowly towards customs.

"Hey Bryan, have you ever thought about having children of your own and a wife?" Amy asked.

"Sometimes I dream about having a partner who would hunt with me and we would be partners for life and both she and I would worship each other, etc. Kids, well, it cannot hurt to have younglings.

Why? Are you asking me for my hand in marriage?" Bryan asked in a confused way.

"No, of course not. I mean, will you ever find someone who loves you dearly and who would love to worship and love you?" even though Amy meant herself, but she wanted to wait for a while.

"So far, I'm not really a lucky man. I am not into feelings and I am not really a good listener. I would take care of someone if they were in physical pain and were about to die," Bryan said with a desperate sigh.

"Sounds lovely," Amy murmured. "Anyway, whatever happened to that Giselle girl? You have not broken up with her because of me, have you?"

"No, it is just, she is a bit too girlish for me. I love a tomboy." That was what Amy was going for. She did not care about getting manicures or pedicures and shopping with her friends. She preferred to just keep her distance and play sports. Amy would rather work in a shop and wear a uniform than become a model, even though she had the model look.

I wonder if Amy is the perfect girl for me. I would want to know more about Amy. Maybe I should call Amelia up to see what she saw in Amy's head. I have been with Amy more than Giselle. Amy seems like a cool girl to hang out with. Bryan thought as he walked hand in hand with Amy over to their gate. Raymond came over to Bryan and pulled him ahead of everyone. "Bryan, what the heck are you thinking?"

"Cut it out Raymond, you had your chances with that other girl," Bryan retorted.

"What about Giselle weren't you guys still dating?" At that point, Bryan jumped on Raymond and beat him crazy. His eyes went black with rage and his nails got longer. Alistair took off his jacket and put it over Bryan's face, so nobody would see him like that. People looked shocked and scared at the scene that was going on. Raymond roared from his chest and got on his feet. "Raymond!" Alistair shouted.

Raymond stopped for a moment and saw what had happened to him. Humans pointed and stared at them. "Monsters!" yelled the humans. The children cried, and some women fainted. "Kill the monsters!" shouted some people.

"Say, Darcia, want to leave this airport and come back at an appropriate time?" Alistair asked.

"I am right ahead of you, Alistair," Darcia snapped. The seven of them ran very fast out through the windows and ran out very fast till they got to the nearest woods, which took them thirty minutes running. "You guys, what happened back there? You almost got us killed!" Alistair yelled.

"We are truly sorry for the way we acted. This will be the last time we will ever do that again. Maybe we can travel in the cargo? We can stand the cold," Bryan said teasingly.

"Yes, but a human will die!" Alistair snapped.

"Amy is already different from the average human," Bryan murmured.

"Bryan shut up. We are not going to do that. We will run over to a motel for a few hours and change into each other's disguises and go back to the airport."

"What about our passports?" Darcia asked.

"Amy didn't do anything. We did. We can easily get on that airplane and Amy can run in the back of us and get on the airplane herself because the most important thing is to get Amy back home. We can get to Oregon another way. Trust me," Alistair responded.

Amy felt like screaming, but it didn't come out of her mouth. "Amy, you are going to get home this evening, whether I have to carry you on my back," Bryan said.

"Bryan shut up again. We need to run back to another airport and see if we can get on the next flight. We have our passports?" Alistair snapped.

"But not Amy's duffle bag. What do we do now?" Bryan moaned.

"Bryan, bring Amy back to the airport so she can fly back home alone without us. If Gabriel or someone else bothers Amy, I know she can defend herself." Alistair sighed, knowing the truth about Amy's bloodline.

"Alistair, that sounds terrible. If that is the only thing we can use, let's do it." Darcia snapped. Amy did not really care anymore except for being in Oregon.

"Sounds good," Bryan said before he kissed Amy. Then he carried Amy on his back to the airport and dropped her off and she went through customs. The airport was sort of cleaned up and Amy went and got in line, boarding the airplane.

"May I see your boarding pass and passport, please?" asked a flight attendant. Amy grabbed her passport and boarding pass, handing them to the flight attendant. "Enjoy your flight. Good evening sir, may I see your passport?" Amy suddenly realized that she was alone on the airplane. No Bryan, or Darcia or anybody. She sat down on her seat and put her passport in her backpack, and looked out the window, sighing. "Amy Ambrose," a whisper that sounded familiar.

"Adrian!" Amy shrieked. She tried to get out of her seat until he grabbed her by her hand.

Adrian shushed her. "Amy, just listen to me. You do not have to do anything except listen to me. Gabriel just wants to talk to you. He is wearing his disguise a few rows down," Adrian said, while nodding toward the back of the plane.

"Amy, just hear me out. I have something important to tell you. It's very important," Adrian whispered. Amy could hardly pay attention to what Adrian was talking about.

Amy, hello are you there? Bryan asked through his thoughts, though it sounded like he was near. *Amy, whatever you do, do not go over to the dark side.*

"Bryan, where are you?" but there was no response. Adrian walked back to Amy to keep her company and knowing that Bryan could communicate to her through his mind to Amy's.

"Gabriel asked me to chaperon you." Amy just nodded and put her earphones in her ears so she could listen to her music.

"Amy, Gabriel wants to give you this red pendant," Adrian said, as he placed the pendant on Amy's table.

"I'm sorry Adrian, but I am not going to go over to your side."

"You do have some form of hunch about your connection with Gabriel, do you not? Do you not remember gasping out daddy when Gabriel used his powers on you? Gabriel can show you. Look, if it makes you feel comfortable, he can make sure it won't hurt a bit," Adrian whispered.

"Um, let me give it some thought, um… no. Now go back to your master and wait till we arrive. I'm going to collect my luggage and take a bullet train back home where I will get lots of hugs and kisses and people will shed tears of joy etc." Vladimir came by and sat in the empty seat next to Adrian and whispered some stuff in an ancient language. A few moments later, Adrian put his hand over Amy's mouth. Then he grabbed a needle and stabbed it into Amy's neck. She yelped softly, and some people looked over to see why she did that. Vladimir and Adrian smiled

"Medicine," Vladimir said, as he used his persuasion powers on them. The humans returned to watching movies and reading books.

The flight attendant made their arrival announcement. Amy did not really listen because she knew everything she had to do. When the plane got to the gate, Amy waited till everyone got off and walked fast to the luggage belt and waited. She was getting impatient when she saw Gabriel, Vladimir, and Adrian walking towards the belt. "Amy, why did you run off like that? We need to stick together because you remember what happened to your brother that other time we split up in an airport." Amy scowled at Gabriel and walked down the luggage belt to get into the crowds so she would not have to deal with those people. She saw them standing there smiling at her with those sinister grins on their faces. Amy felt this nauseous feeling and felt this pain where Adrian stabbed her with a syringe.

She was getting weak and tired, but she fought it and continued waiting for her duffle. Her eyes were getting weaker by the second. She had to stay awake. She fell down on her knees and pushed the ground.

"Help! There is a young woman in pain!" screamed some of the people. Some people were giving her CPR, but she pushed them aside and got on her feet, leaning on this woman's shoulder. "There is an ambulance on its way. Hang in their ma'am," said a middle-aged woman with short dark brown hair, who she was leaning on.

"No, I do not need a hospital. I need to go back home and get some rest." The crowd ignored Amy and carried her on the gurney and wheeled her out of the airport to the nearest hospital. "Hang on a second, folks. The girl is coming with us since we are her family," Gabriel said with a charming smile.

"Are you like the uncle?" asked a paramedic.

"More like a father. Please give her to me so I can bring her back to our place and nurse her to health," Gabriel said while using his persuasion powers on them.

"Thank you, Mr...."

"Gabriel. Just Gabriel." The crowd cheered and clapped for Gabriel. Then they walked out of the airport covered in cloaks.

"Wait, Gabriel, what about her duffle bag? She will hate you for leaving her stuff there," Adrian said as he followed Gabriel from behind.

"She already hates me now. We should teleport back to our castle. We cannot stay at a hotel or anywhere else." A few seconds later, they were back in the castle. Gabriel carried Amy over to the guest room and walked over to the kitchen to discuss what would happen next.

"So we finally have her, ladies and gentlemen. Tomorrow let the ceremony begin," Gabriel said.

"You know what I finally have in mind? Amy has an older sister named Ginger," Lucien said as he entered the kitchen.

"Yes, they both take after me and her mother." Gabriel sighed out of joy.

"Gabriel, what are you going to do to Amy after the ceremony? Tell her the truth about who she actually is and who you are?" Katrina asked as she entered the kitchen.

"I will wait to tell her till I know it is safe and Amy is detained," Gabriel responded.

"Did someone watch too many vampire movies lately?" teased Katrina.

"Well, in our case, it's sort of the same: vampires, werewolves, and other immortal creatures and witches," Gabriel snapped. While they were having their discussion, Alistair and the five others were outside the castle thinking of ways to get Amy out there before it was too late. As Gabriel was preparing for the evening, Alistair and his group managed to return to Romania within a few minutes.

"Alistair, my love, what's our plan of action?" Darcia asked, while she was controlling her breathing.

"They will know who and what we are. We need to get some humans to go in and stall them while we get Amy out. Gabriel is the head person of all parties in this world. Our mission is to get humans?" Alistair said.

"We still have twenty more hours before Amy goes through her transition. We do not have to get humans here for another ten hours. She is saved before they tie her up or hypnotize her or anything. We can walk around for a while and hang out until it is time. Does anyone have any plans?" Bryan whispered.

"Hey Gabriel, isn't that Alistair and Darcia standing in front of the gate over there?" Katrina asked while pointing at the window.

"You are correct. We need to send them away before they steal Amy from us."

"Gabriel, aren't you the smartest, most powerful, and the head of all groups?" Adrian asked.

"Yes, but sometimes I make stupid mistakes. In the end, I do always win," Gabriel, said. The three of them walked downstairs to see what they wanted, even though they already knew. They did not want Alistair and Bryan to know what they were up to. "Hey Alistair, Darcia, and the rest of the family, what brings you to this neck of the woods?" Gabriel asked with a charming smile.

Alistair smiled. "It's such a beautiful night, we wanted to walk around for fresh air and exercise," Alistair said.

"I see Amy is not with you. Is she okay? She did not get hurt, did she?" Gabriel asked.

"She went back to Oregon and we're sort of finished with the whole journey. We were wondering if we could come in and visit for a while since we're family and we do not have anywhere to go," Alistair said, while he held Darcia's hand.

"We are sort of in the middle of something and we don't feel like being bothered with all due respect," Gabriel responded with a smile on his face.

"I guess we could just continue our stroll and enjoy the nice cool weather here," Alistair responded with the same smile on his face. Gabriel, Adrian, Vladimir, and Katrina went back into the castle and continued planning. Alistair rang the doorbell of the castle.

"Alistair, we're busy. Bye now." Before Alistair could say anything, Gabriel shut down all the doors to the castle. "How are we going to get into the castle? He shut down all the doors and windows," Bryan screamed.

"We're going to have to create a diversion. Come on, I have a plan. Let's get back into the car and drive somewhere quiet. Let's get some humans and use them as bait so they can taste the sweet, juicy human blood. Then when they come out, Bryan runs up quickly to where Amy is and jumps out the window and runs quickly. Then we can drive over and meet those two and drive off somewhere private and check to see if Amy is all right," Alistair said.

"Okay, but where are we going to find humans? We're in an area where there aren't many houses or anything," Bryan moaned while walking around to find any humans.

"We still have some time. Let's drive around till we see anything interesting. Hang on. My cell phone is ringing. Hello?" Alistair said, as he was fumbling for his phone in his jacket pocket.

"Alistair, I have changed my mind. Come into the castle. We really need to talk about something," Gabriel said over his call box.

"Really?" Alistair asked in a confused way.

"No, just listen. I've got Amy here, held hostage. I only need her to hear the truth. If that becomes too much for her, I will release her back to the mortal world," Gabriel said over the phone.

"No, I disagree with that, Gabriel. Give Amy to us quickly and quietly and you will never hear from us ever again," Alistair snapped.

"Farewell, Alistair. I know what your plans are next and let me tell you something, it's not going to work because we already ate. "Goodbye," Gabriel snapped before he hung up.

Alistair sighed with frustration. "Let's go around the castle. I remember there was a wooden door that led to the basement and we could sneak into the castle," Bryan said.

"Great idea," Alistair said sarcastically. "He's not human, and he is way better than us put together."

"So, Darcia, have you got any other plans? Just wait outside and see if Amy comes running outside in hysteria or decides to stay inside?" Alistair asked with a snicker.

"Bring it on Alistair," Darcia said, challenging him out of anger.

"You both stop it. You're not helping one bit. Let's drive off for a while so they might think we have given up, but then four hours before it all happens, we disguise ourselves as humans wearing gross perfume and cologne and other stuff. They will get confused and invite us in. The four of us are now going into the car and you guys will have to fight, run, or think whether you are part of this family. Should we bounce, brothers?" Bryan asked while walking towards the van.

"Alistair, he's right. I'm sorry for getting angry with you. I'm scared too," Darcia whispered. As soon as the four guys took the car, Alistair and Darcia made up. They then grabbed each other's hands and ran as fast as they could to catch up with their sons. As soon as they caught the human air, they ran towards it, finding the five boys with a group of eight girls standing against the wall smoking. Alistair and Darcia walked into the nightclub and saw tons of beautiful humans looking at them with interest. "Hey sugar, would you like to have a drink of whisky with me?" a female bartender asked.

"Sure I'm Alistair," Alistair said with his charming, seductive smile.

"Would your pretty lady also like to have a drink with me?" Darcia rolled her eyes and followed them to the bar. She could not stand the smell of whisky and smoke, but she didn't want to stand out, so she inhaled and took a sip. She wanted to spit it out, but instead she forced herself and swallowed it.

"You guys aren't drinkers are you?" The girl chuckled while drinking shot glasses.

"I prefer to stay healthy and live long without any problems that could occur," Darcia said in an annoyed tone.

"Well, it was nice meeting you guys, but I have to work behind the bar right now," said the girl before she walked towards another crowd.

"Alistair, get her to come with us. She is perfect for you know who," Darcia said.

"Um, Jennifer, would you like to come out with me for a moment? I need to ask you a question between you and me?" Alistair said without using his charm.

"I wish I could, but my boss is standing right there staring at me telling me to work or else I'm fired. Please go before he calls security and has you guys thrown out. Look, here is my phone number. I will be finished at midnight and then you and I can talk, but now you really need to go."

They were on their way out finding the car gone and no boys or girls that were out here. *Bryan, where are you guys?* Asked Alistair in his mind.

We are on our way to the castle to use these girls as bait so we can get Amy out of there. Bryan said through his mind. *Just run after us so you will not miss one moment of the excitement!*

"But Bryan…"

"Now, father. Do not waste any time right now!" Alistair and Darcia ran after the trail, and a few moments later they were two blocks away from the castle. They still had six more hours before Gabriel would help Amy with her transition. "So Bryan, are these the girls that were smoking outside the building?" Alistair asked.

"Yes, father. Remember, we are immortals. We can kill these people and disguise ourselves as these girls, walk in and take Amy out of there," Bryan said with confidence in his voice.

"So when do we kill these girls, and where?" Alistair asked.

"We will go our different ways and bite them. When they scream, we will have to suck fast and put our hands over their foreheads and visualize us as them. Now let's go!" When they got out, they followed the plan and got into their female form and walked over to the gate and pressed the button. "May I help you?" Gabriel asked through the call box.

"Um," said Bryan, disguised as one of the girls. "Our car died a block away, and we were wondering if we could use your phone to call for a service?"

"Of course. Please enter the gate and ring the doorbell. A woman wearing a maid outfit came to the door.

"Come in, please." They walked in, finding Katrina and Gabriel standing together holding hands while smiling at the group. The maid walked over to the living quarter and came back with a phone. The disguised group of girls dialed a wrong number and there was no reception. Raymond, who was disguised as another girl, chuckled.

"Oh shoot. Perhaps that number no longer exists." The other group started laughing. Gabriel and Katrina shook their heads.

"Silly, silly little boy. I knew it was your group, but I wanted to see if you guys really thought I was that mental," Gabriel said, as he felt his canines sharpening.

Alistair and the others went back to their original form. "Gabriel, just listen. Amy does not concern you. If Amy finds out about you and her past, how do you think she is going to take it?" Alistair asked desperately.

"mhm. Now please come downstairs and I can tell Amy the truth about who she actually is," Gabriel said as he gestured for Alistair to join him.

"All right, that sounds like a great plan, but I have a better one. How about I take Amy and bring her back to Oregon?" Bryan asked.

"I am afraid I can't let you do that, Bryan. Please leave or I'll have to kill you in front of your precious Amy," Gabriel said with sadness in his eyes.

"Bite me, Gabriel," Bryan snapped. Gabriel's eyes went black with rage and his nails got longer. He started growling and crouching. Bryan sort of did the same thing, only his eyes got red, and he was ripping his clothes, getting ready to attack Gabriel. Alistair heard all the commotion, but Katrina and a few other guards formed a circle around them. Bryan jumped on Gabriel, but he rolled back up and threw him across the room that caused Bryan to smash into the wall. Gabriel got up and got ready for Bryan's attack. Raymond dodged Lucien's punch and jumped over him and ran upstairs to defend Bryan. Gabriel almost killed Bryan when Raymond ran over and jumped on Gabriel's back and bit him in the neck real hard. Gabriel grabbed Raymond by the collar and threw him against the wall next to Bryan. They were both moaning in pain and helped each other up.

"Gabriel, please, Amy is useless to you. You need to earn her affection and have her love you for real or else you won't get anything out of her," Alistair said desperately.

Chapter 8

Misery

Everyone's body healed very fast. Katrina and her group were downstairs fighting Xander, Joshua, Silas, Alistair, and Darcia. "Katrina, let's stop fighting," Gabriel shouted, before hitting the red button on this remote and sent the group flying out the castle.

"No!" Bryan screamed when he landed on his knees on the grass. "I was so close! I was so close!"

"Bryan, would you calm down? I came up and saved you. I could've let you die, but no, I let you heal while I bit Gabriel, and now I feel stronger after that one bite, so please! We need to forget Amy for now. It's over, so let's see where everyone is before we already draw conclusions," Alistair snapped before the others walked over, seeing everyone stand in line thinking about their next plan.

"Well done, Gabriel. Let's get Amy into her childhood room and let her slumber till tomorrow night," Katrina said.

"Hang on," Gabriel said. "We need to assemble all of our guards. I have one question for you. Some great covens know what we're doing and some of them don't like your plan, Gabriel. Are you going to be the person everyone hates in your family?" Katrina asked with raised eyebrows.

"Not really, because I've created all those people and so, and if they were to hate my plan, they'd be able to take me down with full force right at this minute. Since I am the leader, they wouldn't even dare to attack me," Gabriel said with a smirk.

While Gabriel was with Amy and Katrina, Alistair and Bryan were recovering from the attack. Moments later, Bryan and Alistair climbed on the house and dropped through this shutter and opened the door really quietly. Katrina heard them. "Gabriel, send seven people upstairs to deal with Bryan and Alistair," Katrina whispered. The guards had no powers, so in a matter of moments they were all lying on the floor in agony. Darcia and Raymond went through the shutters along with Xander, Silas, and Joshua. Gabriel sent Katrina and another ten guards upstairs to fight them off. Katrina let out a scream that broke some of the windows, so Gabriel ran upstairs to help her.

The five guys were paralyzed on the floor with Darcia in a neck hold and Alistair in a fighting position with five other wolf guards around them. Alistair used his telekinesis to free Bryan so he could save Amy. Gabriel was about to run after Bryan until Alistair tackled him to the ground. Gabriel fell to the floor with Katrina next to him. "Amy, where are you?" Bryan screamed. He found her in her bed, sound asleep. Bryan broke the window with his arms and carried Amy out into the moonlit courtyard.

Alistair and Darcia jumped out the broken window with the four other boys and ran until they got to the van and drove off very fast. "I'll get Alistair some day with Raymond. They'll die at the same time as me!" Gabriel yelled.

"It's okay Gabriel. We all make mistakes and you'll get them. No worries," Katrina said while she helped him back on his feet and looked around, seeing dead corpses and bloodstains.

"Let me go after them right now. I can easily kill them!" Gabriel screamed.

"Wait for the opportunity, Gabe. Maybe you misread something, but just take the time off right now. Oh, and Gabriel, I must tell you something. Amy is with children. The serum Adrian gave her on the airplane caused her to get pregnant," Katrine said as she was shaking her head.

"Why did you use that serum?" Gabriel snapped while glaring at Katrina.

"My goodness, but she will be turning nineteen and I have no idea why she was given the pregnancy serum. With all the medicine everyone around the world gave Amy, I don't understand."

"Well, congratulations now. We should just wait till she finds out and gives birth," Katrina murmured as she walked over to the phone to call Alistair.

"Katrina, we're not speaking to your flock. Bye-bye," Alistair snapped.

"Adrian gave Amy a pregnancy potion and she'll have one baby on her twentieth birthday," Katrina said cheerfully.

"What!" Alistair screamed. Katrina heard the car screech and smiled for a moment. "How did this happen? Who's the father of those babies? Not Adrian, is it?"

"Well, actually, he did put his own blood in the mixture so she'll be a hybrid with the same powers as Gabriel," Katrina said with a chuckle.

"My goodness," Alistair said on the phone.

"Oh, my," said everyone in a chorus except for Amy, still being drowsy and sick.

"What's going on?" asked Amy, knowing something bad was going on and she didn't actually want to know. Since it appeared that serious that everyone seemed shocked, it made her want to ask.

"Hang on Amy, we need to get you to a hospital before something bad happens to you," Alistair said before he hit the gas pedal to go fast.

"Amy, you're pregnant," said Bryan out of fury.

"Bryan!" everyone screamed the whole car.

"What, she has a right to know what happened during the hassle and she should be prepared for the future or else things might not go as planned?"

"Wha…" said Amy, petrified. "I'm pre… pre… pregnant?"

"Yes, you are, and we need to see how bad it is. If it's not as bad as we think it is, you're in for a wonderful surprise on your twentieth," Alistair said, while keeping his eyes on the road.

"I'm going to conceive on my twentieth? Whoa, stop the car. I need to get out and get some fresh air. Please stop, Alistair!" Amy screamed.

"Amy, the sooner we get to the hospital, the better. We don't want to waste any time right now, so let's just get you on that gurney," Alistair snapped.

"Amy, do you have any health insurance or identification on your person?" Darcia asked.

"I'm afraid I left all my stuff in my duffle bag. The last thing I remember, Adrian gave me a shot, and I passed out. They probably left all my stuff at the airport in Oregon, and now I don't have anything. Perfect," Amy moaned.

"Calm down, Amy, it's not as bad as you think it is. You're not even showing right now. You're away from Gabriel and his guards. You're safe in the car and as soon as we get more information you'll be back at home safe with your family and you'll live happily ever after," Alistair said in a soothing tone. Amy scowled at Bryan and looked outside, seeing the interstate and other cars passing. As soon as they got to the hospital, they walked Amy over to the reception desk and asked for a doctor. "Good evening. We need to see a doctor right this minute," Alistair said, while controlling his breathing.

"Wait a moment, sir. Our doctor is indisposed for a while; please take a seat in the waiting room," a dark-haired female receptionist said. The entire hospital looked empty. "Please sit... sir," the receptionist said a bit more sternly. The seven of them walked over to the waiting room and sat down. Moments later, a tall male doctor with short light brown hair and tennis shoes walked over to the receptionist in a white coat. "All right Ms. Martin, the doctor will see you now," said the receptionist.

"Can my boyfriend come in as well, since he's also part of my problem?" Amy asked.

"Ah yes, the new couple have come and follow me into my office." When they got to his office, they took a seat next to each other. "I know why you are here. Here's a pregnancy test and go into that bathroom. Your husband and I will discuss pregnancy stuff," said the doctor.

"We're not married," Amy snapped. Bryan stared at Amy while he had his index finger to his lips. As soon as Amy locked the bathroom, they started discussing forms that needed to be filled out and discussing appointments. When Amy got out, they were both staring at her. "So what does it say?" Bryan asked.

"It's not ready yet. It might take a while for the test to tell me whether I'm pregnant," said Amy as she sat down in the chair next to Bryan.

"I would like to talk to you about what your husband and I have been discussing. When we're finished, I would like you to sign in agreement form," said the doctor.

"What! I'm not going to conceive in Romania, I'm not carrying any babies," Amy snapped.

"Of course you are, but I need to explain some pregnancy stuff. Here is a package filled with information about what you need to eat and how to take care of you and your children. Oh, look, there's a tiny pink plus, it's a miracle!" the doctor said with excitement.

Amy got out of her chair and walked out of the office to her group. "Amy, how did it go and what just happened?" Darcia asked.

"Long story and I really need to go. It's just so upset right now. I just want to go back to Oregon, finish high school, go to college, get a good job and eventually die. How does that sound?" Amy snapped.

"Oh dear, it didn't go so well. I'm sorry, of course. We'll take you back to your home so you can decide what you want to do with it," Alistair said with concern.

"Amy, wait," the doctor, said as he walked towards her. "You need to come back to my office so we can go through these papers you left on my desk, so please come along."

"I don't think so. I'm going to leave back home. Adieu," Amy snapped feeling tears forming in her eyes. She grabbed Bryan's hand and pulled him with her outside to the van.

"Amy, we're very sorry that they got you pregnant, but when you're twenty, you might want to have children and you don't even have to have romantic relations," Bryan said with humor.

"Can we please just go? I want to go back to my parents so badly!" said Amy, teary-eyed.

"Of course. My family is coming out of the hospital and we will go back to Oregon this time without any problems and reunite you with your family," Bryan said in a comforting tone, holding Amy's hand.

"You promise?" Amy asked.

"Yes, and I have this locket I want you to have as a promise of my protection towards you and if you open it up, you'll see a picture of you and me together. If you get lonely or depressed, remember me by this necklace and you'll be happy again and that goes for exams or other stuff," Bryan said with a smile.

"Bryan, I was never mad at you. I am just upset, because hearing that I'll have children in one year isn't my cup of tea," Amy said, feeling herself choke on her tears.

"I'll always see you as the beautiful, sweet woman who I will always love, no matter if you swear at me or smack me across the face. Come on, let's get back on that airplane and see your family again." They kissed each other and cuddled. When they got into the airport and got their money back from the car rental, they got to their gate and boarded the plane back to Oregon.

"Well, Amy, I've already asked you this question. Are you ready to see your parents again? Oh, and Amy, promise me you won't tell any weird stuff about this trip to your parents," Bryan said, keeping his eyes on Amy's.

"Like the whole pregnancy thing, the potion thing, and that I was almost food? It never happened. But what happens if I do accidently tell them?" Amy asked.

"Well, you could write it in your diary or write it down and burn it, but whatever you do, don't tell them," Bryan said, while holding Amy's hand.

"But what happens if I do accidently tell them? Will Gabriel come and kill me? Will I get sent somewhere bad? Will I get a horrific disease? What?" Amy snapped, feeling her blood boiling inside of her.

"It just makes us look really bad and I'm not really supposed to tell you this, but we're not actually going to…" at that moment Alistair covered Bryan's mouth.

"Bryan, you and Xander are switching seats. You and Amy will be able to contact each other through email or post. Xander, please come and sit next to Amy."

"No, dad, I promise I won't mention anything again. Please don't split Amy and me up," Bryan said.

"Bryan, you can't spill any information, no matter how hard it is. One more time and you and Amy will split up till we think you're ready to see people again."

"Yes, father," Bryan, moaned. He grabbed a magazine out of the compartment in front of him and gazed at it till Amy was occupied with a movie. Then he grabbed a brown bag with fresh blood in it and went to the lavatory. When they approached Oregon, they went to the luggage belt and went to the information desk to find Amy's duffle bag. "What does the duffle bag look like, Ms. Martin?" the information desk lady asked.

"It's red and it has blue and purple ribbons on it with my information on it," Amy said.

"I'll send one of our security guards to check for you," she said.

"Is it possible if I went with them so I can immediately see my duffle bag because I've had a very long and horrible day and now I just want to get home."

"I'm sorry, but the airport policy says I can't just let passengers inside the luggage compartment. Next!" the information desk woman said. Amy stepped out of line and waited for them to arrive with her luggage. The security guard didn't seem like he knew what he was doing; by the way, he was staring out into the open. Amy didn't feel comfortable having someone like him to look for her luggage, so she asked Bryan and Joshua to watch her back while she followed him as far as possible into the luggage room. He pressed a code Amy sort of forgot and waited outside till he arrived.

She heard weird noises inside, like glass breaking and him banging his elbows against metal poles. "Aha, there you are, my precious." He grabbed something and walked out. What he came out with was a black suitcase and saw Amy. "Excuse me, ma'am, but what do you think you're doing, stalking me?" the man asked.

"Well… I…" Amy stuttered.

"Nice try. You're coming with me inside and you're going to stay here till I get the squad to take you to the airport jail," the man said.

"Wait…" but it was too late for Amy to get out because he had already locked the door. Amy saw an air duct in the corner and piled all the suitcases on each other, and stood on the top one and pushed her way through the air duct and followed the tube. It was dirty, and it smelled like gasoline. "Yes, she's in the luggage compartment. You had better arrest her for trespassing," the man said.

She crawled until she saw an opening. She crawled and crawled till she came and looked down, seeing nobody. She let herself fall and landed on her hands and knees. She ended up in an office where people lost their luggage and walked out very fast to where everyone was and walked through the exit. "There she is," the security officer yelled, pointing at Amy. Amy made a run for the train and jumped on before the doors closed. Amy was panting like crazy and leaned against the door, closing her eyes. As soon as she opened her eyes, people were staring at her like she was having a heart attack.

When the doors opened, she ended up in the final concourse and stepped out. She took the escalators up and saw her group standing there with her duffle bag and backpack. "Amy, what happened there? Let's go before something bad happens. There's a taxi waiting for you, Bryan and Alistair outside. Some of us are already saying goodbye to you, Amy, and by tomorrow Bryan will leave you. Well, boys, give her a big hug and I will also be leaving going back home so we can sort through some things," Darcia said. Amy felt like someone had stabbed her in the stomach with a knife. "Well, farewell Amy, we really loved hanging out with you in this world and enjoying your company. You still have another seven lessons to go till you're finished with school and you've got pretty good grades," Raymond said.

"Thank you all so much," Amy said, half sobbing.

"Take care Amy and remember the good moments and never the bad parts and I've taken some pictures of you and Bryan walking along the borders and eating ice cream," Darcia hugged Amy really tight and kissed her on her cheek and stepped back.

"Well, come along Amy. The taxi is waiting and your parents are longing to have you back home," said Alistair. Amy walked between Bryan and Alistair to the taxi and drove off, waving goodbye to everyone. "Hey Amy, I know how hard it is for you to say goodbye to people who've been there for you for like ten months. I'll stay with you till tomorrow morning, hugging you farewell." Amy was looking outside the car weeping softly so nobody would hear her, but Bryan did. He didn't want to bring up Amy's crying in front of the taxi guy. When they got to the house, Athan, Emma, and Ginger had a banner. Amy got out of the taxi and walked over to her family, hugging them.

Amy felt like crying and cried on her father's shoulder and hugged Ginger and her two dogs. Athan shook hands with Alistair. "Thank you so much for taking care of Amy, but what happened to Gabriel? I thought he wanted to have her back?" Athan asked, as he looked at Alistair and then at Bryan.

"Plans have changed. For now, she will finish her junior year and then we'll see what Gabriel has planned," Bryan said, holding Amy close to him.

"He's not going to harm us, right?" Athan said, causing Alistair to close his eyes and shake his head while mouthing no.

The four of them walked into the house to talk about what had happened and drank wine and water while smiling at each other. Amy felt like crying and walked up to her room. She covered her face with her pillow and cried. Bryan ran up and hugged Amy real tight and told her everything was going to be okay. He stayed up in her room until Alistair came in. "Well, Bryan," Alistair said. "I'm taking off back home. I know I told you we'd be staying here in the distance so Gabriel can't get her. We're really going back to Romania and stay with them. I expect you to be back tomorrow so you can let Amy continue with her life and get good grades," Alistair said. He then walked out the door and ran towards the woods.

"Bryan, what was he talking about? Is that what you were going to tell me on the airplane?" Amy asked, feeling tears falling down her cheeks.

"We're going to Romania. We'll keep Gabriel in Romania until you're twenty, and we might see you when you give birth to your children," Bryan murmured. Amy cried again for another few minutes until Emma ran upstairs.

"Sweetie, oh my poor baby. Come here to mommy," Emma whispered. Bryan left the room and walked downstairs to talk to Athan to talk to him about Amy. "Hey Amy," Emma said. "Guess what? Larry called, and he's on his way with Jenna bringing you a welcome back cake. They should be here any moment and we've set up a room for Bryan. Your teachers called to tell me you're doing really great at school!" Emma cheered.

The doorbell rang. Emma ran downstairs. "Amy, your friends are here! Hey you guys, Amy's not really in a good state, so could you try to make her happy?" she asked. Jenna smiled, holding a white-sheet cake and placed it on the kitchen counter.

"Oh course, Mrs. Martin. She can have the first square of this white sheet cake," Jenna said with a chuckle. Amy walked down with a tissue and teary eyes and ran over to Jenna and hugged her tight.

"Hey Amy, we ordered you this white sheet cake with cheesecake filling and it says welcome back. We haven't told the school yet, so both you and the school will be in for a big surprise. We're happy you're back in Oregon. I've about died when you left," Jenna chuckled.

"Thank you both," Amy whispered. She hugged Larry and walked over to the dining room where everyone was sitting around waiting for the cake to be served. "Well Amy, to make things less sad when Bryan leaves, you'll be going back to school tomorrow. It'll be hard, but it's best that way, so you'll get adjusted fast. I've already made your lunch and we're going to go through your books fifteen minutes before you leave for school. Bryan, I just want to thank you again for taking care of Amy and give Darcia and your brothers my regards. After cake and after your friends have left, I would like you to go upstairs to your room and try to sleep. Bryan can stay with you and wish you good luck tomorrow," Athan said before he brought some empty plates to the kitchen.

Amy felt empty and drained and couldn't blink or do anything, and sat there with the cake in front of her. When everyone was finished, Jenna and Larry drove off and Bryan carried Amy up to her room and sat in her office chair, handing Amy her pajamas. "So, want to watch some TV or a movie?" Amy's eyes began to water and covered her face in her hands. "Come on, Amy, it's not as bad as you think. You should actually be mad at me for letting Gabriel get you pregnant and remember when we laughed at you when we departed for Australia?" Amy continued crying till twelve o'clock. Her parents came up and hugged her. "Good night Amy and you too, Bryan. Do you need any sleepwear?" Emma asked.

"No, I'm not sleeping tonight. I'll just watch over Amy while she sleeps and go back to Romania in about eight hours. So Amy, maybe you should try to sleep. I'll sing a lullaby to you." He was singing his song and used his sleeping powers on her. The next morning, Aaron came into the room to wake her up at seven.

"Hey Amy, why don't you come downstairs and eat some breakfast with Bryan before he takes off. He'll drive with us to your school one last time. Come down in pajamas and you can sit next to him. We're eating pancakes." Amy felt her stomach cringe and walked downstairs and sat next to Bryan, who was already finished with his breakfast.

"Good morning Amy. While you were asleep, I organized your backpack and looked at your schedule. You won't have to worry about anything, so just eat a pancake and go to school," Bryan said. Amy grabbed a flapjack and some syrup. After breakfast, Amy went up to her room to get dressed. "Come on Amy, let's go before you're five minutes late, but the principal will make an exception for you. Jenna will walk with you upstairs!" Athan yelled.

When Amy and Bryan got into the car with Athan, they drove off to school. Amy and Bryan hugged each other tight and kissed for a minute and waved goodbye to each other. Amy burst into tears and crouched down. "Amy, please don't do this to me," Bryan mouthed before Athan drove off to the woods area and dropped Bryan off. They both shook each other's hands before Bryan ran off. Jenna ran over to Amy and grabbed a tissue for her. "It'll be okay Amy, just breathe in and out. Come on," Jenna said.

They walked into the school and walked up the stairs, and opened the door. "Welcome back Amy!" screamed the whole school, with confetti flying through the school. Amy was surprised and grabbed hold of Jenna's hand and walked through the crowd of students and teachers till they saw the principal holding a little cupcake with Amy's picture on it and a candle. "Go ahead Amy! Blow, I'm so sorry about your grandma and Jenna emailed me, saying that we had to plan a welcome back party for you," the principal said with a smile on her face.

Amy couldn't talk, but smiled and nodded and looked around, seeing happy faces. She sort of forgot about Bryan. Hours later, everyone was allowed to go back home due to Amy's welcome back party. Everyone waved goodbye to Amy and walked back home. She saw a group of teenagers smoking tobacco. "Hey, do any of you guys have a cigarette?" Amy asked.

"How old are you, little girl?" asked one of the guys, wearing a leather jacket and aviators.

"Nineteen and I need to smoke because I just got dumped and need something," Amy's voice was shaky.

"Here, have one and here's a lighter. Hey, tonight we're having this awesome party and you should totally come. There will be a lot of people and alcohol." said another guy.

"Sure I'll be there. See you guys there." Amy murmured. She continued to smoke and walked back home. When she got home, her mother hugged her. "Hey baby, what are you doing home so soon?" Emma asked.

"We got out because of my welcome back party," Amy said.

"Amy, you smell like cigarette smoke. What were you doing?" Emma asked.

"When I left, I stopped for a smoke with some friends out of grief and I'll be staying out at Jenna's tonight. I need to be with a friend tonight."

"Sure Amy, did you ask Jenna?" Emma asked.

"Yeah and her mom is okay with it and I'm going to take a shower and grab my stuff," Amy snapped.

"First you're going to tell me why you were smoking behind our backs and why are you upset, because Bryan left you?" Emma asked, keeping her gaze on Amy.

"Mom, the reason I was smoking is because Bryan left me and I'm not over him. I can't lie to you. I was planning on going to a party and getting drunk," Amy whimpered. Suzanne sighed and shook her head.

"The answer is no, Amy. Go upstairs." After Amy closed her door, she walked over to her window and burst into tears and went to grab her phone when she found a note.

Dear Amy,

I am deeply sorry about Gabriel and your life without me, and I want to let you know that I will always think about you, even when I'm hunting. Awkward I know. Anyway, if you say my name, you and I can contact each other through thoughts. In a year, we will be celebrating your twentieth birthday and, hopefully, your children will turn out so beautifully. I'll always be there for you if you want me. Alcohol is so gross and I prefer blood. Anyway, love you always B.

After Amy read the letter, she thought of Bryan and burst into tears again. *Amy, is that you?* Bryan thought.

"Bryan?" Amy asked with a shaky voice.

Wow Amy, congratulations on finding out one of your powers that you own.

Bryan! Oh my goodness, I miss you! Amy thought through her mind.

I'm sorry Amy, but just focus on your work and when you're finished, you can come back to us real soon unless there's another suitor. I'm in the family room reading the family law book and everyone around the world is staying at the castle, discussing plans. Alistair just entered, so I have to go, but see if you can contact Darcia. Just say her name and see if she replies, but we'll talk later. Bryan thought.

She walked over to her bed and turned on the TV. Her favorite TV show was on and she decided to get her mind off of Bryan. When a commercial came on, she decided to think of Darcia.

Hey Amy, Bryan told me about your new gift and he's thinking about taking Gabriel's place and you have to be here in one year. Darcia thought through her mind.

Yes, anyway, I miss you guys so much and I can't stop crying. Amy thought through her mind.

It'll pass soon. Just think about your TV show and about getting good grades so you can come back to us. I will help you and Bryan will soon be reunited. Darcia thought.

Thanks Darcia. Amy thought. *I'm not ready to get married to an older guy and you know that Bryan and I were meant to be together?*

Yes and so does Alistair, and that's what we're about to discuss, so I have to go now, but good luck tomorrow!

Amy's mom opened the door. "To whom were you talking to?" Emma asked. "I understand how this whole situation makes absolutely no sense. When Gabriel dropped you and Ginger off at our home, we were not sure what to think." Amy looked at her confused. "Now that you are back, I do not know what else to think. I am glad to have you back home," Emma said before she smiled and kissed her on top of her head. The next morning, Amy woke up and went to school. As she was walking through the hallways, she saw a picture of her and this guy named Carl who had a crush on Amy during his freshman year as prom king and queen. Heather and her group laughed at Amy as she walked passed them, but she ignored them and walked over to the principal's office.

"Excuse me, ma'am, I don't mean to sound hysterical, but since when did everyone already pronounce the prom king and queen?" Amy asked, while controlling her emotions.

"That's not possible Amy; prom isn't till another two months." Amy showed a picture of the poster she took with her cell phone.

"You should ask the janitor or someone else to take it down for you because I'm kind of busy with some paperwork," the principal said.

"Do I need to get my mom in here? Or are you going to get it down for me because, in my eyes, I find it stupid, embarrassing, immature." Amy snapped.

The principal shook her head. "Amy, I understand that you are back from your little family gathering, but that is no way to talk to me. I will have the janitor take them down before the day is over," the principal said. Amy nodded and forced a smile.

"Thank you ma'am," said Amy sarcastically, and walked out the office. She walked into the girls' bathroom to call up Emma.

"Hello Amy, is everything okay?"

"No. As I was walking down the school corridors, I saw a poster of Carl and me for homecoming king and queen. The principal refused to take it down."

"You want me to call her up and talk to her?"

"Please come and pick me up from school if I call you next for backup."

"We'll see Amy. Now go back to your classes and make good choices."

"Bye." Amy hung up and walked over to her calculus class.

"Amy, you're late but I'll exempt you from this week. Please take a seat," the male teacher with dark hair and dark eyes said.

"Hey Amy, do you have a boyfriend in your life?" asked a male student next to her.

"No, but let's pay attention to the teacher before we get into trouble."

"I broke up with my girlfriend to get back to you. Jenna told me everything and Heather heard everything and wants to make your life a living hell at school."

Amy pretended she was interested in calculus until the bell rang. Amy stormed out of the school and pulled the same male student with her. "Tell me everything while I was indisposed." He thought about whether to tell Amy the truth or to lie to her.

"While you were gone, Heather was sort of happy about you leaving, and the teachers didn't believe a word you said. Jenna was kind of sad after you left, so she decided to hang out with Heather." Amy listened to everything the boy was talking about and walked over to Jenna, who was grabbing her books from her locker.

"Say Jenna, could I talk to you for a moment?" asked Amy. "It's rather important."

"Sure," said Jenna. They walked back to the spot where Amy and the boy stood. "So what did you want to talk to me about?" Jenna asked with a smile.

"While I was gone, did you tell Heather about what was going on with me?"

"Why do you ask? So what if I did? She does seem nicer to you."

"So you did tell her?" Amy snapped knowing that her best friend told her worst enemy her biggest secret ever.

"Yeah, it accidently slipped out because while you were gone I didn't have anyone to sit with. Heather and Sharon were sitting together, so I thought I would sit with them because if the teachers see you sitting alone or smoking alone, you have to make appointments with the school psychologist and I don't have time for that. The principal told your mother she wants you to see her so you can discuss the loss of your grandma."

"Jenna," Amy moaned. "What else did you tell her? And what's up with the posters? Why couldn't you go with me to the principal and ask to take them down?" Amy whimpered.

"I wanted to be cool sometime and Heather thought it would be funny to see your picture with Carl."

"Aren't we friends or something?" Amy asked. "A good friend like me would stick to her friend's side and defend her from anything."

"Nothing else, I swear." Amy scanned Jenna's facial expression for a while before they walked back inside.

"Ahem Ms. Martin," said the principal. "May I have a word with you in the office? Jenna, go over to your next class." As soon as Amy was in her office, she took a seat in front of her desk. "I just received a call from your mother. I took the posters down. Next Friday we'll be having a parent-teacher student conference and we can discuss what we can do with you. Your grades are pretty good and maybe we can already give you a senior test for you to do."

"Really, I would love to do that," Amy said feeling excited.

"Anyway, you still have twenty more minutes of psychology." Amy walked out of the office with a smile on her face and skipped over to psychology. She saw Heather going through her purse. "Hey Heather, may I talk to you for a moment?"

Heather rolled her eyes as she was going through her bag. "Okay."

"Did you, by any chance, hang up those posters on the wall?" Heather didn't respond. "Heather, did you put those posters on the walls everywhere?"

"I think you and Carl make a good pair," Heather said with a chuckle.

"What did I do to deserve this, Heather? Did I steal your precious item? Did I ever call you a bad name? Did I put red paint on your pants to make it look like you got your womanly times?" Heather cut Amy off before Amy continued. "Whatever Amy. I have to go inside." She opened the door and closed it behind her. Amy was getting furious as she walked into the classroom and took a seat next to Jenna.

"Thanks for joining us, Amy," the female teacher said. "Now class, let's get back to page one hundred and ninety and answer these questions. When you're finished, bring your notebook up to me and you may leave for your next class." After Amy finished, she walked up with her notebook and walked over to a classmate, Martha. "Hey Martha, want to hang out after school today?"

"What! Me! Of course, I've been waiting for someone to ask me to hang out."

After school, Amy and Martha got into Amy's car. They went over to the mall. When they got to some of these teenage clothing stores, they bought a pair of jeans and a shirt and went over to another store and bought more stuff and went to a couple of shoe stores. Amy dropped Martha at her house before she went home. Athan was inside waiting for her.

"So Amy how was your shopping trip? Next time please let us know. I was worried about you," Emma said. Amy sighed and took her clothes and backpack up to her room. After she placed her stuff on the floor, she saw a note on her bed.

Dear Amy,

I really need you to listen to our story. When you were born, your mother, Arabella, died in childbirth, leaving both you and your sister in my care. Because of being an ancient immortal with no experience of childcare, I placed you and your sister up for adoption in the care of Athan and Emma. The fact that you are now pregnant with children due to a mixture of many serums you have taken, I look forward to your return to Romania. Love, your father Gabriel

Amy looked shocked and confused at the letter and shook her head. She grabbed the letter and threw it in her trashcan. Emma went into her room. "Hey Amy, I thought about it for a moment and I know you're still getting adjusted to our lives again," Emma smiled and hugged Amy.

"Thanks mom. Now I must finish my homework and go on my evening walk with our doggies," Amy said. Emma left her room

My goodness where did that come from? I should contact Bryan to see what he's up to. Bryan, Bryan, Bryan, Amy thought as she sat down and hugged her pillow tightly.

Amy! What on Earth are you doing? Bryan snapped in his thoughts.

Amy sighed and composed herself. *I received a letter from Gabriel telling me that both Ginger and I are his daughters. Is this true?* Bryan remained silent. *If it is true, what must I do?* Bryan cleared his throat, thinking about what he was going to do in this situation.

Amy, could you give me a moment? Alistair and Darcia have just entered the living quarter and I will get back to you. Bryan ignored and blocked out Amy's pleas. Alistair and Darcia rolled their eyes at him.

"What?" He snapped. "I never mentioned anything regarding Gabriel or Ginger or Amy and their relationship," Bryan snapped. Alistair sighed before he sat down on one of the red velvet couches.

"Gabriel is trying his best to win over his children, but the silly old fool should never have given them up. He could have put the maids and servants in a trance with his powers. I think he probably did not ever care about having children in the first place," Alistair murmured. Darcia sat next to Alistair and placed her hands on his.

Darcia cleared her throat. "I find this whole situation ridiculous in the first place. Amy just met all the covens? Why did he not want Ginger to join us?" Darcia said before Bryan got to his feet.

"What should we do about this situation?" Bryan asked. "I feel the need to help out, but I am not sure if that would help." Alistair shook his head. "What?"

"I have many mixed thoughts going through my mind and I am not sure which sounds smarter. I feel the need to bring Amy and Ginger back to Romania and help her with her mental transition back into Gabriel's life. On the other hand, he did willingly give them up to humans," Alistair whispered.

As Alistair, Darcia, and Bryan were creating a plan, Amy sat on her bed, trying to calm herself. Ginger entered the room and sat down next to her. "Did I hear you talking to someone, Amy?" Ginger asked. Amy shook her head and rolled her eyes. "I want to tell you something weird that I have been dealing with during your absence, Amy," said Ginger. Amy looked up at Ginger with curiosity. "I have been having weird dreams and also the same dreams about a man with dark hair and you were in my dreams, and how we are actually his children." Ginger shook her head. "I don't know what to think anymore." Amy placed her hand on Ginger's hand and smiled. "It may not have been a dream at all, Gin," Amy said. Amy grabbed the note from the trashcan and handed it to Ginger.

Ginger's eyes went wide. "Amy, what is this?" She gasped. "Who is this, Gabriel?" Ginger looked scared at Amy. "Is this true?" Amy smiled as a response to all of her emotions and shrugged.

"I have no idea anymore, Ginger. This whole trip did a giant number on my psyche, that I do not know what to think anymore. From unexpected traveling to injections to drinking potions, and now this? And that I will soon become a mother within a year?" Amy said with a chuckle, causing Ginger to look disgusted.

"Amy," Ginger whispered. "Are you…" Amy nodded. "Who's the father?" Amy chuckled, as a response to her question.

"I don't even know that part, either." Just then, Emma called them both down for dinner. After dinner, Ginger and Amy returned to Amy's room. Once it was going on eleven in the evening, Amy and Ginger both got under the blankets. Suddenly, there was a loud noise in the garage that caused the dogs to bark.

When both Amy and Ginger snuck down slowly, the dogs looked like they were going to attack someone or something. Ginger slowly opened the door and turned on the light. There was nothing to see. "Quiet, you don't want to wake up our parents," Ginger whispered. When she closed the door, Amy saw a human figure standing in front of them. "Amy! Ginger," said a shadow with a feminine voice.

"I'm not seeing or hearing this," Amy whispered to Ginger. The figure walked closer to them. "Audrey?" Amy snapped, remembering her from Australia. Audrey smiled and beckoned for them to come closer. Ginger and Amy kept their distance.

"Rumors back home in Romania were spreading about Amy carrying children. Congratulations to you, my sweet child," Audrey said cheerfully. "Gabriel sent me out to protect and care for you. It seems that Alistair and his group just up and abandoned you." Amy looked around to make sure none of the neighbors were around. Audrey smiled at Ginger. "And look at you, Ginger Ambrose! How beautiful you look. You have his eyes." Ginger looked over at Amy in disbelief.

"Amy," Ginger said. "Shouldn't we just deal with this person inside before someone sees us?" Amy smiled and nodded.

"Let's go up to my bedroom before someone wakes up. Can I get you something to drink?" Amy asked as Audrey entered the house.

"Do you have fresh blood for me?" Audrey asked as she looked around at the modern human house.

"No," Amy said. "We do have a hospital that is about twenty minutes from here," Amy said as she gestured to the door. Audrey smiled and shook her head.

"I can't leave you two alone. Gabriel's orders. Why don't you two join me for a nice evening snack?" Audrey asked with a smile that turned stern. Amy sighed.

"Let me put some clothes on. Ginger, please join me upstairs. Audrey, please try to be quiet," Amy, whispered before she walked off. Audrey nodded and sat on one of the dining room chairs. A few minutes later, Amy and Audrey got in the back seat of the car and let Ginger drive Athan's car.

When they arrived at the hospital parking lot, Ginger pulled the key out of the ignition. "We'll wait right here, so you can go and sneak into the blood bank," Amy said. Audrey shook her head. "Seriously?" Amy asked.

"Gabriel's orders. I cannot let you two out of my sight. "Please, come and join me. Perhaps you two might want a little sip?" Audrey asked. Once they got into the blood bank, Amy and Ginger sat outside while Audrey sucked down a few blood packs. "Much better," Audrey whispered. "Now, I will not stay with your human parents, but I will keep my eyes out for you from a distance," Audrey said as they left the hospital.

Audrey took off a few minutes later. Amy and Ginger managed to get a few hours of sleep. The next morning, Athan woke Amy up for school. "Hey Amy, were you up last night and did you drive somewhere?" He asked. Amy forgot about how she had to go with Audrey to the hospital.

"Um, no," Amy said as she saw Ginger enter the dining room, pouring herself some coffee. Amy quickly ate her oatmeal and left the house before she would get more questions thrown at her.

When she arrived at the school parking lot, it was an overcast day. Amy parked the car and quickly entered the school, to avoid any suspicious questions from other students that were staring at her. Amy saw Jenna at the lockers.

"Hey Amy, do you remember that tonight is a parent-teacher conference?" Jenna asked excitedly. Amy looked surprised at Jenna and shook her head.

"Today? I totally forgot about that. I will have to call my parents and see if they can come," Amy moaned with irritation. Jenna chuckled and looked around.

"Say Amy, I was wondering if you and I could talk somewhere private?" Jenna asked.

"Sure Jenna," Amy said. Both girls walked over to an empty part of the hallway.

"Amy," Jenna started. "I want to apologize for my whacky behavior. I did not want to give you the feeling of me betraying you. Would you like to go homecoming dress shopping with me? I'll drive us to this newly designed mall. We can then get something to eat, if you like? And if you don't have someone to go with, I would be happy to go with you?" Jenna asked, waiting for Amy to respond. Amy smiled.

"Sure, Jenna. Since I have been gone, I have had nobody ask me to the dance," Amy said with a chuckle. That evening, all the students and their parents were gathered, waiting to have a chat with their guidance counselors and the principal. The principal beckoned for both Emma and Athan to enter her room. "Mr. and Mrs. Martin, I must say how impressed I have been with Amy's dedication to her work. High marks in her assignments. I was wondering if she would like to take some advanced exams during the summer and consider college?" Athan gave Amy a pat on her back. "Congratulations, Amy." Her parents cheered. "How does that feel, Amy?" the principal asked.

"Great, I guess," Amy whispered, remembering how those guys were the ones that did her homework. "Mom, dad, if I promise to keep you two in the loop of my plans tomorrow, could I go dress shopping with Jenna?" Her parents smiled and nodded. The next morning, on a Saturday, Jenna showed up at Amy's house to pick her up.

When Jenna and Amy got to the mall, there were sales going on in many stores. Both girls walked over to each store to try on different dresses. Since Jenna has dark brown hair and green eyes, she decided to go with a long dark green dress with ruffles and a Greek design on the bottom. Since Amy had light brown hair, she decided to go with a long blue dress with short sleeves. After they paid for the dresses, they went to look at their shoes. Around five in the evening, they walked back to Jenna's car, finding Adrian and Daniel leaning against the door, smirking at Amy.

"Hello Amy," said Adrian, "We heard that Audrey came over as some sort of chaperon." Amy glared at them both and pushed Jenna behind her. Daniel looked over at Jenna and smiled.

"I think it's time you both left now," Amy snapped while holding onto Jenna's arm, feeling her heart racing.

"Amy," Jenna whispered. "Should I get security?" Jenna looked scared and started to run inside of the building. Amy kept her cool.

Amy scoffed at them. "Remember the code of all immortals, boys? There will be no spectacles in front of humans. Otherwise, you will be in trouble with Gabriel." Once the security guard walked through the doors outside, Adrian and Daniel ran off and disappeared. Amy smiled at Jenna, who looked horrified at her.

"It's okay. I handled the situation with no problem." Jenna shook her head with fear.

"Who were those guys, Amy?" Jenna asked, while looking around to make sure nobody was going to attack her from behind.

Amy smiled and beckoned Jenna into the car. "Nothing you ever have to worry about." Jenna's hands were still shaking as she was trying to get the key into the ignition. After Jenna dropped Amy off at her house, Amy waved Jenna goodbye and entered the front door. The rest of the evening, Amy modeled her dress in front of her parents and Ginger.

The next morning, Amy walked to school with her agenda and purse without her books. "Good morning students, welcome to the end of the year exams. Don't be scared or worried, since they're all multiple-choice questions. You may go to your classrooms without your backpacks. Good luck and next month, a week before the end of the year, you'll receive your grades in the mail. You may be dismissed," said the principal over the intercom. All the students walked into their classrooms and took their seats till the teachers came in with a stack of paper. "Welcome. Once you have all received your exam, you may start. There will be no breaks. Good luck," said the teacher before she sat down at her desk.

Chapter 9

The Conference

On Monday morning, Amy woke up to get ready for her prom date with Steven, who called her up the morning of prom. Even though she felt reluctant to go with someone who hadn't spoken to her for a while, she decided to see what he had been up to. She took her dogs out for a jog with them. When she reached the forest, she felt happy and upbeat about life. When nobody was around, she squealed really happy, and spun around in circles and threw tennis balls around for her dogs to chase after. Two hours after her outing, she went back home to eat her brunch.

"Morning baby, how are you feeling today, getting ready for your dance tonight? Need some help with your hair and makeup?" Emma asked in a concerned manner.

"Maybe, so anyway. I was thinking about calling Steven up to see what he's planning," Amy said excitedly.

"Um, what?" Emma responded. "Steven? You're going with Steven?"

"Yeah, is there a problem?" Amy asked in a confused manner.

"No, it's just, he broke your heart and six months later you're back with him? What happened to Larry?" Emma asked.

"Yeah, I know, isn't it a coincidence?" Amy scoffed and walked up to her room to take a shower.

"Hey Amy, you are a boy magnet. Ginger said as she walked past her and sat on the edge of Amy's bed.

"Not now. I have to get ready for the dance tonight," Amy said while going through her closet.

"It's one in the afternoon. Why does it take you seven hours to get ready? So, how did you do with your calculus?" Ginger asked in the presence of Emma.

"It's only one day when I get to relax and sit back and not have to do anything."

"Guess what I get to do today?" asked Ginger excitedly.

"What?" Amy asked in a bored tone, since she did not really care what her college sister gets to do.

"I get to pick out covers and bed sheets and look at all sorts of crazy things."

"Have fun with that. Can I ask you something?" asked Amy.

"Sure, what seems to be the problem?" asked Ginger curiously.

"There's no problem, except for I might be getting back with Steven, but I want to be with Bryan or someone else outside of these people. I don't want to go to a motel with Steven and do it."

"Follow your heart Amy, but don't force yourself because, he wants to," Ginger said while looking over at Emma.

"I know. Now leave so I can take a shower without having someone in my room."

"Whatever, Amy," Ginger said before she walked downstairs. When Amy got out of the shower, another hour had passed. Amy walked downstairs in her robe and slippers. She grabbed an apple and took a big bite out of it and walked over to Ginger's room. "Hey sis, you should come to the dance this evening," Amy said.

"No thanks, I am a lone wolf who loves to watch re-runs and do yoga and walk the dogs on their evening walk" Ginger said while keeping her focus on the television.

"Everyone would be happy to see you after a year after you had graduated."

"No," snapped Ginger. "Now leave me."

"Suit yourself." As Amy walked back to her room, she saw her three teenagers with skateboards and caps skateboarding alongside her house. "Hey Ginger, I just spotted your boyfriends."

"Funny," Ginger said sarcastically. When Amy got to her room, she got her hairdryer and put her curling iron on the sink and dried her hair. Then she got her curling iron and sprayed hair spray in it and put her hair up in a bun. She walked downstairs to eat a sandwich before makeup, dress, and brushing her teeth.

"So Amy?" asked Athan. "Are you excited about tonight?"

Not really, thought Amy. "Of course I've been waiting for this day for a few months."

"Is your date going to give you the night to remember?" Athan asked while smiling at Amy before realizing the deal he made with Gabriel when she was just a few days old.

"I hope so," Amy said with a smile.

"So who's your date, by the way?" Athan asked while admiring Amy and trying to remember her growing up.

"Steven," said Amy.

"The guy who dumped you? Why are you guys getting back together again?"

"I don't know. He seemed stressed out and depressed about his breakup with his other girlfriend and needed a shoulder to cry on," Amy said with a sigh.

"By the way, your hair looks beautiful, and I can't wait to see you when you're ready. Will Steven give you a corsage?"

"I hope so. Anyway, got to continue getting ready for this night." She walked up to her room and grabbed a razorblade to shave her legs and moisturize them. At five o'clock, Amy walked over to the bathroom to wash her face and put her makeup on. At seven, Amy waited on the couch, waiting for her date to arrive. Thirty minutes went by and still no Steven. Amy was getting annoyed and worried that he wouldn't show up. She called him and got his answering machine. Then Jenna called her up.

"Hey Amy, why aren't you at the homecoming dance tonight?" Jenna asked in a concerned tone.

"I have this feeling that Steven chickened out and stayed home," Amy moaned.

"I'm sorry, sweetie, would you like one of us to drive you over to school?" Just then, the doorbell rang. When Amy opened the door, she saw Steven holding a blue corsage in his hand and putting it on Amy's wrist.

"Smile," said Emma, with a camera in her hands.

"Mom, no embarrassing pictures," Amy moaned.

"Sorry, I have to," Emma said, causing Athan to chuckle. Amy yanked Steven out of the house and they got into his car and drove off to the prom.

"Wow, Steven. For a second, I thought you weren't going to go with me."

"What can I say? I'm a pretty mysterious guy," Steven said before he started the car.

"Does your phone work or something? Because I tried to call?" Amy asked, while looking at her phone, seeing how many times she had been trying to reach him.

"Yeah, I missed it while shaving," Steven said while keeping his eyes on the road.

"Thank you for the corsage. How did you know what color my dress was going to be?"

"Lucky guess." Amy felt weird and uncomfortable, but she had this smile on her face. When they got to the school parking lot, Steven held the door open for Amy to get out and locked the car doors. Amy grabbed Steven's arm, and they walked into the building and up the stairs till they got to the gymnasium.

"May I have this dance?" Amy asked with a smirk on his face.

"Of course," Steven said with this charming smile that caused Amy to stare at him in a confused way, not realizing that Steven had never went out dancing with her when they dated in the past.

"And again, I am amazed at how you can dance. I never knew you could dance."

"And again, I am a mysterious guy," Steven responded with a smile.

"Oh, look, there's Martha sitting there with a depressed look because she doesn't have a date or it bailed on her," Amy said with compassion in her voice.

"So what have you been up to lately?" asked Steven.

"Not much. I am so happy those exams are behind me. Now I can wind down till senior year," Amy smiled while slow dancing.

"Attention boys and girls, I have a special announcement for everyone. The teachers and I were discussing how we could make this a special night for everyone. We were going to have a dance competition and the winners of this dance will be receiving a twenty-five dollar coupon to any store of a person's choosing," said the principal, who was also dressed up in her white floral gown and silver shoes.

"Boo!" yelled some of the students.

"The winners of the next dance get a package of candy bars. Thank you," the principal stepped away from the microphone and walked over to some of the parents.

"Those are lame prizes to hand out, but who can say no to chocolate? Are you all right, Steven? You look a bit pale and your eyes seem glassy?" Amy asked, turning her gaze back to Steven.

"No, I'm fine. I need to talk to you outside the gymnasium," Steven asked while rubbing his eyes.

"Sure." When they walked outside, Heather and her two friends walked by, smirking at Amy.

"Amy, if I wasn't Steven, would you still be interested in me?" Amy laughed.

"What are you talking about? You are Steven." She continued to laugh.

"Please stop laughing. I need to tell you something big. I am not Steven. Remember the immortal you met in Australia, with Logan and the other ones?"

"Yeah, I believe his name was Caleb," Amy said with a smile on her face that slowly faded.

"Right. Could we take this outside the building in the parking lot because this is something nobody can blurt out?" Caleb asked while looking around, making sure there was nobody watching them.

"Are you on drugs? Are you some weird creature or something?" Amy asked while feeling uncomfortable about being outside in the dark with Caleb.

"Sort of, Amy. Can I trust you?" Before he finished his sentence, his phone rang.

"Hello," Caleb said over the phone, feeling jittery and anxious.

"Caleb, come back right now!" the voice on the phone yelled.

"But..." Caleb said, slowly backing away from Amy, walking toward his car.

"Now!" the voice on the phone yelled.

"Caleb? You're the kid who was flirting with me in the hallway?"

"I guess so," Caleb said. Amy took a few steps back and started running back inside the school. She was looking around the room to see if she could spot Jenna or anyone who she could trust.

"Amy! Over here." Waved Jenna. "So, why were you with Steven? I thought you and I were going together," Jenna said in a concerned way.

"Well, I'm here now," Amy, said.

"Are you okay? You look like you exercised before coming here. Where is he?"

"He and I are through again. Can I talk to you for a moment in the girls' bathrooms?" Amy asked, while controlling her emotions.

"Is this about peer pressure or anything like that?" Jenna asked.

"No! I have to go right now. I can't say anything anymore."

Amy grabbed Jenna's arm pulling her in the direction of the bathrooms. "What is this really about?" Jenna asked.

"Jenna, you're my best friend, right?" Amy asked while looking around to make sure nobody was in earshot.

"Ever since kindergarten and middle school," Jenna said with a smile.

"So I can tell you something, no matter how stupid or idiotic it sounds?"

"Try me. I promise not to laugh," Jenna said while walking with Amy into the girl's bathroom.

"Okay, here I go. Remember that time I left school?"

"Yeah, it was something about your grandma? Is she okay?"

"Well, I didn't go because of my grandma. She's been dead for three years."

"So why?" Jenna asked with a concerned look.

"You promise not to leave this friendship or tell anybody or laugh or make a mockery of it?" Amy asked with worry in her eyes.

"Just shoot. How bad could it be?" Jenna asked with eagerness in her tone.

"Can we take this out into the parking lot?"

"Why, it's so cold and dark outside."

"Because this isn't what you say in a girls' bathroom where girls walk in and out."

"Fine, let's go outside where we might get killed or kidnapped, but who cares?" Jenna said sarcastically.

"Very funny Jenna." When they got out of the building, Amy stood still for a moment and relaxed.

"What?" Jenna sighed while looking at Amy as if she was going crazy.

"Okay. I am not who you think I am."

"Is this a riddle?"

"No, I was gone because a group of immortals wanted to meet me and ask me to join their group, but suddenly this guy wants me to marry him and he's like about a thousand years of age."

"Huh?" asked Jenna with a questioning look on her face. "What are you talking about?"

"Wait a minute; so anyway, we traveled around the world so other family members can meet me, etcetera. They gave me potions to keep me alive, but they were actually powers so I could protect myself."

"My goodness, you're on drugs, I knew it!" Jenna said while backing away from Amy.

"Jenna! Please!" Amy said hysterically.

"You know what? I still want to be friends with you, so no worries, but what you just told me. I don't know, I mean, half of me is in shock and the other half is like, what the heck did I just hear? Next week, we're going to hand in our books and receive our test scores at home and some students will say goodbye when they're leaving school. Others will wish each other a nice summer vacation."

"Will we still see each other and hug each other goodbye?" asked Amy.

"Hopefully, but maybe after the summer vacation we can hang out with each other and chat about homework and teachers and so on. For now, I think we should either go back inside or go home because this was too much for me to handle," Jenna said, feeling herself getting irritated.

"Really?" Amy snapped, causing Jenna not to respond.

"Well, I'll see you next week while handing in our books," Jenna said.

"I'm going to shove off and walk back home and go to sleep," Amy said, calling up Ginger to have her pick her up from the school parking lot.

"See you later Amy!" They waved each other goodbye. Amy saw Heather and her friends standing by the door. Ginger honked her horn before Amy turned to walk to her and got into her car. When she got back, everyone was still awake and her parents were playing chess with one another. "Hey Amy, where's Steven?" asked Athan, muting the television.

"He and I broke up," Amy said as she sat down on the couch.

"Sorry to hear that. Did you have a good time?" Emma asked while holding a magazine in her hands.

"Sure. I'm going upstairs," Amy moaned. When she got upstairs to her room, she saw Caleb sitting on the edge of her bed, staring at her. Amy gasped and locked the door.

"Amy, I know everything and I want to tell you that I won't harm you whatsoever. I am the son of Gabriel. I'm sure you have thousands of questions you'd like me to answer."

"Yes, I do have a thousand questions," Amy snapped while keeping her voice down.

"Go for it. Before you continue, you look beautiful in that dress. You should wear it on the airplane or at one of those fancy dinner parties we'll be having."

"Who are you, and what are you?" Amy snapped with anger in her voice.

"Well, I am a shape shifter and hunt humans in the woods. I am a male and love females my age or younger. When I was a human, I went to top schools and got myself a scholarship to become whatever I wanted to be till Gabriel found me. He couldn't have sons of his own and he's been spying on me for a long time and helped me to get good grades like I did to you and I can walk in the sun and shadow."

"Why did you come to school as an ex-boyfriend?" Amy snapped.

"I'm going undercover as a high school student to get closer to you. My airplane leaves tomorrow. From the moment I saw you, I fell in love with you, Amy. Bryan hates my guts because I refused him to become one of us till we met Alistair and Darcia. Slowly, they wanted kids of their own and got their five boys."

"I'm flattered, but Bryan and I were meant to be together when we left for Australia and other places. I don't know what I'm doing in life right now. I can't make any plans anymore because I am actually Gabriel's daughter. Correction, Ginger is also his daughter, too. We are just one big immortal and shape-shifting family, correct?" Amy snapped while taking her heels off.

"He hasn't told you?"

"What?" Amy asked with irritation in her voice, as she tried to balance herself while taking off her shoes.

"Oh my goodness, when he told you he and you were getting married, he implied me. He is such an idiot who has no brains, but he just got caught in your beauty and he wants you and me to be together." At that moment, Amy walked off to the bathroom with her pajamas and came back still with her makeup on. Caleb was watching her every move. "Amy, I am sorry for everything that has happened to you. From Gabriel abandoning you to you getting yanked out of your human routine. Have you not noticed anything different? Like how your hearing is amazing, your eyes are strong, dreams, thoughts, or even feelings?" he asked. Amy sighed.

"I don't know what to believe anymore or if I should trust you for entering my bedroom. Yes, I have had dreams of being in a beautiful castle. Yes, I have sharp eyes and ears. Yes, I can also walk outside in the light with no problems at all," Amy, snapped. Caleb nodded and waited for Amy to finish.

"Your mom, Arabella, was human before she became immortal. Have you heard of her, Amy?" Caleb asked. Amy shook her head. "Perhaps it is not the best time for me to mention this, but then again, there never is a good time to talk about important topics, such as your life or even Ginger's," Caleb said while walking to the window.

Amy sat down in her chair and watched Caleb, just staring out into the darkness. "Aren't you worried about Alistair, Darcia, or even Bryan showing up to protect me? You did mention that there were problems between them and you?" Amy asked. Caleb turned around to face Amy and smiled while shaking his head. "Gabriel would not allow any harm to come to me," Caleb said with a smirk. "I must say, on a side note, that you are taking this quite well. You have not had any fainting spells or trauma, correct?" he asked. Amy smiled and laughed.

"What makes you think I haven't, Caleb, if that is your actual name? I went numb. I get yanked out of my comfort without my sister being present on the journey. Some unknown variable tells me that I am his daughter. I get lied to by a group of traveling companions. I was scared and crying a lot, but nobody can really tell since I kept it mostly to myself. Bryan noticed my emotions. Suddenly, I get asked by an ex-boyfriend to go to prom and it turns out to be my father's son, so does that make us siblings?" Amy asked with her eyes darkening with rage.

Caleb faced the window again and sighed. "None of this makes sense to me, either, Amy. I really thought that me coming here to tell you the truth would help, since Gabriel should never have given either you or Ginger away. Yet, it happened, and he wants you back now. I understand where Katrina gets her anger. She was not told the truth, either. Gabriel's wife, Arabella, dies and now he has a new woman who also knows nothing about him. I can't help the situation that much by just apologizing on his behalf. I do want to mention that once the time comes, whether it's before you are fully pregnant or after, that once you are back in your routine of being in Romania again, everything will make more sense. With this, I will bid you farewell for now. Perhaps we will cross paths again," Caleb said and jumped out of the window.

Amy felt stunned after what had happened. She didn't know whom to turn to. She didn't want to keep bothering Bryan, Alistair, or even Darcia with her constant complaints. Amy tried to take her mind off of the situation by listening to some of her music and letting herself doze off into a deep sleep.

The next day, Amy got to hand in her schoolbooks to the library. At seven thirty, Amy got into her car and drove off to school. She saw Jenna, Martha, and some other classmates standing outside the building with their books. "Is the school open yet?"

"Yes, so Amy, where were you yesterday?" asked Jenna.

"I don't exactly know. So why are you guys waiting outside the building?" Amy asked.

"We just arrived and we're about to walk inside." As soon as they got to the library, there was a long line for every student to hand in their books. "We should've arrived an hour early. Oh well, it's not like we're doing any work," Jenna said.

"That would be six thirty and there's no way in heck I'd ever wake up at six thirty to drop off some books," Amy said with a chuckle. Thirty minutes later, there were still five more students to go.

"This is not right. How long does one need to drop off books?" asked Amy.

"Well, when you drop off your books, you get a school keychain and a bottle of water to start the day off, and then we have an assembly about this week," said the vice principal as she walked by.

Another twenty minutes had passed and twenty kids were still in front of Amy. "Oh come on already, is someone intentionally slowing us down or something because it seems a bit too long for students to hand in their books and receive some things?" Amy moaned. All the students and faculty turned towards Amy. She smiled cutely and crouched down. Five minutes had passed and Amy finally got to hand in her books.

"Well, congratulations Ms. Martin, we'll be looking forward to seeing you here in twelfth grade," said the principal, while grabbing a keychain out of the box.

"Thank you, ma'am." She walked out of the room to the gymnasium. There were still some balloons and party stuff from yesterday. Just then, Amy got a text from an anonymous caller.

Dear Amy, I'm looking forward to seeing you. Some girls have already picked out your wedding dress and I must say it looks quite beautiful. Anyway, I just wanted to let you know that I'm thinking about you on my way to the airport. I'll be spending the night there since my airplane leaves at six. Love, Caleb.

After Amy put her phone away, she sat at the top of the row so she could leave the building as fast as possible. She thought of Bryan.

"Bryan," Amy whispered.

Yes Amy?

Caleb came over to me last night as my fake prom date and told me about Gabriel and my mom. This is all getting too much. Amy thought.

What? Did he try to do anything or hurt you, Amy? Did he ask you to invite him, or did he just waltz into your room? Bryan thought.

When I got back from prom, he was up in my room and he just kept talking, Bryan. Amy's facial expressions of her communication caused some of the other students to look over and whisper to each other.

Whatever you do, Amy, do not return to Romania. It will only make things worse. Go with your human parents on your summer break and my family and I will take care of the situation from here. Bryan thought.

Caleb sat down as Steven, next to Amy. "Amy?" whispered Caleb, "What's going on?" Caleb asked with a smile on her face.

"Caleb?" whispered Amy with horror in her eyes.

"Ahem, Ms. Martin, are you disrupting my end speech?" asked the principal.

"No, Ma'am." She covered her face.

"Anyway, tomorrow we'll be…" continued the principal.

"Amy! If you're talking to Bryan, leave it to me to get rid of him," Caleb whispered, trying to avoid drawing attention to himself.

Amy! Get away from Caleb Amy! Bryan snapped in her thoughts. Amy walked out of the gymnasium and ran out of the school building into her car. She drove off to the airport. She went over to the information desk with a shocked, scared face.

"Ma'am, you need to calm down and relax. We'll get you some help," said an airport personnel.

"No!" Amy snapped. "I don't need help, well actually I do, but it's not in anyone's concern."

"Is there a problem here?" asked a security guard who was in the area.

"Nope, no problem." She saw Caleb walk in with a suitcase as a prop and walked past Amy. "Caleb!"

"Yes, I'm Caleb, but I don't know you," Caleb said with a confused look.

Amy sighed and tried to regroup. "I can't go with you or anyone back to Romania. It does not feel right." Caleb looked at her with frustration and grabbed her hand and took her away from the other passengers.

"Gabriel needs you back, Amy. You are not a regular person. You have his blood and his lifestyle. Come back home before something worse can happen." Some passengers walked by, staring at them. Amy focused her attention back on Caleb and released herself from his grip.

"What am I to think and say, Caleb? This whole situation makes no sense. I am scared, tired, angry, frustrated, and a little hungry. I can't just up and leave for Romania," Amy whispered as she felt his strong hand around her wrist again.

Caleb stepped back and shook his head. "You are your mother's daughter, Amy. You get your temper from her." Amy was so angry that she smacked him across the face. Caleb recomposed himself and walked off, leaving Amy in the middle of the check-in area. She stood in line, waiting for the flight attendant to call her, and checked in. "I'm sorry, Ms. Martin, but your flight isn't till tomorrow," said the attendant.

"Is there a place I can stay at?" Amy asked in a pleading manner.

"We can't just check you in right now, but we can provide a nice hotel that is in the first concourse and you may stay there if you'd like."

"Okay," Amy sighed and took her stuff off the belt and walked in the direction of the hotel. She got out her phone and dialed her house.

"Hello, this is Ginger. Amy, what the heck are you doing? Mom and dad just got out a search party for you. Get your butt back home so they can stop eating sugar and jumping around crazy," Ginger snapped.

"Ginger, I'm in a messed up situation and I need your help! Please come with me to Romania and protect me."

"So you're in the airport," Ginger said in an irritated manner.

"Yes, I'm renting out a room till it's time for me to leave and then I will see what will happen to me. If it's either dying or getting tortured. Please!" Amy pleaded.

"Amy, I'm already on death row for telling you. I am expected to go, so I'll tell mom and dad that you're staying over at Jenna's and I'll call Jenna to tell her. Wait for me at the airport so we can stick together like sisters," Ginger snapped before she hung up.

"Thanks Ginger." After Amy got off the phone, she left to look around the shops and to get herself some snacks. An hour later, Ginger arrived at the airport and walked over to the hotel that Amy described.

"Amy, thank goodness I found you before mom and dad. So let's get some food." When they got their food and sat down, Amy began talking about the conflict between Caleb and Bryan. "After that, they were bickering like crazy and I ran out of the school screaming. Caleb is in a different part of this airport, or maybe in this hotel. Ginger, could you somehow stop this nonsense? It's really killing me," Amy said in a hushed but anxious tone.

"What would you like me to do? Be an older and responsible sister who looks after her younger sister," Amy said sobbing softly so nobody would pay attention to her. Ginger sighed and wrapped her arms around Amy.

"Amy, it'll be okay in the end. It's like in those fiction books you read. First it's boring and okay, then it gets scary and dangerous, and eventually the main characters always survive. That'll be us and we'll live happily ever after."

As Amy was looking around, she noticed Caleb sitting in a booth two booths ahead of her and her sister. He looked up and pretended they didn't know each other. "Ginger," whispered Amy.

"What?"

"Caleb is sitting two booths down eating human food."

"I think it's best for us to leave right now," Ginger whispered and grabbed Amy's hand. "When I say run, we should run, okay?" she said, while keeping her eyes on Caleb.

"What?" asked Amy?

"Run, now!" Ginger yelled. Both of them grabbed their purses and ran as fast as they could back to their rooms. When they got there, they locked the door and hugged each other on the bed.

"Ginger, I'm scared!" shrieked Amy.

"It's okay Amy. We are safe. I will not let you get harmed whatsoever, do you understand?" Amy nodded in fear and waited for a moment. "Amy? Maybe we should drive some place else."

"Are you kidding?"

"With this jerk here, you won't be safe, and it's best for both of us to be away from everybody. Get your purse and follow me out of the hotel. We're not dealing with actors this time; we're dealing with real killers. If we're going to do this, we're going to do it right. Now follow me slowly and if you see any of them, start running. If they get hold of you, fight!" Ginger said, Amy nodded again and followed Ginger. When they opened the door, there was no one in sight. They crawled on the floor until the coast was clear. They grabbed each other's hand and walked down the stairs to the lobby.

They saw passengers walking around looking happy, tired, and sad.

When they got to another information desk, Ginger showed them their passports and handed them two five hundred-dollar bills that Ginger kept in her safety deposit box under her bed. "Please, ma'am, we're not criminals or anything. We need to go to Romania for some personal reasons."

"Let me check the monitor. There's a three o'clock flight, but there's only one seat left."

"We'll take a seat."

"That'll be about sixteen hundred dollars."

"We only have a thousand. Could you just spare us six hundred bucks because it's sort of an emergency to get on this plan?" Ginger asked pleadingly.

"I'm deeply sorry, but I can't let you on this airplane. Please step aside. Next!" screamed a blonde female flight attendant.

"Hey Amy, I've got a plan. Follow me this way," Ginger whispered. They walked up to a group of six college students that were waiting in line.

"Hey y'all, are you going somewhere?" Ginger asked while using her powers of persuasion.

"We're going back to Odessa to finish our last years of college," said one of the male students with blue eyes and blonde tussled hair, wearing a college hoody.

"I go to college in Oregon. Here's the deal, brother. You got six hundred bucks on you?" Ginger asked, feeling the energy pouring through her body.

"Are you into drugs?" the same guy asked, while looking confused at both Ginger and Amy.

"No, but we need to get on this airplane to Romania for some personal reasons and we only have a thousand dollars and the check in lady won't let us through."

"We got two dollars each to spare on college."

"Please, sirs, we really need that six hundred bucks or else we'll both suffer some great consequences if we do not make this important family gather," Ginger said with another tactic of her powers. The guy looked dazed and confused and snapped out of it.

"Well, okay. Here is three hundred from me." He looked over at the other students, who grabbed their wallets and handed both Amy and Ginger six hundred dollars.

"Oh, thank you!" Ginger said. Then she and Amy walked back to the check in and handed them the money.

"Welcome aboard. Here's your gate number and time and enjoy your flight," said another ground attendant.

"Wow Ginger, you rock!" Amy shrieked. They walked through customs and security and ran over to their gate. They had another two hours, so they sat there and looked around. When the moment came when all passengers boarded the plane, Ginger and Amy were placed separately from each other till Ginger used her powers again to allow a fellow passenger to switch seats with her.

"When we arrive at the airport, we need to get to that castle and take care of the situation," Ginger said reassuringly.

One of the flight attendants came by with some drinks. "Would you like anything to drink?"

"Sure, two sparkling waters with lemon and ice blocks." As they received their drinks, Caleb was sitting on the other side of the plane.

"Ginger, don't look to your left!" They were both frozen till the next drinking load came around. Eight hours seemed to pass very slowly. Caleb walked off and Amy felt like screaming, but shoved her emotions down.

When he got back, they stared at the seat in front of them. They were in shock and horrified when he smirked at them. They still had another four hours to go until they landed in Romania. Caleb fell asleep and the two girls walked into the lavatory with their purses and sketched out a plan. They couldn't smile or scowl. They swallowed some relaxation pills and walked back to their seats. Caleb was gone, and they sat down, staring some more ahead of them. Four hours seemed to pass a bit faster than they thought and sooner or later, they ended up in Romania. They walked through the exit to find Caleb hugging an old woman and they walked over to her car.

Ginger and Amy asked for a cab to drive them without paying. Amy added some drama to get him to say yes. "So, what brings you two to Romania?" asked the taxi driver.

"Family business," Ginger said in a fast manner.

"That's nice," said the taxi driver. When they arrived at the castle, they got out and rang the doorbell.

"Amy? Ginger?" asked Hildegard, Gabriel's maid.

"Yes?" Ginger responded.

"Come in through the gate. Alfred will come and open the door for you."

When they got in, Gabriel, Katrina, and Bryan, and a few other members that Amy was never introduced to were standing there.

"Hildegard will show you your rooms. When you're finished, please come down to the conference room. When they arrived at their rooms, Hildegard gave them a purple and pink dress they could borrow.

Gabriel cleared his throat. "The meeting has begun with Amy and Ginger Ambrose. This is very awkward for me to say, but why so early? We would've been happy to send Daniel and Lucien to pick Amy up. Ginger. Your mother died at birth and I took both of you into my care and put you in a foster home. Want to know why? I couldn't handle the pressure of taking care of the two girls. When you were two years of age, your foster parents came and took you into custody. When I held you in my arms, I whispered I'd find you and gave you some special gifts. You will be my little minions. My son, Caleb, saw you two lying there cooing and squeaking and fell in love with you, Amy. I loved both of you as daughters and wanted to reunite with you. Amy, maybe you are a bit too young to handle the big boy thing. We will have a vote next Monday with everyone around the world to see what everyone thinks about this problem. For now, you girls will stay here in this castle. I will call everyone that you two are here," Gabriel said in his powerful, strong voice.

Gabriel turned his attention to Amy and Ginger. "Amy, Ginger, I know you are in a terrible mess, and I would be happy to turn your frown upside down. I won't pay you money or buy you clothes to win your happiness, but Caleb really loves you, Amy," Gabriel said.

"But what about my happiness, my future, my life?" Amy asked in a pleading manner.

"I was getting to that. If it makes you feel any better, we got you into a top quality online school and the message will be sent in a year."

"But what about my happiness back then? I started off as a normal girl and turned into some monster."

"It passes really soon," Gabriel said, without any emotion in his voice.

"I don't know what to say. Is there any loophole or something that could get me out of this mess?" Amy asked, before she looked at Ginger in a pleading manner.

"I'm thinking. I could assemble everyone over the computers and cameras and discuss this with them. If it really makes you feel any better, I could see if I could bend the rules for you," Gabriel responded, as he shifted his gaze to Ginger.

"Really?" Amy asked in a high-pitched tone, not realizing for that moment how awkward she sounded.

"Yes, I'll try!" Gabriel said with a smile, playing on Amy's emotions.

"Thanks," Amy said. She walked out of the room to find Ginger talking to Lucien and Vladimir. "Hey Amy, we're going to talk about your future?"

"Yes."

Gabriel cleared his throat again. "Attention members of this castle. Tonight we'll be having a conference about Amy and Ginger. I've already informed everyone around the world and they'll be a part of this conversation and they'll arrive on Monday. Thank you."

"Well, got to go and talk about your future. Catch you later," Lucien said. When they got to the conference room, there were cameras from leaders around the world.

"The meeting will start in five, four, three, two, one, go. Welcome to another talk from Gabriel," said Gabriel. "Amy and

Ginger arrived four hours ago and Amy doesn't want to get married. We need to vote. I will call your name and you will say yes or no. Rome: No; Athens: Yes; Australia; Yes; and Romania: Yes. Well, it looks to me that Amy will get married and continue online." Gabriel said with glee. "Amy Ambrose, you will get married to Caleb next Tuesday. Congratulations!"

Amy screamed in agony and ran up crying into her room and locked the doors. She cried and cried for about four hours straight until she heard someone knocking on the door. "Amy, may I come in?" asked Bryan in a glum voice, knowing that he had caused more trouble instead of fixing her problem.

"Go away!" cried Amy.

"Please let me talk to you about this."

"Just leave," Amy whimpered. Bryan managed to unlock the door and ran over to Amy.

"Bryan, I thought you were going to rescue me, not leave me for Caleb!"

"Have patience, Amy."

"Patience for what? Your friends or sisters are taking me shopping and decorating for the beautiful ceremony!"

"Amy!" shouted Bryan, "I have a plan, but you can't know about this."

"What?" sobbed Amy.

"Just be you. Go with the flow for a while and don't let anyone know you're okay," Bryan whispered.

"Why?" asked Amy, sobbing.

"Because then they know we're up to something."

"Could you tell me the plan right now?"

"Sorry Amy, it's confidential for now." He walked out the door over to their car and drove off with everyone in his group in it. Daniel walked into the room where Amy was sobbing in and sat next to her.

"Amy, are you in the state of talking, or do you want to be left alone?"

"No. Stay. My life is totally ruined, and I'm not acting like those other teenagers who overreact."

"Life will be better when Caleb and you are married. You might feel awkward or uncomfortable walking down the aisle with me and Gabriel next to you. For now, just rest and relax till the ceremony. Guess what? Caleb and you are the same age and we've just discussed it. You and Caleb are going to one of the best schools next year and you will visit us during the holidays, plus your human family and friends," said Daniel.

Amy cried again, so he left and Ginger came in.

"Gosh, Amy, I am so sorry for you, but Bryan has a plan going on, but I can't tell you even though we're sisters."

"Ginger, we never lied or kept secrets till this huge nightmare started. You know what? I'm going to kill myself so I can end up somewhere peacefully!"

"Amy, they shut down all the doors and windows. Bryan will take care of things, but I don't know about the rest of them."

"This is not fair! When I was in third grade, I told myself that I was going to live a happy life and now I'm engaged to someone who's going to turn me into a monster!" Amy whimpered.

"Didn't you hear me? Bryan will take care of things. Just play along and wait for the opportune moment," Ginger snapped.

"Till when? What if he's too late?"

"I don't know."

"What do you mean, you don't know?"

"Look Amy, whatever they're doing right now is probably helping you out of this mess, so please do me a favor and shut up." Amy ran out of the room in tears and ran somewhere where nobody would see her cry. She ran into Gabriel.

"Amy, are you okay? You're not crying over the decision we made?"

"No, these are tears of joy!" Amy responded sarcastically, while drying her eyes with her right sleeve.

"Ah, it's good to see you happy about this plan. I need to talk to you about your wedding details. Did you want anything special prepared for the ceremony?"

"No," Amy said feeling herself feeling weak and out of body.

"Perfect! We will have the ceremony in our chapel that is a twenty-minute walk from here. It's on the other side of where we are, only we need to set it up."

"Gabriel, I don't think I can do this?" Amy whimpered.

"What do you mean, my dear?" Gabriel asked with sympathy in his voice.

"This marriage. This is not how I wanted to spend the rest of my life. I wanted to explore the world on my terms and end things on my terms," Amy said as she felt her throat hurting by the second.

"You're having second thoughts. No worries, Caleb will propose to you in ten minutes and I'll take a picture of you receiving the engagement ring."

"Please understand me. I don't want to go through with this. Is there any other way of postponing this thing?" Amy begged.

"I'm afraid not. I've tried talking to them, but they would love to have some excitement ever since I transformed Caleb. Just breathe in and out and you'll be fine. Anyway, are your human parents coming?" Gabriel asked with a smile on his face.

"I haven't told them yet," Amy moaned, feeling defeated at this moment of her life.

"Well, you better contact them now before it's too late," Gabriel said as he was creating the whole wedding ceremony.

"Where will I spend my ceremony?" Amy asked as she was looking around to see if Alistair, Darcia, or Bryan were around.

"Here. We have a little cottage for you two lovebirds. You will stay there for one month and come back and you will fly back to Oregon and continue the rest of your vacation, do your senior year and come back to us," Gabriel said cheerfully.

Amy walked off and bumped into Caleb. "Amy! Oh, I am so glad to see you. You ready Gabriel?" Caleb asked with anxiety in his voice.

"Of course, my son," Gabriel said as he handed Caleb an engagement ring and placed his hands on Amy's shoulders, watching Caleb getting on one knee.

"Amy Rose Ambrose, will you marry me?" he held out this wedding ring and slid it over her finger.

"Well, Caleb, I'm very flattered to hear someone in my life ask me this question, but it's a bit too soon," Amy responded sarcastically.

"Gabriel, you did talk to her, didn't you?"

"Yeah, but she's going through some marriage anxiety. She'll get over it soon," Gabriel said, as his hands remained on Amy's shoulders.

"Caleb? You asked him to talk to me about this?" Amy snapped.

"Yeah. I understand, but you've got to believe me!" Amy threw the ring on the floor and ran off to the entrance.

"Somebody please help me!" screamed Amy, "Please!" She was banging on the door and windows, but there was just silence everywhere. "Please!" Ginger walked down the stairs into the kitchen to drink some water.

"Amy! What's all this commotion?" Ginger screamed out of fear.

"Caleb proposed to me and I rejected him!"

"Oh no Amy, this is part of our plan. Now you're just acting stupid. March back up to Caleb and accept his proposal or else you will end up in a much worse situation!" Amy crouched down and tried to hold in her emotions.

"Can't you marry him, Ginger?" Amy asked as she felt tears forming in her eyes.

"Me? He doesn't love me for some weird reason. I mean guys at school always smile and carry my books for me, but I'm no girl for Caleb. I'll walk you upstairs and you can try it again," Ginger said before she grabbed Amy's hand and yanked her up to Caleb and Gabriel. "Amy just felt her stomach cringe, and would like to redo it again."

"Amy Rose Ambrose, will you marry me?" Amy looked at Ginger and she nodded.

"Yes, Caleb," Amy murmured. He smiled and slid the ring on her finger and hugged her.

"I knew you'd change your mind, Amy!" Gabriel took several pictures of Amy and Caleb in different positions. After that, Ginger walked down for a drink. She sat down and looked at a homeowner magazine when she saw a picture of Caleb's face smiling. She read his article about how a lot of girls love him and would give up their lives and valuables just to be with him.

What a joke thought Ginger as she was looking through the pages where she saw tons of his pictures in front of cars and walking dogs and kissing female models. What is so awesome and spontaneous about his fellow? He's just a regular model who seems to love attention. Maybe I should show this to Amy. While she was on her way, she bumped into Katrina.

"Who are you supposed to be, the maid?" Katrina snapped before she realized it was Ginger.

"No, I'm Amy's sister Ginger, who's going to be here for the marriage ceremony."

"So the rumors are true. You know Caleb actually likes you better than Amy. I mean, you should see what that girl was wearing today," Katrina said with a chuckle.

"Don't talk about my sister like that. I mean, I agree that I am prettier than she is, but she is my sister and I love her deeply," Ginger snapped.

"You're just as bad as she is. Anyway, I need to go down to the spa and relax. See you later."

"Oh, heck no!" Ginger screamed before she grabbed Katrina's hair and smashed her face into a wall. Katrina dug her nails into Ginger's face. Ginger jumped on Katrina and bit her on her neck and sucked her till Katrina couldn't move.

"Don't ever mess with the Ambrose girls!" She walked up to Amy to tell her about Caleb. "May I come in, Amy?" Ginger asked politely.

"Sure," said Amy in a monotone voice, seeing Amy sitting on the edge of her bed, staring at the ring Caleb had given her.

"Wait till you see what I've got to show you," Ginger said with a chuckle as she opened up the magazine.

"What?" Amy asked out of curiosity.

"Read page number six through twenty. You'll find all the information about your future husband!"

"What happened to your face?" Amy asked in a high-pitched tone.

"Katrina. She's such a mean person when it comes to this," Ginger snapped, as she touched her face softly.

"She's not going to be my maid of honor, is she?" Amy snapped before she grabbed the magazine from Ginger's hands.

"No. All the teenage girls around the world whom we know will be flower girls and bridesmaids. Gabriel will walk you down the aisle. I will be your maid of honor and help you with your dress. Athan and Emma will arrive in two days just in time for the wedding," Ginger said. Even though this was a serious moment, Ginger couldn't help but chuckle at the whole ridiculous situation.

"Oh, man, they're not mad at me, are they?" Amy murmured.

"Mom and Dad started acting weird again, so it's hard to tell."

"Oh, goodness, I feel terrible and messed up. Are you sure Bryan will take care of things?" Amy asked, feeling her heart pounding hard inside of her.

"Absolutely!"

Chapter 10

The Transition

When Ginger left the magazine with Amy, she walked over to her room to pick out a dress or look through the dress catalogue. "Knock, knock," said Daniel, the same brother of Gabriel. "How's Amy doing? I heard her scream."

"She's just having a hard time adjusting to her new life. The truth always hurts," Ginger said while placing a dress on her bed.

"So I've heard. So, looking at a dress for the ceremony?" Daniel asked.

"Yes. They all seem very beautiful and elegant. What did you say your name was?" Ginger asked while keeping her gaze on the man.

"Daniel," the man said, with short black hair that was parted sideways. His black eyes and marble complexion caught Ginger's attention.

Ginger smiled and nodded. "I am Ginger, as you know. I must tell you, and perhaps Gabriel is listening through the walls, but this whole situation makes no sense to me. Why did Amy even go through all the traveling? What makes her the special one in the family?" Daniel shrugged.

"You would have to ask Gabriel. He is the main father figure of our group."

Ginger sensed Amy and shook her head in despair. "Daniel, I have a feeling this whole wedding planning is a complete disaster. I never even heard of Caleb and only just briefly saw him at the airport in Oregon," Ginger whispered. Daniel nodded in agreement.

"I understand, Ginger. I was completely against Gabriel going about this plan. Having children, placing you both up for adoption, now Caleb, and now with Katrina. Arabella was a beautiful soul. So loving and beautiful in many ways." Daniel smiled and looked at his watch. "I had best get ready for the ceremony myself. Good luck to you both." He smiled and left the room.

Hours went by and the entire living quarter was transformed into a wedding chapel. A priest that also looked like one of Gabriel's members stood at the altar, getting his book and stuff ready for Amy and Caleb's wedding. Ginger remained upstairs with Amy while Katrina, Claudia, and Audrey were helping Amy prepare her hair, makeup, and the dress. Ginger did have to admit that Amy looked very beautiful as a bride. Then she shook her head and remembered how ridiculous the whole situation was. When the time came, Ginger grabbed both her and Amy's bouquets and let Amy walk out of her bedroom and down the flight of stairs, where Gabriel was waiting in his tuxedo.

Gabriel smiled at Amy and saw Lucien holding the wedding rings in his hands. Amy stopped at the end of the stairs with fear in her eyes. "I can't do this," Amy said in a hoarse voice. Gabriel shook his head and extended his hand.

"It's time," Gabriel said. "Please come down, Amy." Amy overcame her rage and stepped down, taking Gabriel's hand and walking with him toward the altar. The bridal theme was being played as Gabriel's group sat in a small gathering, watching Amy and Gabriel in awe. Caleb was standing at the head of the altar, smiling at Amy. Ginger took her place across from him as Amy's maid of honor and accepted Caleb's ring for Amy to give to Caleb at the end. Before Gabriel released Amy, he put his hands on her shoulders and nodded.

"You look like your mother when she and I got married years ago," Gabriel said before he leaned in and kissed her cheek. "Reverend, please proceed," Gabriel said before he released Amy and joined his group. Amy kept looking around through her veil to see where there was an escape, but it seemed impossible. The reverend was talking about eternal love and how joining families was a blessing. Amy was not paying attention until the reverend stopped and both he and Caleb looked over at Amy.

"Ms. Ambrose, could you repeat what I just said?" the reverend asked with a slightly frustrated expression. Amy looked up at him in fear and shook her head. "Okay, I guess we'll start with Mr. Ambrose." Caleb repeated the words that the reverend had used and turned to Lucien for Amy's ring. Amy felt a slight tug on her arm and felt a cold ring slide on her finger. Amy started crying, which caused the audience to go into awe. "Now it is your turn, Ms. Ambrose. Please repeat after me." Amy looked over at Gabriel with tears in her eyes. Gabriel smiled and nodded.

Repeat the words, Amy. Amy heard his voice in her head. *We can remain in this position for hours, but you will comply with this simple request.* Amy inhaled and exhaled before she repeated the words. Instead of turning toward Ginger, Amy remained frozen in anger and let Ginger hand the ring over to Caleb instead. The reverend finished with that Caleb could kiss the bride. Caleb pulled the veil over Amy's head, grabbed her by her neck till they suddenly heard a loud bang outside of the castle with several explosions following.

Gabriel got up in anger and his eyes went black with anger and his nails were sharp. The other members joined in and they all hovered behind Gabriel, preparing for another attack. Katrina walked over to both Amy and Ginger. "You two finish the ceremony!" She shrieked. Caleb faced Amy, but Amy was already halfway through the room, running towards the doors toward the patio. Amy opened up and ran outside with her wedding dress still on. She took off her white heels and ran in the direction of the woods.

Amy ran without looking back and noticed a full moon was shining down on her. Suddenly, she started feeling very hot and clammy. She wiped the sweat off of her forehead and felt her heart pounding fast. Then she started feeling this feeling that she had only read about in books. Her body was changing. The snapping of her bones in her legs was transitioning into a crouching position. She started feeling this intense thirst building inside of her. She looked at her nails, which looked long and sharp. She felt her canines growing fast and hard. She felt her teeth and pricked her right index finger on one of her teeth. Amy started crying and heard Ginger and Caleb's voices behind her. She remained in a crouching position. Ginger looked at her with fear and put her hands over her mouth. Caleb looked at Amy as if he had seen a ghost.

Amy cried as she looked up at Ginger. "What's happening to me?" She screamed. In the distance, she heard screaming of Bryan, Alistair, Gabriel, Darcia, and Katrina. Amy kept crying till she stopped and placed her hand on her throat. "My throat is burning," she said as she got up and took some steps backwards. Ginger looked over at Caleb with horror.

"Amy," Caleb said. "Your time has come. You're in the transitioning phase of your life. You take a lot after Gabriel." Amy started to calm down and felt like she was going to faint. "Those potions that you had taken were not to protect you from us, but to help you with your transition for your nineteenth birthday," Caleb said as he continued explaining the whole situation from her birth till now. Ginger felt her rage and started crouching as well, feeling her bones snapping and her eyes burning and her canines growing. "And the same went for Ginger, though I have no idea why you had to skip the potions," Caleb whispered as he shook his head, watching both girls in pain.

"Amy!" Bryan screamed as he ran in their direction. "Amy, what happened? Are you okay?" he screamed. Amy started running away, but tripped over her feet. When Bryan had arrived, he looked at both Amy and Ginger in horror. He then looked at Caleb, who gave him a soft smile and hissed at him. Caleb responded with a growl and they both crouched down in a fighting position. "What happened?" Bryan snapped as his eyes went black. Caleb didn't respond, which caused Bryan to lunge at him and pin him down. Caleb pushed Bryan off of him, causing Bryan to fly against a tree.

Caleb stood up and got into a fighting position again. "What makes you think I did anything?" Caleb growled. Bryan regained his composure and walked toward Ginger, who was whimpering. "They are Gabriel's kids, you know. He is the one who turned them into everyone. Perhaps Ginger still has Arabella's human genes inside of her." Caleb murmured. Bryan's appearance went back to normal. He walked over to Amy and moved her hair out of her face and saw black eyes with tears and her marble complexion. He smiled at her.

"Welcome to the life of immortality, Amy," he said, and looked over at Ginger. "And Ginger." he whispered. Amy clung to him and let Bryan pick her up bridal style. "I am here for you, Amy." He held Amy in his arms for a few hours. Alistair and Darcia ran over to Amy and Bryan. Raymond, Silas, and Xander remained at the castle with Gabriel's brothers. Darcia gasped when she saw both Amy and Ginger.

"Ginger," Darcia gasped. "It has been so long since I have seen you. Look at you both." Amy looked over at Darcia with anger in her eyes. Alistair walked over to Amy and stroked her forehead softly.

"I guess there was no better time than this," Alistair said, as he looked deep into Amy's eyes. He then looked over at Ginger, who was leaning against a tree, still in disbelief at what had just happened. "At least we stopped the wedding between you and Caleb," Alistair said before he took a few steps backwards. "How families lie to one another over topics that would easily have been taken care of."

Darcia kept her focus on Amy and shook her head in sadness. "Poor girls. We had no idea about any of this. I just remember the day we heard about Arabella's pregnancy. The day you both came into this world." Darcia inhaled and exhaled before she walked over to Ginger and looked her over. "Whenever you are ready, I believe Gabriel wants you both back inside," Darcia said before she walked back in the direction of the castle to see how her sons were doing. Alistair remained with Bryan.

"Caleb, would you mind giving us some personal time, where it is just Bryan, Amy, Ginger, and myself?" Alistair asked. Caleb nodded and walked back to the castle. Alistair sat down on a tree stump. "There is no easy way in life, my dear girls," he said. "How we come about in this world to where it all goes, but what we have to remember is that even when situations like this do not go as expected. It's important to remain as calm as possible. My boys had immortals, Darcia and myself, to help them through the transition, where you both lost your mother and you had a father who was so frightened and angry with Arabella's passing that it just broke him. He placed you both up for adoption in the care of Emma and Athan's care, just in case he killed you both. Why he never decided on Darcia or myself is because he didn't want to break our coven if his emotions got the best of him. We would not have died, but it would have caused a great number of problems." Amy and Ginger kept looking at him with interest. "No plan is ever the best plan. And perhaps another reason would be that caring for our leader's children also puts a strain on our focus. If anything definitely had happened to you, we would definitely have died at his hands," Alistair said. Amy sighed and cleared her throat.

"What needs to happen right now, Alistair?" Amy asked. "I still don't understand any of it. How did we not transition while we were in Oregon? How did we manage to go out into sunlight? How did we not crave human blood or flesh?" Amy felt herself getting emotional and angry while her voice was rising. "How does any of this make any sense?" Amy felt tears falling down. "Nothing makes sense, from what I am hearing." Ginger looked up at Alistair with confusion.

"I agree with Amy," Ginger said with anger in her voice. "I am just as confused as she is. I went out with my friends to college. I only had dreams about a man with dark hair whom I recently met. He is my father, Gabriel… Ambrose was his name?" Alistair sighed and nodded. "I don't know if I want to go back to the castle. Why isn't Gabriel the one telling us all of this? He sounds more like a coward to me. A father whose wife dies and gives up his children for his own selfish reasons. He has Hildegard, and he had other coven members that would have helped out. You know what? I will approach him myself since he seems too weak to come over to us." Ginger got to her feet and jogged in the direction of the castle. Amy looked at her and asked Bryan to take her to the castle.

"Gabriel!" Ginger screamed when she entered the door from the patio. Nobody was to be seen, not even Darcia or Raymond.

Ginger walked over to Amy's bedroom and saw Hildegard making Amy's bed. Hildegard smiled at Ginger.

"Your bedroom is next to Amy's," she said, with a smile on her face. Ginger sighed and walked over to the other bedroom. She saw a closed letter on the bed with her name on it.

Dear Ginger,

I remember when you came out of my womb and I held you in my arms, crying out of joy. Your father was very happy to see you. I was, of course, in a great deal of pain, but you took it away. You and your sister are the two most wonderful girls in the world. I want to congratulate you on finishing your school years. I am so proud and happy for you. I won't be there for Amy, but tell her that I love you both! I wish I could see you in person. Somehow, you need to get me up to a sort of heaven or happy place. Don't say anything to anybody about this. This is between you and me and no other. Love forever, mom.

Ginger looked at the ink and it was as if it was written a few minutes ago. She put the note in her pocket. Ginger walked back to the living quarter and saw Gabriel sitting in a throne-like chair looking over at Ginger.

"What is this, Gabriel?" She snapped as she approached him. Lucien looked over at Ginger and then at Gabriel. Gabriel nodded at Lucien and Lucien relaxed again. Gabriel reached into the pocket of his blazer and pulled out a key, and raised it for Ginger to take it.

"It's the key to my chamber, Ginger," Gabriel whispered. Ginger ran down into his office and opened the door to his closet. The door opened onto a stairway. Ginger walked into the stairway and walked down, following the stairs. She was getting kind of scared, the way everything was put, but she knew she wasn't in any kind of danger. About fifteen minutes after walking down the stairs, there was a door and it opened by itself when Ginger was in front of it. There was a hallway ahead where she saw a closet. She ran down to see it and used the key to open it. There were at least thousands of pictures of when Gabriel was with her mom. It made Ginger's eyes water when she saw her mom for the first time. She had dark brown hair with brown eyes. She was slender, wearing jeans and an orange plaid shirt, hugging Gabriel.

"Ginger," Gabriel started. "I want to apologize in many ways for what has happened to you both. There is no excuse for my behavior, my acts, and the whole plan. I may be head of all covens, but that does not mean that someone like me goes without mistakes. I only did what I did out of love for you both." Amy followed down and saw Gabriel. She rolled her eyes and leaned against the couch.

"Before you continue, giving us a cup of blood will not take the edge off my anger, you know," Amy said. "What kind of father does that? Out of love, you decide to lie to us for eighteen years, causing me to get pregnant, and now I am immortal? Ginger never had to drink potions, never had to leave our parents in Oregon. I don't know if I want to stay." Before Amy got up, Ginger pulled her back down.

"I was getting to that, my child," Gabriel said with his convincing power. "Years before we had you, I was an immortal that was created for unexpected reasons. I have been around many humans but no immortals. I have witnessed many humans being born and dying for various reasons. I had nobody to be with. When I grew up, I had no parents, no family to support me. It was just unexpected that I became who I am today. I was just as scared, frustrated, and angry as I am witnessing you two. A hundred years later, I came across your mother, Arabella, who was about to be engaged to a lord in her home country. I met her at one of her father's galas and fell in love with her. Of course, the story regarding her family did not end well, especially since her fiancé didn't like me courting your mother, which ended his life. Then her parents found out who I was one evening when I killed her siblings out of hunger. I had no control over my actions, which resulted in her calling me a monster. I used my powers on her to quiet her mind and, eventually, I explained to her that there was a plague going on, which at the time was one of the great plagues our world was dealing with. She eventually understood, and that's kind of how we met. I wished it would have gone easier and smoother, but it wasn't. I then created Lucien, Claudia, Audrey, and the other members of our coven. I sent them across to different countries from Rome and Athens, to avoid too much attention towards Romania. The common country of mystical creatures and how people were talking about vampires in our world," Gabriel sighed before he cleared his throat.

"Eventually, your mother was pregnant with you two. I was very shocked how that was even possible, but then there were no answers to why I was the only immortal in this world. Nothing made sense to me. I managed to read fiction books and science books about how there are humans allergic to the sun and was able to find out from healers from different eras about what the cause of sun allergies were and how humans would treat that. Eventually, I got a serum that Emma and Athan had you two injected with, which resulted in you two being able to go into sunlight. Years were going by and I felt so bad about what I had done. I wanted you both back home, but was not sure what I could do. I waited for both your eighteenth birthday to have Alistiar and Darcia bring you both back home to me," Gabriel said. Ginger felt nauseous and angry. "Any questions so far?" He asked while looking at both Amy and Ginger.

Amy chuckled out of response to her anger. "How did Ginger manage to go to college and I am a junior in high school?" She asked out of confusion. Gabriel smiled.

"I did not want to draw too much attention to two beautiful girls being at the same school. Plus, Ginger was first born, and she has a sharp mindset, where she probably also used her persuasion powers to enter into college, as Alistair and Darcia had told me," Gabriel said with a chuckle. Amy felt herself getting angrier.

"What are my powers, Gabe?" She snapped. "How does Ginger have powers and I don't?" Gabriel quieted Amy down and waited till Amy was relaxed again. "You have your own powers. Have you ever tried any of your powers, Amy?" he asked. "What about strength, mind reading, speed?" He asked with interest. "I remember Arabella was able to shape shift. Perhaps you have some of her skills?" Amy shook her head before she crossed her arms. "Now where was I?" he asked as he was going through his story. "Ah, yes," he said. "You two were considered humans in the human world and you ate. That could be a transitioning phase where you didn't know about human blood yet. However, do you not remember those hospital visits that you took those children to when you were a babysitter? That could have been your way of wanting to be close to the blood packages?" he asked with a reassuring look on his face. "It makes sense to me." he added.

Amy raised her hand before she talked. "How are we to actually believe everything you have told us, from Arabella, to now?" she asked. "For eighteen years you have lied to us and now you want us to be a happy family again?" Amy asked. Gabriel looked concerned at Amy. "What?" she asked with frustration.

"That transition should be enough for you to not want to return to your human life, right?" he asked. "Yes, my plan was not smart or easy for either of us, but yet it happened. Me, being an immortal, happened. The killing of Arabella's family happened. And me having two daughters also happened," Gabriel snapped as he felt himself getting frustrated with the situation and drank down another cup of blood.

Amy felt his tension and softened a bit. "I don't want to anger you, Gabriel, but it really is not all that convincing to me. Athan and Emma told me that we were a family. We took family portraits, went on family vacations, and ate as a family at restaurants. Suddenly, I am the only one that had to travel to meet the other covens? Why me?" she asked in a whisper. Gabriel nodded and waited for the moment to talk.

"Ginger already had her powers, and Alistair and Darcia reported to me that your powers were not inside of you yet. I got concerned as to what was going on with you, so I had the covens give your body a bit of a kick start to help with your transition, which took longer than I had expected. That is why I had Alistair and Darcia take you around without Ginger." Amy sighed and closed her eyes, feeling helpless and angry. "I understand that this is a big step, and a major transition for you both. Soon, which I am hoping will not take longer than a few months, you two will be comfortable and happy to be back home," Gabriel said as he leaned back. Ginger looked over at Amy.

"What is happening now?" Ginger asked while sipping from her cup. Gabriel smiled and sighed. "We can go back upstairs and meet up with the other covens, and take it from there." Ginger rolled her eyes and sat up.

"I have nothing more to say," Ginger said as she placed the empty cup on the table and got to her feet. She walked toward the door of Gabriel's chamber and waited for Amy. Amy remained frozen with anger and looked over at Gabriel with betrayal.

"Amy," Gabriel said as he extended his hand to her, which made her flinch. "I will go upstairs. Take your time with what I just said and hopefully we can start over." Gabriel got to his feet, grabbed the bottle and put it in his cooler. Then he opened the door and walked upstairs with Ginger in front of him. Amy got on her feet and walked upstairs to see everyone in the living quarter on the sofas waiting for Gabriel.

Chapter 11

First Lesson

Once Amy arrived at the main quarter, she did not know what to think or feel. Her mind and body went numb. Amy walked over to Bryan and took his hand and led him toward the front door, and stopped. "I don't know what to think or say, Bryan. I have no idea what I should do, but for some reason, being here in Romania does not feel right. I turned into this weird monster creature and I am the daughter of an immortal leader," Amy murmured. Bryan smiled and held Amy in his arms, letting her rest against his chest.

Bryan turned around to see everyone looking at them. *I think it's best if we leave.* Bryan thought before he opened the door and took off running, causing everyone to run after him in shock. "Stop!" Gabriel yelled. Gabriel looked over at Alistair and Darcia in shock. "Bring them back," he snapped. Alistair and Darcia shrugged. "Lucien, grab Ginger and bring her to my quarter." Lucien overpowered Ginger and took off with her. The lights in Gabriel's lights were flickering, and she heard a feminine voice in the room, but could not see anyone. "Katrina?" Ginger gasped, but the voice did not respond. "Who's there?" Ginger snapped. Suddenly, a ghost-like figure appeared before Ginger. "Mom?" Ginger whispered.

"Ginger," the ghost figure said. "It is I, your mother." Ginger looked at her in horror, but also felt her stomach turn and her eyes water. "Mom. How is this possible?" She asked while approaching her slowly. Arabella smiled and opened her arms to her, knowing that she could not hold her. "I don't understand," Ginger said.

"Nothing of this makes any sense." Arabella lowered her arms and floated toward Ginger.

"You should never have come over here, Ginger. Your father has no intentions of helping you. This immortal lifestyle should have never happened," Arabella said while looking Ginger up and down. "Your father murdered my family so he could get my family's fortune. If you and Amy have anything to say about it, all of my fortune should go to you two and none to anyone else. Promise me that you will, my dear Ginger." Ginger felt tears falling down her cheek. Arabella's ghost hand touched her cheek, causing Ginger to flinch from the cold. "I wish I could hug you, mom," Ginger whimpered. Arabella smiled.

"I held you in my arms before I died, my dear child," Arabella said. "I am glad I have got to see you right now." Arabella started backing away. "I must go now, but remember, there is good inside of both you and Amy." Arabella started dissolving inside the room.

"Mom, wait!" Ginger screamed, but Arabella's ghost was gone. Lucien came into the room with a serious expression. "What?" Ginger snapped. Lucien walked outside of her room again, locking it.

Bryan kept running with Amy and noticed that nobody else was behind them. Bryan stopped and panted from running. Amy stood by him in shock and looked around in fear. "I think we are okay for now," Amy said. "What do I need to do, Bryan? I can't return to Oregon after my transition, but I also don't want to stay here. Could I perhaps join your team for a while?" she asked. Bryan regained his composure, inhaling and exhaling. Bryan nodded and grabbed Amy's hand.

Suddenly, they heard some shrubs rustling and Caleb came out. "Bryan!" said Caleb. Amy looked at him in fear and stood behind Bryan, whose eyes went dark and his canines extended. "Wait. Please, listen to me for a moment. You cannot take Amy with you anywhere. She is meant to stay with Gabriel. Whether you or Amy want to. Amy can, of course, decide that she wants to live her own life. However, since she is no ordinary human, she could end up in more dangerous situations," Caleb said. Amy grabbed Bryan's hand.

"Amy," Caleb started. "Please understand this situation. It was the worst and most monstrous situation that Gabriel may have put you in, but you are his daughter, his offspring, and future princess and queen of all immortal beings, if anything were to happen to him. The same applies to Ginger, since she is the older sibling. You are not human and you must. Well, perhaps I could use a nicer term. It is advised that you stay away from humans since you are on top of the food chain, like any of us," Caleb said with a smile. "Bryan, I understand how you love her. The whole arrangement with her and I was never going to work out, anyway." Bryan scoffed and started walking away.

"Amy is old enough to make her decisions and does not need her father's approval. If Amy wants to be with us, Gabriel cannot forbid her from wanting to be with us. Especially when it comes from you," Bryan snapped before he led Amy away from him. Caleb sighed and walked back in the direction of the castle. Amy looked over at Bryan with a smile. "Thank you, Bryan," Amy said before she kissed his hand and leaned into his embrace. When Bryan and Amy were on the open road, they headed toward the scent of Alistair and Darcia.

Once they arrived at their scene, Amy saw Ginger standing outside of the castle in shock. "Ginger," Amy whispered before walking toward her. Bryan looked around to see if this was not a trap. When he felt it was safe to approach Ginger, both Amy and Bryan walked over to her. "Ginger? What's going on?" Amy asked. Ginger shook her head in disbelief. "What?" Amy asked.

"I saw our mother in the form of a ghost, Amy," Ginger said as she controlled herself. "She's dead, but also alive enough." Amy looked confused at her and then at Bryan. Lucien was standing in the distance, watching them. Amy approached Ginger and hugged her. "I find that it's best that we stay, Amy. Or at least, I will stay. I am not sure if I want to return to Oregon and continue on living the life as Ginger Martin, a college girl, whereas I can probably go on a killing spree whenever I have an appetite," Ginger said while putting a lock of hair behind Amy's ear. "My advice to you is to wait and see how it goes in Romania." Amy whimpered while shaking her head. "What did Gabriel do to you?" she whispered.

Ginger gave Amy a concerned look. "Ames," Ginger said. "I know how hard it is to go from one moment to another in a short amount of time, but I'm starting to understand it a bit better." Amy felt her eyes water, as if her own sister had just stabbed her with a dagger. "Bryan, I am at a loss. Whatever she decides, please take good care of her." Bryan nodded and placed his hands on Amy's shoulders, steadying her. Amy walked away from Ginger slowly, feeling her legs giving up on her. Bryan picked her up bridal style and walked her over to Alistair and Darcia, who were with Gabriel on the other side of the castle in the courtyard.

Gabriel looked confused at Bryan. "Bryan, what's going on? Have you returned my daughter?" he asked while looking at Amy, who had her eyes closed. Bryan shook his head.

"I think it is best if Amy would live with our coven for a while, Gabriel. Amy is in complete shock at the news. Plus, it was also Alistair, Darcia, the other ones, and I that were mostly there for Amy during her trip. She probably feels more comfortable with us." Gabriel glared at Bryan and then at Alistair, who remained quiet.

Gabriel scoffed. "She is my flesh and blood, Bryan. I have made this great mistake, but that does not mean I should now suffer the consequences," Gabriel snapped as he walked towards Bryan, who started backing away. "Bryan, I can easily rip her from your grasp and defend myself from Alistair and let Lucien take Darcia, if I must." Suddenly they heard some familiar voices entering the courtyard. Audrey and Claudia entered the courtyard. Then Lucien and a few of Gabriel's members left the castle to stand behind Gabriel.

"Gabriel, you already have Ginger, who is willing to stay with you," Bryan said. "Let me keep Amy for a while and see how she fares before she ends up trying to escape from you." Ginger came running into the courtyard.

"Father!" Ginger said with a raised voice. "I saw mom as a ghost, in your bedroom." Gabriel gave Ginger a confused look. "Arabella," Ginger said. "Why is she a ghost, and why is she in your room?" Ginger asked with a concerned expression. Gabriel sighed and returned his gaze to Bryan. Suddenly, Arabella appeared before them, causing all the members to gasp. Arabella smiled and floated towards Gabriel.

"My love," Arabella said. "I think it may be best for you to release Amy to Bryan. Can you not see how much they love each other?" Arabella said while gesturing to Bryan and Amy. "Remember how you fell in love with me? How horrible it is in hindsight, but how I did see how well you treated me in the end," she said. Gabriel started to feel himself lost in this battle. Arabella kept smiling at Gabriel and nodded. "Ginger has made her decision, so please let Amy make hers." Gabriel growled and got into a fighting position with his sharp nails and black eyes. Arabella looked over at Bryan. "Run!" She screamed before Gabriel lunged at Bryan.

Suddenly, Gabriel's members and Alistair's group were in a big fighting battle. Bryan threw Amy over his back and ran at a fast pace through the woods and onto the main roads, where he saw cars driving around. Gabriel was close enough to catch up to Bryan and tripped him, causing Amy to fly off the side of the road and into a shrub. Gabriel grabbed Bryan and threw him against a tree, and lunged at him again. Bryan quickly moved over, causing Gabriel to crash into the same tree, toppling it over. Bryan lunged at Amy and grabbed her. Gabriel tackled them both again and pinned Bryn on his back.

Ginger came running at them and grabbed Gabriel from behind, and pushed him aside. "Stop!" Ginger yelled in a high-pitched screech, causing some car windows to break. Gabriel grabbed Ginger by her throat and growled before throwing her into another shrub. Amy got on her feet and suddenly used her powers of combusting into flames and blasting Gabriel very hard. Gabriel flew across the road and was scorched temporarily. Then his body had regenerated quickly. Gabriel got to his feet with a smile. He then placed his hands on his knees, catching his breath.

"I concede, for now, Amy," Gabriel said with a sigh. "Well done," he said, while regaining his composure. "You have finally mastered your power. How does it feel?" Gabriel asked with a smile on his face. Amy looked at him in horror and then at Ginger, who was healing slowly. "I guess as your father, I must let you decide who and where you want to be, don't I?" he said in a neutral tone.

Amy nodded and wrapped her arms around Bryan. "Let me be with you for a while," Amy said, and Bryan picked her up and carried her over to Alistair and Darcia. Ginger walked over to Gabriel and smacked him across the face. "How dare you, father?" Ginger snapped. "That did not just physically hurt, but also emotionally." Ginger walked behind Amy and Ginger in the direction of the castle and saw Alistair and Darcia inside a rental van, watching the other boys enter the van. Amy went inside with Bryan and they both looked at Ginger. Ginger shook her head and the door to the van closed. Alistair turned on the ignition and they drove off, leaving Gabriel's group and Ginger outside the castle. Gabriel entered the castle and watched Hildegard come out to spray away the blood and flesh. Gabriel walked over to his living quarter and grabbed his bottle of blood and sat back down on the sofa.

Ginger walked over to the living quarter, analyzing each team member. Katrina came up from her living quarter in her silk nightgown and feather robe, holding a glass of blood in her hands. "So, the oldest daughter remains loyal to her father?" she asked with a hint of anger in her tone. Ginger looked over at her and shook her head.

"It's not like that, Katrina," Ginger said hoarsely. I had just finally met the ghost of my birth mother and I was convinced. Katrina scoffed and sat down on the sofa near Ginger. "What about you and your children, Katrina?" Ginger asked in a provocative way.

Katrina glared at Ginger. "I don't have any children. Gabriel never wanted any more children with other women. I guess you two are the only heiresses to his throne," Katrina said with sadness in her voice. Ginger sat down on the opposite sofa.

"Do you think I enjoy being here, Katrina?" Ginger asked in an empathetic tone. "I get told the biggest lie after all these years of being alive. I witnessed my sister transforming into an immortal creature. I experienced the same pain and suffering. I never wanted to be an heiress to an immortal family. I left my human home in Oregon, where I had friends and a human couple that gave me a feeling that I was loved. Soon I will become an aunt to Amy's children and still have no idea who the father is. Never knew that part about Amy, either," Ginger said with a chuckle.

Katrina rolled her eyes. "I was also lied to with a fake promise from Gabriel. When I was human, he told me that I was the most precious jewel in his life. I was his one true love. He never mentioned anything about his daughters, Arabella, or what immortal life was also about. It all seemed exciting at first, with this new beautiful experience, and then it slowly started becoming boring and very frustrating." Ginger nodded in agreement.

"Gabriel is not that trusting or even handy when it comes to such plans, I guess," Ginger murmured while looking at Katrina's cup. Ginger started feeling herself getting this intense thirst. Katrina rolled her eyes and sighed.

"I think I know what you need," Katrina said and got up with her cup to refill it, bringing Ginger her own cup of blood. Once Ginger saw the cup of blood in front of her, she took a sip and slowly gulped it down in one setting. Katrina chuckled and sipped from her own cup.

Back in the van, Alistair and Darcia drove over to this motel and booked themselves four rooms, where each room had two beds inside of it. Amy got out of the van and waited for Bryan to get out. "Bryan, my throat is burning. What should I do about it?" Amy asked hoarsely while pressing down on her throat. Bryan looked over at Alistair and then at Darcia. "I guess we could have our meal in the great outdoors," Alistair said with a chuckle. Bryan smiled and wrapped his arms around Amy's shoulders. "We should wait till it's late in the evening when there is hardly anyone outside," Alistair said as he opened the door to one of the rooms, where Darcia followed.

Amy and Bryan entered their room. Amy sat down on one of the beds that made her bounce. "Say Amy, I noticed that you hardly mentioned Larry for a while. Is there a reason?" Amy looked up at him, concerned. "Not that I want to lure out your inner immortal, Amy," Bryan said. Amy rolled her eyes and looked away.

"How could I, Bryan?" Amy asked. "This whole situation made no sense. Nothing makes sense to me. I just have to accept these questions with frustration?" Amy asked as she touched her throat. Bryan looked at his hand and bit open a wound, giving it to Amy. Amy backed away in fright. "No, absolutely not!" Amy snapped.

Bryan licked his wound, and it healed within a few seconds. "Suit yourself, but I just want to help you," he said with despair in his voice. Bryan sat down on the other side of the bed to lie down. He closed his eyes and let himself go into a resting position for a few minutes. Amy joined him and wrapped her arms around him, snuggling close to him. Hours went by and there was a knock on the door.

Bryan got up to open the door and saw Alistair and Darcia standing outside.

"Is our guest ready for her meal?" Alistair asked in a cheerful manner. He looked at Amy, who looked pale with dark rings around her eyes. "It appears she might be. Shall we?" Bryan nodded. The group got back into the van and dove over to a park where they saw people jogging, couples walking, and dog walkers. Amy felt her mouth water at the sight of those humans.

"Easy now," Alistair whispered as he placed his left hand on Amy's shoulder. "Remember how we did it?" he asked as he looked down at Amy. Amy looked up at him and remembered how they would chat with those people, take them to an abandoned area, and feast off their bodies. Amy nodded and Alistair smiled before he gave Amy a pat on the back. "Bryan, would you do the honors and show Amy how it is done? Try out that man, walking his dog over there," Alistair said, gesturing with his head over to the man. Bryan sauntered over to the man and stood in front of him while the man was tying his shoelaces. The man looked startled at Bryan, who gave him a soft smile.

"It's a lovely night, isn't it?" Bryan asked, while keeping his gaze on the man. The man nodded and looked behind Bryan and started to leave. "Wait, don't go," Bryan whispered as he used his seduction power on the man. "My friends and I were wondering if you wanted to join us for a meal?" Bryan asked. The man nodded and smiled. "Good," Bryan said and led him over to Amy. "Amy, would you like to join us?" Amy smiled in an excited way and walked over to this abandoned area of the park where nobody was around and sunk her teeth into the man's throat and drank from him. The dog started to bark until Bryan used his powers on the dog. "Go," Bryan whispered, and the dog ran away.

Amy practically drank all the man's life force and let him fall to the ground afterwards, feeling this euphoric, warm, and amazing feeling flowing through her. Bryan chuckled and wrapped his arms around Amy, holding her close to him. "Well done, Amy," Bryan said with a chuckle before he released her. "How do you feel?" Amy looked at him with euphoria in her eyes.

"Amazing," Amy whispered as she wiped her mouth with her fingers and licked them afterwards. Bryan walked Amy back to the van where the others were slowly returning. The whole group clapped for Amy, which made her smile with pride. "Your first human victim," Darcia said before she hugged Amy tightly. "Next time, you can lure them to you," she said before releasing Amy. The other guys chuckled at Amy before they got inside the van.

Once they returned to the motel room, Amy took a shower to get herself clean and dried herself off. Bryan was lying on the bed waiting for Amy to return. "So Amy, perhaps this might not be the right time to be asking this question, but how do you feel about returning to Oregon?" Bryan asked out of curiosity. Amy sighed and shook her head.

"I'm not so sure anymore, Bryan. I actually felt like a new person after that feeding. Is that how all everyone feels after their first feed?" Amy asked as she sat down next to Bryan. Bryan smiled.

"I'll tell you about how I handled my first experience. I was born immortal. Gabriel created Alistair and Darcia and they were still able to conceive children, just like you are, Amy. There is something special about the womb of our females. Gabriel still has no idea how women can still have children. I remember when I was fifteen, four years younger than you are, Amy, I got to experience my first feeding. Not from a human body, but from a medical pack. It tasted sweet for blood, but I remember how Alistair laughed at how I just tore into that blood pack and got blood all over my face, like some children get ice cream all over their faces at birthday parties," Bryan said with a chuckle. Amy smiled and continued listening. "Ever since, then Raymond came into the picture, then Silas, and last, Xander was the last child that Alistair wanted to have. A big family, but that also means that we support each other," Bryan said.

Amy wondered if Gabriel just wanted two kids at the time. "I remember how Raymond got his blood pack, and he cried at first, because of how he felt so horrible at seeing humans as his meal. Silas was a champ, and Xander didn't feel much. When we heard about how Arabella gave birth to two children, I was so happy and excited about who Gabriel could father in his life. I was then very upset when he put you two up for adoption. I felt this intense feeling of wanting to snatch you both and protect you, but Alistair and Darcia denied me that chance," Bryan said with a sigh. Amy grabbed Bryan's hand and held it in her right hand. "I wonder what Ginger is doing right now," Amy said as she closed her eyes and pictured Gabriel and Ginger sitting in the living quarter with a bottle of blood.

Back at the castle, Gabriel smiled at Ginger as he leaned against the back of the sofa, holding his cup of blood in his hands. "You look so much like Arabella, my dear child," Gabriel said with a smile on his face. "I believe that Amy has her temper more than you do," he chuckled. Ginger started to feel sad about Amy's absence and looked around. "Amy made her decision, my sweet girl. I am glad you decided to stay with me," he said as he extended his hand to Ginger.

Ginger smiled and accepted his hand in his and smiled in return. "I think I made the right decision," Ginger said as she leaned back against the sofa again. "I do wonder what Amy is doing. I cannot see her anywhere," Ginger said with sadness in her face. Gabriel got off his side of the sofa and sat next to Ginger, comforting her.

"She will find a reason to want to return, Ginger. I know what Amy has been doing, and she is transitioning into a beautiful creature," Gabriel said as he pressed Ginger to his chest. Ginger rested her head on his shoulder and closed her eyes. "Perhaps you and I can have some bonding time in the days to come. I can show you more of your past if you like?" Gabriel asked. Ginger nodded, and he got up off the sofa and called to Lucien and Adrian, who both entered the room. "Care to join us for an evening walk?" Gabriel asked, with a hint of sternness in his eyes. The other two smiled and nodded.

"I think it is time to show our beloved guest who she is and what she is capable of doing," Gabriel said, with a smile on his face. The four of them left the castle. Katrina watched them from a window of her bedroom and scoffed at the whole scene. Ginger walked next to Gabriel while the other two walked behind them. "Say Ginger," Gabriel said while he put his left arm around her shoulders. "How are you feeling right now?" he asked while keeping his gaze ahead of them. Ginger looked up at him and in the direction he was looking, and saw a young woman jogging toward them. "Care for a little treat?" he asked while pushing her gently in her direction.

Ginger looked at him with horror. "Like," she whispered. "To kill her?" she asked. Gabriel smiled and nodded. "I don't know, father," Ginger said with a sigh. "I can't take life away right now. I thought that the blood in the cup tasted okay." Gabriel laughed and led Ginger in the woman's direction, who was walking slowly away from them.

"Here, let me show you how it is done." Gabriel walked over to the woman and cleared his throat. The woman turned around in horror and started to run. Gabriel grabbed the woman and bit down on the back of her neck, causing the woman to scream, and dragged her body over to Ginger. "Try her," Gabriel whispered with blood flowing down the corner of his mouth.

Ginger felt insecure and afraid, as if she was being forced. Ginger placed her mouth on the open wound and took a sip. Then she grabbed the woman's body and started drinking from her till there was no drop left inside of her. Ginger straightened up and dropped the woman on the ground. Gabriel cheered and clapped and had the other two join him at this celebratory moment. "Your training is now complete, my dear child." Gabriel wrapped his arms around Ginger and hugged her tightly. Ginger clamped onto him and held him close to him. "Welcome home, my child," Gabriel said before he released Ginger from his grip and cupped her face to let his eyes stare deep into hers.

"Don't worry about Amy right now," Gabriel said as the four of them walked back to his castle. "She will probably be joining us again really soon. I can sense her force and her power." He walked through the front door. When Ginger entered her sleeping quarter it was filled with gold wallpaper, gold bedding, and a chestnut closet with fresh dresses inside of it. The carpet was a beige color that looked completely fresh, as if nobody had ever stepped foot inside of the room. Ginger walked over to the balcony and saw the stars sparkling outside. She looked around in the darkness, seeing how clear everything looked. Suddenly, there was a knock on the door.

"Come in," Ginger said, with fear in her voice. Gabriel had entered her room with a box. Ginger approached the bed where Gabriel laid the box and sat down next to him.

"Here is a box of your mother's jewelry when she was alive," Gabriel said as he opened the pearl box with necklaces, bracelets, earrings, and her wedding ring. "Since you are my firstborn daughter, I want you to be the first of the Ambrose bloodline to have her jewelry." Ginger looked at it with wide eyes. Gabriel chuckled and grabbed a golden bracelet with the name Ambrose engraved on it and placed it around Ginger's right wrist. "I have a replica bracelet I want to give to Amy once she returns." Ginger admired the bracelet on her arm and smiled at Gabriel. Gabriel leaned over and kissed her on top of her hair. "When the time comes for Amy's children to be born, Amy can pass her jewelry over to them, if she wishes," Gabriel said before he got off the bed. "I will leave you to look at those jewels. If you need me, I will be in my quarter." Gabriel left the room, leaving Ginger to admire the jewelry.

Chapter 12

Last Moments

As Ginger was going through her mother's jewelry, Amy sat in the motel room, feeling the urge to want to do something positive. "Bryan," Amy said. "I think I did something really bad at my prom months ago." Amy was fidgeting with her hair. Bryan looked at Amy with confusion. "I think I may have exploited our family secret to my friend Jenna. I told her that the reason I left was not because of my grandma, but because of the immortal family." Bryan rolled his eyes and sighed. "I couldn't help it. I started feeling very guilty and ashamed of lying," Amy said out of desperation. Bryan shook his head in despair.

"Amy, how many people were around when you told them?" Bryan asked with a sigh. "We might need to take care of this problem before people start to think that all immortal creatures could be the reason for anyone's death or why there is a blood shortage in hospitals. Let me talk to Alistair and Darcia about this," Bryan said, before he got up to leave the room. Amy moaned in desperation.

"Wait, please," Amy said. "I didn't mean it." Bryan shook his head and left the room. Amy waited pensively on the bed, biting her well-manicured nails.

Minutes went by and Bryan returned with Alistair and Darcia. "Amy," Alistair said, with worry in his eyes. "Who did you tell, and who else was in the vicinity?" Amy gulped and sighed.

"Jenna, my best friend, was who I had told the truth. There might have been other people, like Heather, who I really hate and a few other people in the area." Amy avoided Alistair's eye contact and leaned back against the bed. Darcia looked at Amy, and then at Alistair again.

"I think we might have to go to Oregon just one last time. Otherwise, Emma and Athan could end up in a lot of trouble. All because Amy felt the need to be honest," Darcia said, feeling anxious. Amy's eyes started tearing up. Darcia placed her left hand on Amy's shoulder. "It can be taken care of without too much trouble," Darcia said in a reassuring way.

Amy! Amy heard Gabriel's voice inside of her. *What did you do to our family?* Gabriel snapped. Amy covered her ears and didn't answer. *Why, Amy? Why did you feel the need to tell us about our family? It could jeopardize not only us but also you.* Amy whimpered and shook her head.

"Stop it!" Amy yelled before she got out of bed and walked over to the front door. "I didn't mean any of it. I didn't know about you or who was chasing me. I get told this lie and I feel bad when I see my friends all worried about me." Amy's tears were flowing down her cheeks. "I'm sorry! So very sorry!" Amy cried as she kept covering her ears. "Alistair and Darcia will help me take care of this situation. Please! Leave me alone!" Amy cried. Then it was silent.

Alistair looked over at Bryan and sighed. "I think it's best we go back to Oregon one last time. This time, Amy can bring back anything she wants. She can also say farewells to all of her friends and we'll just charm them, so they will all forget Amy ever existed," Alistair said.

"What should I do about Gabriel?" Amy asked, trying to breathe in and out as much as possible. Alistair smiled and chuckled.

"Nothing needs to be done about Gabriel. We have just taken care of this problem and we'll be back in Romania before you know it," Alistair said. "I'll get our sons and we'll be off back to Oregon in a few minutes." Alistair left the room, and Darcia followed. Amy moaned before she let herself drop on the bed. The other boys came into the room and sighed with irritation. "I'm sorry for this inconvenience," Amy said with guilt in her voice. "I didn't think this through at all." The boys shook their heads, and they waited for

Bryan and Amy to enter the van. Once they all got in, they headed for the airport.

As Amy was looking at the humans walking around with their suitcases, her throat started to burn fast. Alistair pulled Amy to him and held her close to him. "We didn't think of this too well, did we?" Alistair asked while looking over at Darcia, who looked scared. "Amy," Alistair said, as he remained calm. "I will feed you from my blood just to curb your craving right now. Darcia, wait in line with the boys, I will return momentarily with Amy." Alistair led Amy to an abandoned area of the airport, bit his hand and held it for Amy to place it in her mouth to drink from him. Amy moaned and felt herself getting happy and euphoric from his blood. Alistair quickly snatched his hand back to lick the blood from his hand and wiped Amy's mouth with a handkerchief from his pocket.

Amy and Alistair returned to the line that was closer to the security checkpoint and handed the male assistant their passports. Once they passed through, they walked over to the gate and saw groups of people hovering at different gates. Amy's heart was beating faster than she had expected. Alistair kept her close to him. "Amy," Alistair whispered. "I will teach you the skill of self-control. Let's first sit down and I will help you regain control of this urge." Once they sat down, the four boys walked over to the window to look at the different planes. Bryan sat down next to Amy and Darcia sat on the other side of Amy. Alistair crouched down in front of Amy and made Amy close her eyes. "Listen to my voice, Amy. Just don't think of anything else but my voice. Inhale and exhale, Amy." Alistair watched Amy obey. "Just keep breathing and relax your muscles. Every muscle in your body." Amy's back and neck muscles started to relax after a minute. "Good," Alistair said. "Continue with your breathing." Bryan looked at Darcia and smiled.

"Now," Alistair said. "Relax your throat and mind. You are not hungry. You are just stressed and anxious about your new lifestyle. Blood is your new source, but now, you need to understand that you are not thirsty right now." Amy started resisting that thought. "Easy," Alistair said. "Relax your mind again, Amy." Alistair felt Amy's body relax again. "Okay, let's try this again. You are not thirsty. You are just anxious. Both anxiety and thirst are not the same." Amy started resisting again.

"I can't," Amy whimpered as she opened her eyes again. Some passengers walked by in confusion. Darcia walked over to them and whispered something to them that made them walk away. "Amy," Alistair said. "We have all the time to help you. Please close your eyes again." Amy closed her eyes and felt herself tense.

"Relax your mind, Amy. Just focus on the sound of my voice. You are safe. There is no danger. You are okay." Alistair used his charm to increase the chance of Amy succeeding this time. "Relax," Alistair whispered while holding Amy's hands. "Relax." He repeated. Amy started to feel herself relaxing again. "Okay, let's try this again." Alistair whispered while holding Amy's hands. "You are not thirsty. Humans are your friends. You are just scared, but you are not thirsty. You do not want to feed right now." Amy did not resist this time. Alistair smiled with excitement. "Good. Now repeat after me, Amy," Alistair said. "I am not thirsty." Amy inhaled and exhaled. "Amy," Alistair said, and waited for Amy to respond. Amy inhaled and exhaled again.

"I am not thirsty," Amy said. Alistair smiled and nodded. "And again," Alistair said with a smile.

"I am not thirsty," Amy said. Alistair looked over at Darcia in a reassuring way. Darcia looked at Bryan and Bryan smiled at his brothers. Alistair waited for a moment and released Amy's hands.

"Now open your eyes," Alistair said. Alistair got up and saw Amy slowly opening her eyes. "How are you feeling?" Alistair asked, while his eyes remained on Amy.

"I'm okay," Amy said. "I feel much better than I did before we came over here." Alistair sat down next to Darcia and leaned back to close his eyes. Bryan put his right arm around Amy and held her close to him.

"Well done, Amy. You finally mastered your first lesson of self-control. You did way better than any of us," Bryan said with a chuckle. Moments later, the plane to Oregon was boarding. This time, Alistair decided not to use any charms on anyone and sat back in his chair to slumber. Darcia curled up in his embrace, and they both closed their eyes throughout the entire flight. Amy grabbed an airplane magazine and saw that her eyes could spot every greasy detail on every page and the fingerprints on the cover.

"My goodness," Amy whispered. Bryan heard Amy and chuckled. "This is so gross." she snapped and put the magazine back in the compartment.

"Getting used to your new lifestyle?" Bryan asked as he chuckled before he grabbed Amy's hand. Amy heard Alistair's voice in her head and was able to remain relaxed throughout the entire flight. Once they arrived in Oregon, Amy felt a sense of reluctance to see her human friends and foster parents again. Bryan kept Amy close to him and they all walked over to this big taxi and they drove over to Jenna's house first. An hour later, Alistair and Amy both walked over to Jenna's front door and rang the doorbell.

Jenna's father answered the door and smiled at Amy. "Amy, it's so nice to see you again." Amy smiled sheepishly and looked at Alistair. Alistair extended his hand to Jenna's father.

"Alistair," Alistair said with a smile. "I am Athan's brother, Amy's uncle. She never mentioned us since we mostly kept to ourselves at home, but we thought it would be nice to finally see Amy again."

"I'm Gerry. Would you both like to come inside? Jenna is upstairs in her bedroom if you want to go up and say hi?" Alistair looked concerned.

"Would it be possible for Jenna to meet us here? We are kind of in a rush to take Amy back home, if you don't mind?" Alistair asked, using his charm on Gerry.

Gerry smiled. "I'll go and get her. Jenna!" Gerry screamed before he walked off. Seconds later, Jenna came to the front door.

"Amy! So nice to see you again." Jenna hugged Amy tightly. Amy could smell her shampoo and shower gel on her. "I wasn't really expecting any visitors, but would you like to come inside?" Amy cleared her throat and looked up at Alistair. Alistair smiled and used his charm of persuasion on Jenna.

"Whatever Amy told you about her true identity is incorrect. Amy is just a regular high school girl. She is not immortal. Do you understand?" Alistair asked. Jenna nodded. "Good. Now, it is best for us to leave now. Say your goodbyes Amy." Amy felt this intense need to want to hug her, but instead waved her goodbye and got in the taxi.

Amy felt her stomach turn. "That hurt so much," Amy said as she felt tears forming in her eyes. Bryan grabbed Amy's hand and held it close to him. "Thank you," she whispered, wiping the tears away. Then Alistair requested that the taxi drive them over to Heather's place. Heather and Amy got out of the car again and walked toward the front door. Alistair rang the bell. Heather's mom answered the door.

"Yes?" Heather's mom asked with a smile. "Can I help you?" Alistair smiled and used his powers on her requesting Heather. "Oh darn, she is not here right now. She had just left for the mall with her friends. Is there anything I can help you with?" Alistair shook his head. "She will be home this evening, hopefully." Alistair nodded, and he took Amy back to the taxi and got in. "Amy, are you sure this Heather girl heard you?" Amy shrugged. "What we can first do is stop by Athan and Emma and have you say your farewells to them, and maybe we can wait for Heather to return in the evening," Alistair said. Amy nodded, and the taxi drove them over to her old house. This time, Alistair, Darcia, Bryan, and the other boys got out of the taxi and walked over to the front door. Alistair rang the bell and they heard the golden retriever dogs barking.

Emma walked over to the entrance, shushing the dogs, and opened the door with a surprised expression. "Amy," Emma said with a gasp. Amy smiled and opened her arms to hug her. "You look so beautiful and different." Emma looked confused at Darcia and then Alistair. Alistair smiled and nodded.

"Yes, she is different. She transitioned a few days ago and had her first victim," Alistair said with a chuckle. Emma remained horrified and beckoned them inside. "I never mentioned this to any of my neighbors, so please come in." After Emma closed the door behind Raymond, they all walked into the dining room and sat down. "What brings you here and where is Ginger?" Emma asked while preparing the coffee machine.

"She met Gabriel, and she is now with him," Alistair said with a smile. "We don't want to take up too much of your time, Emma. Especially since Athan is not here as well, but Amy wants to bid you farewell forever," Alistair said, with his arm around Amy's shoulders. "Gabriel met Amy and Amy transitioned into an immortal. We have been going around Amy's friends and now we are letting you know of the plan. We'll let Ginger know of your regards," Alistair said.

Emma looked at Amy with sadness and pain. "You two gave Athan and me the best moments of our lives. The dogs will miss you both. I just remember when Gabriel handed you both into our care. Athan and I were constantly hoping that Gabriel no longer wanted you both until we saw Alistair and Darcia show up. Athan and I could never have kids and we were so blessed to have had you two in our lives. If there is anything you would want to take back with you, whether it's pictures, stuffed animals, clothes, jewelry," Emma said with a chuckle. "Feel free to gather as much as you want."

Amy felt this sense of sorrow flowing through her while remaining calm and relaxed. Tears started to form. Amy wiped her eyes and kept herself together. "It has been wonderful to have had a mother that went shopping with me. Celebrate all occasions of birthdays and other holidays. You really gave me a sense of security and love. Before I even knew that my own birth mother had died, Emma, you have been so wonderful to me. I would love to take as much of anything I can back to Romania with me." Emma smiled and to her feet.

"Would any of you like some coffee?" Emma asked, while looking at Alistair and Darcia.

"Sure," Alistair said, while looking at the other members, except for Amy. "Since Amy is still adjusting, it might be best for her to stick to her new diet, unless you do want some, Amy?" Amy shook her head and got to her feet. Emma grabbed three mugs for Alistair, Darcia, and herself. The other boys just leaned against their chairs, looking around at the house. Bryan followed Amy up to her old room and saw Amy standing frozen by her bed. Bryan walked over to Amy and hugged her close to her. Amy started to cry softly. Bryan held her close to her and stroked her back.

"I know, Amy," Bryan whispered while holding her close to him. "I know the pain you must be going through." Amy pulled back gently to look up at him, teary-eyed. Bryan gently stroked Amy's face and kissed her on her forehead. "It will get better, Amy. I promise you." Amy started to relax a bit. "I'll see if Emma has a suitcase for you." Bryan left the room and returned minutes later with a big dark purple suitcase. Amy sat on the edge of the bed, looking at this picture of her with her two dogs. Bryan smiled and placed the suitcase on the bed. "Do you need any help?" Amy shook her head.

Bryan sat on the edge of the bed next to Amy. "I feel so sick right now Bryan," Amy whispered. Bryan put his arm around Amy and held her close.

"Take all the time you need, Amy," Bryan whispered as he let Amy lean on his right shoulder. Bryan kissed her on top of her head and let her rest against him. A few minutes later, Emma came up to her room with sadness, holding a picture album in her hands. Amy opened her eyes and smiled.

"I have all of your baby pictures and growing up pictures all in this album for you, if you like?" Emma asked with sadness in her voice.

Amy got off the bed and walked over to Emma to take the book from her hands and place it in the suitcase. "It will be quiet without having you and Ginger around," Emma said with a chuckle. "The dogs will miss you both terribly" Amy nodded and packed some pictures, some of Emma's jewelry, and some of her clothes. After Amy had finished, Bryan brought the suitcase down for her so Amy could walk around the upper area of the house one last time. Amy felt numb and tired. She returned downstairs and saw Alistair and Darcia waiting for her at the door. Emma stood by them and waited for Amy. Once Amy was at the bottom of the stairs, she walked over to both of her dogs and they whimpered when she hugged them.

"Be good doggies," Amy whispered before she got to her feet. Then she walked over to Emma and hugged her very tightly. "Thank you again for everything, Emma. You are a wonderful person in every single way. I'm sorry this all happened to both you and Athan," Amy whispered. Emma didn't want to let go, but she saw Alistair tapping his wrist and nodded. Emma wiped her eyes and stepped back.

"Good luck and take good care of yourself, Amy," Emma said, holding back her tears. "Tell Ginger she was also an amazing girl and that we are saddened that we couldn't say our goodbyes." Emma waved Amy and the other ones off and watched them take off in the taxi. After she closed the door, she walked to the living room and sat on the couch to cry. The dogs both joined her with their cries and she hugged them both. "Athan will not be happy about missing Amy's final departure, but this was so unexpected," Emma said.

Amy leaned against her seat in the taxi, doing breathing exercises to help keep her calm. "Alistair," Amy said. "The craving is starting to hit me. What do I need to do?" Alistair looked over at the taxi in panic, and then at Darcia.

"Sir, could you pull over for a moment?" The taxi looked back with confusion. "Sir?" Alistair asked, with worry in his voice.

"Okay," said the taxi driver, and he waited till he was able to park somewhere and stopped. Alistair pulled Amy out of the taxi and ran off into the bushes and crouched down with her and bit open his hand again. Amy placed his hand on her mouth and started drinking." Alistair felt himself getting tired, but tried to remain focused on the moment.

After Amy had enough for the moment, Alistair licked his wound and wiped Amy's mouth with his handkerchief, and they both returned to the taxi. The taxi driver looked concerned at Amy and then at Alistair. "We're good. If you can take us back to this address, it is about going in the evening time for humans… or I mean people. We can see if that Heather girl is around yet," Alistair said. The taxi driver drove them over to Heather's address again and let Alistair and Amy get out.

Alistair rang the doorbell again. Heather's mother showed up at the door again. "Oh, it's you two again," she said. "Heather is still not back yet, but if you want to wait for about fifteen minutes, she did call that she was on her way." Alistair nodded and walked inside with Amy. Heather's house was a small boxy house with basic furniture, a flat-screen television. Heather's mom walked over to them. "Could I offer you two something to drink?" Alistair shook his head.

"No thank you, ma'am," Alistair said. "We were just hoping for Amy to say her farewells to Heather. She will be transferring schools after the summer, so Amy thought it would be nice to see her one last time." Amy rolled her eyes at that comment. Heather's mom smiled and sat down across from them in an oak chair without armrests. Heather's mom smiled at them both and it all went silent. About a half hour later, the door opened and Heather came back with a shopping bag while wearing a crop top, skill capris, and white tennis shoes.

"I'm back, mom," Heather said in a half moaning tone. "What's for…" before Heather could finish her sentence, she stared at Amy with confusion. "What's this?" She asked, pointing at Amy and Alistair. Heather's mom chuckled nervously.

"Alistair said that Amy wanted to say farewell to you," Heather's mom said as she looked up at Heather. Heather looked annoyed at Amy and shook her head.

Alistair nudged Amy to create a fake story, so he could use his powers on her. "Say, Heather, you are looking like yourself today," Amy said with a smirk on her face. Heather glared at her and rolled her eyes. "You look… different." Heather snapped. "What, Halloween has come earlier this time of year?" Heather asked sarcastically. Amy smiled while controlling her anger. It was perhaps very good that Alistair had fed her earlier, because if she had no control, she would have gone after Heather.

"I'm leaving you forever, Heather," Amy said with a smile. "No worries about seeing me again." Heather's mom looked confused at Alistair. Alistair smiled and got to his feet. Then he walked over to Heather's mom and used his powers on her first.

"You will not remember this moment. As far as you remember, Heather came back home, and then your boyfriend, and you never knew Amy in any way," Alistair said. Heather's mom nodded blankly. Alistair walked over to Heather, who started to back away slowly. "Heather," Alistair said, which caused her to panic and grab her phone. Alistair grabbed her wrist with his left hand and grabbed Heather's chin with his right hand, forcing Heather to look at him. "You will not ever remember Amy or what you may have heard about her. Amy never existed in your life. Understand?" Alistair asked in a stern tone. Heather nodded blankly. Alistair released her and grabbed Amy. "It was nice meeting you both," Alistair said with a smile and they both walked out of their house.

The sun was slowly setting. Suddenly, a car pulled up to the house. That was probably the boyfriend. Alistair and Amy walked by him and smiled at him before they got into the taxi. The taxi drove off. "Where shall I go now?" the taxi driver asked. Alistair looked over at Darcia with a smile.

"To the airport," Alistair said. The taxi driver dropped them off at departures. "That will be about eighty dollars," the taxi driver said. Alistair rolled his eyes and grabbed his wallet and pulled out a hundred-dollar bill.

"Keep the change," Alistair said, before everyone left the taxi and walked inside.

Amy walked with Bryan and they all headed toward the gate and waited to board their flight. *Amy,* Gabriel said in his thoughts. Amy gasped and felt her heart race. *Are you prepared to come back to me? I really want to redo our meeting and our life over again. Please give me another chance.* Amy looked shocked around, as if she was going crazy. Bryan held Amy close to him as they walked and smiled at the other passengers.

Please, my darling girl. Gabriel said pleadingly. *I want to make both you and Ginger a blood oath and give you the biggest promise of being a better father to you both.* Amy looked at Bryan in horror. Bryan smiled at her and waited at the gate.

"Darcia, could you hold Amy for a moment? Alistair, could you and I have a chat for a moment?" Bryan asked. After Darcia switched places with Bryan, Alistair and Bryan walked over to an empty gate. "Alistair, what do we need to do? I don't want to give Amy up to Gabriel." Alistair sighed and took a step back.

"Amy needs to make this decision herself, Bryan. Gabriel is her actual father, and it is up to Amy to decide this one. We cannot do much about this situation. I will not fight Gabriel over Amy. Alistair looked at Amy, who clung to Darcia.

"Let's find out what Amy will decide, Bryan," Alistair said, as he walked back to their gate. Bryan reluctantly followed him back to Amy and sat down next to Amy. Amy closed her eyes and tried to relax as much as possible. "What's going on, Amy?" Alistair asked. Amy opened her eyes and sighed.

"I think Gabriel is honest about his proposal of a blood oath. Ginger seems convinced about being there, so I guess I am the missing puzzle piece," Amy said with sadness in her voice. Bryan got up in agitation and walked away from the gate with a growl. Alistair got up and saw the other boys looking at him with concern.

"Bryan," Alistair said with a raised voice. "Please come back." Bryan kept walking away in anger. Alistair ran after him and grabbed him from behind, holding him as Bryan tried to struggle free from his embrace. "It's okay, Bryan," Alistair whispered as he lowered Bryan to the floor of the airport. Other passengers tried to ignore the scene as Bryan was choking on his tears. Alistair adjusted his position to hug Bryan in his arms. "I know this is painful." Bryan put his face against Alistair's chest and sobbed. Alistair didn't say anything. He just held Bryan in his arms.

Suddenly, they heard their flight in the process of boarding. Alistair got to his feet and extended his hand for Bryan to take it. Bryan got on his feet and let Alistair put his left arm around his shoulder and they both walked back to the gate. Darcia looked scared and sad at Bryan while she held Amy close to her. Bryan sat down next to Amy in silence. Minutes later, they boarded the flight. Bryan sat in the window seat and let Amy take the aisle. "Bryan, please say something. At least look at me," Amy whimpered. Bryan stared outside in the dark and remained silent. "Bryan, please, don't do this to me," Amy said with sadness in her voice. Bryan then looked over at her and felt tears forming in his eyes.

"I can't believe this," Bryan said with anger. "How did you let Gabriel persuade you to return to him? The guy abandoned you and lied to you, and you're going back to him?" Bryan returned his gaze to the window while biting his thumb nail on his right hand. The doors of the plane closed and the safety talk was given. Then the plane was ready for departure and the plane took off. Of all the flights she had been on, this flight took the longest.

Chapter 13

Nightmare

When the plane had arrived at the airport, Amy undid her seatbelt and stood up. Since there were hardly any passengers on the plane, they got out within a few minutes and waited for a taxi to drop Amy off at the castle. When the taxi stopped before the gate of the castle, Bryan got out first and waited for Amy. "Amy," Bryan said. "Please reconsider this plan of yours." Amy looked at him and shook her head. "Please," Bryan whispered while gazing deep into Amy's eyes.

"I don't know what to think anymore, Bryan. Why would Ginger finally be convinced?" Amy whispered.

Alistair sighed and walked over to Bryan and pulled him away from Amy. "Let her go, Bryan. Let Amy make her decision. It's time to release her. We had some good moments with her around the world. Now it's time, son," Alistair said. Bryan's eyes watered and he walked back into the taxi. Darcia hugged Amy one last time and wiped her eyes afterwards. Alistair finally hugged Amy and held her a few seconds longer. "You did excellent, Amy. From being a regular teenager in Oregon to now being an immortal in Romania. You were so brave." Alistair released Amy and took a step back.

The gates to the castle opened and Amy grabbed her purple suitcase and walked toward the gates and waited for the gates to close before she walked inside. "Feel free to leave whenever you want to," Amy said as she choked on her words. Alistair smiled and got into the taxi, and the taxi started to leave. Amy placed her hands on the bars of the gates and felt tears falling down her cheeks, but with no one to comfort her. She felt nauseous and pain was flowing through her body. As she was walking towards the front door, the door opened and Hildegard stood at the entrance.

"Your father is waiting for you in the living quarter, Amy," Hildegard said. "Please let me take your bag." Amy smiled and wiped her eyes. "Welcome home, Amy Ambrose," Hildegard said after Amy walked over the threshold. Amy tried to regain her strength as she walked toward the living quarter. Gabriel sat in his throne-like chair with a soft smile on his face. He got to his feet, as Amy was closer to him, and hugged her tightly.

"Welcome home, my child," Gabriel whispered in his velvety soft voice. Amy closed her eyes and wrapped her arms around him. Ginger went into the living quarter and walked over to Amy to hug her. "You have changed, my dear Amy," Gabriel said as he looked at Amy. Amy nodded, but could not smile. Ginger looked at Amy with astonishment and smiled. "So have you," Amy said to Ginger. Gabriel smiled at Ginger and sat back down in his chair, waiting for his daughters to sit down with him. Amy's throat felt raw and scratchy. "What is happening now?" Amy asked as she tried to look at Gabriel.

"We are complete, my dears," Gabriel said. "We can do whatever you want to do," Gabriel said with a smile. "Would you both be interested in our family's bloodline? I had Adrian and Lucien find some important artifacts and memorabilia of my upbringing, if you are interested?" he asked as he was looking at Ginger and then at Amy. Amy sighed. "Or would you both like to rest for a bit and take it slowly?" Amy nodded. Gabriel smiled. "Hildegard, are both my daughters rooms ready for them?" Gabriel asked while watching Hildegard enter the room in her light blue dress. Hildegard nodded and Gabriel smiled. "Perfect."

Just then, Caleb went into the living room and sat next to Amy on the sofa. "My goodness Amy," Caleb said. "You look so beautiful. How did the transition go?" Caleb smiled while looking at Ginger. "And you as well, Ginger?" Ginger chuckled. "For me, it was interesting. Gabriel killed this woman, and I felt this sadness inside of me. Then, once I tasted her life force, I felt this excitement inside of me," Caleb said with a chuckle as he looked back at Amy. Amy shook her head in embarrassment.

"Alistair, Darcia, and Bryan showed me how they charmed people into doing their bidding. Bryan got this man under his spell and I drank from him and felt this euphoric feeling inside of me. Something I would have never felt in my entire life," Amy said with a chuckle. Caleb chuckled and placed his hands on Amy, which caused her to flinch.

"I'm sorry. Perhaps my hands are still a bit too cold," Caleb said as he rubbed his hands together. Gabriel watched the three of them with curiosity.

Katrina came into the room and sat next to Ginger while wearing the same nightgown and robe. "You two girls are so beautiful. The transition went okay, I hope?" Katrina asked. Both Amy and Ginger nodded. "Good. I remember when Gabriel taught me about this new lifestyle. I felt scared and uncertain. With Gabriel's soft words and support, it also went quite well for me, too," Katrina said. She then winked at Gabriel. "What are your plans for now?" Katrina asked, while leaning against the sofa. Gabriel smiled and cleared his throat.

"I think my girls want some time for themselves. Perhaps later on or in the days to come, they want to see some of the ancient artifacts." Katrina looked over at both Ginger and Amy with a smile.

"That sounds exciting. I might want to tag along for some of the stories that Gabriel has to share. They are quite interesting," Katrina said before she got on her feet. "I will get myself something to drink. Does anyone want anything?" Both Amy and Ginger shook their heads, but Gabriel accepted a drink. Katrina went over to their cooling area to fetch two cups. Gabriel got to his feet and walked over to Ginger and kissed her on top of her head, and did the same to Amy afterwards.

Amy smiled softly at Gabriel and got to her feet. "I will see what Hildegard has done with my bag," Amy said as she walked towards the staircase. Ginger got to her feet and followed. Once they both arrived in Amy's room, Amy closed the door and felt this intense anger inside of her. "How did Gabriel manage to convince you, Gin?" Amy snapped as she walked towards her. Ginger looked at Amy in a confused way.

"What are you talking about? You are here, too," Ginger responded with anger in her voice.

Amy rolled her eyes. "I came here to check up on you. I am still not convinced. I had to lie to Alistair and Darcia to have them drop me off at Gabriel's home, just so I could see you. How did you even manage to accept the transition?" Amy asked, feeling sadness inside of her. "Is this our new life? Immortal girls that can also walk in daylight? How is this even possible? I thought we would be burning like in those fiction books," Amy whispered. "I'm so confused about everything, Ginger." Ginger walked over to Amy and hugged her. Amy hugged her back, and they stood in that position for a few minutes.

"I saw our mother in a ghost form, Amy. That is what probably convinced me that. I still don't understand many of the things that happened to us and how Gabriel doesn't know how he became an immortal and if there is even a cure for it. Why would he even lie to us, Amy?" Amy scoffed and took a step back. "Either he is telling us the truth or you are gullible," Amy snapped. Ginger laughed. "What?"

"Look at us, Amy. Is this not evidence enough that we are his? We are beautiful and we drink blood. How many humans can actually say the second thing?" Ginger asked, with humor in her eyes. Amy shook her head in frustration.

"That's why it makes no sense. It all happened too fast for me to even grasp reality," Amy said. Ginger nodded.

"Let's say that if Gabriel said is the truth. How can I actually believe it, Ginger?" Amy whispered as she sat on the edge of the bed. "How is this all possible?" Ginger smiled and sat next to her.

"It probably takes time, Amy. Right now, we are both in a shocked state from being lied to, you traveling without me, and now we meet the father of all. That is what I just think. It will take time for us to get adjusted to this new reality. As hard and perhaps impossible as it may seem, I think we are meant to be where we are now," Ginger said before she got to her feet. "I'm going to see what Hildegard has done to my sleeping quarter," Ginger said before she left Amy alone in her room.

Ginger walked over to her living quarter and saw Caleb sitting on her bed with a worried expression. "Caleb, what's going on?" Ginger asked while keeping a distance from him.

"I think this whole situation was a mistake, Ginger. Your ghost mother did say that you should never have come here, right?" Caleb asked. Ginger felt this cold sensation around her and nodded.

"Why would Gabriel want you both back home when your mother has another idea?" Caleb whispered. "I think he may have a secret agenda for you two." Ginger closed the door and walked over to him. Just then, there was a knock on the door.

"Come in," Ginger said. Gabriel entered the room and closed the door. "Father, what a surprise," Ginger said with concern in her voice. Gabriel grabbed one of the chairs in the bedroom and placed it in front of them. Ginger felt her heart race.

Gabriel waited a few seconds before he spoke. "I have good hearing, you know. Caleb, what is going on? Why are you trying to send my girls away from me?" Caleb stuttered in shock.

"I don't like hearing lies being told in this family." Ginger scoffed in anger. "Outside of the lie, I told you and your sister to protect you," Gabriel snapped. Ginger felt anger inside of her.

"Protect us from what, exactly?" Ginger asked in a harsh whisper. Gabriel got to his feet and took a step back. "Protect you from myself. When you find out that your life partner dies and leaves you with two children, without even realizing how it was all possible, I was distraught. I was not the best person to be a father of two beautiful children. You two would not have survived in this family. That's why I had you both raised by two warmhearted humans. I never gave up on having you return to me. I may be thousands of years old, but that does not mean I am the smartest, strongest, or best father. You both might have been so frightened of me. Yes, I made a terrible mistake. I am willing to suffer ten times how you feel right now, but now, I want to make it all up to you in any way I can. Please give your old man a chance," Gabriel said with desperation in his voice.

Ginger felt her anger disappear and relaxed on the bed. Gabriel looked over at Caleb. "Son, you have no right to use their past as a means of talking about me behind my back like that. I have changed in many ways and I am willing to change for the sake of Amy's children. I will be a way better leader, protector, father, and soon to be grandfather to all children in our family." Caleb looked at him with sadness. "Have I ever given you, Caleb, the feeling that I would do you harm as well? I gave you this new gift of life?" Caleb shook his head and got on his feet. "Where are you going?" Gabriel snapped. "We are not done yet. Obviously, you need to hear this again," Gabriel snapped. Caleb felt this intense sadness in his throat and sat back down. "Now, Ginger, if you need someone to talk to, I welcome you to come to me whenever you feel the need. Come dawn or dusk. I will be there for you and Amy." Gabriel got on his feet and placed the chair on the same spot it was before and waited a few moments. "Is everything okay now?" Gabriel asked in a stern but loving way. Both Ginger and Caleb nodded. "Good," Gabriel said, before he left the room.

Katrina walked over to Gabriel and wrapped her arms around him. "It will take some time, my love. Ginger and Amy just need some patience in their lives. Hopefully, within a few months, they will love you again," Katrina said with a smile before she kissed him softly. Gabriel returned a kiss to Katrina and carried her off to his sleeping quarter.

Amy overheard the entire conversation and sighed while placing Emma's belongings on the top of the mahogany chest of drawers. Once she felt it looked okay, she walked into the washroom and saw how tired she looked. Amy splashed some water on her face and rinsed her mouth with water. Then she looked inside the closet to find dresses and nightgowns. Suddenly, the lamp in her sleeping quarter flickered, and she started to see a ghost-like figure appear.

"Amy," said Arabella. "It's me, your mother." Amy looked at her with horror and backed up to the wall. "Don't be scared, my child," Arabella said. "I wanted to see you again." Amy's eyes began to water.

"Mom?" Amy asked. "Is that really you? What's going on?" Amy whispered. Arabella walked toward Amy until they were twelve inches apart. "How is this possible?" Arabella smiled at Amy and placed her hand against Amy, which caused her to flinch. Amy walked in a past face over to the other side of the room.

"Amy," Arabella said in her feathery voice. "Why have you come? I need you and your sister to leave," Arabella said. Amy shook her head. "Please, my dear child."

"Why? What will Gabriel do to us if we stay?" Amy whispered in anger and sadness.

"Immortal women do not survive when they give birth to children. Our bodies are too frail to handle it." Arabella looked at Amy's belly, which had not formed yet. "I know it sounds scary, but you must not have children. You will end up dying and living like a ghost in this place. You need to release yourself from Gabriel's grasp," Arabella said as she looked at Amy again. Amy started to become overwhelmed.

"I didn't choose this," Amy whispered as she felt tears falling down her cheeks. "I don't want to live like this. How can I become human again?" Amy sobbed, letting herself fall against the wall. "Please mommy. Help me. What must I do?" Amy asked as she choked on her words.

Arabella floated over to Amy and got down on her knees, facing Amy. "There might be a potion that could help," Arabella said. Amy looked up at her, remembering all the potions she had to consume in Rome and Athens. "Those potions were to help you with your transition, but there are other potions that could perhaps reverse immortality." Amy shook her head in anger.

"No. Absolutely not. I am never consuming anything ever again. I am not going through that trauma," Amy snapped as she walked back to the other side of the room. "Please leave mom," Amy said with tears in her voice. "I need to be alone." Arabella felt hurt by Amy's response and nodded. "If you ever need me, just call out my name." With that, Arabella disappeared.

As dawn was approaching, Amy felt herself feeling tired and crawled into bed with one of the cotton nightgowns that hung in her closet. Amy closed the curtains and crawled into bed. Amy dreamt that she was back in Oregon and it was snowing outside. Her dogs were outside playing in it, and Emma and Athan were walking around. Amy walked outside, and it started to get dark. She beckoned for her dogs to come in, but there was something in their eyes that shocked her. They transformed into her two babies. Amy could not speak, but started to back away till she felt Gabriel behind her. "Dad! What's going on?" Gabriel smiled and pointed at the children and gave her a bottle of blood inside of it. "No, my children will not take part in this. Please, no! No!" Amy screamed and woke up and saw that it was dark outside again.

Ginger came running into Amy's room and hugged her tightly. "It's okay Amy. It was just a bad dream. Please focus on me, Amy," Ginger said as she was stroking her back and arms. "I'm here," Ginger said in a soft tone. Amy calmed down and looked around.

"I had a nightmare. I was back home in Oregon and then it was snowing. The dogs were there, but then they transformed into my children, and then Gabriel was there holding a bottle of blood. It was so horrific, Ginger," Amy whimpered. Ginger hopped into bed with Amy from the other side and got under the covers.

"Remember how we used to sleep in the same bed when we were younger?" Ginger chuckled. "We used to read each other those romance books and giggle at the absurdity of it." Amy chuckled as she felt herself relax against the bed. "Having a nightmare the first night you arrive doesn't sound like a good start. I was not really able to sleep, until I heard your scream. We have each other, and that's the most important thing," Ginger whispered. Amy smiled as she took Ginger's hand in hers and closed her eyes.

Back at the motel, Bryan kept pacing back and forth in the same room where his brothers were. "I can't seem to relax, knowing that

Amy and Ginger made a bad choice. How can we convince them to choose differently?" Bryan snapped. Raymond looked up at Bryan.

"What could we have done differently, Bryan?" he asked, while chewing on his nails. "It seems pretty obvious that she wanted to go back to her father," Raymond said.

Bryan glared at Raymond and scoffed. "Yeah, right. Gabriel must have done something to them." There was a knock on the door, and Alistair and Darcia walked into their room. "Alistair, something doesn't feel right. Look at the situation. How did Gabriel convince them to change their minds?" Alistair shrugged and sat down on one of the chairs.

"I do agree with you on that, Bryan. Something doesn't feel right about this situation at all. There is, sadly, nothing we can do about it for now. Whether he charmed the girls or that there was something inside of those potions that Amy took that could contribute. For now, we need to give them their space and see if anything happens," Alistair said, while looking up at Darcia. Darcia smiled before she sat down on another chair.

"Alistair, I can sense that there is something not right. I know I can be dramatic in many ways, but my senses regarding this moment is telling me that we need to protect them." Alistair didn't respond. "So that's it? Nothing? We just sit and wait?" Bryan scoffed and left the motel room. Alistair remained in the chair and shrugged.

"He'll be back. Bryan was not dumb enough to challenge Gabriel right now. If you are all ready for a bite, I will be heading out myself," Alistair said before he opened the door and saw the other ones follow him. The five of them walked out of the motel and walked in the direction where Bryan was headed. "He might be hungry," Alistair said with a smile.

The five of them kept following his scent and saw him in the distance, talking to a group of teenagers who were celebrating someone's birthday. Alistair smiled and approached the group. Before they got closer, Bryan growled and grabbed the first guy near him and tore into him. Alistair and Darcia ran towards them as the group ran in different directions and managed to chase them down. "Bryan!" Alistair yelled before he returned. "What was that? You know you first have to charm your target before you go forth with your feeding." Bryan glared at Alistair and dropped the man.

"I couldn't help it, Alistair. This whole situation with Amy and Gabriel got to me," Bryan whispered. Alistair grabbed more firewood and increased the fire that the teenagers had built, and they placed the bodies on it. "I just wished that Amy and I were together. I love her. I fell in love with her when I laid my eyes on her when we were in Oregon. I want her back," Bryan said before he let himself fall on the grass. Darcia walked over to Bryan and placed her hand on her shoulder.

"I think we could eventually visit both Amy and Ginger really soon, once the tension starts to fade." Darcia looked over at Alistair with a questioning look. Alistair shook his head.

"For now, it is best for us to remain low and not draw attention anymore to us. Perhaps I will look into the blood banks around here and stock up for a while. We cannot have humans start targeting us. Gabriel made it clear to us as well that there should be no spectacles. I will be going back to the motel room to rest and we'll take it each day at a time," Darcia whispered. Alistair started to walk off. Raymond, Silas, and Xander followed him. Bryan remained on the ground. Darcia crouched down next to him.

"Take all the time you need, but we'll see Amy and Ginger soon. Right now, there is tension all around. Once everyone feels more relaxed, I think Gabriel will allow us to see them again." With that, Darcia started walking toward the motel. Bryan got to his feet and caught up with Darcia.

"Thanks," Bryan whispered. "Your motherly words to help me, Darcia. I sometimes feel that I don't appreciate you, but I do." Darcia chuckled before she grabbed Bryan's hand and held it in hers.

"Come on, Bryan. I know you well enough that you care about the family. You don't always have to tell me, because I feel the love you have for us all." Once Darcia and Bryan returned to the motel, Bryan stayed in the same room with Raymond, Xander, and Silas. They all fell asleep in their beds and waited for nightfall.

Back at the castle, Amy and Ginger walked down in their robes and slippers and saw Gabriel pouring them two cups of blood. "Good evening, my dears," Gabriel said. Katrina, Lucien and Adrian also entered the sleeping quarter with their cups and sat down next to Amy and Ginger on the sofas. "How was your first slumber?" Gabriel asked as he leaned against the back of his chair. Amy looked at Ginger.

"The bed is comfortable Gabriel," Ginger said and smiled at him. Amy nodded. "Yes, the bed is very comfortable. I slept quite deep."

Gabriel smiled and nodded. "Very good. We get our furniture imported from good quality manufacturers. Nothing but the best for my family," Gabriel said with a smile. "I was thinking about having you two girls join me in a little history. What do you two say about this suggestion? I want to build this trust again and tell you everything about who we are and how you two came about. I will be honest with you both about everything," Gabriel said as he refilled his cup.

Amy and Ginger both nodded. Gabriel smiled. "Excellent. When you two are done with your drink, the three of us will go down to the lower part of the castle, where I keep all personal items behind a locked door. Gabriel waited for Amy and Ginger to finish and the three of them walked over to a staircase going downward.

Gabriel pulled out a chain he kept around his neck with a small black key and put it into the lock. The door opened, and the entrance was pitch dark. Gabriel pressed a button, and the lights turned on. There was another door ahead of them. On the walls, there were two paintings. One that looked like Gabriel and another that looked like Arabella. Both the girls analyzed Arabella's painting. Gabriel stood by them and smiled. "She was so beautiful. You would have loved her," Gabriel said as he smiled before he turned to the second locked door.

The door opened up to another pitch-black room. Gabriel turned on the light and this room was twice as big but with more paintings and chestnut chests with drawers. There was a big table with two chairs. Gabriel led the girls into the room and they both sat down on the chairs. "Now, before I continue," Gabriel said. "I need your full attention and no distractions of any kind." The girls looked at him in confusion. "I keep everything private and personal in these chests." The girls nodded for him to continue.

"Okay," Gabriel said as he started with the first right chest. He grabbed another key from his pocket and turned the lock on the first drawer, and pulled out a book. "This book is about me and how I grew up. There are no pictures, but it is a diary that I wrote in," Gabriel said as he placed the book on the table in front of them. "Feel free to read through it, if you want." Gabriel closed the drawer and opened up the second drawer next to it and pulled out another book. "Here is another diary of how I met your mother," Gabriel said as he placed the second book on the table. Gabriel turned back and walked this time over to the second chest and grabbed out a jewelry chest.

"This is a chest of family jewelry. Your mother's necklaces and jewelry and my family's jewelry and rings. I want you girls to have it all," Gabriel said as he grabbed Arabella's wedding band and held it in his hands, analyzing the diamond on it. "This was the ring I gave to your mother when I had proposed to her." He then looked at the other wedding ring that Arabella had given him. A golden band with a smaller diamond on it. Then he compared it to the ring Katrina had given him and chuckled. "I will have Adrian and Lucien find a way for you to have the same keys as I have to this room. I want you to feel that this home is yours. For now, I will leave you two to read, analyze, and feel comfortable about me. For any questions, I want you to always come to me. No matter how easy or hard they are. Always come to me when you feel the need to. I want to be the father that I wished I could have been for you two," Gabriel said before he smiled and looked at the room. "I'll take my leave for now." Gabriel left the girls alone in the room with pictures, jewelry, and books.

Chapter 14

Conflict Resolution

Katrina and Caleb walked over to Gabriel, who had just been up the stairs. "Gabriel, what are your intentions with Amy and Ginger?" Caleb asked. "I cannot help but feel that this is all just some kind of trick." Gabriel walked past Caleb without responding to him. "Gabe," Caleb said in annoyance while looking at Katrina. Katrina smiled and followed Gabriel into the dining quarter.

"My love, is there something wrong?" Katrina asked as she wrapped her arms around Gabriel from behind. Gabriel released her grasp and walked over to the cooler to pour himself some blood from a wine bottle.

"Nothing is wrong, my dears. I do have someone I must deal with. Arabella has apparently been talking to my daughters and trying to get them to leave. When I showed up in Amy's dream, I was hoping that she would be convinced of her true identity. Arabella is now poisoning their minds. I must try to stop her from going any further. Ginger finally understood her true identity, but it seems that Amy is still resisting her life." Gabriel sighed as he closed his eyes, leaning against the door of the cooler, trying to keep himself together.

Caleb took a few steps closer to Gabriel. "Do you think I could play a part in this situation, Gabriel?" Caleb asked with a smile on his face. "I mean Amy is carrying my children, is she not? How did that even work?" Gabriel scoffed and shook his head.

"You ask hard questions, Caleb. How does anything even work? How am I immortal? There are questions that do not always have an answer, so it is best to move on," Gabriel said, while controlling his frustration. Katrina smiled and grabbed herself a cup of blood.

Back in the basement, Amy and Ginger were reading from one of Gabriel's diaries with smiles and laughs. "Gabriel does have nice handwriting, doesn't he," Ginger said with a chuckle. "Some of the parts are hard to even read." Amy smiled and looked through Arabella's jewelry and saw different types of stones, pearls, diamonds, and different colors.

"Gabriel did dote upon our mother," Amy said. "I mean, all of this must have cost him a lot." Ginger smiled and continued reading other sections of his first diary. "I wonder how Bryan and the other guys and Darcia are doing. They must be relieved to have their old lives back. No more responsibility of taking a girl traveling. Protecting a vulnerable person like myself." Amy sighed at the last part.

Ginger closed the book and adjusted her seat to face Amy. "Would you like to see them again? I would be interested to see what they have been up to after they dropped you off," Ginger said as she looked at Amy and then at the jewelry.

"As a matter of fact, I never got to see Emma or Athan again. How were they when you saw them?" Amy looked confused at Ginger.

"How do you know that? I never mentioned that I went back to Oregon," Amy said. Ginger smiled.

"Gabriel told me. He was worried that you had told our family secret to your human friends." Amy felt herself getting irritated. "Not that I don't blame you, of course, but I just realized that we will never be amongst humans anymore," Ginger said. Amy shook her head in frustration.

"I was worried that such news would spread like the plague," Amy whispered. "I never knew that the situation was that terrible. Plus, when I told Jenna, she didn't seem all that worried about me. She thought I was on drugs and wanted to avoid me at our prom that night till I came across Caleb," said Amy. "How did Caleb ever show up at our hometown, Ginger? Did Gabriel have a chaperon check up on us?" Amy asked with sarcasm in her voice. "I can't believe it."

Ginger sighed. "I know. I mean, how I ever made it to college and how we managed to survive in the sun. Nothing makes sense to me, either. Why would our mother not want us to be here?" Ginger asked with curiosity. "Obviously, she would be happy that you and I are still alive, right?" Amy smiled and shrugged.

"I wondered about that, as well. Plus, why did I even have that dream with Gabriel in it, holding a bottle of blood for me?" Ginger shrugged and looked around. "I mean, a thousand-year-old father who abandoned us out of fear of killing us? Where is the fatherly love with that? He sounds more like a narcissist that loves power and didn't even want daughters, since he created Caleb," Amy snapped. Amy got up and walked toward the entrance of the door. "I think I have had enough for today from looking at this stuff. I might want to go out for some fresh air, since it is dark enough." Ginger nodded and got to her feet as well, and they both left the basement area.

Back upstairs in the dining quarter, Gabriel was pondering his plan on how he was going to deal with Arabella. Ginger and Amy walked up to the floor he was on and entered the dining quarter, seeing him looking pensive. "Father," Ginger said in a concerned tone. Gabriel looked up with curiosity and then smiled. "Is it okay if Amy and I walk outside in the courtyard?" Gabriel chuckled and nodded.

"Of course, you never have to ask me, but since it is your official first day here, I appreciate you both coming to me." Ginger smiled and led Amy out through two doors that they closed from the outside and walked down a flight of stairs into the courtyard.

Gabriel had designers place two porcelain lions at the bottom of the stairs. The grass was well manicured and there was a path of pebbles that took them around the outside of the castle. It was a dark, cool evening, but warm enough for Amy and Ginger to walk without heavy layers. They analyzed the statues and shrub designs that the designers had created under Gabriel's request with amazement. "I must say, for someone who doesn't seem to be honest with his flesh and blood, he does take good care of his property," Amy said with amazement. Ginger chuckled and looked around.

"Or was that more of Arabella's doing?" Ginger asked as they walked around. Amy laughed as she looked at the different designs. "Perhaps."

Back inside the dining quarter, Arabella showed up in her ghost-like form. "You summoned me, Gabriel?" Arabella said. Gabriel sat down in his chair while he watched Arabella float around.

"What have you been telling Ginger and Amy?" Gabriel snapped. "I have excellent hearing, you know. I find it wrong that you are trying to have my daughters leave me." Arabella scoffed and shook her head in frustration. "What? You disagree?" Arabella exhaled before she continued. "I was not the one who gave up on our daughters, you know. When you even found out that we were having daughters, you probably hated it. Now you have a son that is not even your flesh and blood. It was not my fault that I had died. I wished I could have been the mother I was meant to be for those two girls," Arabella snapped. Gabriel scoffed and got off his chair.

"What, you think it was my fault that I died? How dare you, Gabriel Ambrose!" Arabella screamed. "I have no idea why I had to be the one to die." Gabriel looked shocked at Arabella. "What does that mean? You had to be the one to die? Are you saying I should have?" Gabriel asked with anger. "How dare you even say that to me! I wanted to have a partner for life and this happened. I'm sorry you died, but then again, I also never got to have the happy childhood I wanted, either. I was placed in darkness my entire life. I was in isolation for many years. I never knew that there were actual humans in this world and that I had become the oldest immortal creature. Not human, but a creature in this world. So give me a break," Gabriel snapped before he sighed and sat down again.

Arabella floated closer to Gabriel and rolled her eyes. "Why did you want them back, Gabe?" Arabella asked with sadness in her voice. "How did our Amy actually get pregnant? Her life is going to be harder, you know." Gabriel placed his right hand over his forehead and closed his eyes. "That's your plan? Not responding to my question and sitting there in silence?" Gabriel did not respond and sighed. "If you want to talk again, you know where to find me. If there is a plan to even jeopardize our daughters futures, may you suffer twice as much as how my family had died in your grasp," With that, Arabella disappeared.

Gabriel relaxed against the back of the chair and sighed. "This was actually a bad idea. To bring my daughters back. To even be here. I am not sure if I want to continue anymore. Nobody should ever have to suffer in this life. Life is hard enough," Gabriel murmured. Just then, Lucien and Adrian came into the room with concern.

"Gabriel?" Lucien asked with empathy. "Are you all right?" Both he and Adrian sat down on the sofa. "What are your plans with Amy and Ginger?" Lucien asked. Gabriel smiled.

"I don't know anymore. I was hoping to have my daughters be brought up to their highest skill of immortality and become the new queens of our kind and abdicate, but perhaps I might not do that," Gabriel said. Adrian walked over to Gabriel and crouched down next to him.

"What about us, Gabe?" Adrian asked as he grabbed Gabriel's left hand. "We care about you, a lot." Gabriel looked at Adrian with humor in his eyes. "What? It's true. You are our brother, Gabe. We love you." Gabriel waved Adrian away and got on his feet. Lucien got up and stood eight feet away from him.

"Please don't do anything scary, Gabe. I feel that I cannot let you leave before you promise me that," Lucien said with fear. "So you had a bit of a setback in this plan. Nothing ever goes according to plan. Not even Arabella's death was planned, right?"

Gabriel glared at him and growled. "Never mention that name to me," Gabriel said before he walked past Lucien. "That name is forbidden in this household!" Gabriel yelled before he ran down to the basement and locked the doors. Lucien and Adrian exchanged confused glances. Gabriel closed his eyes and regained his composure before he relaxed his body again. "Arabella, how could you? Your words have weakened me." There was silence. "I never meant for anything to happen. I never meant to exist in this life." Still no response. "I love our daughters. I loved them enough to protect them from me. That was and still will be the reason for me handing them over to humans. I could not trust the other groups to take care of them. Doesn't that still make me a good father?" Gabriel said in a whisper.

Arabella showed up in her spirit form. "Gabriel, what's going on? Does my presence bother you?" she asked as she floated towards him. "Or did common sense finally smack you?" Arabella chuckled. Gabriel shook his head and felt sadness fall over him.

"I feel terrible for what has happened. To what happened to you, your family, and all the immortals I have created. I wished for none of this to have ever happened. Yet, it did happen and I feel so much regret and guilt inside of me that I have no idea what I should be doing. Perhaps I should release Amy and Ginger back into the human world. Perhaps not. Katrina cannot ever replace you, Arabella. I hope you know that," whispered Gabriel. Arabella placed her ghost hand on Gabriel's cheek, which had no impact on his reaction, and smiled. "I miss you incredibly. That's why I had you placed in this castle, so I could still see you," Gabriel whispered. Arabella sighed before she leaned into his body and wrapped her arms around him.

"I know, Gabriel. I know," she said in a calm, reassuring voice. "I was thinking. Since you have no idea how you came about, perhaps there is a sorcerer or some form of magic potion that could perhaps bring me back to life?" Gabriel smiled, with tears flowing down his cheeks. "I wished I could have held Amy and Ginger in my arms for a longer time. I wish I could have watched them grow up in Romania. That's why I fear for Amy's life, as well. That she might not survive this childbearing." Arabella floated backwards.

"My love, what would you advise me to do in this situation? Ginger may also be pretending. Amy still has this uncertainty about me. I want to regain their trust and be there for them. Whenever I talk, they look at me with fear and anger," Gabriel whispered. Arabella sighed and nodded.

"It will not be easy. It may be, or it doesn't have to be, impossible. I would talk to them every day. I would do family activities with them and try to get them to bond with you," Araballa said with a smile.

Gabriel nodded in agreement and smiled. "You were always my greatest support, my love. I never meant to do you any harm. I just wanted to find a lifelong mate that would suffer along with me," Gabriel said with a chuckle, which then made Arabella chuckle. "The suffering was the only thing that came out of it," Gabriel said as he returned to sadness. Arabella smiled.

"The girls will soon be back from their walk. Try to bond with them through funny memories. Loving memories. Perhaps you can even take them to our favorite areas in Romania. Where we first kissed. Perhaps that might work for them. Then expand the area by traveling with them and perhaps playing games and getting them engaged in all forms of activity that could also take their minds off of their anger. I did notice that you brought them artifacts and jewelry, but then you do walk away from them, leaving them to figure it out for themselves. Engage more with them. Like you even say, be there for them. Let them know that your presence is there," Arabella said as she started to fade. "For now, I will leave you with that. Take care Gabriel."

Gabriel was alone in the basement and mustered up the courage and strength to approach Amy and Ginger. Later in the evening, Amy and Ginger returned, feeling happy and relaxed. Gabriel saw them walk inside and approached them. "Girls," Gabriel said with a smile. "How would you two like to spend the rest of the evening together?" Gabriel asked as he clasped his hands together, like a prayer. The girls rolled their eyes. "We were thinking about resting, father," Ginger said. "Perhaps tomorrow?" she asked. Gabriel smiled and nodded. The girls walked up to their sleeping quarter, leaving Gabriel alone. Then he sat down and felt deflated from his attempt.

"It's hopeless," he whispered as he closed his eyes. "Arabella, I have no connection with them." It was silent.

Back at the motel rooms, Bryan was biting his nails on his left hand in agitation. "Bryan," Alistair said, as he sat on the footstool in front of him. "What can Darcia and I do to make you more at ease with this situation?" Bryan shook his head and remained silent. "I wished we could have had Amy with us. I wished it was your children she was carrying, but I had no control over the situation." Bryan got out of the chair and walked over to the edge of his bed. "Shall I go and give you some space?" Alistair asked. Bryan didn't respond again. Alistair sighed and walked out of the room, back to where Darcia was.

Bryan wanted to communicate with Amy, but was afraid that Gabriel would come after him. He sat alone in his room with tears in his eyes. "I wish for Amy to be back with me," Bryan whispered softly. "I need her back. I want her back. I love her." Just then, there was a knock on the door. Bryan got up and walked slowly toward the door and opened it to see the other guys waiting for him outside.

"Want to go for a walk, just us guys?" Raymond asked with a smile. "It doesn't help to sit in a dark room, just thinking about Amy." Bryan rolled his eyes and walked outside.

The guys walked away from the motel and walked over to this empty park, where the fountains were still running. "What's the purpose of this outing?" Bryan asked. Raymond wrapped his right arm around Bryan's shoulder and held him close.

"We don't like seeing our brother so sad. I found the entire journey of dealing with Gabriel's daughters unnecessary and wrong. They did not seem that smart when I saw them. Whatever happened to that Larry guy, anyway? Does Amy ever mention him?"

Bryan scoffed and stopped at his pace. "I don't care about that guy. Why would you bring him up?" Bryan snapped. Raymond sighed and smiled.

"I think he might be in the area, if you want to get rid of him?" Raymond asked with a sneer. Bryan furrowed his brown with confusion.

"I may have invited our little guest to Romania and told him that Amy wanted to see him at Gabriel's castle, but instead, I asked him to meet us here. Would you like a little evening snack?" Raymond asked with a smile. Bryan shook his head and chuckled. Just then, Larry showed up in the area where they all stood.

Larry looked over at the boys with concern and waited in silence. Bryan looked over at Raymond and Raymond chuckled. "You must be Larry. Amy's boyfriend, was it?" Larry looked at them with fear and started to back away. "Wait," Raymond asked in a raised voice. "Don't you want to see her?" Larry scoffed and walked off. "Bryan, what do you think?" Bryan felt his hunger build inside of him.

"My brother asked you a question, Larry. Why are you walking away from us?" Bryan asked with a growl. "Don't you turn your back on us when I'm talking to you." Larry turned around and then started to run. Bryan started to jog after him and then ran in a sprint after Larry. Larry kept running through the trees and in zigzag runs. The other boys joined Bryan on his run. Bryan transformed into a wolf and started increasing his pace till he tackled Larry.

Larry fell with Bryan on top of him, growling at him. Then Bryan got off of Larry and returned to his human form. "Why did you run, Larry? What's with the rush?" Larry gasped and coughed while trying to get to his feet. "What is Amy to you, anyway?" Bryan snapped, getting into a fighting position. "Answer me!" He yelled. Larry got on his feet and shook his head with humor. "What's so funny?"

"I have no idea who you are, but a little introduction would have been nice," Larry said sarcastically. Bryan growled and took a step closer to Larry.

"What can I call you?" Larry snapped as he got into a fighting position. Bryan felt confused, but remained in his fighting stance. "You don't know? Amy never mentioned me or…" Looking back at his brothers. "Us?" He asked. Larry shook his head and rolled his eyes.

"No, but after what I just saw, I feel like I am dealing with a schizophrenic dream. You are a shape shifter?" Larry asked. "Does our world even have mystical creatures?" Bryan chuckled and relaxed his body. Larry smiled and relaxed his stance. "What are you?"

Bryan ignored that question and started to walk away. "Not so scary now, are ya, puppy?" Larry snapped. Bryan looked back and bared his canines. Bryan returned and shoved Larry into a tree, which caused Larry to chuckle.

"I should kill you, you filthy piece of trash," Bryan snapped before he released his grip. Larry regained his composure. "I want to, but I don't have the energy inside of me." Larry scoffed and remained by the tree. "What is your relationship with Amy?" Bryan growled.

Larry shook his head and chuckled. "Last thing I remember was that she was becoming my girlfriend. She even shared my bed with me." Bryan's mind went blank with rage and he turned around and twisted his neck. Bryan returned to his wolf form and howled at the sky. The other boys joined in with their transformation into wolves and did the same. Just then, Alistair and Darcia came running at them with horror.

"Bryan!" Darcia yelled. Bryan turned around with fear and started to run. Alistair and Darcia got into their wolf bodies and chased Bryan down.

Bryan, stop! Alistair screamed in his thoughts. *This is your last chance, son. Come back to us, now!*

Bryan stopped and returned to his human form and broke down crying. "I'm so sorry, Alistair… and Darcia," Bryan sobbed. "I didn't mean to kill that kid. I would never have done it, had Raymond not called him up and had him fly over to see Amy." The other boys returned to their human forms. Alistair glared at Raymond and growled. "Don't blame him, father." Bryan panted. "It was my fault in the end." Darcia walked over to Bryan and held him in her arms, shushing him.

Alistair relaxed and shook his head. "I feel like we are at a loss, my family. I never wished for any of this to have happened," Alistair whispered before he sat down on a tree stump and looked out into the woods. The boys stood by him and looked over at Bryan occasionally.

"I'm sorry, father," Raymond, whispered. He put his hand on Alistair's shoulder and remained silent. Alistair looked up at Raymond and chuckled.

"I blame myself for not being harder on you boys. Gabriel disapproves of public spectacles, but I disapprove of these intentional acts."

"What should we do?" Raymond asked. "Tell his family about his death?" Alistair got up fast and placed his hands on Raymond's shoulders.

"No, son," Alistair said. "We will continue on and go back to the motel. Deaths are all around us. As long as there were no bite-marks on his body, we should be okay. He could have just gone for a walk and caused his neck to twist somehow, but we need to keep ourselves low key for a while," Alistair said with a smile before he released Raymond from his grasp. Alistair headed back in the direction of the motel, and the others slowly followed him.

Back at the castle, Gabriel was in his sleeping quarter, creating a plan until he heard Caleb knock on his door. "Enter, Caleb," Gabriel said in a stern tone. Caleb walked into his quarter with a smile.

"I couldn't help but overhear your conversation with Arabella about your plans with Amy and Ginger. Perhaps I can help you, Gabe?" Caleb asked with a smirk. "I can be quite persuasive if you want some support?" Gabriel scoffed and shook his head.

"No, Caleb. I just need you to remain low for a while. I feel like I messed up and don't want to create more lies and deceptions anymore. I want to rebuild my relationship with my daughters with honesty, love, and support."

Caleb chucked and shook his head. "The things you say, Gabe. How do you even sleep?" Caleb sat down on another chair in Gabriel's quarter. Gabriel glared at Caleb and leaned forward.

"What does that mean? You think I'm still lying to you about my plans? Arabella had changed my mindset about this situation," Gabriel snapped.

"If you don't want to help, I'll leave," Caleb whispered. He then rolled his eyes and left Gabriel's quarter. Caleb decided to walk over to Amy and Ginger, seeing them sitting together in Amy's sleeping quarter. Caleb knocked on Amy's door and waited for her to respond before he entered the room.

Amy looked at Caleb with anger. "What? Gabriel has you now spying on me, to make sure I stay in his home?" Amy snapped. Caleb smiled and shook his head. "No. I came here to check up on you both, to see how you are managing in this castle." Ginger looked at Caleb and then at Amy. "If you ever want to talk with me about anything, you can bother me whenever you feel like it," Caleb said. Ginger chuckled.

"Tell me, Caleb, how did you ever become Gabriel's stepson?" Caleb felt exposed and sat down in one of the chairs.

"I don't know," Caleb started. "I just remember how fast it went. I barely felt any pain. It was probably the shock that didn't help. Suddenly, I end up in this castle, all exhausted and in pain." Ginger chuckled at Caleb's response. "Now Gabriel will not tell me about how Amy, you…" Caleb gestured to Amy. "Is carrying my children." Amy choked and coughed, as if she had swallowed something hard.

"Children? Why not the word, child?" Amy snapped. "How many are growing inside of me?" Caleb shrugged in desperation. Amy got to her feet and walked towards the door. "Where are you going?" Amy ignored Caleb and walked down to where Gabriel was.

"Gabriel, I must speak with you," Amy snapped, before Gabriel even responded. Gabriel gestured for Amy to sit in one of the chairs and waited. "What is this about the word, children, and not child? How many of Caleb's kids are inside of me?" Gabriel sighed as he formulated his response.

"Three," Gabriel whispered. "Two girls and one boy." Amy backed away in shock. "No!" Amy snapped. "No! No!" She started to see dark and then blacked out from her emotions.

Gabriel picked Amy up and took her up to her room and tucked her in her bed. "Ginger, you can stay with her as you wish. Caleb, why did you have to talk to them? I never gave you the go ahead to talk to them. I told you, just like everyone else in this family, that I would handle it myself. I'll go back down to my quarter and give Amy the space she needs, but please, do not do anything on your own accord without my approval." Caleb nodded and left the room to go over to his own quarter. Ginger got under the covers with Amy and held her in her arms, comforting her.

Chapter 15

The New Dawn

The next day, Amy woke up and felt her body feeling very heavy. Ginger wasn't in the room. "Ginger! Ginger!" Amy screamed before Ginger came running into her room. "Where were you?" Amy whimpered. Ginger got on the edge of the bed and held her in her arms.

"I got thirsty. Katrina poured me a cup of blood," Ginger said. "I'm starting to enjoy it.

"What happened to me, Ginger?" Amy whispered, as she was feeling her body to make sure she wasn't paralyzed. Ginger gently stroked Amy's face. "What happened?" Ginger walked over to Amy's door to close and walked back.

"You fainted, Amy. I think this adjustment is going to take longer than Gabriel had expected," Ginger whispered, making sure nobody was around. "Our father, Gabriel," Ginger cleared her throat. "Has great hearing, so it makes it hard to have conversations in this castle."

Amy looked around and saw how dark it was, except for her night lamp. "Am I still…" Amy hesitated for a few seconds. "Pregnant?" Ginger nodded. "How? I never had any relationship with anyone, Ginger. How do these things happen like that?" Ginger shrugged. Just then, there was a knock on the door. Amy got back under the covers. "I don't want to see anyone. Please send them away," Amy whispered.

Ginger got off the bed and walked over to the door, and opened it. Gabriel stood by the door with a concerned look. "Could I have a word with Amy?" Gabriel asked. Ginger sighed and looked over at Amy, who looked like a lost pup.

"It might not be the best time, Gabriel," Ginger whispered. "She's still overwhelmed." Gabriel walked into the room, anyway.

"Amy," Gabriel sighed. "I think it is time that you and I had a one-on-one talk without Ginger." Amy shook her head. "I feel the need to explain this situation to you." Amy looked at Ginger with fear.

"I could also just remain quiet as a form of compromise?" Ginger asked. Gabriel looked at Ginger.

"It's about Amy's children. I really want no distraction when I explain the situation to her. Why don't you go down and visit Katrina for a while?" Gabriel asked. Ginger felt that Gabriel was not going to allow her to be present at that moment and sighed.

"Okay," Ginger whispered. "If anything happens to Amy, I will not make the rest of our time together easy," Ginger snapped before she left the room. After the door had closed, Gabriel sat in a chair, facing Amy, and formulated what he was going to say to Amy.

"Amy, whatever you heard from your mother regarding your pregnancy is incorrect. The reason she died was because she was still human. How I managed to get her pregnant is still a mystery to me. How you got pregnant is what I am willing to explain to you." Gabriel adjusted his seat and cleared his throat. "I never turned Arabella, but tried to when I saw her heart slowing. I never wanted her to die."

Amy sat up in bed, leaning against the back of the bed. "Nothing makes sense to me," Amy snapped. "Why did you give up on us when we were at our most vulnerable? You were perhaps going to be a thousand years old, and yet you acted like a child." Gabriel shook his head and got to his feet. Amy didn't want to have any more talks with him, but Gabriel didn't leave her room.

"Amy," Gabriel started off. "I never meant to have you two placed up for adoption in the human world. The reason I had you and not Ginger meet those other members was because they were all against me even having children and I had Alistair and Darcia take you to meet them. There were many lies, I will admit, but would you have gone with them if you had heard the truth from them? Would you have been scared if I was the one that showed up at their house in the evening?" Amy rolled her eyes. "There is a grey area about telling someone a lie. You either tell them to spare their feelings and you also tell them, so they can go forth with a plan that I had created. Yes, I was not the best parent to father you and your sister. Yes, I am willing to admit many of my faults. Yes, for everything."

Gabriel started feeling himself getting angry, as his voice was getting harsher. "I only did that to protect you and your sister. I know this is your third day of being in our castle, but I want you to understand the reasons behind my actions. I was so distraught by seeing your mother lying on the table, watching her light dim out. I was so angry, but mostly at myself," Gabriel snapped as he was pacing back and forth.

Amy started to feel this fear building inside of her by Gabriel's behavior. Amy was looking at the door to her bedroom and thought about creating a plan before Gabriel relaxed and sat down again. "Forgive me, child. Sometimes I go overboard with my anger," Gabriel whispered as he leaned against the back of the chair. "Any questions?" Ginger asked, watching Amy's eyes with fear.

Amy rolled her eyes and crossed her legs. "Many, Gabriel. I have many questions to ask you, but before I continue, how much time do you have?" Amy snapped. Gabriel smiled.

"All the time you want, Amy." Gabriel whispered as he leaned against the chair and kept his gaze on Amy. "Feel free to ask any question you want." Amy sighed and formulated a few questions.

"Am I going to die giving birth to these triplets?" Amy asked, with anger in her tone.

"No, Amy," Gabriel said in a soothing tone. "You are immortal. It only happens to human women," Gabriel said, with a gentle smile.

"Okay. So, what happened to Arabella, our mother? Why is she a ghost? Do all immortals become ghosts or does that only apply to our family?" Amy asked, feeling this intense hunger inside of her. Gabriel smiled.

"Before I answer that, would you like something to eat?" Gabriel asked in the same soothing tone. Amy sighed and shook her head. "I'll have Hildegard bring something for us. I could use a little drink myself." Amy nodded. Gabriel grabbed a little rectangular machine that looked like a remote and pressed a green button on it. That was the sign that Hildegard was meant to bring up Gabriel's drink, but she knew that Amy was with him. Moments later, Hildegard came up with an unlabeled bottle and two cups.

Gabriel undid the cork and poured Amy a cup and handed it to her. Then he poured himself a cup and placed the bottle on Amy's night table. "Where were we?" Gabriel asked after he took his first gulp. Amy gulped down the cup and felt this relaxed feeling inside of her.

"Why is Arabella a ghost, Gabriel?" Amy asked. Gabriel smiled and nodded before he placed the cup on Amy's night table.

"My group and I put a spell on Arabella, to keep her in some form of limbo, where she can't leave. I was so upset by her death that I couldn't let go of her. Plus, she does still give me support and advice when I need it," Gabriel said, remembering how beautiful Arabella had looked.

"That sounds perverse," Amy moaned as she reached for the bottle to pour herself some more. "Not letting go of the dead and keep our mother confined for your own insecurities?" Gabriel couldn't help but feel this anger at that comment. Amy looked up at him and wondered how this was going to end. Gabriel took another sip and relaxed.

"You sounded like Amelia and Daniel when I proposed that plan, Amy," Gabriel sighed. Amy couldn't help but chuckle at that comment.

"Great minds think alike, right?" Amy said with a chuckle, which caused Gabriel to chuckle.

"Right," Gabriel said with a smile. He was wondering if this talk was helping him with his connection to Amy. Amy looked away from Gabriel's smile and redirected her gaze to the pictures of her with her dogs. Gabriel followed Amy's gaze and sighed.

"Do you miss humans, Amy?" Gabriel asked, causing Amy to return to reality. Amy looked at the pictures and shrugged.

"Perhaps, but I felt this hunger and this sense of power when I hugged Jenna and Emma when I went back to Oregon to correct my mistake," Amy said with a hint of sadness. Gabriel smiled and got off the chair to sit next to Amy, which caused her to flinch.

"Apologies, Amy. I didn't mean to cause any discomfort or awkwardness. I wanted to hug you," Gabriel said before he returned to the chair. Amy felt this sense of guilt, but then snapped out of that feeling and leaned against the bed again. "Any other questions, or have I made the situation as clear as crystal?" Gabriel asked with a questioning look.

Amy didn't know what to think or ask anymore, so she shook her head. "For now, I think it's clear to me. Oh, I forgot one question. How did I ever get pregnant and what was the whole wedding ceremony with Caleb and who is Caleb?" Amy asked with panic.

Gabriel relaxed and used his powers to calm Amy down. "Relax. We have all the time for your questions," Gabriel said in a soothing voice. "There is a serum that Amelia had created that we would give to immortal women to impregnate them without any intercourse. After my sorrow at losing Arabella, I vowed to keep our women alive when they wanted children," Gabriel said in a hushed tone. Amy rolled her eyes.

"Why me at this age and why not Ginger?" Amy snapped, feeling her anger build inside of her body. Gabriel had to formulate his words again and sighed.

"When you were born, I wasn't ready to be a father to daughters, as I mostly saw women as vessels, rather than partners." Amy spat out some of the blood that sprayed on her fresh sheets and coughed.

"What!" Amy screeched before she was coughing. "How could you even think like that? What about Audrey, Arabella, Claudia, Amelia, Ginger, or even Darcia?" Amy snapped. Gabriel held up his hands to quiet Amy. "No, don't hush me up. This is the most ridiculous mindset I have ever heard from you." Amy got out of bed and headed for the door, to find that Gabriel grabbed her from behind and held her close. "Release me!" Amy snapped, but Gabriel kept holding her. "Please!" Amy shrieked, feeling tears inside of her. "Please." Amy whispered, till she felt herself being pulled away from the doorknob.

"Amy," Gabriel whispered as he held her in his arms, holding her close to him. "I never and could ever think of you or Ginger as a vessel. You two are the most powerful and strongest women I have ever had the honor of having. You two are so beautiful and smart. I was a fool in many ways. Amelia was perhaps the best woman after Arabella," Gabriel said with a chuckle. Gabriel released his hold on Amy and let her take a few steps away from him.

"So why me?" Amy asked, wiping tears away from her eyes. "What makes me so special?" Amy whispered.

Gabriel closed his eyes and shook his head. "Because of Larry Harrison," Gabriel snapped. "I know you have met him and Amy. I am so sorry that you had to deal with that creature. He is one of our enemies in this world." Amy gasped when she heard that name and started to feel dizzy and let herself drop onto her bed.

"When I was young and naïve with my powers and strength, I killed this one mortal, but did not fully kill him. I think he has it out for me, Amy. That's why he found out where you were, as they all have different powers of mind reading to sniff out with their strong noses. They tried to have you killed, Amy," Gabriel whispered. "I think your friend Bryan may have taken care of him, as they lured him to Romania and snapped his neck." Gabriel whispered.

"How did that happen?" Amy whispered as she tried to focus on an object to keep herself from getting dizzy. "I got a weird feeling from that Larry guy and wondered who he actually was. He kept mentioning you and he had his family give me some type of potion," Amy whispered as she was remembering that moment of being in his family's mansion in Oregon.

Gabriel nodded. "Those baby immortals that are growing inside of you are keeping you alive by giving you their strength. Those potions that our family gave you were to keep you alive and strong. You already have your gifts, Amy. I felt the need for these lies to protect you and your sister," Gabriel said in a hushed tone. "Is there any way I can help you overcome any doubts or uncertainties about your true identity, Amy?" Gabriel asked.

Amy shook her head. "Did Alistair and Darcia know about Larry and their family?" Gabriel thought about that question for a moment and furrowed his brow.

"I would have to ask Alistair about that, because why would they even bring you over to them if they knew about their intentions towards Gabriel's daughter?" Gabriel murmured to himself. "Until that question is resolved, would you and Ginger like to go outside with Daniel, Lucien, Vladimir, and me for an evening walk?" Gabriel asked.

Amy felt the need to leave the room from all the news and lies that were pouring out and nodded. "Good. I'll see what everyone else is up to and feel free to ask Ginger." Gabriel whispered before he leaned down to kiss Amy on top of her head. Amy couldn't help but smile at his comforting and loving response. After Gabriel had left the room, Amy walked over to Ginger and saw Ginger reading the second of Gabriel's entries.

Ginger looked up at Amy with curious eyes. "I'm starting to feel better, Ginger. Would you like to join us for an evening walk?" Amy asked as she leaned against the wall near the door. Ginger smiled and got up.

"How did the talk go?" Ginger asked, as she placed the book on her night table and grabbed her shoes.

"Much better than I had expected, Gin." Amy sighed as she watched Ginger. "I can't help but wonder how much of what I was told is a lie and what is the truth," Amy whispered. Ginger walked over to Amy and hugged her.

"Follow your intuition, Amy," Ginger whispered as she held Amy in her arms. "Whatever doesn't feel right usually isn't right."

Back in the motel room, Bryan felt this hunger inside of him, like he had never felt before. Alistair came into the room Bryan and

Raymond were in. "Sons, we need to retrieve Larry's dead body. Could you tell me where you had him killed?" Alistair asked, as Darcia went into the same room. Bryan looked at Raymond, who chuckled. "Show me," Alistair snapped as he opened the door to let Bryan and Raymond walk out. Xander and Silas were outside, waiting for everyone.

When they got to the park, Raymond led the group to the area where Larry had died, but they couldn't find his body. "Raymond, are you sure it was here?" Alistair asked, feeling himself getting impatient. Raymond looked around the area and couldn't find the dead body of Larry. He started to panic as he was pacing around. "Raymond, what's going on?" Alistair asked.

Just then, they heard a growl from behind them. Larry stood there, crouched down with his teeth barred and his nails sharp. Alistair couldn't help but chuckle at the situation. "Raymond, did you know about this?" Alistair asked as he stood in front of his sons. "Remember him? Larry from Oregon?" Alistair said in a snide tone. "Gabriel warned us about you. Why we even allowed Amy to get in contact with you was such a foolish mistake of mine, but then again, I was hoping Amy could have softened the situation. Your anger was, and perhaps still is, at Gabriel. Amy was never a target of yours, Larry," Alistair said in his soothing tone.

Larry remained in the position and kept growling. "Gabriel deserves to die. For what he did to me," Larry snapped. Darcia looked confused at Alistair, who kept his gaze on Larry.

"What did he even do to you, Larry?" Darcia asked in a soft tone as she turned her gaze to face Larry.

"He turned me. He got so hungry and lost himself and only drank where I just remained alive. Then came the transition, and I became this horrible monster. Gabriel refused to help me or even guide me. He just ignored my calls and my pleas, leaving me in this mess of being this horrible creature," Larry said in a saddened tone. "Now I want him gone. I never meant to harm his little girl, though she did make for a nice treat. Bryan crouched down and barred his teeth after hearing that comment. Alistair held his hand up to Bryan to hold him back.

"No, son," Alistair hissed. "Not right now." Bryan moaned before he returned to his human form.

Larry looked over at Bryan and growled, moving one step closer. "Keep your distance, Larry," Alistair hissed as he crouched down, barring his teeth. "We have no quarrel with you. If you want Gabriel, you'll have to go to him yourself, but leave us alone. We are part of his family, but we are not the ones you want." Larry straightened his body and retracted his canines before he returned to his human form.

Larry moaned as he walked off into the darkness and ran through the park. Alistair returned to his human form, but kept his teeth barred for any unexpected attacks. The seven of them looked around, letting their ears and senses remain sharp. "I wonder what Gabriel is actually doing, right now," Alistair whispered as he thought about Amy.

Darcia took Alistair's hand in hers and smiled. "I'm sure there is some family drama taking place, my love. I am honored at the fact that our family was chosen to escort Gabriel's daughters, well, mostly Amy around. She reminds me so much of Arabella in many ways. The sharpness, but also the softness of being so innocent and pure. I can understand how you boys fell for her. She is quite a special woman," Darcia said before she kissed Alistair on the top of his hand.

"I guess we should return to our motel rooms, where we are confined until further notice," Alistair said, before they walked back in that direction.

"How did we not know that Larry was actually an immortal, but a bit younger than Gabriel? Did any of you all notice anything when we dropped Amy off at his family's mansion?" Alistair asked, as he stopped before them. They all looked confused and deep in thought.

"Perhaps we'll find the reason really soon, my darlings," Alistair said with a smile before he continued to walk. "Raymond," Alistair said, as he beckoned for him to walk with him. "What made you actually lure Larry over to Romania?" Alistair asked with a confused look. Raymond sighed, remembering that he could read people's minds and their thoughts.

"Mind reading," Raymond mumbled as he kept his focus on the path they were walking on. Alistair chuckled. "What?" Raymond chuckled.

"Why did you let us drop Amy off at his mansion and allow their family to poison our leader's daughter?" Alistair said before he stopped in front of Raymond. Raymond shook his head in panic.

"It's not like that. I thought that Larry was part of Amy's journey. Yes, I knew about the whole adoption and meeting the other covens, but I really thought…" Raymond raised his right hand to show his honesty. "That their group was part of Amy's strength building. I had no intention of seeing Amy get harmed at all," Raymond said in a pleading manner.

Alistair pulled Raymond into his arms and held him. "Son, I would never see you or your brothers as ill-minded individuals. Perhaps this was an honest mistake, but then, what was the reason of you bringing him here?" Alistair asked, with irritation in his voice. He released Raymond, but kept his hands on his shoulders.

"I wanted him dead. He would not let go of the thought of Amy ever being his. I love Amy and I know Bryan loves her, and perhaps Silas and Xander, as well," Raymond said with sadness.

Alistair closed his eyes and exhaled. "It's okay. We came across Larry and found out his true intentions. Now we'll see what happens next. We can't have any spectacles in this family anymore. That scenario at the airport was already the worst part of our plan. We cannot have other humans know about us," Alistair said in a whisper. He then released his grasp on Raymond and continued to walk with Darcia in front of the boys.

Raymond felt this intense guilt and shame washing over his body as he kept his eyes on the ground. Bryan came up and put his left arm around Raymond and walked with him in silence. "It'll be okay, brother," Bryan whispered. "These things just happen. I am quite impressed by how you managed to bring that creature over to us. It did feel good to go after him," Bryan said with a chuckle. Raymond remained quiet and kept walking in silence.

Back at the castle, Gabriel, Lucien, Vladimir, Daniel, Amy, and Ginger walked out through the balcony doors, out into the courtyard and walked in the dark, where the stars were out. "Such a beautiful night for a walk, isn't it?" Gabriel asked as he took the lead in their walk. Amy grabbed Ginger's hand and held it tightly. Vladimir, Daniel, and Lucien walked together behind the girls to keep both sides protected. Gabriel started sensing another presence and looked around. It was quiet, but his sharp hearing noticed something off about the quiet air.

"Brothers, please form a triangle around my daughters. I think we may be expecting an unknown presence." The three brothers formed a triangle around both Amy and Ginger. Then the growling and panting came closer in front of Gabriel till Larry sprang out from the bushes toward Gabriel. Gabriel's speed caused Larry to fall behind him. Amy gasped and looked shocked at Larry's appearance.

"What happened to you?" Amy asked as she covered her mouth in shock. Larry looked up at Amy and growled before he returned to his human form. "Father, did you change him, too?" Amy asked in a whisper.

Gabriel sighed and crossed his arms. "I did, but it was not intentional to turn him into an immortal," Gabriel snapped. Larry's breathing remained heavy and fast as he kept ten feet away from them. The four brothers remained still. "How did you find me?" Gabriel asked, keeping himself composed.

"It wasn't that easy, but a little bird by the name of Alistair had brought me here to see your precious daughter," Larry snapped.

Gabriel looked over at Amy with confusion. "Amy, what is he talking about? Do you know Larry?" Amy gasped and remained frozen with fear.

"Um..." Amy stuttered. "Yes, and no." Larry rolled his eyes and scoffed. "How did it even happen?" Amy asked in a high-pitched tone. Larry moved over to the other side to get closer to Amy.

"Your monster father had turned me, just like what he had said. I was living a decent human life till I feel this heavy body and sharp teeth on my flesh. He left me to die like this. I knew who you were,

Amy Ambrose. I thought I could actually end your life, like your father had ended mine, but then I smelled you. The rotting flesh of an immortal," Amy looked hurt by that comment and looked over at Ginger, who furrowed her brow and glared at Larry. Gabriel moved closer to Amy while keeping his gaze on Larry.

"Well," Gabriel said as he looked back at Amy. "What do you think should happen?" Larry chuckled as he crouched down, barring his teeth. "Do you have any feelings for this Larry fellow, Amy?" Gabriel asked as he returned his gaze to Amy. Amy felt so overwhelmed again.

"I don't know. Larry, why didn't you tell me the truth? Did you want to protect me, like my father?" Amy snapped as she felt herself getting angry. Larry relaxed his body and returned to his human form.

"I was actually going to have you killed and see what Gabriel would have done. He didn't seem like a good father, by abandoning both you and Ginger at birth. Especially for what he did to me. Out of lust and hunger," Larry snapped.

Amy felt bad for what happened to Larry. "What should we do about this situation, Larry? For some reason, I don't feel that having my father killed in this moment." Gabriel smiled when he heard Amy use the word father. "But then again, I feel bad for what he did to you. Would you like to come into our home for a drink?" Amy asked before she looked up at Gabriel.

"Perhaps another time, Amy," Larry said. "I just wanted you to know what your father had done to me. Back in Oregon, you were innocent and pure that I didn't want to scare you. Perhaps I might want to see you alone sometime when the tension has simmered." Larry regained his composure and started to back away.

Gabriel wrapped his arms around both Amy and Ginger and waited till Larry was out of sight. "Perhaps it's time we return home. What say you, my dears?" Gabriel asked as he pulled Amy and Ginger gently backwards.

Chapter 16

The Moment of Truth

Once the doors to the castle had closed, Gabriel pushed his daughters into the living quarter and had Hildegard bring down the bottle that was still in Amy's room. Gabriel sat down in his throne-like chair and placed his hand under his chin, formulating his words. Lucien, Vladimir, and Daniel sat across from Amy and Ginger on the opposite couch. "That was very displeasing," Gabriel murmured as he kept his gaze on the ground. "How did he ever find me?" Gabriel asked, looking at his brothers.

Amy kept holding Ginger's hand as they both walked back to the living quarter, sitting down in the same sofa they had sat on before. Ginger kept looking at Amy, who remained frozen with fear. "Larry is an immortal?" Amy whispered as she squeezed Ginger's hand. Ginger remained silent, not knowing how to handle the situation, except just being there for her sister.

"I can't wrap my mind around it. It makes sense, but how should I've known, Gin?" Amy whispered when she looked at Ginger. "I just…" Amy closed her eyes and leaned into Ginger's arms. "I feel so sick right now, Ginger," Amy whispered. Caleb came into the living quarter with a confused look.

"What's going on? Did Amy get hurt?" Caleb asked as he looked around in confusion. "Is Gabriel around?" Ginger pointed in the area Gabriel was at. Caleb walked over to him.

"I hate this feeling, Ginger. I feel so lost, alone, tired, sick, like I want to give up. I have children inside of me for unknown reasons.

I met this guy who I was going out with, without realizing our own father made him. I feel so overwhelmed, Gin," Amy whispered. Ginger kept helping her relax by stroking her back, listening to Amy, holding her in her arms, even though Ginger felt the same.

"I don't know what to say, Amy," Ginger whispered. "I wish there were answers and help out there, but I think for now, it's best to keep as relaxed and try not to get overworked over questions. None of this makes sense to me, either. None of it makes sense whatsoever. I feel the exact anger and frustration you are feeling. I want to be there for you, Amy." Amy looked up at Ginger and smiled.

"The same goes for you too, Ginger." Amy whispered as she wrapped her arms around Ginger.

Gabriel came into the room with guilt and shame in his eyes. He sat down in this throne-like chair and watched his daughters. "Amy, Ginger," Gabriel whispered. "I feel very bad and guilty for what I've put you two through. It was never my intention to have it result at this moment. Perhaps I should've been a better parent and more supportive of my daughters. I should've put aside my own needs and lusts to protect you two better." Ginger and Amy looked up at him with sadness. "I want to be a better parent to you two from now on. Do you trust me enough to know that I am being honest?" Gabriel asked with a tiny smile on his face.

Ginger smiled back and nodded and then looked over at Amy, who was reluctant. "As the old saying goes that the road to hell is paved with good intensions," Gabriel said with a chuckle. Ginger smirked, and Amy looked at him with a tiny smile.

"I don't want to have any problems with you, Gabriel," Amy said in a hoarse voice. "I never meant for any of this to happen, either. I just feel so overwhelmed, especially since our first meeting also went quite bad, where you had this hunger for me."

Gabriel nodded with guilt in his eyes. "I was not prepared for that meeting, either. You still had your human-like scent on you and seeing humans as just a nutritional source didn't help," Gabriel whispered. Ginger looked up at Gabriel with concern.

"You tried to kill Amy?" Ginger asked, with shock in her eyes. Gabriel nodded and shrugged. "And now?" Ginger snapped, tightening her grip on Amy.

Gabriel cleared his throat. "Absolutely not," he said. "You two have the immortal scent that just makes me feel very proud," Gabriel said with a smile. "I must ask Alistair and Darcia why they didn't know about Larry and his intentions for Amy. Please excuse me, my dears," Gabriel said before he got off his chair to leave for his sleeping quarter.

Amy and Ginger remained in each other's arms till Caleb returned. "So," Caleb said with a chuckle. "How are you two managing?" he said with a smile. Amy rolled her eyes at him and remained in Ginger's arms. Ginger looked at him with distrust, but returned her gaze to Amy.

"Fine," Ginger said in a monotone voice. "We're just tired, that's all." Caleb smiled. "Care for a drink?" he asked. Amy and Ginger both nodded before Caleb left for the cooler to grab a new bottle. When he returned with three cups and the bottle, he sat on the opposite sofa and undid the cork.

"So, how did you and Larry even meet?" Caleb asked, as he was pouring the three cups. Amy looked up at Ginger with uncertainty. Amy sighed and released herself from Ginger's grasp, to sit up against the back of the sofa.

"He wrote me a letter to ask me to meet him months ago. I thought this was some type of joke, but I guess it wasn't in the end," Amy said in a hushed tone, looking at the cups.

Caleb nodded and smiled. "I remember Gabriel mentioned him briefly, but then refused to even talk about him. I never knew much about this Larry fellow, except that he hates Gabriel," Caleb said as he handed both Amy and Ginger their cups. Both the girls accepted the cups and took a sip. Caleb took a sip from his own and exhaled in euphoria. Amy chuckled.

"How did you feel about Gabriel turning you?" Amy asked, as she kept her gaze on Caleb.

"I felt this weird, uncertain, scared, and angry feeling inside of me. I felt alone and angry about why I got chosen to be a son of an immortal man," Caleb said before he took another sip. "Probably how you two are feeling right now. If you ever need someone to help you through the process, I may have some experience with this situation," Caleb said in a soothing voice.

Ginger chuckled and gulped down her cup before she poured herself another. Amy looked at how Ginger was drinking down the blood with irritation. "Perhaps sometime," Amy whispered before she gulped down her cup and set it down. "I want to first see if these feelings will disappear on their own without too much pressure from help. I do know how good it felt when Alistair helped me with my transition and how I could control myself amongst humans," Amy said as she kept her focus on the bottle.

Caleb looked up with interest. "Tell me about that? I wonder if it's something I could benefit from, as well." Amy smiled and chuckled.

"There was just something about Alistair's voice that made me feel so relaxed and happy about being an immortal. I hope this doesn't mean I'm falling in love with him. There was just something that made it okay for me," Amy said as she looked over at Caleb.

Ginger put down her cup and looked over at Amy with interest. "Alistair helped you cope with your urges?" Ginger asked. Amy smiled and nodded. "How?" Amy exhaled and looked back at when she was at the airport, going back to Oregon to fix the human situation that she had created. "He sat me down at our gate and just started repeating words of that I was only scared and not thirst," she said.

Ginger smiled. "I wish I could've experienced something like that. I could use some type of mindfulness tactic to help me cope with my problems in this world. And now, family," Ginger said with a chuckle. Caleb chuckled and leaned against the sofa. "Do you notice a difference between how you feel now and how you felt at the airport?"

Amy smiled and exhaled. "Yes. I feel more darkness being in this castle and felt more relaxed and happy when I was with Bryan,

Alistair, Darcia, and the other guys," Amy said with sadness in her voice. Gabriel came back into the room they were in with anger in his eyes.

"We have a problem," Gabriel snapped before he sat down in his chair. Lucien, Vladimir, Daniel, Amelia, Adrian, Katrina, Audrey, and Claudia all came into the room they were in and sat down in separate chairs, waiting for Gabriel to talk. "It appears that our extended family, Alistair and Darcia, knew about Larry and his intentions for Amy, but yet they didn't do anything to protect my daughter from harm," Gabriel said in a raised voice. "The deal was when I handed you two over to Alistair, and Darcia was that you would be protected and not put in any form of danger," Gabriel snapped, as he looked up at his group. Lucien looked up at Gabriel and raised his hand. "Questions can be saved for later, unless you have a suggestion?" Gabriel asked. Lucien lowered his hand and continued to listen to Gabriel. "That doesn't make me happy in any way." Gabriel snapped. "I will invite them and see what the other covens have to say about the fate of Alistair and Darcia. I will contact them tomorrow evening and we'll decide the fate of that family. Amy, I am so sorry this even happened to you, as well. Did you get injured in any way?" Gabriel asked, focusing his gaze on Amy, who looked like a frightened deer in the headlights.

Amy nodded and cleared her throat. "They gave me a potion. It scared me, but Alistair and Bryan did eventually come to my rescue. Then I did hang out with Larry and he even came over to Emma and Athan's house when I had arrived back to Oregon," Amy said in a hushed tone. From the news Gabriel was hearing, he put his head against his temple and massaged it.

"Well, thank you for being honest with me about that, Amy. We will make sure that you or Ginger will remain safe here," Gabriel said before he smiled at them.

Back at the motel, Alistair and Darcia were in their room, feeling anxious and tired. "My love," Darcia whispered as she placed her right hand on Alistair's left hand. "What should we do about this situation?" she whispered. Alistair looked at Darcia with guilt and pain.

"I don't know. We tried out best, trying to be the best protectors of the Ambrose daughters, but instead, we may've created a bigger problem for ourselves. If anyone needs to be punished, I'll take the blame and have you relocate with our sons to another country," Alistair said. Darcia shrieked and wrapped her arms around Alistair.

"Never!" Darcia cried as she felt this hard feeling in her stomach. "I won't let you die. We can always relocate together. Perhaps tonight?" Darcia whimpered. Alistair cupped Darcia's face to plant a soft kiss on her lips. "No, Alistair," Darcia whispered as she held him close to her. "Please. Leave here, with us."

Alistair held Darcia in her arms tightly. "I don't know what to do anymore, Darcia. We did our duty. We brought the girls back to Gabriel. Perhaps it is time that we did relocate to another home," he whispered before he loosened his grip on Darcia.

Raymond, Bryan, and Joshua, and Xander came into their room with somber faces. "What's this about Alistair wanting to get executed for his crimes?" Raymond asked, with guilt in his eyes. Darcia looked over at her sons.

"Nothing is going to happen, my boys," Darcia said in a soothing tone. "Nobody is going anywhere and nobody is going to die." Alistair scoffed at that comment.

"Yet," Alistair whispered. Darcia punched Alistair softly. "Ouch, what was that?" Alistair snapped.

Darcia glared at him before she got to her feet. "As far as I am concerned, nobody saw this situation coming. The situation with Larry is over. Yes, the moment when Amy spent the night at his family's mansion and how he came back to Romania. As far as I am concerned, there is nothing we have to worry about," Darcia snapped.

Just then, Alistair's phone rang. Alistair looked and saw an anonymous caller and hesitated before he answered it. "Hello?" Alistair asked in a stern voice, not wanting to sound vulnerable over the phone.

"Alistair," Gabriel said in a calm tone. "I need you and Darcia to come to the castle, without your sons." Alistair looked up at Darcia with horror and shook his head. "Whatever happened in Oregon regarding Larry needs to be addressed," Gabriel snapped.

Darcia's eyes started to water as she started to fear for the worst. Darcia mouthed the words no to Alistair. "Okay, Gabriel. When would you like Darcia and me to be there?" Alistair asked.

"Tomorrow evening, at eight o'clock," Gabriel said before he hung up the phone. Darcia screamed and held Alistair close to her. "No!" Darcia screamed. "You can't die!" Alistair felt so overwhelmed that he shoved Darcia off of him and got to his feet.

"This is insane. We didn't put Amy's life in jeopardy on purpose. I wonder if this is some type of setup. Amy should at least know that we had no intention of harming her or that we knew about Larry's existence," Alistair snapped before he walked out of the room. Darcia was crying on the edge of the bed, till Bryan walked over to her and wrapped his arms around her.

"I'm sure it'll all be okay, Darcia," Bryan said with a smile. "Perhaps Gabriel just needs a little explanation of why Larry showed up. As long as we know that we didn't do anything intentional, we have nothing to worry about." Darcia held Bryan in her arms and couldn't stop crying. Bryan used his sleep powers on Darcia and sent her off to a deep slumber. When Alistair had returned from his walk, the sun started to break through. He closed the curtains and got on the same bed Darcia was sleeping in, but couldn't fall to a slumber.

Back at the castle, Amy and Ginger were in Ginger's room, reading more from Gabriel's diaries. "Our father did travel a lot when he was young," Amy said with interest in her voice. "He's been throughout most of Western Europe and to some states in America. Where did he even get the money to survive? He must've stolen it from his victims, wouldn't you think?" Amy asked, looking at Ginger.

"Whatever he did, he managed to survive all of this time and purchase himself a nice, big castle in Romania," Ginger said with a smile.

Amy! Amy heard Bryan's voice in her head and with a shock she got to her feet. "Bryan?" Amy whispered, causing Ginger to look up at Amy with confusion.

Amy, you must listen to me. Pleas be honest about your answer to what I am about to ask you. Can you do that?

Bryan, what's going on? Are you okay?

Amy, did you tell Gabriel that we knew about Larry and had you intentionally harmed by his family?

Bryan, what's going on? No, of course not. Why would you even ask such a question?

Gabriel is having my parents over at the castle tomorrow evening, and Darcia fears that Gabriel might have Alistair killed for putting you in harm's way.

That's absurd. Why does my father…Gabriel even think you tried to have me killed intentionally?

Larry showed up in Romania. My brother Raymond called him over and we had a bit of a situation between us.

Amy choked on her own saliva, which caused her to cough hard. *Bryan, I don't understand. How did Larry even show up at Romania and why did you tell him?*

I didn't. It was Raymond's doing. He thought it would've been best if I… well, how can I phrase this properly, to get rid of him my way. Bryan thought, as he was sitting with Raymond in his room, with the curtains closed.

What? You tried to get rid of him? Bryan, perhaps we need to see each other about this situation, because I can't really picture the whole situation.

Bryan sighed and cleared his throat. Raymond sat on the other bed, staring at Bryan with anger. "Bryan, what are you doing? Having me killed, as well?" Bryan waved Raymond off and got to his feet, walking towards the bathroom of the room. Raymond got off the bed and walked over to the bathroom, where Bryan was standing. "Stop making me look like the bad guy, Bryan," Raymond snapped. "I had no intention that this would even happen."

Bryan looked over at Raymond with frustration and rolled his eyes. "I know that, Raymond. I was only asking Amy if she knew about Gabriel's plans or not.

Bryan, are you still there? Please don't ignore me right now.

Amy, we are afraid that Gabriel is going to have Alistair killed with a vote from all the covens you have met. Has Gabriel mentioned anything to you about his plan?

Amy sat back down in shock. "Alistair is going to die because of me?" Amy asked, causing Ginger to close the book and sit next to Amy.

"Amy, what's going on?" Ginger asked with worry. "Please talk to me." Amy looked up at Ginger and felt her eyes tear up.

"Alistair might die because of me," Amy whimpered as she got on her feet. All because of my meeting with Larry.

"What?" Ginger snapped. "Why would he do or even think that, Amy?" Amy turned to face Ginger and shrugged before she started to bite her fingernails.

"Amy, whatever is going on, we have until tomorrow evening as well. Alistair isn't going to die." Amy scoffed and headed for the door. "Amy, please don't walk away while we're still talking. Amy turned around and glared at Ginger.

"Yes, mommy," Amy snapped before she walked back to Ginger and stood five feet away from her. Ginger rolled her eyes and shook her head.

"I hardly doubt this will be the end of Alistair. I don't believe he or Darcia would intentionally have you harmed." Amy moved her gaze over to the window and saw how light it was getting through the curtains. "What does your intuition say? Perhaps Gabriel is just being an overprotective father to us, Amy, and with a decent conversation, it will be cleared up in no time," Ginger said before she smiled at Amy.

Amy shrugged. "I hope so. I don't want to have anyone's death on my conscience, Ginger. I think I'll go back to my room and see if my body is willing to slumber for a bit." Ginger walked over to Amy and hugged her tightly. "Thanks, Ginger. I don't know how I would've been without you," Amy said before she released her hold on Ginger.

When Amy got to her bed, she got under the covers and closed her eyes. To her surprise, she did manage to fall asleep. She was walking through the castle and saw how clean and fresh it was from the inside. Everyone looked happy and relaxed. Gabriel and Katrina were in their sleeping quarter and Ginger was in her sleeping quarter. Amy decided to go outside where it was bright out, but noticed how she wasn't burning or how she couldn't feel any different from she had before. As she was walking, she saw Bryan, Darcia, Alistair, and Raymond walking towards her. Instead of remaining in their human form, they transformed into wolves.

"Bryan?" Amy asked as he kept running towards her. "Please, stop!" Amy screamed. Bryan kept running till he jumped over her, causing Amy to duck and saw another figure that looked like Larry under Bryan's body.

"What's going on?" Amy whispered as she saw the four of them around Larry, who was cowering in shock. "Stop! Larry is innocent! You can't have him!" Amy screamed before she woke up screaming in her bed. Ginger came running into Amy's bedroom with shock.

"Amy! What happened?" Ginger screamed. "Amy, it's okay. You are safe." Amy looked at Ginger with horror. Amy looked around at her dark room and felt this cold feeling around her.

"I had this weird dream where I saw Bryan, Alistair, Raymond, and Darcia running towards Larry and attacking him. I couldn't stop the situation, Ginger," Amy whimpered. "It felt so real."

Ginger stoked Amy's hair gently and tried to calm her down. "It's okay, Amy. It was just a nightmare. Nothing more." Amy got out of bed and grabbed her robe before she headed out. "Where are you going, Amy? It's only four in the morning." Amy ignored Ginger and walked down to the cooler to get herself a cup of blood. Ginger followed.

"I suddenly got this intense thirst, for some reason, Ginger. I needed to calm myself. When Caleb handed me that cup of blood yesterday, I felt much better." Ginger chuckled as she watched Amy gulp down a cup of blood.

"I think I could use some of that stuff, as well, Amy. Could you pour me a cup?" Amy grabbed a cup for Ginger and poured her from the same bottle that Caleb had opened.

"We still have four hours till Alistair's trial," Amy said. "I feel the need to be present during the talk with Gabriel and the other covens. Do you think he'll allow that?" Amy asked as she looked at the blood inside the cup. Ginger shrugged.

"You can always ask. It might be important to be there to vouch for Alistair and Darcia's good behavior," Ginger said before she gulped down her cup.

Back at the motel, Alistair managed to sleep for a bit and woke up from Darcia's hand over his chest. He gently removed her hand and got up to splash some water on his face. "This is so absurd. How Gabriel first puts his trust in us and then he suddenly has mixed feelings?" Alistair whispered to himself. He heard Darcia moan and walked back to the bed to see her eyes open.

"My love," Darcia whispered. "I don't feel so well about this whole trial that we could be facing." Alistair smiled before he sat on the edge of the bed and leaned down to kiss Darcia on her forehead.

"It'll happen as it happens, my beloved wife," Alistair said as he stroked Darcia's hair. "If we must, I'll propose that we never have any contact with Amy or Ginger ever again, if that means that none of us will die." Darcia's eyes started to water again. "Shh, my beloved. Nothing bad will happen to us. We just have to be honest and hopefully, it'll all be over before we know it. Tomorrow we can celebrate with a nice evening hunt," Alistair said before he kissed Darcia tenderly on her lips.

Bryan knocked on Alistair and Darcia's room and waited to enter. "Son, what are you doing up? Shouldn't you still be slumbering?" Alistair asked. Bryan felt his eyes water and his throat clogged.

"You can't go alone. If anyone is to blame for Amy being with Larry and Larry's anger, it should be me. I was Amy's main protector. I watched over her. I sat with her on those flights. It should be me, father," Bryan said before he sat down on a chair.

Alistair sighed. "Son, nothing bad is going to happen. You or your brothers are not coming with us. Gabriel explicitly asked for Darcia and me. Please, do us a favor and remain here with your brothers. If you must, take your brothers over to a bar or a club and claim yourselves a nice girl or guy to snack on," Alistair said as he placed his hand on Bryan's shoulder.

"As far as I am concerned, we are all innocent in this situation with Larry. We didn't intentionally put Amy's life in any danger. Amy is okay now, so there is nothing we need to worry about. We have about three hours left, but your mother and I will leave in about two hours to show up on time. Please, Bryan. Don't do anything that you might regret. Darcia and I will be back before you know it, and we'll celebrate," Alistair said with a smile.

Darcia kept fidgeting with her hair as she sat tense on the edge of her bed. Alistair walked over to sit next to her and wrapped his right arm around her shoulders. "We'll be fine. Okay?" Alistair said with a reassuring smile. Bryan nodded but couldn't get himself to smile. "Good. Now, could you give your mother and me some privacy for a moment?" Alistair asked, causing Bryan to gag at that request and leave the room. Alistair chuckled after the door closed.

"My love, how can you be so relaxed right now? I feel that this is our final moment together. I can't seem to relax myself."

Alistair placed his hands gently on Darcia's face. "Listen to my voice, Darcia. Just listen to me. Please close your eyes." Darcia closed her eyes and relaxed her shoulders. "Good. I want you to relax and do some breathing exercises. Inhale when I ask you to and exhale when I ask you to. Are you up for this little exercise?" Alistair asked. Darcia nodded while keeping her eyes closed. "Good. Now I want you to inhale." Darcia inhaled and waited about ten seconds. "Good, now exhale." Darcia exhaled. "Very good," Alistair said, before he planted another kiss on Darcia's lips. "Again, inhale." Darcia inhaled and then waited. "Exhale," Alistair said. Darcia exhaled. "Please do this for the next five sessions." Darcia repeated the inhaling and exhaling and started to feel more relaxed. "Good. Now please open your eyes."

Darcia opened her eyes and her eyes looked calmer than they were before. "Let's go prove, Gabriel, that we are the best family that he has ever had the honor of creating," Alistair said with glee in his eyes and extended his hand to Darcia, who took Alistair's hand and walked out of the motel together.

Chapter 17

The Trial

After Gabriel had awoken from his slumber, he put on his black suit and tie and shiny shoes with laces and turned into quite the honorable gentlemen when he walked up from the basement area. His brothers followed him seconds later and the living quarter got turned into a trial where there was a big television screen with all the coven leaders on them. It was fifteen minutes before the trial started and the doorbell rang. Hildegard walked over to the door and welcomed Alistair and Darcia into the castle.

There was a fresh bottle of blood and nine cups with eight chairs around the table. Gabriel sat in his throne-like chair and waited for his group to arrive. "In five minutes, the trial will start. Amy and Ginger, I need you to be present in the back. Please, keep quiet till after the trial. Try to remember your questions and comments until the trial is over. I'll discuss the verdict with all the leaders and the decision will then be final," Gabriel said, as he looked at all the group members.

It was eight o'clock and the grandfather clock in the living quarter had chimed. "Let's begin," Gabriel said before he got to his feet. "Alistair and Darcia stand trial in Romania because of the dangerous peril they put Amy in when they were in Oregon. How do you two plead? Alistair, you may begin," Gabriel said as he focused his gaze on Alistair.

"Innocent," Alistair said in a stern but also calm tone. Gabriel nodded to Darcia.

"Innocent," Darcia said in the same tone as Alistair. Gabriel nodded and focused his attention on the television screen.

"It appears that the opposing party declares themselves innocent. I want to hear stories from all of you leaders. We'll start with Dante. Please tell us how you perceived Alistair and Darcia when they were with Amy?" Dante cleared his throat and the screen focused on him.

"When I met Darcia and Alistair, they seemed like sweet and immortals. A couple that were friendly and easy-going," Dante said. Gabriel remained silent so Dante could continue.

"I did notice that they did keep their distance away from Amy and let her sleep alone, even though I recall hearing Bryan telling Amy he would watch over her, but instead, he would go hunting with Alistair and Darcia, and our group." Gabriel looked over his shoulder at Alistair and glared.

"Anything else, Dante?" Gabriel asked. Dante shook his head. "Okay. Now I want to hear from Alarick. What do you have to say about your perception of Alistair and Darcia?" Alarick swallowed hard, remembering how Adrian showed up during their hunt. "Alarick, please answer the question," Gabriel said with impatience in his voice.

"Alistair and Darcia seemed very loving toward Amy. Bryan was quite protective of Amy when they had visited us. There was just a moment where we thought it was going to go wrong," Alarick said with guilt in his voice. Gabriel's ears peaked. "When we went hunting, or at least when Alistair and Darcia's group went out hunting with Amy, something had happened to Amy, and Amy ran off and got injured somehow." Gabriel gasped and looked at Alistair with anger.

"Then what happened?" Gabriel snapped as he kept his gaze on Alistair. Adrian looked over at Alistair, and then at Gabriel.

"Perhaps I can add my part to the story, Gabe?" Adrian asked as he held his hand up. Gabriel looked confused at Adrian. "I was there."

"Go on, brother. What happened?" Adrian sighed and formulated his answer in his head.

"I saw Amy, and I may've scared her when I was in wolf form," Adrian said quietly. Gabriel recomposed himself and cleared his throat. "That was just my part. Then I did hear Bryan and Darcia come for her," Adrian said before he leaned against his chair. Gabriel chuckled and looked back at Alistair.

"From what I'm hearing, Adrian did the right thing. He ran to Amy first, before you got the chance to help her." Adrian looked concerned at Alistair. "We'll continue," Gabriel snapped.

"Thank you, Alarick. Now I want to hear from Kristjan. How did you perceive Alistair and Darcia?" Gabriel said with anger in his voice. Kristjan waited a few seconds.

"They seemed like decent, good immortals. Bryan did make Amy feel comfortable and happy. I just remember seeing how happy they looked together. I didn't think much about Alistair or Darcia, except that they were well-mannered." Gabriel smiled and nodded. "However, there was a moment where Gregory almost attacked Amy." Gabriel's eyebrows rose. "Yes. I remember now. Gregory had this intense hunger for Amy and almost killed her. I apologize for that, master," Kristjan said.

"Well, Kristjan. Thank you for your honesty Well, it seems that there are mixed feelings regarding this trial. I think it's time we take a break, as we have been here for an hour," Gabriel said before he left the room. The other members just remained seated. "Before we finish off, Gregory gets the death sentence after Amy's children are born."

Darcia started to feel this fear inside of her again and grabbed Alistair's hand. The other members of the group looked at them with pity. Amy and Ginger then came into the circle. "That whole incident of me running away from you was my fault," Amy said with sadness in her eyes. "I should've never run away. You were just doing what you were meant to do. Hunt for humans." Darcia smiled and shrugged.

"Let me talk to my father," Amy said. "I think I can settle this better than having anyone get hurt." Amy walked in the direction of where Gabriel was at and saw him with his back to her, drinking from another bottle. "Father," Amy whispered. Gabriel turned around with surprise and wiped his mouth with the back of his right hand.

"Amy, what are you doing here?" Amy shook her head in sadness. "Amy," Gabriel whispered and wrapped his arms around Amy, holding her close. "My child, what's wrong?" Amy looked up at him with tears in her eyes.

"Please don't hurt them, father," Amy whispered. Gabriel chuckled and released his grasp from Amy.

"For every action, there is either a positive reaction to a reward or a punishment for being bad. When I handed you and Ginger over to Alistair and Darcia, they vowed they would never see you come to harm. We haven't even discussed the situation with Larry. When I return, that's the next topic on the list."

Amy felt as if Gabriel betrayed her. "Please, father. Darcia and Alistair were wonderful to me. Bryan was, or actually still is an amazing guy. He was there for me when I cried. He was there for me when I found out I was pregnant. He was there for me for the past year. I love him, father. I wish to be with Bryan. Have him become my mate and the father of these children," Amy said. Gabriel furrowed his brow.

"We'll talk about that soon, Amy. Right now, the trial will continue. You can either wait in the back and remain silent or I'll have you placed in your room for a while." Amy felt anger boiling in her. "Excuse me, my child," Gabriel said before he placed the bottle back in the cooler and walked back to the room.

The group was silent when Gabriel entered the room again. "Okay, to be continued," Gabriel said. "Where did we leave off? Oh yes. The topic of the immortal Larry," Gabriel said with humor in his voice. The entire group remained quiet. "Do you all remember, Larry? The man who I snacked on, about five hundred years ago?" The group looked at each other, as if they were seeing if anyone knew who Larry was. "Well, okay. When I was about five or six hundred years old, I came across this charming young man who was studying, I believe. I was so hungry and had no self-control. To make a long story short, I fed off of him, but didn't kill him."

The group looked at Gabriel with confusion. "Yes, that was very wrong of me, but he transitioned into one of us. I saw him about two days ago when I was going for my walk out in the dark with my daughters and I saw him pounce on me. Of course, due to my speed, he didn't touch me. My daughter, Amy, appeared to have recognized him. Apparently, she met him in Oregon, where he pretended to be human, just to get close to my daughter," Gabriel said as he crossed his arms. "Apparently, Alistair and Darcia thought it was okay for Amy to spend the night with Larry, knowing that he was immortal," Gabriel said sarcastically.

Alistair sighed and waited for the moment to speak up. "I'll let Alistair take it from here," Gabriel said before he sat down. Alistair looked at Darcia, who looked at him with fear. Alistair patted Darcia's hands before he got to his feet.

"Yes, we allowed Amy to spend the night at Larry's mansion, but I never knew Larry was immortal. My son Raymond, however, just recently told me the news. He even had Bryan try to kill him."

Amy squeaked when she heard that. The whole group looked at Amy with surprise. "Sorry," Amy whispered. Alistair looked at Amy and went back to his story.

"If the fact that Raymond knew something that I didn't, I'm willing to take blame for what Larry had done to Amy and accept my fate," Alistair said. Darcia got up.

"No, Alistair! You cannot do this to us!" Darcia screamed. "Gabriel, please. Alistair or Raymond would never harm Amy. They love her. They saw her as family. Raymond and Bryan even fought each other over Amy when we were at the airport." Just then, Darcia remembered how there was a human spectacle.

"Yes," Gabriel whispered. "Then I came for Amy that afternoon and had her brought back home." Gabriel nodded. "I've heard enough." Just then, Darcia raised her hand. "Yes?" Gabriel asked with annoyance.

"I remember when we had brought Amy back you to months ago, that she had fainted, and you snapped at Alistair that you had almost killed her, because she smelled too much of human." The group looked back at Gabriel with confusion. "Alistair never did any of those. That one time where Amy ran off, that was a flaw on our part, but we never saw Amy as food," Darcia said.

Alistair looked at Darcia with pride. "Exactly. Before you even consider us to be the evil ones of this coven, please remember your part in it as well." Gabriel scoffed and got to his feet. "What do you want me to say? Case closed, and have you two leave?" Gabriel snapped. Alistair and Darcia nodded simultaneously. Gabriel looked at his group, who looked at him with confusion. "Case closed. Amy and Ginger are safe, but there is still this Larry creature that needs to be dealt with," Gabriel said.

Alistair and Darcia started to head for the door. "Before you leave, here are my terms, since there have been scary moments in Amy's journey. Your group is not allowed to see Amy till after she's had kids. Do you understand?" Gabriel said with anger in his eyes. Alistair walked back a few steps.

"Or what? You'll have us killed? As far as I am concerned, my group and I have been a better family to Amy than you have, Gabriel. You gave them up, because you were going to have them killed? What father even thinks like that? You were ruthless when you grew up. You even had Caleb turned, as well," Alistair snapped.

Gabriel walked in the direction where Alistair was standing. "Or there will be funerals to be planned," Gabriel snarled. Darcia grabbed Alistair's hand and tugged on it.

"Come, Alistair. We shall go back to our sons. They must be worried about us," Darcia said. Alistair let himself be led by Darcia, and they both left the castle.

Back at the motel rooms, Bryan was pacing back and forth in horror. "What if they don't return? What if they are dead?" Bryan murmured. Raymond came back into the room with glee. "Yes?" Bryan asked.

"It's all okay, Bryan. Alistair and Darcia are on their way back. There is a problem, though. You are not to see Amy till after she's had her kids," Raymond said. Bryan looked up at him with anger.

"What?" Bryan snapped, walking towards Raymond. Raymond walked back up to the door and held his hands up. "That's ridiculous. Why would he even say such a thing?" Raymond moved inward to close the door.

"Gabriel had all the leaders on this big television screen and they mentioned the situation that took place in Athens, where Amy ran down the hill and Adrian was there." Bryan rolled his eyes and shook his head.

"Unbelievable. We were actually protecting her. We did arrive before Adrian could do anything and we took care of her afterwards."

Raymond shrugged. "That's all I could hear from my mind reading ability, Bryan. On a positive note, our parents are returning any moment now. And see them walking in the distance?" Alistair and Darcia came running toward the motel. Raymond opened the door for them to enter. "Mom, dad?" Raymond asked. "I hope everything went okay?" Raymond asked before he looked at Bryan.

"Yes, son," Alistair said. "Hey Bryan, we are okay. Just like we promised you," Alistair said before he hugged Bryan. "It's going to be okay for us." Darcia smiled and hugged Bryan and Joshua as well. Bryan took a step back.

"What about Amy?" Bryan asked. "Raymond said I can't ever see her for a while?" Alistair and Darcia exchanged glances. "What?"

"Yes son," Alistair said. "That is correct. Only for about eight months from now, or perhaps sooner." Bryan scoffed and walked towards his bed to sit down on. Darcia sat down next to Bryan and held him close to her.

"I know you love her, Bryan," Darcia whispered. "I loved her like a daughter. She reminded me so much of Arabella, didn't she, Alistair?" Alistair smiled.

"Yes. Such a beautiful angel, she was. For now, let's say we all go out for a ceremonial hunt?" Alistair asked with happiness in his voice.

Silas and Xander came into the room to hug Alistair and Darcia. "We're so happy to have you back with us," Silas said as he was wiping his eyes. "I got so worried about you both." Darcia leaned over to kiss them both on their foreheads.

"Nothing could ever kill our group," Darcia chuckled. "We're very strong, especially together." The six of them left the motel rooms to go out on their hunt.

Back at the castle, Gabriel remained in his chair and kept going back to the moment he saw Amy for the first time after eighteen years. "I have no idea what happened to me that day," Gabriel said as he kept his gaze on the floor. "How did that even happen?" Katrina walked over to him and sat on his lap.

"You were new to this situation, Gabriel. Please don't be so hard on yourself. I even had this hunger inside of me." Gabriel furrowed his brow. "I have no intention of harming your daughters, you know, but I know that feeling."

Gabriel nudged Katrina off of his lap so he could get to his feet. "Well, now that this hectic situation is over, we now have Larry to deal with and then Amy and Caleb's offspring," Gabriel murmured. He walked over for another cup of blood. Amy and Ginger remained together. Amy watched Gabriel walk past her and quickly moved her gaze back to Ginger.

"Ginger, I am so relieved that the trial is over and that Alistair and Darcia are okay. I was so worried that Alistair may have died just for the sake of that incident in Athens," Amy whispered.

"Me too, Amy. Me too," Ginger whispered before she walked over to see what Gabriel was doing. "Father?" Ginger asked. Gabriel looked at Ginger and forced a smile. "How is this going to play out? Are we going to have a battle where it's us against Larry?" Gabriel scoffed.

"No, my child. This is mostly Larry against me," Gabriel said with a smile. "You and Amy will have nothing to worry about. It will all be okay." Ginger smiled and looked at the floor.

"I'm worried about Amy's wellbeing, though. I can understand how the whole trip was Alistair's responsibility, but Bryan did his best to care for Amy as much as he could." Gabriel gulped down the last drops of blood and placed the cup on the counter. "Amy loves Bryan. Probably the same way how you loved our mother."

Gabriel kept his gaze on Ginger. "I just want to keep my girls with me for a while, before I allow a son-in-law to enter the family," Gabriel said. "Alistair and Darcia are still alive, including their boys. I will not back down from my verdict of keeping Amy and Bryan separated." Ginger rolled her eyes and walked away from Gabriel.

Gabriel growled before he placed the bottle back in the cooler and walked back to the living room quarter. He saw his brothers and the females still together. "I will go down for a little nap," Gabriel said before he left them. When he got into his own bed, he laid on his back, staring at the ceiling, and remembered how beautiful Arabella looked in her wedding gown. Just then, Arabella's ghost form showed up.

"Gabriel," Arabella said. "I am very proud of you for how you handled the trial. You were a great host and honorable leader of the group." Gabriel smiled and sat up on the edge of his bed.

"I was just so scared and worried about Amy's wellbeing, Arabella. I really wanted to keep my daughters safe, but instead, I think I may've made things worse," Gabriel said, with remorse in his voice.

Arabella floated closer to Gabriel and hovered a few inches from him. "I know. I know how awful it must've been to have seen my heart slowing and being stuck with two children. You have them back and they seem to do much better than they did the first night you had them here. If Amy does love this Bryan guy, let them live a happy life together. Caleb has no intentions of ever being a husband to Amy. This was done out of pure force," Arabella said. "If you love our daughters enough, please let them make their own decisions and live their own lives. Once you set something free, there is a chance that they will return."

Gabriel scoffed and got to his feet. "I have already let them go and live their own lives for a while. Then Larry shows up," Gabriel snapped. "What must I do about him, my love?" Gabriel asked.

Arabella smirked. "You're Gabriel Ambrose. Leader of all covens. If those other groups have any respect for you, then you will be protected." Gabriel chuckled. "You're strong. You can handle a youngling like Larry," Arabella said with a chuckle.

Gabriel looked at Arabella as if he had fallen in love with her again. "I wish there was a way to bring you back into my world again, my wife." Arabella floated to Gabriel and wrapped her ghost arms around her.

"If there is a way to put me in limbo, there should be a way to bring me back, right?" Arabella asked. Gabriel remembered the book that Amelia was reading from and decided to run up to Amelia.

Back at the motel, Alistair and Darcia walked over to their room and locked the door this time. "I need you, my beloved wife," Alistair said as he guided Darcia over to the bed.

Bryan, Raymond, Joshua, Silas, and Xander were in Bryan's room, watching television, to avoid hearing their parents. "Some night, wasn't it, brothers?" Silas asked, as he turned his gaze to Bryan and Raymond. "You both were so scared," Silas said with a chuckle. Raymond looked over at Silas and smirked.

"Oh yeah, mister cry baby? I saw the way you wiped your eyes when they came running into the room." The five boys all chuckled.

"I missed our moments like this," Bryan said as he looked at his brothers. "Just the four of us, hanging out. Perhaps a break from Gabriel's flock will do us some good," Bryan said. The four boys were sitting around reminiscing about their past and occasionally laughing.

Back at the castle, Gabriel walked over to Amelia, who was talking with Daniel. "Amelia," Gabriel snapped. Amelia looked over at Gabriel. "Do we still have that book where we put Arabella in limbo? The spell book?" Amelia thought about it for a few seconds.

"Yes. It's in our library," Amelia said. "Why?" Gabriel ignored her question and walked over to the library and saw various books, from law books to science books, and then what looked like a spell book.

Daniel and Amelia walked into the library. "Are you going to do some spell casting?" Amelia asked. "It might not work this time." Gabriel looked at the chapters and saw a spell on how to reverse ghosts. "Gabriel, what are you planning?"

"I'm going to try to bring Arabella back to our world, Amelia," Gabriel said before he grabbed the book and brought it back to the basement area. He was looking at the materials he needed. He placed the book on his bed and thought of Arabella. Gabriel grabbed a knife to draw blood in his hand. "I'm calling for Arabella Ambrose, wife and lover of Gabriel," Gabriel said. "With this knife, I will draw blood and swear on my blood that I will protect, love and care for Arabella if she returns to her old form in this world," Gabriel said.

Gabriel closed his eyes and cut open his hand and felt his blood trickle down his hands. "Arabella, with this blood oath, I promise to love, protect, care, and always be there for you when you return to me in my arms." Gabriel remained in that position for a few minutes. Then he looked at the spell book and saw some ancient words he had to speak. Gabriel memorized the words and closed his eyes, repeating the words.

Then he opened up his eyes, and nothing happened. "Arabella, please come home to me. Please," Gabriel begged before he got on his knees. "On my blood, I need you back home with me. Please." Gabriel felt his eyes starting to water. Still, nothing happened. "Fine. I guess these spells have no value anymore," Gabriel growled before he tossed the book off his bed and walked back to the living quarter.

Amelia and Daniel waited for him when Gabriel came up. "Did anything work, Gabriel?" Amelia asked. Gabriel shook his head. "I'm sorry, Gabe. I really wish there was such a thing as bringing people back from the dead. I never even knew it was possible to put people in limbo," Amelia whispered.

Amy and Ginger were up in Amy's room reminiscing about their memories of being in Oregon. "Emma and Athan were kind of odd in their own way, wouldn't you think?" Amy asked with a chuckle. Ginger chuckled.

"Aren't all parents odd in their own ways?" Ginger asked before she felt a cold presence near her. "Amy, did you feel that?" Ginger asked as she looked around the room. "We may not be alone."

Amy scoffed at that comment and shook her head. "I have no idea what you are talking about, Ginger," Amy said with a chuckle. Ginger got off the bed and looked around. "Ginger, you're scaring me. What are you doing?" Amy asked before she got off the bed.

Ginger didn't feel anything anymore and looked outside to see nothing but darkness. "Perhaps it was just a brief moment," Ginger murmured. Ginger walked over to where Amy put pictures of Emma and Athan, and the dogs. "They were good to us, you know?" Ginger asked. "I did make it to college for a while. Mostly because of my powers of persuasion. I wonder why you didn't do that?" Amy looked at Ginger, confused. Amy shrugged and looked back outside to see nothing but stars and black skies.

"I wonder what they have been doing lately," Amy murmured to herself. "Probably doing their routine of work, dog walking, eating, and sleeping." Amy chuckled. "At least that's what I remembered about them." Ginger walked in the direction of her door.

"I think I will lie down for a bit, if you don't mind," Ginger said. Amy nodded and smiled. "Sweet dreams, if I don't see you." Amy waved at Ginger before she herself got into her bed. Even though it was morning for them, Amy felt quite tired. Probably because of the trial and still adjusting to her new life. Amy looked up at her ceiling and felt her eyes close. Amy got out of bed and stood on the other side of the room.

Back at the motel, Raymond suddenly looked up in shock at the sky. "Brothers," Raymond said in a panicking tone. "I think we may be facing something more. I feel this feminine presence entering our lives real soon. I cannot really picture who it could be. It couldn't be Amy, Ginger, or Amelia. I think there is someone out there." The other boys exchanged looks with each other.

"Raymond, whatever you know, please tell us," said Bryan. Raymond looked back at his brothers in shock that slowly turned into a smile. "I can't say much, but I may have a good feeling about who we could be seeing real soon." Bryan rolled his eyes.

"I know about Amy's pregnancy, okay?" Bryan snapped. "I don't need to know which children will look like Caleb." Raymond chuckled but didn't respond.

Epilogue

As Amy was falling asleep, there was suddenly she heard a knock on the door. It was probably not Ginger who would return. Could it be Larry? Amy felt this intense fear inside of her and remained quiet. The knocking repeated another two times. "Come in," Amy said shakily. The door opened and there was a woman standing in the doorway, smiling at Amy. The woman reminded Amy of her mother.

"Mom?" Amy whispered. "Is that really you?" Arabella came walking into her room, wearing a long blue dress, with her long brown hair and brown eyes.

"Amy," said the voice.

Amy got out of bed and walked to the opposite side of the room. "Who are you?" Amy snapped, feeling fearful. Arabella smiled.

"It is I, your mother. Arabella Ambrose. Wife of Gabriel Ambrose. I believe your father brought me back from the dead." Amy looked at her with confusion and horror. "Fear not, my child. Please, come to me." Amy felt hesitant but suddenly felt this need to know if it was true.

Amy walked into Arabella's arms and felt this warm feeling around you. Amy's eyes started to tear up. Ginger heard the commotion and entered the room with surprise. "Mom?" Ginger asked. Arabella turned around and opened her left arm for Ginger to enter. "Mom!" Ginger screamed before she ran into her arms. "How is this possible?" Ginger asked as her eyes were forming tears.

Arabella's eyes were on both Amy and Ginger's eyes. "Your father may've brought me back from the dead. How? I am unsure. Why he never thought to do this earlier, he might explain. For now, let me look at my beautiful girls. How grown up and beautiful you both have become," Arabella said as she wiped her eyes. "Such exquisite creatures."

Amy looked at the open door and heard footsteps coming up the stairs. "I think father might be surprised to see you," Amy said. "Father?" Amy asked. Gabriel entered the room and looked at Arabella in a shocked manner.

"Arabella, is that you?" Gabriel asked as he approached Arabella, who had tears of joy running down her cheeks.

"Yes, my love," Arabella said as she walked over to hug Gabriel. Gabriel wrapped his arms around Arabella and held her in his arms. "Are you still human?" Gabriel asked as he analyzed her body. Arabella shrugged.

"It's hard to tell, my love," Arabella said. Gabriel took a step back with concern in his eyes. "What's wrong, my love?" Arabella asked. Gabriel looked at Amy and Ginger and then at Arabella again.

"How do you not know if you're human, Arabella? What should I do to see if you are not immortal, like us?" Arabella looked at Gabriel in a concerned manner. "What should we do?" Arabella asked. "I could try to drink some of your life force, my love?"

Gabriel scoffed and walked to the other side of the room. "Before I do that, I might want to try something else with you," Gabriel said. "I'll fetch some of my personal blood supplies and see how you react to it," Gabriel said before he left the room to fetch some bottles. Amy and Ginger hugged Arabella again.

"It's been too long," Ginger said as she sobbed through her words. "I missed you so much, mom." Ginger sniffled. Arabella kissed Ginger on her forehead.

"We're together again, my dearest loves. Amy, you were so brave to meet all the covens without having your father or me present. How proud I am for how you coped with the situation."

Amy was sobbing as she clung to Arabella. "We are a family, again," Arabella whispered to both her girls. "We will be together for a very long time." Gabriel came back into the room and placed two bottles of blood on Amy's night table. "Girls, if you could give me a moment?" Amy and Ginger stepped aside to let Gabriel approach Arabella. Gabriel opened the bottle and handed it to Arabella. "Try to drink this, my love. See how your body responds to it."

Arabella sniffed at the bottle and flinched. "It smells like pennies," Arabella said. Gabriel kept his gaze on Arabella. Arabella took a sip from it and it made her feel happy inside. "Much better," Arabella said with a smile. Gabriel smiled.

"Perhaps I might want you to do something with me. Please join me for our evening walk, my love," Gabriel said as he placed the bottle back on Amy's night table and led her outside of the castle.

Lucien and Amelia exchanged glances before they follow Arabella and Gabriel out the door. "She's back? My goodness," Amelia said. "I didn't know that would even be possible." Amelia smiled and hugged Lucien. Gabriel led Arabella over to a couple that were sitting in a park and saw another female jogger running in their direction.

"Want to do this like old times, my love?" Gabriel asked as he pushed Arabella in the direction of the woman. Arabella walked slowly over to her direction and stopped.

"Excuse me, ma'am, my husband and I were wondering what brings you to this area of the park?" The woman took her earphones out.

"I'm sorry, I didn't hear what you just asked me," said the woman with blonde short hair in a ponytail with blue eyes, wearing blue yoga clothes. "Do you come here a lot?" Arabella asked as she kept her gaze on the woman. The woman looked confused at her and then at Gabriel. Gabriel approached her and smirked.

"It's now or never, my love. Here, let me help you," said Gabriel grabbed as he woman from behind and bit her on her throat while covering her mouth to block out her screams.

Arabella placed her mouth against the wound and felt this warm sensation going through her body. Gabriel let go of the body, so Arabella could take over and watched Arabella start the transition. "Welcome to my world again, Arabella Ambrose."

About the Author

I started writing True Identity when I was 16 years old. I have always enjoyed writing, whether it be poetry, stories, or other forms. I was born in Amsterdam with dual citizenship for the Netherlands and the United States. I have always considered myself a creator, in not only writing but also in music. I live with my family and three beautiful cats, two  Ragdoll cats and 1 Burmese kitty, who is just over a year old. My hobbies include morning and evening walks outside. I also enjoy nature walks from which I gain a great deal of inspiration for my writing, especially when I am alone with my thoughts.

I have a Bachelor's Degree in Criminal Justice and a Master's Degree in Information Technology Management in the United States, but I decided to pursue my ambitions in a more creative setting. For my undergraduate and graduate years, I was student speaker for the Winter Commencement Ceremonies in 2020 and 2021, in this role I was able to write two of my greatest speeches which gained many views on YouTube. Being able to write a good story, whether it is a speech or a book may seem daunting, but it is an act of being creative and I love nothing more than creating a compelling story for my readers.

I hope to visit Australia someday, as my mother used to be a violinist in the Queensland Symphony Orchestra. She has told me of all her beautiful adventures of being an American in Australia. She, my brother, and I plan on visiting a friend someday soon in Sydney.